THE HUNTED AND THE HAUNTED

In his next instant of awareness, Franz heard a hollow *chunk* and a faint tinkling, and he was searching the dark sea of roofs with his naked eyes to try and locate anywhere a swift brown thing stalking him across them and taking advantage of every bit of cover: a chimney and its cap, a cupola, a water tank, a penthouse large or tiny, a thick standpipe, a wind scoop, a ventilator hood, hood of a garbage chute, a skylight, a roof's low walls, the low walls of an airshaft.

His heart was pounding and his breathing fast. . . .

Other Tor Books by Fritz Leiber

The Wanderer

Ship of Shadows (A Tor Double with *No Truce With Kings* by Poul Anderson)

Ill Met In Lankhmar (A Tor Double with *The Fair in Emain Macha* by Charles de Lint)

FRITZ LEIBER

CONJURE WIFE

OUR LADY OF DARKNESS

TOR
fantasy

A TOM DOHERTY ASSOCIATES BOOK
NEW YORK

Tor SF Double No. 36

CONJURE WIFE

OUR LADY OF DARKNESS

A Tor Book
Published by Tom Doherty Associates, Inc.
49 West 24th Street
New York, N.Y. 10010

Cover art by Wayne Barlowe

ISBN: 0-812-51296-0

First edition: August 1991

Printed in the United States of America

0 9 8 7 6 5 4 3 2 1

CONJURE WIFE

I

Norman Saylor was not the sort of man to go prying into his wife's dressing room. That was partly the reason why he did it. He was sure that nothing could touch the security of the relationship between him and Tansy.

He knew, of course, what had happened to Bluebeard's inquisitive wife. In fact, at one time he had gone rather deeply into the psychoanalytic undertones of that strange tale of dangling ladies. But it never occurred to him that any comparable surprise might await a husband, and a modern husband at that. A half-dozen handsome beaux hanging on hooks behind that door which gleamed so creamily? The idea would have given him a chuckle in spite of his scholarly delvings into feminine psychology and those brilliant studies in the parallelisms of primitive superstition and modern neurosis that had already won him a certain professional fame.

He didn't look like a distinguished ethnologist—he was rather too young for one thing—and he certainly didn't look like a professor of sociology at Hempnell College. He quite lacked the pursed lips, frightened eyes, and tyrannical jaw of the typical faculty member of that small, proud college.

Nor did he feel at all like a good Hempnell, for which he was particularly grateful today.

Spring sunshine was streaming restfully, and the balmy air sluicing gently, through the window at his elbow. He put in the last staccato burst of typing on his long-deferred paper. "The Social Background of the Modern Voodoo Cult," and pushed himself and his chair away from his desk with a sigh of satisfaction, suddenly conscious of having reached one of those peaks in the endless cycle of happiness and unhappiness when conscience sleeps at last and everything shows its pleasant side. Such a moment as would mark for a neurotic or adolescent the beginning of a swift tumble into abysses of gloom, but which Norman had long ago learned to ride out successfully, introducing new activities at just the right time to cushion the inevitable descent.

But that didn't mean he shouldn't enjoy to the full the moment while it lasted, extract the last drop of dreamy pleasure. He wandered out of his study, flipped open a bright-backed novel, immediately deserted it to let his gaze drift past two Chinese devil-masks on the wall, ambled out past the bedroom door, smiled at the cabinet where the liquor, Hempnell-wise, was "kept in the background"—but without wanting a drink—and retraced his course as far as the bedroom.

The house was very quiet. There was something comforting this afternoon about its unpretentious size, its over-partitioned stuffiness, even its approaching senility. It seemed to wear bravely its middle-class intellectual trappings of books and prints and record-albums. Today's washable paint covered last century's ornate moldings. Overtones of intellectual freedom and love of living apologized for heavy notes of professorial dignity.

Outside the bedroom window the neighbor's boy was hauling a coaster wagon piled with newspapers. Across the street an old man was spading around some bushes, stepping gingerly over the new grass. A laundry truck rattled past, going toward the college. Norman momentarily knit his brows.

Then in the opposite direction, two girl students came sauntering in the trousers and flapping shirt tails forbidden in the classrooms. Norman smiled. He was in a mood to cherish warmly the funny, cold little culture that the street represented, the narrow unamiable culture with its taboos against mentioning reality, its elaborate suppression of sex, its insistence on a stoical ability to withstand a monotonous routine of business or drudgery—and in the midst, performing the necessary rituals to keep dead ideas alive, like a college of witch-doctors in their stern stone tents, powerful, property-owning Hempnell.

It was odd, he thought, that he and Tansy had been able to stick it out so long and, in the end, so successfully. You couldn't honestly have called either of them the small-college type. Tansy especially, he was sure, had at first found everything nerve-racking: the keen-honed faculty rivalries, the lip-service to all species of respectability, the bland requirement (which would have sent a simple mechanic into spasms) that faculty wives work for the college out of pure loyalty, the elaborate social responsibilities, and the endless chaperoning of resentfully fawning students (for Hempnell was one of those colleges which offer anxious parents an alternative to the unshepherded freedom of what Norman recalled a local politician having described as "those hotbeds of communism and free love"—the big metropolitan universities).

By all expectations Tansy and he should either have escaped to one of the hotbeds, or started a process of uneasy drifting—a squabble about academic freedom here, a question of salary there—or else tried to become writers or something equally reclusive. But somehow, drawing on an unknown inward source, Tansy had found the strength to fight Hempnell on its own terms, to conform without losing stature, to take more than her share of the social burdens and thereby draw around Norman, as it were, a magic circle, within which he had been able to carry on his real work, the researches and papers that would ultimately make them independent of Hempnell and what Hempnell thought. And not only ultimately, but soon, for now with Redding's retirement he was assured of the sociology chairmanship, and then it would only be a matter of months until one of the big universities came through with the right offer.

For a moment Norman lost himself in sudden, sharp admiration of his wife, as if he were seeing Tansy's sterling qualities for the first time. Damn it, she had done so much for him, and so unobtrusively. Even to acting as a tireless and efficient secretary on all his researches without once making him feel guilty in his gratefulness. And he had been such unpromising material to start with: a lazy, spottily brilliant young instructor, dangerously contemptuous of academic life, taking a sophomoric pleasure in shocking his staid colleagues, with a suicidal tendency to make major issues out of minor disputes with deans and presidents. Why, there had been a dozen times during the early years when he had teetered on the brink of the academic downgrade, when there had loomed some irreparable break with authority, yet he had always managed to wriggle out, and almost always, he could see, looking back, with Tansy's clever, roundabout aid. Ever since he had married her, his life had been luck, luck, luck!

How the devil had she managed it?—she, who had been as lazy and wantonly rebellious as himself, a moody, irresponsible girl, daughter of an ineffectual country minister, her childhood lonely and undisciplined, solaced by wild imaginings, with little or nothing of the routinized, middle-class stuffiness that helped so much at Hempnell.

Nevertheless she had managed it, so that now—what a paradox!—he was looked upon as "a good, solid Hempnell man," "a credit to the college," "doing big things," close friend to Dean Gunnison (who wasn't such a terrible sort himself when you got to know him) and a man on whom platitudinous President Pollard "depended," a tower of strength compared to his nervous, rabbit-brained department colleague Hervey Sawtelle. From being one of the iconoclasts, he had become one of the plaster images, and yet (and this was the really wonderful thing) without once compromising his serious ideals, without once knuckling under to reactionary rulings.

Now, in his reflective, sun-brightened mood, it seemed to Norman that there was something incredible about his success at Hempnell, something magical and frightening, as if he and Tansy were a young warrior and squaw who had blundered into a realm of ancestral ghosts and had managed to convince those grim phantoms that they too were properly buried tribal elders, fit to share the supernatural rulership; always managing to keep secret their true flesh-and-blood nature despite a thousand threatened disclosures, because Tansy happened to know the right protective charms. Of course, when you came down to it, it was just that they were both mature and realistic. Everybody had to get over that age-old hump, learn to control the childish ego or else have his life wrecked by it. Still . . .

The sunlight brightened a trifle, became a shade more golden, as if some cosmic electrician had advanced the switch another notch. At the same moment one of the two shirt-tailed girls, disappearing around the corner of the house next door, laughed happily. Norman turned back from the window and as he did, Totem the cat rose from her sun-warmed spot on the silk comforter and indulged in a titanic yawn-and-stretch that looked as if it surely would dislocate every bone in her handsome body. Grateful for the example, Norman copied her, in moderation. Oh, it was a wonderful day all right, one of those days when reality becomes a succession of such bright and sharp images that you are afraid that any moment you will poke a hole in the gorgeous screen and glimpse the illimitable, unknown blackness it films; when everything seems so friendly and right that you tremble lest a sudden searing flash of insight reveal to you the massed horror and hate and brutality and ignorance of which life rests.

As Norman finished his yawn, he became aware that his blissful mood had still a few moments to run.

At the same instant his gaze happened to swing to the door of Tansy's dressing room.

He was conscious of wanting to do one more thing before he buckled down to work or recreation, something completely idle and aimless, a shade out of character, perhaps even a little childish and reprehensible, so he could be amusedly ashamed afterwards.

Of course, if Tansy had been there . . . but since she wasn't, her dressing room might serve as a proxy of her amiable self.

The door stood enticingly ajar, revealing the edge of a fragile chair with a discarded slip trailing down from it and a feathery-toed mule peeking from under. Beyond the chair was a jar-strewn section of ivory table-top, pleasantly dusky—for it was a windowless small cubicle, hardly more than a large closet.

He had never in his life spied on Tansy or seriously thought of doing so, any more than, so far as he knew, she had on him. It was one of those things they had taken for granted as a fundamental of marriage.

But this thing he was tempted toward couldn't be called spying. It was more like a gesture of illicit love, in any case a trifling transgression.

Besides, no human being has the right to consider himself perfect, or even completely adult, to bottle up all naughty urges.

Moreover, he had carried away for the sunny window a certain preoccupation with the riddle of Tansy, the secret of her ability to withstand and best the strangling atmosphere of catclawed Hempnell. Hardly a riddle, of course, and certainly not one to which you could hope to find the answer in her boudoir. Still . . .

He hesitated.

Totem, her white paws curled neatly under her black waistcoat, watched him.

He walked into Tansy's dressing room.

Totem sprang down from the bed and padded after him.

He switched on the rose-shaded lamp and surveyed the rack of dresses, the shelves of shoes. There was a slight disorder, very sane and lovable. A faint perfume conjured up agreeable memories.

He studied the photographs on the wall around the mirror.

One of Tansy and himself in partial Indian costume, from three summers back when he had been studying the Yumas. They both looked solemn, as if trying very seriously to be good Indians. Another, rather faded, showed them in 1928 bathing suits, standing on an old pier smiling squintily with the sun in their eyes. That took him back east to Bayport, the summer before they were married. A third showed an uproarious Negro baptism in midriver. That was when he had held the Hazelton Fellowship and been gathering materials for his *Social Patterns of the Southern Negro* and later "Feminine Element in Superstition." Tansy had been invaluable to him that busy half-year when he had hammered out the groundwork of a reputation. She had accompanied him in the field, writing down the vivid, rambling recollections of ancient, bright-eyed men and women who remembered the slave days because they themselves had been slaves. He recalled how slight and boyish and intense she'd seemed, even a little gauche, that summer when they'd just left Gorham College before coming to Hempnell. She'd certainly gained remarkably in poise since then.

The fourth picture showed an old Negro conjure doctor with wrinkled face and proud high forehead under a battered slouch hat. He stood with shoulders back and eyes quietly flaring, as if surveying the whole dirty-pink culture and rejecting it because he had a deeper and stronger knowledge of his own. Ostrich plumes and scarified cheeks couldn't have made him look any more impressive. Norman remembered the fellow well—he had been one of their more valuable and also more difficult informants, requiring several visits before the notebook had been satisfied.

He looked down at the dressing table and the ample array of cosmetics. Tansy had been the first of the Hempnell faculty wives to use lipstick and lacquer her nails. There had been veiled criticism and some talk of "the example we set our students," but she had stuck it out until Hulda Gunnison had appeared at the Faculty Frolic with a careless but unmistakable crimson smear on her mouth. Then all had been well.

Flanked by cold cream jars was a small photograph of

himself, with a little pile of small change, all dimes and quarters, in front of it.

He roused himself. This wasn't the vaguely illegitimate spying he had intended. He pulled out a drawer at random, hastily scanned the pile of rolled-up stockings that filled it, shut it, took hold of the ivory knob of the next.

And paused.

This was rather silly, it occurred to him. Simultaneously he realized that he had just squeezed the last drop from the peak of his mood. As when he had turned from the window, but more ominously, the moment seemed to freeze, as if all reality, every bit of it he lived to this moment, were something revealed by a lightning flash that would the next instant blink out, leaving inky darkness. That rather common buzzing-in-the-ears, everything-too-real sensation.

From the doorway Totem looked up at him.

But sillier still to analyze a trifling whim, as if it could mean anything one way or the other.

To show it didn't, he'd look in one more drawer.

It jammed, so he gave it a sharp tug before it jerked free.

A large cardboard box toward the back caught his eye. He edged up the cover and took out one of the tiny glass-stoppered bottles that filled it. What sort of a cosmetic would this be? Too dark for face powder. More like a geologist's soil specimen. An ingredient for a mud pack? Hardly. Tansy had an herb garden. Could that be involved?

The dry, dark-brown granules shifted smoothly, like sand in an hourglass, as he rotated the glass cylinder. The label appeared, in Tansy's clear script. "Julia Trock, Roseland." He couldn't recall any Julia Trock. And why should the name Roseland seem distasteful? His hand knocked aside the cardboard cover as he reached for a second bottle, identical with the first, except that the contents had a somewhat reddish tinge and the label read, "Phillip Lassiter, Hill." A third, contents same color as the first: "J. P. Thorndyke, Roseland." Then a handful, quickly snatched up: "Emelyn Scatterday, Roseland." "Mortimer Pope, Hill." "The Rev.

Bufort Ames, Roseland.'' They were, respectively, brown, reddish, and brown.

The silence in the house grew thunderous; even the sunlight in the bedroom seemed to sizzle and fry, as his mind rose to a sudden pitch of concentration on the puzzle. "Roseland and Hill, Roseland and Hill, Oh we went to Roseland and Hill,"—like a nursery rhyme somehow turned nasty, making the glass cylinders repugnant to his fingers, ''—but we never came back.''

Abruptly the answer came.

The two local cemeteries.

Graveyard dirt.

Soil specimens all right. Graveyard dirt from particular graves. A chief ingredient of Negro conjure magic.

With a soft thud Totem landed on the table and began to sniff inquisitively at the bottles, springing away as Norman plunged his hand into the drawer. He felt smaller boxes behind the big one, yanked suddenly at the whole drawer, so it fell to the floor. In one of the boxes were bent, rusty, worn bits of iron—horseshoe nails. In the other were calling-card envelopes, filled with snippings of hair, each labeled like the bottles. But he knew most of those names—"Hervey Sawtelle . . . Gracine Pollard . . . Hulda Gunnison . . ." And in one labeled "Evelyn Sawtelle"—red-lacquered nail clippings.

In the third drawer he drew blank. But the fourth yielded a varied harvest. Packets of small dried leaves and powdered vegetable matter—so that was what came from Tansy's herb garden along with kitchen seasonings? Vervain, vinmoin, devil's stuff, the labels said. Bits of lodestone with iron filings clinging to them. Goose quills which spilled quicksilver when he shook them. Small squares of flannel, the sort that Negro conjure doctors use for their "tricken bags" or "hands." A box of old silver coins and silver filings—strong protective magic; giving significance to the silver coins in front of his photograph.

But Tansy was so sane, so healthily contemptuous of palmistry, astrology, numerology and all other superstitious fads.

A hardheaded New Englander. So well versed, from her work with him, in the psychological background of superstition and primitive magic. So well versed—

He found himself thumbing through a dog-eared copy of his own *Parallelisms in Superstition and Neurosis*. It looked like the one he had lost around the house—was it eight years ago? Beside a formula for conjuration was a marginal notation in Tansy's script: "Doesn't work. Substitute copper filings for brass. Try in dark of moon instead of full."

"Norman—"

Tansy was standing in the doorway.

II

It is the people we know best who can, on rare occasions, seem most unreal to us. For a moment the familiar face registers as merely an arbitrary arrangement of colored surfaces, without even the shadowy personality with which we invest a strange face glimpsed in the street.

Norman Saylor felt he wasn't looking at his wife, but at a painting of her. It was as if some wizardly Renoir or Toulouse-Lautrec had painted Tansy with the air for a canvas—boldly blocked in the flat cheeks in pale flesh tones faintly under-tinged with green, drew them together to a small defiant chin; smudged crosswise with careless art the red thoughtful lips, the gray-green maybe humorous eyes, the narrow low-arched brows with single vertical furrow between; created with one black stroke the childishly sinister bangs, swiftly smeared the areas of shadowed white throat and wine-colored dress; caught perfectly the feel of the elbow that hugged a package from the dressmaker's, as the small ugly hands lifted to remove a tiny hat that was another patch of the wine color with a highlight representing a little doodad of silvered glass.

If he were to reach out and touch her, Norman felt, the paint would peel down in strips from the empty air, as from some walking sister-picture of Dorian Gray.

He stood stupidly staring at her, the open book in his hand. He didn't hear himself say anything, though he knew that if words had come to his lips at that moment, his voice would have sounded to him like another's—some fool professor's.

Then, without saying anything either, and without any noticeable change of expression, Tansy turned on her heel and walked rapidly out of the bedroom. The package from the dressmaker's fell to the floor. It was a moment before Norman could stir himself.

He caught up with her in the living room. She was headed for the front door. When he realized she wasn't going to turn or stop, he threw his arms around her. And then, at last, she did react. She struggled like an animal, but with her face turned sharply away and her arms flat against her sides, as if tied there.

Through taut mouth-slit, in a very low voice, but spittingly, she said, "Don't touch me."

Norman strained and braced his feet. There was something horrible about the way she threw herself from side to side, trying to break his embrace. There flickered in his mind the thought of a woman in a straitjacket.

She kept repeating "Don't touch me" in the same tones, and he kept imploring, "But Tansy—"

Suddenly she stopped struggling. He dropped his arms and stepped back.

She didn't relax. She just stood there rigidly, her face twisted to one side—and from what he could see of it, the eyes were winced shut and the lips bitten together. Some kindred tightness, inside him, hurt his heart.

"Darling!" he said. "I'm ashamed of what I did. No matter what it led to, it was a cheap, underhanded unworthy action. But—"

"It's not that!"

He hesitated. "You mean, you're acting this way because you're, well, ashamed of what I found out?"

No reply.

"Please, Tansy, we've got to talk about it."

Still no reply. He unhappily fingered the air. "But I'm sure everything will be all right. If you'll just tell me . . .

"Tansy, please . . ."

Her posture didn't alter, but her lips arched and the words were spat out: "Why don't you strap me and stick pins in me? They used to do that."

"Darling, I'd do anything rather than hurt you! But this is something that just has to be talked about."

"I can't. If you say another word about it, I'll scream!"

"Darling, if I possibly could, I'd stop. But this is one of those things. We've just got to talk it over."

"I'd rather die."

"But you've got to tell me. You've got to!"

He was shouting.

For a moment he thought she was going to faint. He reached forward to catch her. But it was only that her body had abruptly gone slack. She walked over to the nearest chair, dropped her hat on a small table beside, sat down listlessly.

"All right," she sad. "Let's talk about it."

6:37 P.M.: The last rays of sunlight sliced the bookcase, touched the red teeth of the left-hand devil mask. Tansy was sitting on one end of the davenport, while Norman was at the other, turned sideways with one knee on the cushion, watching her.

Tansy switched around, flirting her head irritably, as if there were in the air a smoke of words which had grown unendurably thick. "All right, have it your own way then! I was very seriously trying to use conjure magic. I was doing everything a civilized woman shouldn't. I was trying to put spells on people and things. I was trying to change the future. I was . . . oh, the whole works!"

Norman gave a small jerky nod. It was the same sort of nod he gave at student conferences, when after seeming hours of muddled discussion, some blank-faced young hopeful would begin to get a glimmering of what they were really talking about. He leaned toward her.

"But why?"

"To protect you and your career." She was looking at her lap.

"But knowing all you did about the background of superstition, how did you ever come to believe—?" His voice wasn't loud now. It was cool, almost a lawyer's.

She twisted. "I don't know. When you put it that way . . . of course. But when you desperately want things to happen, or not to happen, to someone you love . . . I was only doing what millions of others have done. And then, you see, Norm, the things I did . . . well, they seemed to work . . . at least most of the time."

"But don't you see," he continued smoothly, "that those very exceptions prove that the things you were doing *didn't* work? That the successes were just coincidences?"

Her voice rose a trifle. "I don't know about that. There might have been counter-influences at work—" She turned toward him impulsively. "Oh, I don't know what I believe! I've never really been sure that my charms worked. There was no way of telling. Don't you see, once I'd started, I didn't dare stop?"

"And you've been doing it all these years?"

She nodded unhappily. "Ever since we came to Hempnell."

He looked at her, trying to comprehend it. It was almost impossible to take at one gulp the realization that in the mind of this trim modern creature he had known in completest intimacy, there was a whole great area he had never dreamed of, an area that was part and parcel of the dead practices he analyzed in books, an area that belonged to the Stone Age and never to him, an area plunged in darkness, acrouch with fear, blown by giant winds. He tried to picture Tansy muttering charms, stitching up flannel hands by candlelight, visiting graveyards and God knows what other places in search of ingredients. His imagination almost failed. And yet it had all been happening right under his nose.

The only faintly suspicious aspect of Tansy's behavior that he could recall was her whim for taking "little walks" by herself. If he had ever wondered about Tansy and superstitions at all, it had only been to decide, with a touch of self-congratulation, that for a woman she was almost oddly free from irrationality.

"Oh, Norm, I'm so confused and miserable," she broke in. "I don't know what to say or how to start."

He had an answer for that, a scholar's answer.

"Tell me how it all happened, right from the beginning."

7:54: They were still sitting on the davenport. The room was almost dark. The devil masks were irregular ovals of gloom. Tansy's face was a pale smudge. Norman couldn't study its expression, but judging from her voice, it had become animated.

"Hold on a minute," he interrupted. "Let's get some things straight. You say you were very much afraid when we first came to Hempnell to arrange about my job, before I went south on the Hazelton Fellowship?"

"Oh, yes, Norm. Hempnell terrified me. Everyone was so obviously antagonistic and so deadly respectable. I knew I'd be a flop as a professor's wife—I was practically told so to my face. I don't know which was worse. Hulda Gunnison looking me up and down and grunting contemptuously, 'I guess you'll do,' when I made the mistake of confiding in her, or old Mrs. Carr petting my arm and saying, 'I know you and your husband will be very happy here at Hempnell. You're young, but Hempnell loves nice young folk!' Against those women I felt completely unprotected. And your career too."

"Right. So when I took you south and plunged you into the midst of the most superstition-swayed area in the whole country, exposed you to the stuff night and day, you were ripe for its promise of magical security."

Tansy laughed half-heartedly. "I don't know about the ripe part, but it certainly impressed me. I drank in all I could. At the back of my mind, I suppose, was the feeling: Some day I may need this. And when we went back to Hempnell in the fall, I felt more confident."

Norman nodded. That fitted. Come to think of it, there had been something unnatural about the intense, silent enthusiasm with which Tansy had plunged into boring secretarial work right after their marriage.

"But you didn't actually try and conjure magic," he continued, "until I got pneumonia that first winter?"

"That's right. Until then, it was just a cloud of vaguely reassuring ideas—scraps of things I'd find myself saying over when I woke in the middle of the night, things I'd unconsciously avoid doing because they were unlucky, like sweeping the steps after dark or crossing knives and forks. And then when you got pneumonia, well, when the person you love is near death, you'll try anything."

For a moment Norman's voice was sympathetic. "Of course." Then the classroom tone came back. "But I gather that it wasn't until I had that brush with Pollard over sex education and came off decently, and especially until my book came out in 1931 and got such, well, pretty favorable reviews, that you really began to believe that your magic was working?"

"That's right."

Norman sat back. "Oh, Lord," he said.

"What's the matter, dear? You don't feel I'm trying to take any credit away from you for the book's success?"

Norman half laughed, half snorted. "Good Lord, no. But—" He stopped himself. "Well, that takes us to 1930. Go on from there."

8:58: Norman reached over and switched on the light, winced at its glare. Tansy ducked her head.

He stood up, massaging the back of his neck.

"The things that gets me," he said, "is the way it invaded every nook and corner of your life, bit by bit, so that finally you couldn't take a step, or rather let me take one, without there having to be some protective charm. It's almost like—"

He was going to say, "Some kinds of paranoia."

Tansy's voice was hoarse and whispery. "I even wear hooks-and-eyes instead of zippers because the hooks are supposed to catch evil spirits. And the mirror-decorations on my hats and bags and dresses—you've guessed it, they're Tibetan magic to reflect away misfortune."

He stood in front of her. "Look, Tansy, whatever made you do it?"

"I've just told you."

"I know, but what made you stick to it year after year, when as you've admitted, you always suspected you were just fooling yourself? I could understand it with another woman, but with you . . ."

Tansy hesitated. "I know you'll think I'm being romantic and trite, but I've always felt that women were more primitive than men, closer to ancient feelings." She hurried over that. "And then there were things I remembered from childhood. Queer mistaken ideas I got from my father's sermons. Stories one of the old ladies there used to tell us. Hints." (Norman thought: Country parsonage? Healthy mental atmosphere, not!) "And then—oh, there were a thousand other things. But I'll try to tell them to you."

"Swell," he said, putting his hand on her shoulder. "But we'd better eat something along with it."

9:17: They were sitting facing each other in the jolly red-and-white kitchen. On the table were untasted sandwiches and half-sipped cups of black coffee. It was obvious that the situation between them had changed. Now it was Norman who looked away and Tansy who studied expressions anxiously.

"Well, Norman," she managed to say finally, "do you think I'm crazy, or going crazy?"

It was just the question he had needed. "No, I don't," he said levelly. "Though Lord only knows what an outsider would think if he found out what you'd been doing. But just as surely as you aren't crazy, you are neurotic—like all of us—and your neurosis has taken a darned unusual form."

Suddenly aware of hunger, he picked up a sandwich and began to munch it as he talked, nibbling the edge all around and then beginning to work in.

"Look, all of us have private rituals—our own little peculiar ways of eating and drinking and sleeping and going to the bathroom. Rituals we're hardly conscious of, but that would look mighty strange if analyzed. You know, to step or not to step on cracks in the sidewalk. Things like that. Now I'd say that your private rituals, because of the special circumstances of your life, have gotten all tangled up with conjure magic, so you can hardly tell which is which." He paused. "Now here's an important thing. So long as only *you* knew what you were doing, you didn't tend to criticize your entanglement with conjure magic any more than the average person criticizes his magic formula for going to sleep. There was no social conflict."

He started to pace, still eating the sandwich.

"Good Lord, haven't I devoted a good part of my life to investigating how and why men and women are superstitious? And shouldn't I have been aware of the contagious effect of that study on you? And what is superstition, but misguided, unobjective science? And when it comes down to that, is it to be wondered if people grasp at superstition in this rotten, hate-filled, half-doomed world of today? Lord knows, I'd welcome the blackest of black magic, if it could do anything to stave off the atom bomb."

Tansy had risen. Her eyes looked unnaturally large and bright.

"Then," she faltered, "you honestly don't hate me, or think I'm going crazy?"

He put his arms around her. "Hell no!"

She began to cry.

9:33: They were sitting on the davenport again. Tansy had stopped crying, but her head still rested against his shoulder.

For a while they were quiet. Then Norman spoke. He used the deceptively mild tones of a doctor telling a patient that another operation will be necessary.

"Of course, you'll have to quit doing it now."

Tansy sat up quickly. "Oh, no, Norm, I couldn't."

"Why not? You've just agreed it was all nonsense. You've just thanked me for opening your eyes."

"I know that, but still—don't make me, Norm!"

"Now be reasonable, Tansy," he said. "You've taken this like a major so far. I'm proud of you. But don't you see, you can't stop half way. Once you've started to face this weakness of yours logically, you've got to keep on. You've got to get rid of all that stuff in your dressing room, all the charms you've hidden around, everything.''

She shook her head. ''Don't make me, Norm,'' she repeated. ''Not all at once. I'd feel naked.''

''No you won't. You'll feel stronger. Because you'll find out that what you half thought might be magic, is really your own unaided ability.''

''No, Norm. Why do I have to stop? What difference does it make? You said yourself it was just nonsense—a private ritual.''

''But now that I know about it, it's not private any more. And in any case,'' he added, almost dangerously, ''it's a pretty unusual ritual.''

''But couldn't I just quit by degrees?'' She pleaded, like a child. ''You know, not lay any new charms, but leave the old ones?''

He shook his head. ''No,'' he said, ''it's like giving up drink—it has to be a clean break.''

Her voice began to rise. ''But, Norm, I can't do it. I simply can't!''

He began to feel she was a child. ''Tansy, you must.''

''But there wasn't ever anything bad about my magic.'' The childishness was getting frightening. ''I never used it to hurt anyone or to ask for unreasonable things, like making you president of Hempnell overnight. I only wanted to protect you.''

''Tansy, what difference does that make!''

Her breasts were heaving. ''I tell you, Norm, I won't be responsible for what happens to you if you make me take away those protections.''

''Tansy, be reasonable. What on earth do I need with protections of that sort?''

''Oh, so you think that everything you've won in life is just the result of your own unaided abilities? You don't recognize the luck in it?''

Norman remembered thinking the same thing himself this afternoon and that made him angrier. ''Now Tansy—''

"And you think that everyone loves you and wishes you well, don't you? You think all those beasts over at Hempnell are just a lot of pussies with their claws clipped? You pass off their spite and jealousies as something trivial, beneath your notice. Well, let me tell you—"

"Tansy, stop screaming!"

"—that there are those at Hempnell who would like to see you dead—and who would have seen you dead a long time ago, if they could have worked it!"

"Tansy!"

"What do you suppose Evelyn Sawtelle feels toward you for the way you're nosing out her flutterbudget of a husband for the sociology chairmanship? Do you think she wants to bake you a cake? One of her cherry-chocolate ones? How do you suppose Hulda Gunnison likes the influence you have acquired over her husband? It's mainly because of you that she no longer runs the Dean of Men's office. And as for that libidinous old bitch Mrs. Carr, do you imagine that she enjoys the way your freedom-and-frankness policy with the students is cutting into her holier-than-thou respectability, her 'Sex is just an ugly word' stuff? What do you think those women have been doing for *their* husbands?"

"Oh, Lord, Tansy, why drag in that old faculty jealousies business?"

"Do you suppose they'd stop at mere protection? Do you imagine women like that would observe any distinction between white magic and black?"

"Tansy! You don't know what you're saying. If you mean to imply—Tansy, when you talk that way, you actually sound like a witch."

"Oh, I do?" For a moment her expression was so tight her face looked all skull. "Well, maybe I am. And maybe it's lucky for you I've been one."

He grabbed her by the arm. "Listen, I've been patient with you about all this ignorant nonsense. But now you're going to show some sense and show it quick."

Her lips curled, nastily. "Oh, I see. It's been the velvet

glove so far, but now it's going to be the iron hand. If I don't do just as you say, I get packed off to an asylum. Is that it?"

"Of course not! But you've just got to be sensible."

"Well, I tell you I won't!"

"Now, Tansy—"

10:13: The folded comforter jounced as Tansy flopped on the bed. New tears had streaked and reddened her face and dried. "All right," she said, in a stuffy voice. "I'll do what you want. I'll burn all my things."

Norman felt light-headed. The thought came into his mind, "And to think I dared to tackle it without a psychiatrist!"

"There've been enough times when I've wanted to stop," she added. "Just like there've been times I've wanted to stop being a woman."

What followed struck Norman as weirdly anticlimactic. First the ransacking of Tansy's dressing room for hidden charms and paraphernalia. Norman found himself remembering those old two-reel comedies in which scores of people pile out of a taxicab—it seemed impossible that a few shallow drawers and old shoe boxes could hold so many wastepaper baskets of junk. He tossed the dog-eared copy of "Parallelisms" on top of the last one, picked up Tansy's leather-bound diary. She shook her head reassuringly. After the barest hesitation he put it back unopened.

Then the rest of the house. Tansy moving faster and faster, darting from room to room, deftly recovering flannel-wrapped "hands" from the upholstery of the chair, the under sides of table tops, the interior of vases, until Norman dizzily marveled that he had lived in the house for more than ten years without chancing on any.

"It's rather like a treasure hunt, isn't it?" she said with a rueful smile.

There were other charms outside—under front and back doorsteps, in the garage, and in the car. With every handful thrown on the roaring fire he had built in the living room, Norman's sense of relief grew. Finally Tansy opened the seams of the pillows on his bed and carefully fished out two little matted shapes made of feathers bound with fine thread so that they had blended with the fluffy contents of the pillow.

"See, one's a heart, the other an anchor. That's for security," she told him. "New Orleans feather magic. You haven't taken a step for years without being in the range of one of my protective charms."

The feather figures puffed into flame.

"There," she said. "Feel any reaction?"

"No," he said. "Any reason I should?"

She shook her head. "Except that those were the last ones. And so, if there *were* any hostile forces that my charms were keeping at bay . . ."

He laughed tolerantly. Then for a moment his voice grew hard. "You're sure they're all gone? Absolutely certain you haven't overlooked any?"

"Absolutely certain. There's not one left in the house or near it, Norm—and I never planted any anywhere else because I was afraid of . . . well, interference. I've counted them all over in my mind a dozen times and they've all gone—" She looked at the fire, "—pouf. And now," she said quietly, "I'm tired, really tired. I want to go straight to bed."

Suddenly she began to laugh. "Oh, but first I'll have to stitch up those pillows, or else there'll be feathers all over the place."

He put his arms around her. "Everything okay now?"

"Yes, darling. There's only one thing I want to ask you— that we don't talk about this for a few days at least. Not even mention it. I don't think I could. . . . Will you promise me that, Norm?"

He pulled her closer. "Absolutely dear, Absolutely."

III

Leaning forward from the worn leather edge of the old easy chair, Norman played with the remnants of the fire, tapped the fang of the poker against a glowing board until it collapsed into tinkling embers, over which swayed almost invisible blue flames.

From the floor beside him Totem watched the flames, head between outstretched paws.

Norman felt tired. He really ought to have followed Tansy to bed long ago, except he wanted time for his thoughts to unkink. Rather a bother, this professional need to assimilate each new situation, to pick over its details mentally, turning them this way and that, until they became quite shopworn. Whereas Tansy had turned out her thoughts like a light and plunged into sleep. How like Tansy!—or perhaps it was just the more finely attuned, hyperthyroid female physiology.

In any case, she'd done the practical, sensible thing. And that was like Tansy, too. Always fair. Always willing, in the long run, to listen to logic (in a similar situation would he have dared try reasoned argument on any other woman?). Always . . . yes . . . empirical. Except that she had gotten off on a crazy sidetrack.

Hempnell was responsible for that, it was a breeding place for neurosis, and being a faculty wife put a woman in one of the worst spots. He ought to have realized years ago the strain she was under and taken steps. But she'd been too good an actor for him. And he was always forgetting just how deadly seriously women took faculty intrigues. They couldn't escape like their husbands into the cook measured worlds of mathematics, microbiology or what have you.

Norman smiled. That had been an odd notion Tansy had let slip toward the end—that Evelyn Sawtelle and Harold Gunnison's wife and old Mrs. Carr were practicing magic too, of the venomous black variety. And not any too hard to believe, either, if you knew them! That was the sort of idea with which a clever satirical writer could do a lot. Just carry it a step further—picture most women as glamor-conscious witches, carrying on their savage warfare of deathspell and countercharm, while their reality-befuddled husbands went blithely about their business. Let's see, Barrie had written *What Every Woman Knows* to show that men never realize how their wives were responsible for their successes. Being that blind, would men be any more apt to realize that their wives used witchcraft for the purpose?

Norm's smile changed to a wince. He had just remembered that it wasn't just an odd notion, but that Tansy had actually believed, or half-believed, such things. He sucked his lips wryly. Doubtless he'd have more unpleasant moments like this, when memory would catch him up with a start. After tonight, it was inevitable.

Still, the worst was over.

He reached down to stroke Totem, who did not look away from the hypnotic embers.

"Time we got to bed, old cat. Must be about twelve. No—quarter past one."

As he slipped the watch back into his pocket, the fingers of his left hand went to the locket at the other end of the chain.

He weighted in his palm the small golden heart, a gift from Tansy. Was it perhaps a trifle heavier than its metal shell could account for? He snapped up the cover with his thumbnail. There was no regular way of getting at the space behind Tansy's picture, so after a moment's hesitation, he carefully edged out the tiny photograph with a pencil point.

Behind the photograph was a tiny packet wrapped in the finest flannel.

Just like a woman—that thought came with vicious swiftness—to seem to give in completely, but to hold out on something.

Perhaps she had forgotten.

Angrily he tossed the packet into the fireplace. The photograph fluttered along with it, lighted on the bed of embers, and flared before he could snatch it out. He had a glimpse of Tansy's face curling and blackening.

The packet took longer. A yellow glow crept across its surface, as the nap singed. Then a wavering four-inch flame shot up.

Simultaneously a chill went through him, though he still felt the heat from the embers. The room seemed to darken. There was a faint, mighty roaring in his ears, as of motors far underground. He had the sense of standing suddenly naked and unarmed before something menacingly alien.

Totem had turned around and was peering intently at the shadows in the far corner. With a spitting hiss she sprang sideways and darted from the room.

Norman realized he was trembling. Nervous reaction, he told himself. Might have known it was overdue.

The flame died, and once again there was only the frostily tinkling bed of embers.

Explosively, the phone began to jangle.

"Professor Saylor? I don't suppose you ever thought you'd hear from me again, did you? Well, the reason I'm calling you is that I always believe in letting people—no matter who—know where I stand, which is a lot more than can be said for some people."

Norman held the receiver away from his ear. The words, though jumbled, sounded like the beginning of a call, but the tone in which they were uttered didn't. Surely it would take half an hour of ranting before anyone could reach such a pitch of whining and—yes, the word was applicable—insane anger.

"What I want to tell you, Saylor, is this: I'm not going to take what's been done to me lying down. I'm not going to let myself stay flunked out of Hempnell. I'm going to demand to have my grades changed and you know why!"

Norman recognized the voice. There sprang into his mind the image of a pale, abnormally narrow face with pouting lips and protuberant eyes, crowned by a great shock of red hair. He cut in.

"Now listen, Jennings, if you thought you were being treated unfairly, why didn't you present your grievances two months ago, when you got your grades?"

"Why? Because I let you pull the wool over my eyes. The open-minded Professor Saylor! It wasn't until afterwards that I realized how you hadn't given me the proper attention, how I'd been slighted or bamboozled at conferences, how you didn't tell me I might flunk until it was too late, how you based your tests on trick questions from lectures I'd missed, how you discriminated against me because of my father's politics and because I wasn't the student type like that Bronstein. It wasn't until then—"

"Jennings, be reasonable. You flunked two courses besides mine last semester."

"Yes, because you passed the word around, influenced others against me, made them see me as you pretended to see me, made everyone—"

"And you mean to tell me you only now realized all this?"

"Yes I do. It just came to me in a flash as I was thinking here. Oh, you were clever, all right. You had me eating out of your hand, you had me taking everything lying down, you had me scared. But once I got my first suspicion, I saw the whole plot clear as day. Everything fitted, everything led back to you, everything—"

"Including the fact that you were flunked out of two other colleges before you ever came to Hempnell?"

"There! I knew you were prejudiced against me from the start!"

"Jennings," Norman said wearily, "I've listened to all I'm going to. If you have any grievances, present them to Dean Gunnison."

"Do you mean to say you won't take any action?"

"Yes, I mean just that."

"Is that final?"

"Yes, it's final."

"Very well, Saylor. Then all I can say to you is, watch out! Watch out, Saylor! Watch out!"

There was a click at the other end of the line. Norman gently put the phone back in its cradle. Oh, damn Theodore Jennings' parents! Not because they were hypocritical, vain, reactionary stuffed-shirts, but because they had such cruel pride that they were determined to shove through college a sensitive, selfish, wordy, somewhat subnormal boy, as narrow-minded as they were though not one-tenth as canny. And damn President Pollard for kow-towing so ineptly to their wealth and political influence that he had let the boy into Hempnell knowing perfectly well he'd fail.

Norman put the screen in front of the fire, switched out

the living room lights and started toward the bedroom in the yellow glow fanning out from the hall.

Again the phone jangled. Norman looked at it curiously for a moment before he picked it up.

"Hello."

There was no reply. He waited for a few moments. Then, "Hello?" he repeated.

Still there was no reply. He was about to hang up when he thought he caught the sound of breathing—excited, uneven, choked.

"Who is it?" he said sharply. "This is Professor Saylor. Please speak up."

He still seemed to hear the breathing. That was all.

Then out of the small black mystery of the phone came one word, enunciated slowly and with difficulty, in a voice that was deep yet throbbed with an almost fantastic intimacy.

"Darling!"

Norman swallowed. He didn't seem to recognize this voice at all. Before he could think what to say, it went on, more swiftly, but otherwise unchanged.

"Oh, Norman, how glad I am that at last I've found the courage to speak where you wouldn't. I'm ready now, darling, I'm ready. You only need to come to me."

"Really?" Norman temporized in amazement. It seemed to him now that there was something faintly familiar about the voice, not in its tone, but in its phrasing and rhythm.

"Come to me, lover, come to me. Take me to some place where we'll be alone. All alone. I'll be your mistress. I'll be your slave. Subject me to you. Do anything you want to me."

Norman wanted to laugh uproariously, yet his heart was pounding a little. Nice, perhaps, if it were real, but there was something so clownish about it. Was it a joke? he suddenly asked himself.

"I'm lying here talking to you without any clothes on, darling. There's just a tiny pink lamp by the bed. Oh, take me to some lonely tropical isle and we'll make passionate love together. I'll hurt you and you'll hurt me. And then we'll swim in the moonlight with white petals drifting down onto the water.''

Yes, it was a joke all right, it just had to be, he decided with a twinge of only half-humorous regret. And then there suddenly occurred to him the one person capable of playing such a joke.

"So come, Norman, come, and take me into the darkness," the voice continued.

"All right, I will," he replied briskly. "And after I've made passionate love to you I'll switch on the lights and I'll say, 'Mona Utell, aren't you ashamed of yourself?' "

"Mona?" The voice rose in pitch. "Mona?"

"Yes indeed, Mona!" he assured her laughingly. "You're the only actress I know, in fact the only woman I know, who could do that corny sultriness to such perfection. What would you have done if Tansy had answered? An imitation of Humphrey Bogart? How's New York? How's the party? What are you drinking?"

"Drinking? Norman, don't you know who this is?"

"Certainly. You're Mona Utell." But he had already grown doubtful. Long-drawn-out jokes weren't Mona's specialty. And the strange voice, with its aura of exasperating familiarity, was growing higher all the time.

"You really don't know who I am?"

"No, I guess I don't," he replied, speaking a little sharply because that was the way the question had been put.

"Not really?"

Norman sensed that those two words cocked the trigger for an emotional explosion, but he didn't care. He went ahead and pulled it. "No!" he said impatiently.

At that the voice at the other end of the wire rose to a scream. Totem, slinking past, turned her head at the sound.

"You beast! You dirty beast! After all you've done to me! After you've deliberately roused me. After you've undressed me a hundred times with your eyes!"

"Now please—"

"Corny sultriness! You . . . you lousy schoolteacher! Go

back to your Mona! Go back to that snippy wife of yours. And I hope you all three fry in hell!''

Once again Norman found himself listening to a dead phone. With a wry smile he put it down. Oh, the staid life of a college professor! He tried to think of some woman who could possibly be entertaining a secret passion for him, but that didn't lead him anywhere. Certainly his idea about Mona Utell had seemed a good one at the time. She was quite capable of calling them up long distance from New York for a joke. It was just the sort of thing she'd do to enliven a party after the evening performance.

But not to end the joke that way. Mona always wanted you laughing with her at the finish.

Perhaps someone else had been playing a joke.

Or perhaps someone else really . . . He shrugged his shoulders. Such an asinine business. He must tell Tansy. It would amuse her. He started toward the bedroom.

Only then did he remember all that had happened earlier in the evening. The two startling phone calls had quite knocked it out of his head.

He was at the bedroom door. He turned around slowly and looked at the phone. The house was very quiet.

It occurred to him that from one way of looking at it, those two phone calls, coming just when they did, constituted a very unpleasant coincidence.

But a scientist ought to have a healthy disregard for coincidences.

He could hear Tansy breathing softly, regularly.

He switched out the light in the hall and went to bed.

IV

As Norman walked the last block to Hempnell the next morning, it struck him with unusual forcefulness just how pseudo was Hempnell's Gothic. Odd to think how little scholarly thought that ornate architecture masked, and how much anxiety over low salaries and excessive administrative burdens; and among the students, how little passion for knowledge and how much passion, period—even though of a halting, advertisement-derived, move-stimulated sort. But perhaps that was just what that fabulous gray architecture was supposed to symbolize, even in the old monastic days when its arches and buttresses had been functional.

The walks were empty except for a few hurrying figures, but in three or four minutes the student body would spill out of chapel, a scattering tide of brightly-colored sweaters and jackets.

A delivery van came gliding around the corner as Norman started to cross the street. He stepped back on the curb with a shivery distaste. In this gasoline-obsessed world he didn't mind ordinary automobiles, but somehow trucks with their suggestion of an unwholesome gigantism touched him with a faint irrational horror.

In taking a quick glance around before he started across again, he thought he saw a girl student behind him, either very late for chapel or else cutting it altogether. The next moment he realized that it was Mrs. Carr. He waited for her to catch up with him.

The mistake was a natural one. In spite of her surely seventy years, the silver-haired Dean of Women had a remarkably youthful figure and carriage. Her gait was always brisk and almost supple. Only the second glance revealed the darkened neck, the network of heavy wrinkles, showed you that the slimness was of age not youth. Her manner didn't seem an affectation of girlishness or a pathetic clinging to sex—or, if it were, a very subtle one—but rather a hungry infatuation with youthfulness, with dewiness, with freshness, so great that it influenced the very cells and electrical tensions of her body.

There is a cult of youth among the faculty members of our colleges, Norman began to think, a special form of the great American cult of youth, an almost vampiristic feeding on young eager feelings. . . .

Mrs. Carr's arrival cut him short.

"And *how* is Tansy?" she asked, with such sweet solicitude that for a moment Norman wondered if the Dean of Women had even more of an inside wire on the private lives of the faculty than was generally surmised. But only for a moment. After all, sweet solicitude was the Dean of Women's stock-in-trade.

"We missed her at our last faculty wives' meeting," Mrs. Carr continued. "She's such a gay soul. And we *do* need gaiety these days." Cold morning sunlight glinted on her thick glasses and glowed frostily on her apple-red cheeks. She put her hand on his arm. "Hempnell *appreciates* Tansy, Professor Saylor."

Norman's "And why not?" changed to "I think that shows good judgment" as he said it. He derived sardonic amusement from recalling how ten years ago Mrs. Carr was a charter member of *The-Saylors-are-a-demoralizing-influence Club*.

Mrs. Carr's silvery laughter trilled in the chilly air. "I must get on to my student conferences," she said. "But remember, Hempnell appreciates you too, Professor Saylor."

He watched her hurry off, wondering if her last remark meant there had been an unexpected improvement in his chances of getting the vacant chairmanship of the sociology department. Then he turned into Morton Hall.

When he had climbed to his office, the phone was ringing. It was Thompson, who handled Hempnell's public relations—almost the only administrative duty considered too vital to be entrusted to a mere professor.

Thompson's greeting was exceptionally affable. As always, Norman had the vision of a man who would be much happier selling soap. It would take a psychoanalyst, he thought, to discover what weird compulsion made Thompson cling to the fringes of the academic world. We only know that some potentially great salesmen feel impelled to do so.

"A rather delicate matter," Thompson was saying. Delicate matters were one of his fortes. "Just now one of the trustees phoned me. It seems he had heard a very odd story—he wouldn't tell me the source of his information—concerning you and Mrs. Saylor. That over Christmas vacation in New York you had attended a party given by some prominent but . . . er . . . very gay theatrical people. He couldn't be quite straight about where it happened, the party seemed to have wandered all over New York. In fact it all sounded very unlikely. There was something about an impromptu act staged in a night club, and an academic gown, and an . . . er . . . strip-tease dancer. I told him I'd look into it. But naturally I thought . . . and I was wondering if you'd . . ."

"If I'd issue a denial? Sorry, but it wouldn't be honest. The story's substantially true."

"Oh. . . . I see. Well, that's all there is to it then," Thompson answered bravely after a moment. "I thought you'd like to know though. The trustee . . . Fenner . . . was very hot under the collar. Talked my ear off about how these particular theatrical people were conspicuous for drunkenness and divorce."

"He was right about the former, not the latter. Mona and Welby Utell are faithful to each other after their fashion. Nice folk, I'll introduce you to them some time."

"Oh! . . . That would be interesting, yes," replied Thompson. "Good-by."

The warning buzzer sounded for classes. Norman stopped fingering the little obsidian knife he used for slitting envelopes, swiveled his chair away from the desk and leaned back, amusedly irritated at this latest manifestation of the Hempnell "hush-hush" policy. Not that he had made any particular attempt to conceal the Utell party, which had been a trifle crazier than he had expected. Still, he had said nothing about it to anyone on campus. No use in being a fool. Now, after a matter of months, it had all come out anyway.

From where he sat, the roof ridge of Estrey Hall neatly bisected his office window along the diagonal. There was a medium-sized cement dragon frozen in the act of clambering down it. For the tenth time this morning he reminded himself that what had happened last night had really happened. It was not so easy. And yet, when you got down to it, Tansy's lapse into medievalism was not so very much stranger than

Hempnell's architecture, with its sprinkling of gargoyles and other fabulous monsters designed to scare off evil spirits. The second buzzer sounded and he got up.

His class in "Primitive Societies" quieted down leisurely as he strode in. He set a student to explaining the sib as a factor in tribal organization, then put in the next five minutes organizing his thoughts and noting late arrivals and absentees. When the explanation, supplemented by blackboard diagrams of marriage groups, had become so complicated that Bronstein, the prize student, was twitching with eagerness to take a hand, he called for comments and criticisms, and succeeded in getting a first-class argument going.

Finally the cocksure fraternity president in the second row said, "But all those ideas of social organization were based on ignorance, tradition and superstition. Unlike modern society."

That was Norman's cue. He lit in joyously, pulverized the defender of modern society with a point-by-point comparison of fraternities and primitive "young men's houses" down to the details of initiation ceremonies, which he dissected with scientific relish, and then launched into a broad analysis of present-day customs as they would appear to a hypothetical ethnologist from Mars. In passing, he drew a facetious analogy between sororities and primitive seclusion of girls at puberty.

The minutes raced pleasantly by as he demonstrated instances of cultural lag in everything from table manners to systems of measurements. Even the lone sleeper in the last row woke up and listened.

"Certainly we've made important innovations, chief among them the systematic use of the scientific method," he said at one point, "but the primitive groundwork is still there, dominating the pattern of our lives. We're modified anthropoid apes inhabiting night clubs and battleships. What else could you expect us to be?"

Marriage and courtship got special attention. With Bronstein grinning delightfully, Norman drew detailed modern parallels to marriage by purchase, marriage by capture, and symbolic marriage to a deity. He showed that trial marriage is no mere modern conception but a well-established ancient custom, successfully practiced by the Polynesians and others.

At this point he became aware of a beet-red, angry face toward the back of the room—that of Gracine Pollard, daughter of Hempnell's president. She glared at him, pointedly ignoring the interest taken by the neighboring students in her blushes.

Automatically it occurred to him, "Now I suppose the little neurotic will be yammering to Papa that Professor Saylor is advocating free love." He shrugged the idea aside and continued the discussion with modification. The buzzer cut it short.

But he was feeling irritated with himself. He only half listened to the enthusiastic comments and questions of Bronstein and a couple fo others.

Back at the office he found a note from Harold Gunnison, the Dean of Men. Having the next hour free, he set out across the quadrangle for the Administration Building, Bronstein still tagging along to expound some theory of his own.

But Norman was wondering why he had let himself go. Admittedly, some of his remarks had been a trifle raw. He had long ago adjusted his classroom behavior to Hempnell standards, without losing intellectual integrity, and this morning's ill-advised though trivial deviation bothered him.

Mrs. Carr swept by him without a word, her face slightly averted, cutting him cold. A moment later he guessed a possible explanation. In his abstraction, he had lighted a cigarette. Moreover, Bronstein had followed suit, obviously delighted at faculty infraction of a firmly established taboo. The faculty were only supposed to smoke in their dingy clubroom or, on the quiet, in their offices.

He frowned, but continued to smoke. Evidently the events of the previous night had disturbed his mind more than he had realized. He ground out the butt on the steps of the Administration Building.

In the doorway to the outer office he collided with the stylishly stout form of Mrs. Gunnison.

"Lucky I had a good hold on my camera," she grumbled, as he stooped to recover her bulging handbag. "I'd hate to have to try to replace these lenses." Then brushing back an untidy wisp of reddish hair from her forehead, "You look worried. How's Tansy?"

He answered briefly, sliding past her. Now there was a woman who really ought to be a witch. Expensive clothes worn sloppily; bossy, snobbish, and gruff; good-humored in a beefy fashion, but capable of riding rough-shod over anyone else's desires. The only person in whose presence her husband's authority seemed quite ridiculous.

Harold Gunnison cut short a telephone call and motioned Norman to come in and shut the door.

"Norman," Gunnison began, scowling, "this is a pretty delicate matter."

Norman became attentive. When Harold Gunnison said something was a delicate matter, unlike Thompson, he really meant it. He and Norman played squash together and got on pretty well. Norman's only serious objection to Gunnison was the latter's mutual admiration society with President Pollard, wherein solemn references to Pollard's political ideas and exaggerations of his friendship with national political figures were traded for occasional orotund commendations of the Dean of Men's Office.

But Harold had said, "A delicate matter." Norman braced himself to hear an accounts of eccentric, indiscreet, or even criminal behavior on the part of Tansy. That suddenly seemed the obvious explanation.

"You have a girl from the Student Employment Agency working for you? A Margaret Van Nice?"

Abruptly Norman realized who had made the second telephone call last night. Covering his shock, he waited a moment and said, "A rather quiet kid. Does mimeographing." Then, with an involuntary look of enlightenment, "Always talks in a whisper."

"Well, a little while ago she threw an hysterical fit in Mrs. Carr's office. Claimed that you had seduced her. Mrs. Carr immediately dumped the whole business in my lap."

Norman fought the impulse to tell about the phone conversation, contented himself with, "Well?"

Gunnison frowned and cocked a sad eye at him.

"I know things like that have happened," Norman said. "Right here at Hempnell. But not this time."

"Of course, Norman."

"Sure. There was opportunity though. We worked late several nights over at Morton."

Gunnison reached for a folder. "On a chance I got out her neurotic index. She ranks way up near the top. A regular bundle of complexes. We'll just have to handle it smoothly."

"I'll want to hear her accuse me," said Norman. "Soon as possible."

"Of course. I've arranged for a meeting at Mrs. Carr's office. Four o'clock this afternoon. Meantime she's seeing Dr. Gardner. That should sober her up."

"Four o'clock," repeated Norman, standing up. "You'll be there?"

"Certainly. I'm sorry about this whole business, Norman. Frankly, I think Mrs. Carr botched it up. Got panicky. She's a pretty old lady."

In the outer office Norman stopped to glance at a small display case of items concerned with Gunnison's work in physical chemistry. The present display was of Prince Rupert drops and other high-tension oddities. He stared moodily at the shiny dark globules with their stiff, twisted tails, vaguely noting the card which told how they were produced by dripping molten glass into hot oil. It occurred to him that Hempnell was something like a Prince Rupert drop. Hit the main body with a hammer and you only jarred your hand. But flick with a fingernail the delicate filament in which the drop ended, and it would explode in your face.

Fanciful.

He glanced at the other objects, among them a tiny mirror which, the legend explained, would fly to powder at the slightest scratch or sudden uneven change in temperature.

Yet it wasn't so fanciful, when you got to thinking about it. Any over-organized, tension-shot, somewhat artificial in-

stitution such as a small college tends to develop danger
points. And the same would be true of a person or a career.
Flick the delicate spot in the mind of a neurotic girl, and she
would erupt with wild accusations. Or take a saner person,
like himself. Suppose someone were studying him secretly,
looking for the vulnerable filament, finger poised to flick—

But that was really getting fanciful. He hurried off to his
last morning class.

Coming out of it, Hervey Sawtelle buttonholed him.

Norman's departmental colleague resembled an unfriendly
caricature of a college professor. Little older than Norman,
but with the personality of a septuagenarian, or a frightened
adolescent. He was always in a hurry, nervous to the point
of twitching, and he sometimes carried two brief cases. Norman saw in him one of the all too many victims of intellectual
vanity. Very likely during his own college days Hervey Sawtelle had been goaded by arrogant instructors into believing
that he ought to know everything about everything, be familiar with all the authorities on all the subjects, including
medieval music, differential equations, and modern poetry,
be able to produce an instant knowing rejoinder to any con-
ceivable intellectual remark, including those made in dead
and foreign languages, and never under any circumstances
ask a question. Failing in his subsequent frantic efforts to
become much more than a modern Bacon, Hervey Sawtelle
had presumably conceived a deep conviction of his intellectual inadequacy, which he tried to conceal, or perhaps forget,
by a furious attention to detail.

All this showed in his narrow, shrunken, thin-lipped, high-
browed face. Routine worries ceaselessly chased themselves
up and down it.

But at the moment he was in the grip of one of his petty
excitements.

"Say, Norman, the most interesting thing! I was down in
the stacks this morning, and I happened to pull out an old
doctor's thesis—1930—by someone I never heard of—with
the title *Superstition and Neurosis*." He produced a bound,
typewritten manuscript that looked as if it had aged without

ever being opened. "Almost the same title as your *Parallelisms in Superstition and Neurosis*. An odd coincidence, eh? I'm going to look it over tonight."

They were hurrying together toward the dining hall down a walk flooded with jabbering, laughing students, who curtsied smilingly out of their way. Norman studied Sawtelle's face covertly. Surely the fool must remember that his *Parallelisms* had been published in 1931, giving an ugly suggestion of plagiarism. But Sawtelle's nervous toothy grin was without guile.

He had the impulse to pull Sawtelle aside and tell him that there was something odder than a coincidence involved, and that it did not reflect in any way on his own integrity of scholarship. But this seemed hardly the place.

Yet there was no denying the incident bothered him a trifle. Why, it was years since he had even thought of that stupid business of Cunningham's thesis. It had lain buried in the past—a hidden vulnerability, waiting for the flick of the fingernail.

Asinine fancifulness! It could all be very well explained, to Sawtelle or anyone else, at a more suitable time.

Sawtelle's mind was back to habitual anxieties. "You know, we should be having our conference on the social-science program for next year. On the other hand, I suppose we should wait until—" He paused embarrassedly.

"Until it's decided whether you or I get the chairmanship of the department?" Norman finished for him. "I don't see why. We'll be working together in any case."

"Yes, of course. I didn't mean to suggest—"

They were joined by some other faculty members on the steps of the dining hall. The deafening clatter of trays from the student section was subdued to a slightly fainter din as they entered the faculty sanctum.

Conversation revolved among the old familiar topics, with an undercurrent of speculation as to what reorganizations and expansions of staff the new year might bring to Hempnell. There was some reference to the political ambitions of President Pollard—Harold Gunnison confided that a certain powerful political group was attempting to persuade him to run for governor; discreet silences here and there around the table substituted for adverse criticisms on this possibility. Sawtelle's Adam's apple twitched convulsively at a chance reference to the vacant chairmanship in sociology.

Norman managed to get a fairly interesting conversation going, with Holstrom of psychology. He was glad he would be busy with classes and conferences until four o'clock. He knew he could work half again as hard as someone like Sawtelle, but if he had to do one quarter of the worrying that man did—

Yet the four o'clock meeting proved to be an anti-climax. He had no sooner put his hand on the door leading to Mrs. Carr's office, when—as if that had provided the necessary stimulus—a shrill, tearful voice burst out with: "It's all a lie! I made it up!"

Gunnison was sitting near the window, face a trifle averted, arms folded, looking like a slightly bored, slightly embarrassed elephant. In a chair in the center of the room was huddled a delicate, fair-haired girl, tears dribbling down her flat cheeks and hysterical sobs racking her shoulders. Mrs. Carr was trying to calm her in a fluttery way.

"I don't know why I did it," the girl bleated pitifully. "I was in love with him and he wouldn't even look at me. I was going to kill myself last night, and I thought I would do this instead, to hurt him, or—"

"Now, Margaret, you must control yourself," Mrs. Carr admonished, her hands hovering over the girl's shoulders.

"Just a minute," Norman said. "Miss Van Nice—"

She looked around and up at him, apparently just becoming aware of his presence.

Norman waited a little. Neither of them moved. Then he said, "Miss Van Nice, last night between the time you decided to kill yourself and the time you decided to hurt me this way, did you do something else? Did you by any chance make a phone call?"

The girl didn't answer, but after a few moments a blush appeared on her tear-stained face, overspread it, and flowed

down under her dress. A little later even her forearms were
dull red.

Gunnison registered vague curiosity.

Mrs. Carr looked at the girl sharply, bending toward her.
For a moment Norman fancied that there was something distinctly venomous in her searching glance. But that was probably just a trick of the thick glasses, which sometimes
magnified Mrs. Carr's eyes until they looked fishlike.

The girl did not react as Mrs. Carr's hands touched her
shoulders. She was still looking at Norman, now with an
expression of agonized embarrassment and entreaty.

"That's all right," Norman said softly. "Nothing to worry
about," and he smiled at her sympathetically.

The girl's expression changed completely. She suddenly
shook loose from Mrs. Carr and sprang up facing Norman.
"Oh, I hate you!" she screamed. "I hate you!"

Gunnison followed him out of the office. He yawned, shook
his head, and remarked, "Glad that's over. Incidentally,
Gardner says nothing could possibly have happened to her."

"Never a dull moment," Norman responded, absently.

"Oh, by the way," Gunnison, said, dragging a stiff white
envelope out of his inside pocket, "here's a note for Mrs.
Saylor. Hulda asked me to give it to you. I forgot about it
before."

"I met Hulda coming out of your office this morning,"
Norman said, his thoughts still elsewhere.

Somewhat later, back at Morton, Norman tried to come to
grips with those thoughts, but found them remarkably slip-
pery. The dragon on the roof ridge of Estrey Hall lured away
his attention. Funny about little things like that. You never
even noticed them for years, and then they suddenly popped
into focus. How many people could give you one single definite fact about the architectural ornaments of buildings in
which they worked? Not one in ten, probably. Why, if you
had asked him yesterday about that dragon, he couldn't for
his life have been able to tell you even if there was one or
not.

He leaned on the window sill, looking at the lizard-like yet

grotesquely anthropoid form, bathed in the yellow sunset
glow, which, his wandering mind remembered, was supposed to symbolize the souls of the dead passing into and out
of the underworld. Below the dragon, jutting from under the
cornice, was a sculptured head, one of a series of famous
scientists and mathematicians decorating the entablature. He
made out the name "Galileo," along with a brief inscription
of some sort.

When he turned back to answer the phone, it suddenly
seemed very dark in the office.

"Saylor? I just want to tell you that I'm going to give you
until tomorrow—"

"Listen, Jennings," Norman cut in sharply, "I hung up
on you last night because you kept shouting into the phone.
This threatening line won't do you any good."

The voice continued where it had broken off, growing dangerously high. "—until tomorrow to withdraw your charges
and have me reinstated at Hempnell."

Then the voice broke into a screaming obscene torrent of
abuse, so loud that Norman could still hear it very plainly as
he placed the receiver back in the cradle.

Paranoid—that was the way it sounded.

Then he suddenly sat very still.

At twenty past one last night he had burned a charm supposedly designed to ward off evil influence from him. The
last of Tansy's "hands."

At about the same time Margaret Van Nice had decided to
avow her fanciful passion for him, and Theodore Jennings
had decided to make him responsible for an imaginary plot.

Next morning sanctimonious Trustee Fenner had called up
Thompson about the Utell party, and Hervey Sawtelle, poking around in the stacks, had found—

Rubbish!

With an angry snort of laughter at his own credulity, he
picked up his hat and headed for home.

V

Tansy was in a radiant mood, prettier than she had seemed in months. Twice he caught her smiling to herself, when he glanced up from his supper.

He gave her the note from Mrs. Gunnison. "Mrs. Carr asked after you, too. Gushed all over me—in a ladylike way, of course. Then, later on—" He caught himself as he started to tell about the cigarette and Mrs. Carr cutting him and the whole Margaret Van Nice business. No use worrying Tansy right now with things that might be considered bad luck. No telling what further construction she might put upon them.

She glanced through the note and handed it back to him.

"It has the authentic Hempnell flavor, don't you think?" she observed.

He read:

Dear Tansy: Where are you keeping yourself? I haven't seen you on campus more than once or twice this last month. If you're busy with something especially interesting, why not tell us about it? Why not come to tea this Saturday, and tell me all about yourself?

Hulda

P.S. You're supposed to bring four dozen cookies to the Local Alumni Wives' Reception the Saturday after.

"Rather confused-sounding," he said, "but I clearly perceive the keen bludgeon of Mrs. Gunnison. She looked particularly sloppy today."

Tansy laughed. "Still, we have been pretty antisocial these last weeks. I believe I'll ask them over for bridge tomorrow night. It's short notice, but they're usually free Wednesdays. And the Sawtelles."

"Do we have to? That henpecker?"

Tansy laughed. "I don't know how you would ever manage to get along without me—" She stopped short. "I'm afraid you'll have to endure Evelyn. After all, Hervey's the other important man in your department, and it's expected that you see something of each other socially. To make two tables, I'll invite the Carrs."

"Three fearful females," said Norman. "If they represent the average run of professors' wives, I was lucky to get you."

"I sometimes think the same thing about professors' wives' husbands," said Tansy.

As they smoked over the coffee, she said hesitatingly, "Norm, I said I didn't want to talk about last night. But now there's something I want to tell you."

He nodded.

"I didn't tell you last night, Norm, but when we burned those . . . things, I was terribly frightened. I felt that we were knocking holes in walls that had taken me years to build, and that now there was nothing to keep out the—"

He said nothing, sat very still.

"Oh, it's hard to explain, but ever since I began to . . . play with those things, I've been conscious of pressure from outside. A vague neurotic fear, something like the way *you* feel about trucks. Things trying to push their way in and get at us. And I've had to press them back, fight back at them with my—It's like that test of strength men sometimes make, trying to force each other's hand to the table. But that wasn't what I was starting to say.

"I went to bed feeling miserable and scared. The pressure from outside kept tightening around me, and I couldn't resist it, because we'd burned those things. And then suddenly, as I lay in the dark, about an hour after I went to bed, I got the most tremendous feeling of relief. The pressure vanished, as if I'd bobbed up to the surface after almost drowning. And I knew then . . . that I'd gotten over my craziness. That's why I'm so happy."

It was hard for Norman not to tell Tansy what he was thinking. Here was one more coincidence, but it knocked the others into a cocked hat. At about the same time as he had burned the last charm, experiencing a sensation of fear, Tansy had felt a great relief. That would teach him to build theories on coincidences!

"For I was crazy in a way, dear," she was saying. "There aren't many people who would have taken it as you did."

He said, "You weren't crazy—which is a relative term, anyway, applicable to anyone. You were just fooled by the cussedness of things."

"Cussedness?"

"Yes. The way nails sometimes insist on bending when you hammer, as if they were trying to. Or the way machinery refuses to work. Matter's funny stuff. In large aggregates, it obeys natural law, but when you get down to the individual atom or electron, it's largely a matter of chance or whim—" This conversation was not taking the direction he wanted it to, and he was thankful when Totem jumped onto the table, creating a diversion.

It turned out to be the pleasantest evening they had spent together in ages.

But next morning when he arrived at Morton, Norman wished he had not gotten started on that "cussedness of things" notion. It stuck in his mind. He found himself puzzling over the merest trifles—such as the precise position of that idiotic cement dragon. Yesterday he remembered thinking that it was exactly in the middle of the descending roof ridge. But now he saw that it was obviously two thirds of the way down, quite near the architrave topping the huge useless Gothic gateway set between Estrey and Morton. Even a social scientist ought to have better powers of observation than that!

The jangle of the phone coincided with the nine o'clock buzzer.

"Professor Saylor?" Thompson's voice was apologetic. "I'm sorry to bother you again, but I just got another inquiry from one of the trustees—Liddell, this time. Concerning an informal address you were supposed to have delivered at about the same time as that . . . er . . . party. The topic was 'What's wrong with College Education?' "

"Well, what about it? Are you implying there's nothing wrong with college education, or that the topic is taboo?"

"Oh, no, no, no, no. But the trustee seemed to think that you were making a criticism of Hempnell."

"Of small colleges of the same type as Hempnell, yes. Of Hempnell specifically, no."

"Well, he seemed to fear it might have a detrimental effect on enrollment for next year. Spoke of several friends of his with children of college age as having heard your address and being unfavorably impressed."

"Then they were supersensitive."

"He also seemed to think you had made a slighting reference to President Pollard's . . . er . . . political activities."

"I'm sorry but I have to get along to a class now."

"Very well," said Thompson, and hung up. Norman grimaced. The cussedness of things certainly wasn't to be compared with the cussedness of people! Then he jumped up and hurried off to his "Primitive Societies."

Gracine Pollard was absent, he noted with an inward grin, wondering if yesterday's lecture had been too much for her warped sense of propriety. But even the daughters of college presidents ought to be told a few home truths now and then.

And on the others, yesterday's lecture had had a markedly stimulating effect. Several students had abruptly chosen related subjects for their term papers, and the fraternity president had capitalized on his yesterday's discomfiture by planning a humorous article for the Hempnell *Buffoon* on the primitive significance of fraternity initiations. All in all they had a very brisk session.

Afterwards Norman found himself musing good-humoredly on how college students were misunderstood by a great many people.

Collegians were generally viewed as dangerously rebellious and radical, and shockingly experimental in their morality. Indeed the lower classes were inclined to picture them as monsters of unwholesomeness and perversion, potential murderers of little children and celebrants of various equivalents of the Black Mass. Whereas actually they were more

conventional than many high school kids. And as for experiments in sex, they were a long way behind those whose
education ended with grade school.

Instead of standing up boldly in the classroom and uttering
rebel pronouncements, they were much more apt to be fawn-
ingly hypocritical, desirous only of saying the thing that would
please the teacher most. Small danger of their getting out of
hand! On the contrary, it was necessary to charm them slowly
into truthfulness, away from the taboos and narrow-
mindedness of the home. And how much more complex these
problems became, and needful of solution, when you were
living in an obvious time of interim morality like today, when
national loyalty and faithfulness to family alone were dis-
solving in favor of a wider loyalty and a wider love—or in
favor of a selfish, dog-eat-dog, atom-bombed chaos, if the
human spirit were hedged, clipped, and dwarfed by tradi-
tional egotisms and fears.

College faculty members were as badly misrepresented to
the general public as were college students. Actually they
were a pretty timorous folk, exceedingly sensitive to social
disapproval. That they occasionally spoke out fearlessly was
all the more to their credit.

All of which of course reflected society's slow-dying tendency to view teachers not as educators but as vestal virgins
of a sort, living sacrifices on the altar of respectability, housed
in suitably grim buildings and judged on the basis of a far
stricter moral code than that applied to businessmen and
housewives. And in their vestal-virgining, their virginity
counted much more than their tending of the feeble flame of
imaginative curiosity and honest intellectual inquiry. Indeed,
for all most people cared, the flame might safely be let go
out, so long as the teachers remained sitting around it in their
temple—inviolate, sour-faced, and quite frozen testimonials
to the fact that somebody was upholding moral values somewhere.

Norman thought wryly: Why, they actually *want* us to be
witches, of a harmless sort. And I made Tansy stop!

The irony tickled him and he smiled.

His good humor lasted until after his last class that afternoon, when he happened to meet the Sawtelles in front of Morton Hall.

Evelyn Sawtelle was a snob and a fake intellectual. The illusion she tried most to encourage was that she had sacrificed a great career in the theater in order to marry Hervey. While in reality she had never been able to wrangle the directorship of the Hempnell Student Players and had had to content herself with a minor position in the speech department. She had an affected carriage and a slightly arty taste in clothes that, taken along with her flat cheeks and dull black hair and eyes, suggested the sort of creature you sometimes see stalking through the lobby at ballet and concert intermissions.

But far from being a bohemian, Evelyn Sawtelle was even more inclined to agonize over the minutiae of social convention and prestige than most Hempnell faculty wives. Yet because of her general incompetence, this anxiety did not result in tactfulness, but rather its opposite.

Her husband was completely under her thumb. She managed him like a business—bunglingly, overzealously, but with a certain dogged effectiveness.

"I had lunch today with Henrietta . . . I mean Mrs. Pollard," she announced to Norman with the air of one who has just visited royalty.

"Oh, say, Norman—" Hervey began excitedly, thrusting forward his brief case.

"We had a very interesting chat," his wife swept on. "We talked about you, too, Norman. It seems Gracine has been misinterpreting some of the things you've been saying in your class. She's such a sensitive girl."

"Dumb bunny, you mean," Norman corrected mentally. He murmured, "Oh?" with some show of politeness.

"Dear Henrietta was a little puzzled as just how to handle it, though of course she's a very tolerant, cosmopolitan soul. I just mentioned it because I thought you'd want to know. After all, it is very important that no one get any wrong impressions about the department. Don't you agree with me, Hervey?'' She ended sharply.

"What, dear? Oh, yes, yes. Say, Norman. I want to tell you about that thesis I showed you yesterday. The most amazing thing! Its main arguments are almost the same as those in your book! An amazing case of independent investigators arriving at the same conclusions. Why, it's like Darwin and Wallace, or—''

"You didn't tell *me* anything about this, dear,'' said his wife.

"Wait a minute,'' said Norman.

He hated to make an explanation in Mrs. Sawtelle's presence, but it had to be done.

"Sorry, Hervey, to have to substitute a rather sordid story for an intriguing scientific coincidence. It happened when I was an instructor here—1929, my first year. A graduate student named Cunningham got hold of my ideas—I was friendly with him—and incorporated them into his doctor's thesis. My work in superstition and neurosis was just a side line then, and partly because I was sick with pneumonia for two months I didn't read his thesis until after he'd gotten his degree.''

Sawtelle blinked. He face resumed its usual worried expression. A look of vague disappointment came into Mrs. Sawtelle's black-button eyes, as she would have liked to read the thesis, lingering over each paragraph, letting her suspicions have full scope, before hearing the explanation.

"I was very angry,'' Norman continued, "and intended to expose him. But then I heard he'd died. There was some hint of suicide. He was an unbalanced chap. How he'd hoped to get away with such an out-and-out steal, I don't know. Anyway, I decided not to do anything about it, for his family's sake. You see, it would have supplied a reason for thinking he *had* committed suicide.''

Mrs. Sawtelle looked incredulous.

"But, Norman,'' Sawtelle commented anxiously, "was that really wise? I mean to keep silent. Weren't you taking a chance? I mean with regard to your academic reputation?''

Abruptly, Mrs. Sawtelle's manner changed.

"Put that thing back in the stacks, Hervey, and forget about it," she directed curtly. Then she smiled archly at Norman. "I've been forgetting I have a surprise for you, Professor Saylor. Come down to the sound booth now, and I'll show you. It won't take a minute. Come along, Hervey."

Norman had no excuse ready, so he accompanied the Sawtelles to the rooms of the speech department at the other end of Morton, wondering how the speech department ever found any use for someone with as nasal and affected a voice as Evelyn Sawtelle, even if she did happen to be a professor's wife and a thwarted tragedienne.

The sound booth was dim and quiet, a solid box with sound-resistant walls and double windows. Mrs. Sawtelle took a disk from the cabinet, put it on one of the three turntables, and adjusted a couple of dials. Norman jerked. For an instant he thought that a truck was roaring toward the sound booth and would momentarily crash through the insulating walls. Then the abominable noise pouring from the amplifier changed to a strangely pulsing wail or whir, as of wind prying at a house. It struck a less usual chord, though, in Norman's agitated memory.

Mrs. Sawtelle darted back and swiveled the dials.

"I made a mistake," she said. "That's some modernistic music or other. Hervey, switch on the light. Here's the record I wanted." She put it on one of the other turntables.

"It sounded awful, whatever it was," her husband observed.

Norman had identified his memory. It was of an Australian bull-roarer a colleague had once demonstrated for him. The curved slat of wood, whirled at the end of a cord, made exactly the same sound. The aborigines used it in their rain magic.

". . . but if, in these times of misunderstanding and strife, we willfully or carelessly forget that every word and thought must refer to something in the real world, if we allow references to the unreal and the nonexistent to creep into our minds . . ."

Again Norman started. For now it was his own voice that

was coming out of the amplifier and he had an odd sense of jerking back in time.

"Surprised?" Evelyn Sawtelle questioned coyly. "It's that talk on semantics you gave the students last week. We had a mike spotted by the speaker's rostrum—I suppose you thought it was for amplification—and we made a sneak recording, as we call it. We cut it down here."

She indicated the heavier, cement-based turntable for making recordings. Her hands fluttered around the dials.

"We can do all sorts of things down here," she babbled on. "Mix all sorts of sounds. Music against voices. And—"

"Words *can* hurt us, you know. And oddly enough, it's the words that refer to things that *aren't*, that can hurt us most. Why . . ."

It was hard for Norman to appear even slightly pleased. He knew his reasons were no more sensible than those of a savage afraid someone will learn his secret name, yet all the same he disliked the idea of Evelyn Sawtelle monkeying around with his voice. Like her dully malicious, small-socketed eyes, it suggested a prying for hidden weaknesses.

And then Norman moved involuntarily for a third time. For suddenly out of the amplifier, but now mixed with his voice, came the sound of the bull-roarer that still had that devilish hint of an onrushing truck.

"Oh, there I've done it again," said Evelyn Sawtelle rapidly, snatching at the dials. "Messing up your beautiful voice with that terrible music." She grimaced. "But then, as you just said, Professor Saylor, sounds can't hurt us."

Norman did not correct her typical misquoting. He looked at her curiously for a moment. She stood facing him, her hands behind her. Her husband, his nose twitching, had idled over to the still moving turntables and was gingerly poking a finger at one of them.

"No," said Norman slowly, "they can't." And then he excused himself with a brusque, "Well, thanks for the demonstration."

"We'll see you tonight," Evelyn called after him. Somehow it sounded like, "You won't get rid of me."

How I detest that woman, thought Norman, as he hurried up the dark stair and down the corridor.

Back at his office, he put in a good hour's work on his notes. Then getting up to switch on the light, his glance happened to fall on the window.

After a few moments, he jerked away and darted to the closet to get his field glasses.

Someone must have a very obscure sense of humor to perpetrate such a complicated practical joke.

Intently he searched the cement at the juncture of roof ridge and clawed feet, looking for the telltale cracks. He could not spot any, but that would not have been easy in the failing yellow light.

The cement dragon now stood at the edge of the gutter, as if about to walk over to Morton along the architrave of the big gateway.

He lifted his glasses to the creature's head—blank and crude as an unfinished skull. Then on an impulse he dropped down to the row of sculptured heads, focused on Galileo, and read the little inscription he had not been able to make out before.

"Eppur si muove."

The words Galileo was supposed to have muttered after recanting before the Inquisition his belief in the revolution of the earth around the sun.

"Nevertheless, it moves."

A board creaked behind him, and he spun around.

By his desk stood a young man,, waxen pale, with thick red hair. His eyes stood out like milky marbles. One white, tendon-ridged hand gripped a .22 target pistol.

Norman walked toward him, bearing slightly to the right.

The skimpy barrel of the gun came up.

"Hullo, Jennings," said Norman. "You've been reinstated. Your grades have been changed to straight A's."

The gun barrel slowed for an instant.

Norman lunged in.

The gun went off under his left arm, pinking the window.

The gun clunked on the floor. Jennings' skinny form went

limp. As Norman sat him down on the chair, he began to sob, convulsively.

Norman picked up the gun by the barrel, laid it in a drawer, locked the drawer, pocketed the key. Then he lifted the phone and asked for an on-campus number. The connection was made quickly. "Gunnison?" he asked.

"Uh-huh, just caught me as I was leaving."

"Theodore Jennings' parents live right near the college, don't they? You know, the chap who flunked out last semester."

"Of course they do. What's the matter?"

"Better get them over here quick. And have them bring his doctor. He just tried to shoot me. Yes, *his* doctor. No, neither of us is hurt. But quickly."

Norman put down the phone. Jennings continued to sob agonizingly. Norman looked at him with disgust for a moment, then patted his shoulder.

An hour later Gunnison sat down in the same chair, and let off a sigh of relief.

"I'm sure glad they agreed about asking for his commitment to the asylum," he said. "It was awfully good of you, Norman, not to insist on the police. Things like that give a college a bad name."

Norman smiled wearily. "Almost anything gives a college a bad name. But the kid was obviously as crazy as a loon. And of course I understand how much the Jenningses, with their political connections and influence, mean to Pollard."

Gunnison nodded. They lit up and smoked for a while in silence. Norman thought how different real life was from a detective story, where an attempted murder was generally considered a most serious thing, an occasion for much turmoil and telephoning and the gathering of flocks of official and unofficial detectives. Whereas here, because it occurred in an area of life governed by respectability rather than sensation, it was easily hushed up and forgotten.

Gunnison looked at his watch. "I'll have to hustle. It's almost seven, and we're due at your place at eight."

But he lingered, ambling over to the window to inspect the bullet hole.

"I wonder if you'd mind not mentioning this to Tansy?" Norman asked. "I don't want to worry her."

Gunnison nodded. "Good thing if we kept it to ourselves." Then he pointed out the window. "That's one of my wife's pets," he remarked in a jocular tone.

Norman saw that his finger was trained on the cement dragon, now coldly revealed by the upward glare from the street lights.

"I mean," Gunnison went on, "she must have a dozen photographs of it. Hempnell's her specialty. I believe she's got a photograph of every architectural oddity on campus. That one is her favorite." He chuckled. "Usually it's the husband who keeps ducking down into the darkroom, but not in our family. And me a chemist, at that."

Norman's taut mind had unaccountably jumped to the thought of a bull-roarer. Abruptly he realized the analogy between the recording of a bull-roarer and the photograph of a dragon.

He clamped a lid on the fantastic questions he wanted to ask Gunnison.

"Come on!" he said. "We'd better get along."

Gunnison started a little at the harshness of his voice.

"Can you drop me off?" asked Norman in quieter tones. "My car's at home."

"Sure thing," said Gunnison.

After he switched out the lights, Norman paused for a moment, staring at the window. The words came back.

"*Eppur si muove.*"

VI

They had hardly cleared away the remains of a hasty supper, when there came the first clang from the front-door chimes. To Norman's relief, Tansy had accepted without questioning his rather clumsy explanation of why he had gotten home so late. There was something puzzling, though, about her serenity these last two days. She was usually much sharper and more curious. But of course he had been careful to hide disturbing events from her, and he ought only to be glad her nerves were in such good shape.

"Dearest! It's been *ages* since we've seen you!" Mrs. Carr embraced Tansy cuddlingly. "How are you? How are you?" The question sounded peculiarly eager and incisive. Norman put it down to typical Hempnell gush. "Oh, dear, I'm afraid I've got a cinder in my eye," Mrs. Carr continued. "The wind's getting quite fierce."

"Gusty," said Professor Carr of the mathematics department, showing harmless delight at finding the right word. He was a little man with red cheeks and a white Vandyke, as innocent and absent-minded as college professors are supposed to be. He gave the impression of residing permanently in a special paradise of transcendental and transfinite numbers and of the hieroglyphs of symbolic logic, for whose manipulations he had a nationally recognized fame among mathematicians. Russell and Whitehead may have invented those hieroglyphs, but when it came to handling, cherishing, and coaxing the exasperating, riddlesome things, Carr was the champion prestidigitator.

"It seems to have gone away now," said Mrs. Carr, waving aside Tansy's handkerchief and experimentally blinking her eyes, which looked unpleasantly naked until she replaced her thick glasses. "Oh, that must be the others," she added, as the chimes sounded. "Isn't it *marvelous* that everyone at Hempnell is so punctual?"

As Norman started for the front door he imagined for the crazy moment that someone must be whirling a bull-roarer outside, until he realized it could only be the rising wind living up to Professor Carr's description of it.

He was confronted by Evelyn Sawtelle's angular form, wind whipping her black coat against her legs. Her equally angular face, with its shoe-button eyes, was thrust toward his own.

"Let us in, or it'll blow us in," she said. Like most of her attempts at coy or facetious humor, it did not come off, perhaps because she made it sound so stupidly grim. She entered, with Hervey in tow, and made for Tansy.

"My dear, how are you? Whatever have you been doing with yourself?" Again Norman was struck by the eager and meaningful tone of the question. For a moment he wondered whether the woman had somehow gotten an inkling of Tansy's eccentricity and the recent crisis. But Mrs. Sawtelle was so voice-conscious that she was always emphasizing things the wrong way.

There was a noisy flurry of greetings, Totem squeaked and darted out of the way of the crowd of human beings. Mrs. Carr's voice rose above the rest, shrilling girlishly.

"Oh, Professor Sawtelle, I want to tell you how *much* we appreciated your talk on city planning. It was truly *significant!*" Sawtelle writhed.

Norman thought: "So now *he's* the favorite for the chairmanship.'

Professor Carr had made a beeline for the bridge tables and was wistfully fingering the cards.

"I've been studying the mathematics of the shuffle," he began with a bright-eyed air, as soon as Norman drifted into range. "The shuffle is supposed to make it a matter of chance what hands are dealt. But that is not true at all." He broke open a new pack of cards and spread the deck. "The manufacturers arrange these by suits—thirteen spades, thirteen hearts, and so on. Now suppose I make a perfect shuffle—divide the pack into equal parts and interleaf the cards one by one."

He tried to demonstrate, but the cards got away from him.

"It's really not as hard as it looks," he continued amiably. "Some players can do it every time, quick as a wink. But that's not the point. Suppose I make two perfect shuffles with a new pack. Then, no matter how the cards are cut, each player will get thirteen of a suit—an event that, if you went purely by the laws of chance, would happen only once in about one hundred and fifty-eight billion times as regards a *single* hand, let alone all four."

Norman nodded and Carr smiled delightedly.

"That's only one example. It comes to this: What is loosely termed chance is really the resultant of several perfectly definite factors—chiefly the play of cards on each hand, and the shuffle-habits of the players." He made it sound as important as the Theory of Relativity. "Some evenings the hands are very ordinary. Other evenings they keep getting wilder and wilder—long suits, voids and so on. Sometimes the cards persistently run north and south. Other times, east and west. Luck? Chance? Not at all! It's the result of known causes. Some expert players actually make use of this principle to determine the probable location of key cards. They remember how the cards were played on the last hand, how the packets were put together, how the shuffle-habits of the maker have disarranged the cards. Then they interpret that information according to the bids and opening leads the next time the cards are used. Why, it's really quite simple—or would be for a blindfolded chess expert. And of course any really good bridge player should—"

Norman's mind went off at a tangent. Suppose you applied this principle outside bridge? Suppose that coincidence and other chance happenings weren't really as chancy as they looked? Suppose there were individuals with a special aptitude for calling the turns, making the breaks? But that was a pretty obvious idea—nothing to give a person the shiver it had given him.

"I wonder what's holding up the Gunnisons," Professor Carr was saying. "We might start one table now. Perhaps we can get in an extra rubber," he added hopefully.

A peal from the chimes settled the question.

Gunnison looked as if he had eaten his dinner too fast and Hulda seemed rather surly.

"We had to rush so," she muttered curtly to Norman as he held open the door.

Like the other two women, she almost ignored him and concentrated her greetings on Tansy. It gave him a vaguely uneasy feeling as when they had first come to Hempnell and faculty visits had been a nerve-racking chore. Tansy seemed at a disadvantage, unprotected, in contrast to the aggressive air animating the other three.

But what of it?—he told himself. That was normal for Hempnell faculty wives. They acted as if they lay awake nights plotting to poison the people between their husbands and the president's chair.

Whereas Tansy—But that was like what Tansy had been doing or rather what Tansy had said *they* were doing. *She* hadn't been doing it. She had only been—His thoughts started to gyrate confusingly and he switched them off.

They cut for partners.

The cards seemed determined to provide an illustration for the theory Carr had explained. The hands were uniformly commonplace—abnormally average. No long suits. Nothing but 4-4-3-2 and 4-3-3-3 distribution. Bid one; make two. Bid two; down one.

After the second round, Norman applied his private remedy for boredom—the game of "Spot the Primitive." You played it by yourself, secretly. It was just an exercise for an ethnologist's imagination. You pretended that the people around you were members of a savage race, and you tried to figure out how their personalities would manifest themselves in such an environment.

Tonight it worked almost too well.

Nothing unusual about the men. Gunnison, of course, would be a prosperous tribal chieftain; perhaps a little fatter, and tended by maidens, but with a jealous and vindictive wife waiting to pounce. Carr might figure as the basket maker of the village—a spry old man, grinning like a little monkey, weaving the basket fibers into intricate mathematical matrices. Sawtelle, of course, would be the tribal scapegoat, butt of endless painful practical jokes.

But the women!

Take Mrs. Gunnison, now his partner. Give her a brown skin. Leave the red hair, but twist some copper ornaments in it. She'd be heftier if anything, a real mountain of a woman, stronger than most of the men in the tribe, able to wield a spear or club. The same brutish eyes, but the lower lip would jut out in a more openly sullen and domineering way. It was only too easy to imagine what she'd do to the unlucky maidens in whom her husband showed too much interest. Or how she would pound tribal policy into his head when they retired to their hut. Or how her voice would thunder out the death chants the women sang to aid the men away at war.

Then Mrs. Sawtelle and Mrs. Carr, who had progressed to the top table along with himself and Mrs. Gunnison. Mrs. Sawtelle first. Make her skinnier. Scarify the flat cheeks with ornamental ridges. Tattoo the spine. Witch woman. Bitter as quinine bark because her husband was ineffectual. Think of her prancing before a spike-studded fetish. Think of her screeching incantations and ripping off a chicken's head . . .

"Norman, you are playing out of turn," said Mrs. Gunnison.

"Sorry."

And Mrs. Carr. Shrivel her a bit. Leave only a few wisps of hair on the parchment skull. Take away the glasses, so her eyes would be gummy. She'd blink and peer short-sightedly, and leer toothlessly, and flutter her bony claws. A nice harmless old squaw, who'd gather the tribe's children around her (always that hunger for youth!) and tell them legends. But her jaw would still be able to snap like a steel trap, and her clawlike hands would be deft at applying arrow poison, and she wouldn't really need her eyes because she'd have other ways of seeing things, and even the bravest warrior would grow nervous if she looked too long in his direction.

"Those experts at the top table are awfully quiet," called Gunnison with a laugh. "They must be taking the game very seriously."

Witch women, all three of them, engaged in booting their husbands to the top of the tribal hierarchy.

From the dark doorway at the far end of the room, Totem was peering curiously as if weighing some similar possibility.

But Norman could not fit Tansy into the picture. He could visualize physical changes, like frizzing her hair and putting some big rings in her ears and a painted design on her forehead. But he could not picture her as belonging to the same tribe. She persisted in his imagination as a stranger woman, a captive, eyed with suspicion and hate by the rest. Or perhaps a woman of the same tribe, but one who had done something to forfeit the trust of all the other women. A priestess who had violated taboo. A witch who had renounced witchcraft.

Abruptly his field of vision narrowed to the score pad. Evelyn Sawtelle was idly scribbling stick figures as Mrs. Carr deliberated over a lead. First the stick figure of a man with arms raised and three or four balls above his head, as if he were juggling. Then the stick figure of a queen, indicated by crown and skirt. Then a little tower with battlements. Then an L-shaped thing with a stick figure hanging from it—a gallows. Finally, a crude vehicle—a rectangle with two wheels—bearing down on a man whose arms were extended toward it in fear.

Just five scribbles. But Norman knew that four of them were connected with a bit of unusual knowledge buried somewhere in his mind. A glance at the exposed dummy gave him the clue.

Cards.

But this bit of knowledge was from the ancient history of cards, when the whole deck was drenched with magic, when there was a Knight between the Jack and Queen, when the suits were swords, batons, cups, and money, and when there were twenty-two special tarot, or fortune-telling, cards in the pack, of which today only the Joker remained.

But Evelyn Sawtelle knowing about anything so recondite as tarot cards? Knowing them so well she doodled them? Stupid, affected, conventional Evelyn Sawtelle? It was unthinkable. Yet—four of the tarot cards were the Juggler, the Empress, the Tower, and the Hanged Man.

Only the fifth stick figure, that of the man and vehicle, did not fit in. Juggernaut? The fanatical, finally cringing victim about to die under the wheels of the vast, trundling idol? That was closer—and chalk one more up to the esoteric scholarship of stupid Evelyn Sawtelle.

Suddenly it came to him. Himself and a truck. A great big truck. That was the meaning of the fifth stick figure.

But Evelyn Sawtelle knowing his pet phobia?

He stared at her. She scratched out the stick figures and looked at him sullenly.

Mrs. Gunnison leaned forward, lips moving as if she might be counting trump.

Mrs. Carr smiled, and made her lead. The risen wind began to make the same intermittent roaring sound it had for a moment earlier in the evening.

Norman suddenly chuckled whistlingly, so that the three women looked at him. Why, what a fool he was! Worrying about witchcraft, when all Evelyn Sawtelle had been doodling was a child playing ball—the child she couldn't have; a stick queen—herself; a tower—her husband's office as chairman of the sociology department, or some other and more fundamental potency; a hanged man—Hervey's impotence (that was an idea!); fearful man and truck—her own sexual energy horrifying and crushing Hervey.

He chuckled again, so that the three women lifted their eyebrows. He looked around at them enigmatically.

"And yet," he asked himself, continuing his earlier ruminations, in what was, at first, a much lighter vein, "why not?"

Three witch women using magic as Tansy had, to advance their husbands' careers and their own.

Making use of their husbands' special knowledge to give magic a modern twist. Suspicious and worried because Tansy had given up magic; afraid she'd found a much stronger variety and was planning to make use of it.

And Tansy—suddenly unprotected, possibly unaware of the change in their attitude toward her because, in giving up magic, she had lost her sensitivity to the super-natural, her "woman's intuition."

Why not carry it a step further? Maybe all women were the same. Guardians of mankind's ancient customs and traditions, including the practice of witchcraft. Fighting their husbands' battles from behind the scenes, by sorcery. Keeping it a secret; and on those occasions when they were discovered, conveniently explaining it as feminine susceptibility to superstitious fads.

Half of the human race still actively practicing sorcery.

Why not?

"It's your play, Norman," said Mrs. Sawtelle, sweetly.

"You look as if you had something on your mind," said Mrs. Gunnison.

"How are you getting along up there, Norm?" her husband called. "Those women got you buffaloed?"

Buffaloed? Norman came back to reality with a jerk. That was just what they almost had done. And all because the human imagination was a thoroughly unreliable instrument, like a rubber ruler. Let's see, if he played his King it might set up a Queen in Mrs. Gunnison's hand so she could get in and run her spades.

As Mrs. Carr topped it with her ace, Norm was conscious of her wrinkled lips fixed in a faint cryptic smile.

After that hand, Tansy served refreshments. Norman followed her to the kitchen.

"Did you see the looks she kept giving you?" she whispered gaily to Norman. "I sometimes think the bitch is in love with you."

He chuckled. "You mean Evelyn?"

"Of course not. Mrs. Carr. Inside she's a glamor girl. Haven't you ever seen her looking at the students, wishing she had the outside too?"

Norman remembered he'd been thinking the very thing that morning.

Tansy continued, "I'm not trying to flatter myself when I say I've caught her looking at me in the same way. It gives me the creeps."

Norman nodded. "She reminds me of the Wicked—" He caught himself.

"—Witch in Snow White? Yes. And now you'd better run along, dear, or they'll be bustling out here to remind me that a Hempnell man's place is definitely not in the kitchen."

When he returned to the living room, the usual shop talk had started.

"Saw Pollard today," Gunnison remarked, helping himself to a section of chocolate cake. "Told me he'd be meeting with the trustees tomorrow morning, to decide among other things on the sociology chairmanship."

Hervey Sawtelle choked on a crumb and almost upset his cup of cocoa.

Norman caught Mrs. Sawtelle glaring at him vindictively. She changed her face and murmured, "How interesting." He smiled. That kind of hate he could understand. No need to confuse it with witchcraft.

He went to the kitchen to get Mrs. Carr a glass of water, and met Mrs. Gunnison coming out of the bedroom. She was slipping a leather bound booklet into her capacious handbag. It recalled to his mind Tansy's diary. Probably an address book.

Totem slipped out from behind her, hissing decorously as she dodged past her feet.

"I loathe cats," said Mrs. Gunnison bluntly and walked past him.

Professor Carr had made arrangements for a final rubber, men at one table, women at the other.

"A barbaric arrangement," said Tansy, winking. "You really don't think we can play bridge at all."

"On the contrary, my dear, I think you play very well," Carr replied seriously. "But I confess that at times I prefer to play with men. I can get a better idea of what's going on in their minds. Whereas women still baffle me."

"As they should, dear," added Mrs. Carr, bringing a flurry of laughter.

The cards suddenly began to run freakishly, with abnormal distribution of suits, and play took a wild turn. But Norman found it impossible to concentrate, which made Sawtelle an even more jittery partner than usual.

He kept listening to what the women were saying at the other table. His rebellious imagination persisted in reading hidden meanings into the most innocuous remarks.

"You usually hold wonderful hands, Tansy. But tonight you don't seem to have any," said Mrs. Carr. But suppose she was referring to the kind of hand you wrapped in flannel?

"Oh, well, unlucky in cards . . . you know." How had Mrs. Sawtelle meant to finish the remark? Lucky in love? Lucky in sorcery? Idiotic notion!

"That's two psychic bids you've made in succession, Tansy. Better watch out. We'll catch up with you." What might not a psychic bid stand for in Mrs. Gunnison's vocabulary? Some kind of bluff in witchcraft? A pretense at giving up conjuring?

"I wonder," Mrs. Carr murmured sweetly to Tansy, "if you're hiding a very strong hand this time, dear, and making a trap pass?"

Rubber ruler. That was the trouble with imagination. According to a rubber ruler, an elephant would be no bigger than a mouse, a jagged line and a curve might be equally straight. He tried to think about the slam he had contracted for.

"The girls talk a good game of bridge," murmured Gunnison in an undertone.

Gunnison and Carr came out at the long end of a two-thousand rubber and were still crowing pleasantly as they stood around waiting to leave.

Norman remembered a question he wanted to ask Mrs. Gunnison.

"Harold was telling me you had a number of photographs of that cement dragon or whatever it is on top of Estrey. It's right opposite my window."

She looked at him for a moment, then nodded.

"I believe I've got one with me. Took it almost a year ago."

She dug a rumpled snapshot out of her handbag.

He studied it, and experienced a kind of shiver in reverse. This didn't make sense at all. Instead of being toward the center of the roof ridge, or near the bottom, it was almost at the top. Just what was involved here? A practical joke stretching over a period of days or weeks? Or—His mind balked, like a skittish horse. Yet—*Eppur si muove*.

He turned it over. There was a confusing inscription on the back, in greasy red crayon. Mrs. Gunnison took it out of his hands. to show the others.

"The wind sounds like a lost soul," said Mrs. Carr, hugging her coat around her as Norman opened the door.

"But a rather talkative one—probably a woman," her husband added with a chuckle.

When the last of them were gone, Tansy slipped her arm around his waist, and said, "I must be getting old. It wasn't nearly as much of a trial as usual. Even Mrs. Carr's ghoulish flirting didn't bother me. For once they all seemed almost human."

Norman looked down at her intently. She was smiling peacefully. Totem had come out of hiding and was rubbing against her legs.

With an effort Norman nodded and said, "Yes, they did. But God, that cocoa! Let's have a drink!"

VII

There were shadows everywhere, and the ground under Norman's feet was soft and quivering. The dreadful strident roaring, which seemed to have gone on since eternity began, shook his very bones. Yet it did not drown out the flat, nasty monotone of that other voice which kept telling him to do something—he could not be sure what, except that it involved injury to himself, although he heard the voice as plainly as if someone were talking inside his head. He tried to struggle away from the direction in which the voice wanted him to go, but heavy hands jerked him back. He wanted to look over his shoulder at something he knew would be taller than himself, but he couldn't muster the courage. The shadows were made by great rushing clouds which would momentarily assume the form of gigantic faces brooding down on him, faces with pits of darkness for eyes, and sullen, savage lips, and great masses of hair streaming behind.

He must not do the thing the voice commanded. And yet he must. He struggled wildly. The sound rose to an earth-shaking pandemonium. The clouds became a black all-engulfing torrent.

And then suddenly the bedroom became mixed up with the other picture, and he struggled awake.

He rubbed his face, which was thick with sleep, and tried unsuccessfully to remember what the voice had wanted him to do. He still felt the reverberations of the sound in his ears.

Gloomy daylight seeped through the shades. The clock indicated quarter to eight.

Tansy was still curled up, one arm out of the covers. A smile was tickling the corners of her lips and wrinkling her nose. Norman slipped out carefully. His bare foot came down on a loose carpet tack. Suppressing an angry grunt, he hobbled off.

For the first time in months he botched shaving. Twice the new blade slid too sharply sideways, neatly removing tiny segments of skin. He glared irritably at the white-glazed, red-flecked face in the mirror, pulled the blade down his chin very slowly, but with a little too much pressure, and gave himself a third nick.

By the time he got down to the kitchen, the water he had put on was boiling. As he poured it into the coffeepot, the wobbly handle of the saucepan came completely loose, and his bare ankles were splattered painfully. Totem skittered away, then slowly returned to her pan of milk. Norman cursed, then grinned. What had he been telling Tansy about the cussedness of things? As if to prove the point with a final ridiculous example, he bit his tongue while eating coffee cake. Cussedness of things? Say rather the cussedness of the human nervous system! Faintly he was aware of a potently disturbing and unidentifiable emotion—remnant of the dream?—like an unpleasant swimming shape glimpsed beneath weedy water.

It seemed most akin to a dull seething anger, for as he hurried toward Morton Hall, he found himself inwardly at war with the established order of things, particularly educational institutions. The old sophomoric exasperation at the hypocrisies and compromises of civilized society welled up and poured over the dams that a mature realism had set against it. This was a great life for a man to be leading! Coddling the immature minds of grownup brats, and lucky to get one halfway promising student a year. Playing bridge with a bunch of old fogies. Catering to jittery incompetents like Hervey Sawtelle. Bowing to the thousand and one stupid rules and traditions of a second-rate college. And for what!

Ragged clouds were moving overhead, presaging rain. They reminded him of his dream. He felt the impulse to shout a childish defiance at those faces in the sky.

A truck rolled quietly by, recalling to his mind the little picture Evelyn Sawtelle had scribbled on the bridge pad. He followed it with his eyes. When he turned back, he saw Mrs. Carr.

"You've cut yourself," she said with sweet solicitude, peering sharply through her spectacles.

"Yes, I have."

"How unfortunate!"

He didn't even agree. They walked together through the gate between Estrey and Morton. He could just make out the snout of the cement dragon poked over the Estrey gutter.

"I wanted to tell you last night how distressed I was, Professor Saylor, about the matter of Margaret Van Nice, only of course, it wasn't the right time. I'm dreadfully sorry that you had to be called in. Such a disgusting accusation! How you must have felt!"

She seemed to misinterpret his wry grimace at this, for she went on very swiftly, "Of course, I never once dreamed that *you* had done anything the least improper, but I thought there must be *something* to the girl's story. She told it in such *detail*." She studied his face with interest. The thick glass made her eyes big as an owl's. "Really, Professor Saylor, some of the girls that come to Hempnell nowadays are *terrible*. Where they get such loathsome ideas from is quite beyond me."

"Would you like to know?"

She looked at him blankly, an owl in daytime.

"They get them," he told her concisely, "from a society which seeks simultaneously to stimulate and inhibit one of their basic drives. They get them, in brief, from a lot of dirty-minded adults!"

"Really, Professor Saylor! Why—"

"There are a number of girls here at Hempnell who would be a lot healthier with real love affairs rather than imaginary ones. A fair proportion, of course, have already made satisfactory adjustments."

He had the satisfaction of hearing her gasp as he abruptly turned into Morton. His heart was pounding pleasantly. His lips were tight. When he reached his office he lifted his phone and asked for an on-campus number.

"Thompson? . . . Saylor. I have a couple of news items for you."

"Good, good! What are they?" Thompson replied hungrily, in the tone of one who poises a pencil.

"First, the subject for my address to the Off-campus Mothers, week after next: 'Pre-marital Relations and the College Student.' Second, my theatrical friends—the Utells—will be playing in the city at the same time, and I shall invite them to be guests of the college."

"But—" The poised pencil had obviously been stopped like a red-hot poker.

"That's all, Thompson. Perhaps I shall have something more interesting another time. Good-by."

He felt a stinging sensation in his hand. He had been fingering the little obsidian knife. It had gashed his finger. Blood smeared the clear volcanic glass where once, he told himself, had been the blood of sacrifice or ritual scarification. Clumsy—he searched his desk for adhesive bandages. The drawer where he remembered putting them was locked. He opened it and there was the slim-barreled revolver he had taken from Theodore Jennings. The buzzer sounded. He shut the drawer, locked it again, ripped a strip of cloth from his handkerchief, and hurried tied it around the dripping wound.

As he hurried down the corridor, Bronstein fell into step with him.

"We're pulling for you this morning, Dr. Saylor," he murmured heartily.

"What do you mean?"

Bronstein's grin was a trifle knowing. "A girl who works in the president's office told us they were deciding on the sociology chairmanship. I sure hope the old buzzards show some sense for once."

Academic dignity stiffened Norman's reply. "In any case, I will be satisfied with their decision."

Bronstein felt the rebuff. "Of course, I didn't mean to—"

"Of course you didn't."

He immediately regretted his sharpness. Why the devil should he rebuke a student for failing to reverence trustees as representatives of deity? Why pretend he didn't want the chairmanship? Why conceal his contempt for half the faculty? The anger he thought he had worked out of his system surged up with redoubled violence. On a sudden irresistible impulse he tossed his lecture notes aside and started in to tell the class just what he thought of the world and Hempnell. They might as well find out young!

Fifteen minutes later he came to with a jerk in the middle of a sentence about "dirty-minded old women, in whom greed for social prestige has reached the magnitude of a perversion." He could not remember half of what he had been saying. He searched the faces of his class. They looked excited, but puzzled, most of them, and a few looked shocked. Gracine Pollard was glaring. Yes! He remembered now that he had made a neat but nasty analysis of the political ambitions of a certain college president who could be none other than Randolph Pollard. And somewhere he had started off on that pre-marital relations business, and had been ribald about it, to say the least. And he had—

Exploded. Like a Prince Rupert drop.

He finished off with half a dozen lame generalities. He knew they must be quite inappropriate, for the looks grew more puzzled.

But the class seemed very remote. A shiver was spreading downward from the base of his skull, all because of a few words that had printed themselves in his mind.

The words were: A fingernail has flicked a psychic filament.

He shook his head, jumbling the type. The words vanished.

There were thirty minutes of class time left. He wanted to get away. He announced a surprise quiz, chalked up two questions, and left the room. In his office, he noticed that the cut finger had started to bleed again through the bandage. He remembered that there had been blood on the chalk.

And dried blood on the obsidian knife. He resisted the impulse to finger it, and sat staring at the top of his desk.

It all went back to Tansy's witchcraft aberration, he told himself. It had shaken him much more than he had dared to admit. He had tried to put it out of his mind too quickly. And Tansy had appeared to forget it too quickly. He must thrash it all out with her, again, and again, or the thing would fester.

What was he thinking! Tansy seemed so happy and relieved the last three days, that would surely be the wrong course to take.

But how could Tansy have got over a serious obsession so easily? It wasn't normal. He remembered her sleeping smile. Yet it wasn't Tansy who was behaving strangely now. It was he. As if a spell—What asinine rot! He'd just let himself be irritated by that stupid, hidebound old bunch of women, those old dragons—

His eyes instantly strayed toward the window, but the telephone recalled him.

"Professor Saylor? . . . I'm calling for Doctor Pollard. Could you come in and see Dr. Pollard this afternoon? . . . Four o'clock? Thank you."

He leaned back with a smile. At least, he told himself, he had got the chairmanship.

It grew darker as the day progressed, the ragged clouds

swept lower and lower. Students scurried along the walks. But the storm held off until almost four.

Big raindrops splattered the dusty steps as he ducked under the portico of the Administration Building. Thunder crackled and crashed, as if acres of metal sheeting were being shaken above the clouds. He turned back to watch. Lightning threw the Gothic roofs and towers into sharp relief. Again the crackle, building to a crash. He remembered he had left a window open in his office. But there was nothing that would be damaged by the wet.

Wind swooped through the portico with a strident, pulsating roar. The unmusical voice that spoke into his ear had the same quality.

"Isn't it a pretty storm?"

Evelyn Sawtelle was smiling for once. It had a grotesque effect on her features, as if a horse had suddenly discovered how to smirk.

"You've heard the news, of course?" She went on. "About Hervey."

Hervey popped out from behind her. He was grinning too, but embarrassedly. He mumbled something that was lost in the storm and extended his hand blindly, as if he were in a receiving line.

Evelyn never took her eye off Norman. "Isn't it wonderful?" she said. "Of course, we expected it, but still—"

Norman guessed. He forced himself to grasp Hervey's hand, just as the latter was withdrawing it flusteredly.

"Congratulations, old man," he said briefly.

"I'm very proud of Hervey," Evelyn announced possessively, as if he were a small boy who had won a prize for good behavior.

Her eyes followed Norman's hand. "Oh, you've cut yourself." The smirk seemed to be a permanent addition to her features. The wind wailed fiendishly. "Come, Hervey!" And she walked out into the storm as if it weren't there.

Hervey goggled at her in surprise. He mumbled something apologetic to Norman, pumped his hand up and down again, and then obediently scampered after his wife.

Norman watched them. There was something unpleasantly impressive about the way Evelyn Sawtelle marched through the sheets of rain, getting both of them drenched to no purpose except to satisfy some strange obstinacy. He could see that Hervey was trying to hurry her and not succeeding. Lightning flared viciously, but there was no reaction apparent in her angular, awkward frame. Once again Norman became dimly aware of an alien, explosive emotion deep within him.

And so that little poodle dog of hers, he thought, is to have the final say on the educational policy of the sociology department, Then what the devil does Pollard want to see me for? To offer his commiserations?

Almost an hour later he slammed out of Pollard's office, tense with anger, wondering why he had not handed in his resignation on the spot. To be interrogated about his actions like some kid, on the obvious instigation of busy-bodies like Thompson and Mrs. Carr and Gracine Pollard! To have to listen to a lot of hogwash about his "attitudes" and "the Hempnell spirit," with veiled insinuations about his "moral code."

At least he had given somewhat better than he had taken! At least he had forced a note of confusion into that suave, oratorical voice, and made those tufted gray eyebrows pop up and down more than once!

He had to pass the Dean of Men's office. Mrs. Gunnison was standing at the door. Like a big, oozy, tough-skinned slug, he told himself, noting her twisted stockings and hand-bag stuffed full as a grab bag, the inevitable camera dangling beside it. His exasperation shifted to her.

"Yes, I cut myself!" he told her, observing the direction of her glance. His voice was hoarse from the tirade he had delivered to Pollard.

Then he remembered something and did not stop to weigh his words. "Mrs. Gunnison, you picked up my wife's diary last night . . . by mistake. Will you please give it to me?"

"*You're* mistaken," she replied tolerantly.

"I saw you coming out of her bedroom with it."

Her eyes became lazy slits. "In that case you'd have mentioned it last night. You're overwrought, Norman. I understand." She nodded toward Pollard's office. "It must have been quite a disappointment."

"I'm asking you to return the diary!"

"And you'd really better look after that cut," she continued unruffledly. "It doesn't look any too well bandaged, and it seems to be bleeding. Infections can be nasty things."

He turned on his heel and walked away. Her reflection confronted him, murky and dim in the glass of the outer door. She was smiling.

Outside, Norman looked at his hand. Evidently he had opened the cut when he banged Pollard's desk. He drew the bandage tighter.

The storm had blown over. Yellow sunlight was flooding from under the low curtain of clouds to the west, flashing richly from the wet roofs and upper windows. Surplus rain was sprinkling from the trees. The campus was empty. A flurry of laughter from the girls' dormitories etched itself, a light, harmless acid, on the silence. He shrugged aside his anger and let his senses absorb the new-washed beauty of the scene.

He prided himself on being able to enjoy the moment at hand. It seemed to him one of the chief signs of maturity.

He tried to think like a painter, identifying hues and shades, searching for the faint rose or green hidden in the shadows. There was really something to be said for Gothic architecture. Even though it was not functional, it carried the eye along pleasantly from one fanciful bit of stonework to the next. Now take those leafy finials topping the Estrey tower—

And then suddenly the sunlight was colder than ice, the roofs of Hempnell were like the roofs of hell, and the faint laughter like the crystalline cachinnations of fiends. Before he knew it, he had swerved sharply away from Morton, off the path and onto the wet grass, although he was only halfway across campus.

No need to go back to the office, he told himself shakily. Just a long climb for a few notes. They could wait until tomorrow. And why not go home a different way tonight? Why always take the direct route that led through the gate between Estrey and Morton, under those dark, overhanging ledges. Why—

He forced himself to look up again at the open window of his office. It was empty now, as he might have expected. That other thing must have been some moving blur in his vision, and imagination had done the rest, as when a small shadow scurrying across the floor becomes a spider.

Or perhaps a shade flapping outward—

But a shadow could hardly crawl along the ledge outside the windows. A blur could hardly move so slowly or retain such a definite form.

And then the way the thing had waited, peering in, before it dropped down inside. Like . . . Like a—

Of course it was all nonsense. And there really was no need whatsoever to bother about fetching those notes or closing the window. It would be giving in to a momentary fear. There was a rumble of distant thunder.

—Like a very large lizard, the color and texture of stone.

VIII

"—And henceforth his soul is believed to be knit up in a manner with the stone. If it breaks, it is an evil omen for him; they say that thunder has struck the stone and that he who owns it will soon die—"

No use. His eyes kept wandering over the mass of print. He laid the volume of *The Golden Bough* aside and leaned back. From somewhere to the east, the thunder still throbbed faintly. But the familiar leather of the easy-chair imparted a sense of security and detachment.

Suppose, just as an intellectual exercise, he tried to analyze the misfortunes and fancies of the past three days in terms of sorcery.

The cement dragon would be a clear case of sympathetic magic. Mrs. Gunnison animated it by means of her photographs—the old business of doing things to the image instead of the object, like sticking pins in a wax doll. Perhaps she had joined a number of photographs together to make a *motion* picture. Or perhaps she had managed to get a picture of the inside of his office and had clipped a picture of the dragon to it. Murmuring suitable incantations, of course. Or, more simply, she might have slipped a picture of the dragon into one of his pockets. He started to feel through them, then reminded himself that this was only an intellectual exercise, a trifling diversion for a tired brain.

But carry through on it. You've exhausted Mrs. Gunnison. How about Evelyn Sawtelle? Her recording of the bull-roarer, notable storm-summoner, would provide a neat magical explanation for the wind last night and the storm and wind today—both associated with the Sawtelles. And then the similar sound in his dream—he wrinkled his nose in distaste.

He could hear Tansy calling Totem from the back porch, rattling her little tin pan.

Put today's self-injurious acts in another category. The obsidian knife. The razor blade. The cranky saucepan. The carpet tack. The match that he had let burn his fingers a few minutes ago.

Perhaps the razor blade had been charmed, like the enchanted sword or ax which wounds the person who wields it. Perhaps someone had stolen the blood-smeared obsidian knife and dropped it in water, so the wound would keep flowing. That was a well-established superstition.

A dog was trotting along the sidewalk out in front. He could distinctly hear the clop-clop of paws.

Tansy was still calling Totem.

Perhaps a sorcerer had commanded him to destroy himself by inches—or millimeters, considering the razor blade. That would explain all the self-injurious acts at one swoop. The flat voice in the dream had ordered him to do it.

The dog had turned up the drive. His claws made a grating sound on the concrete.

The tarot-card diagrams scribbled by Mrs. Sawtelle would figure as some magical control mechanism. The stick-figure of the man and the truck had grim implications if interpreted in the light of his old irrational fear.

It really didn't sound so much like a dog. Probably the neighbor's boy dragging home by jerks some indeterminate bulky object. The neighbor's boy devoted all his spare time to collecting trash.

"Totem! Totem!" Followed by, "All right, stay out if you want to," and the sound of the back door closing.

Finally, that very trite "sense of a presence" just behind him. Taller than himself, hands poised to grab. Only whenever he looked over his shoulder, it dodged. Something resembling it had figured in the dream—the source, perhaps, of that flat voice. And in that case—

His patience snapped. An intellectual exercise all right! For morons! He stubbed out his cigarette.

"Well, I've done my duty. That cat can sing for her supper." Tansy sat on the arm of the chair and put her hand on Norman's shoulder. "How are things going?"

"Not so good," he replied lightly.

"The chairmanship?"

He nodded. "Sawtelle got it."

Tansy cursed fluently. It did him good to hear her.

"Make you want to take up conjuring again?" He bit his lip. He certainly hadn't intended to say that.

She looked at him closely.

"What do you mean by that?" she asked.

"Just a joke."

"Are you sure? I know you've been worrying about me these last few days, ever since you found out. Wondering if I were going totally neurotic on you, and watching for the next symptoms. Now, dear, you don't have to deny it. It was the natural thing. I expected you'd be suspicious of me for a while. With your knowledge of psychiatry, it wold be impossible for you to believe that anyone could shake off an obsession so quickly. And I've been so happy to get free from all that, that your suspicions haven't bothered me. I've known they would wear off."

"But, darling, I honestly haven't been suspicious," he protested. "Maybe I ought to have been, but I haven't."

Her gray-green eyes were sphinxlike. She said slowly, "Then what are you worrying about?"

"Nothing at all." Here was where he had to be very careful.

She shook her head. "That's not true. You are worrying. Oh, I know there are some things on your mind that you haven't told me about. It isn't that."

He looked up quickly.

She nodded. "About the chairmanship. And about some student who's been threatening you. And about that Van Nice girl. You didn't really think, did you, that Hempnell would let me miss those delightful scandals?" She smiled briefly as he started to protest. "Oh, I know you aren't the type who seduces love-struck mimeograph operators, not neurotic ones at any rate." She became serious again. "Those are all minor matters, things you can take in your stride. You didn't tell me about them because you were afraid I might backslide from the desire to protect you. Isn't that right?"

"Yes."

"But I have the feeling that what you're worrying about goes much deeper than that. Yesterday and today I've even felt that you wanted to turn to me for help, and didn't dare."

He paused, as if thinking exactly how to phrase his answer. But he was studying her face, trying to read the exact meaning of each familiar quirk of expression around the mouth and eyes. She looked very contained, but that was only a mask, he thought. Actually, in spite of everything she said, she must still be poised close to the brink of her obsession. One little push, such as a few careless words on his part— How the devil had he ever let himself get so enmeshed in his own worries and those ridiculous projections of his cranky imagination? Here a few inches away from him was the only thing that mattered—the mind behind this smooth forehead and these clear, gray-green eyes; to steer that mind away from any such ridiculous notions as those he had been indulging in, the last few days.

"To tell the truth," he said, "I *have* been worried about you. I thought it would hurt your self-confidence if I let you know. Maybe I was unwise—you seem to have sensed it, anyway—but that's what I thought. The way you feel now, of course, it can't possibly hurt you to know."

It occurred to him that it was almost frighteningly easy to lie convincingly to someone you loved.

She did not give in at once. "Are you sure?" she asked. "I still have the feeling there's more to it."

Suddenly she smiled and yielded to the pressure of his arms. "It must be the MacKnight in me—my Scotch ancestry," she said, laughing. "Awfully stubborn, you know. Monomaniacs. When we're crazy on a thing, we're completely crazy, but when we drop it, we drop it all at once. Like my great-uncle Peter. You know, the one who left the Presbyterian ministry and gave up Christianity on the very same day he proved to his satisfaction there was no God. Remember, at the age of seventy-two?" There was a long and grumbling roll of thunder.

The storm was coming back.

"Well, I'm very glad you're only worried about me," she continued. "It's complimentary, and I like it."

She was smiling happily, but there was still something enigmatic about the eyes, something withheld. As he was congratulating himself on carrying it off successfully, it suddenly occurred to him that two could play at the game of lying. She might be holding something back herself, with the idea of reassuring him. She might be trying to protect him from her own blacker worries. Her subtlety might undercut his own. No sane reason to suspect that, and yet—

"Suppose I get us a drink," she said, "and we decide whether or not you leave Hempnell this year, and look for greener fields."

He nodded. She started around the bend in the L-shaped room.

—And yet, you could live with and love a person for fifteen years, and not know what was behind her eyes.

There was the rattle of glassware from the sideboard, and the friendly sound of a full bottle set down.

Then, timed to the thunder, but much closer, a shuddering, animal scream. It was cut off before Norman had sprung to his feet.

As he cleared the angle of the room, he saw Tansy going through the kitchen door. She was a little ahead of him down the back steps.

Light fanned out from the windows of the opposite house into the service yard. It revealed the sprawled body of Totem, head mashed flat against the concrete.

He heard a little sound start and stop in Tansy's throat. It might have been a gasp, or a sob, or a snarl.

The light revealed little more than the body. Norman moved so that his feet covered the two prominent scuffs in the concrete just beyond the body. They might have been caused by the impact of a brick or heavy stone, perhaps the thing that had killed Totem, but there was something so suggestive about their relative position that he did not want Tansy's imagination to have a chance to work on them.

She lifted her face. It didn't show much emotion.

"You'd better go in," he said.

"You'll—"

He nodded. "Yes."

She stopped halfway up the stairs. "That was a rotten, rotten thing for anybody to do."

"Yes."

She left the door open. A moment later she came out and laid on the porch railing a square of heavy cloth, covered with shed hair. Then she went in again and shut the door.

He rolled up the cat's body and stopped at the garage for the spade. He did not spend time searching for any brick or heavy stone or other missile. Nor did he examine closer the heavy footmarks he fancied he saw in the grass beyond the service yard.

Lightning began to flicker as his spade bit into the soft ground by the back fence. He kept his mind strictly on the task at hand. He worked steadily, but without undue haste.

When he patted down the last spadeful of earth and started for the house, the lightning flashes were stronger, making the moments in between even darker. A wind started up and dragged at the leaves.

He did not hurry. What if the lighting did indistinctly show him a large dog near the front of the house? There were several large dogs in the neighborhood. They were not savage. Totem had not been killed by a dog.

Deliberately he replaced the spade in the garage and walked back to the house. Only when he got inside and looked back through the screen did his thoughts break loose for a moment.

The lightning flash, brightest yet, showed the dog coming around the corner of the house. He had only a glimpse. A dog the color of concrete. It walked stiff-legged. He quickly closed the door and shot home the bolt.

Then he remembered that the study windows were open. He must close them. Quickly.

It might rain.

IX

When Norman entered the living room his face was outwardly serene. Tansy was sitting on the straight chair, leaning a little forward, an intent moody expression around her eyes. Her hands were playing absently with a bit of twine.

He carefully lit a cigarette.

"Do you want that drink now?" he asked, not too casually, not too sharply.

"No, thanks. You have one." Her hands kept on knotting and unknotting the twine.

He sat down and picked up his book. From the easy-chair he could watch her unobtrusively.

And now that he had no grave to dig or other mechanical task to perform, his thoughts were not to be denied. But at least he could keep them circling in a little isolated sphere inside his skull, without affecting either the expression of his face or the direction of his other thoughts, which were protectively concentrated on Tansy.

"Sorcery *is*," went the thoughts inside the sphere. "Something has been conjured down from a roof. Women are witches fighting for their men. Tansy was a witch. She was guarding you. But you made her stop."

"In that case," he replied swiftly to the thoughts inside the sphere, "why isn't Tansy aware of what's happening? It can't be denied that she has acted very relieved and happy."

"Are you sure she isn't aware or becoming aware?" answered the thoughts inside the sphere. "Besides, in losing her instruments of magic she probably lost her sensitivity to magic. Without *his* instruments—say microscope or telescope—a scientist would be no better able than a savage to see the germs of typhoid or the moons of Mars. His natural sensory equipment might even be inferior to that of the savage."

And the imprisoned thoughts buzzed violently, like bees seeking escape from a stopped-up hive.

"Norman," Tansy said abruptly, without looking at him, "you found and burned that hand in your watch charm, didn't you?"

He thought a moment. "Yes, I did," he said lightly.

"I'd really forgotten about that. There were so many."

He turned a page, and then another. Thunder crackled loudly and rain began to patter on the roof.

"Norman, you burned the diary, too, didn't you? You were right in doing it, of course. I held it back, because it didn't contain actual spells already laid, only the formulas for them. So in a twisted illogical way I pretended it didn't count. But you did burn it?"

That was harder to answer. He felt as if he were playing a guessing game and Tansy were getting perilously "warm." The thoughts in the sphere buzzed triumphantly: "Mrs. Gunnison has the diary. Now she knows all of Tansy's protective charms."

But he lied, "Yes, I burnt it. I'm sorry, but I thought—"

"Of course," Tansy cut in. "You were quite right." Her fingers played more rapidly with the cord. She did not look down at it.

Lightning showed flashes of pale street and trees through the window. The patter of rain became a pelting. But through it he fancied he heard the scrunch of paws on the drive. Ridiculous—rain and wind were making too much noise.

His eyes were attracted by the pattern of the knots Tansy's restless fingers were weaving. They were complicated, strong-looking knots which fell apart at a single cunning jerk, reminding him of how Tansy had studied assiduously the cat's cradles of the Indians. It also recalled to his mind how knots are used by primitive people, to tie and loose the winds, to hold loved ones, to noose far-off enemies, to inhibit or free all manner of physical and physiological processes. And how the Fates weave destinies like threads. He found something very pleasing in the pattern of the knots and the rhythmic movements which produced them. They seemed to signify security. Until they fell apart.

"Norman,"—the voice was preoccupied and rapid—"what was that snapshot you asked Hulda Gunnison to show you last night?"

He felt a brief flurry of panic. She was getting "very warm." This was the stage of the game where you cried out "Hot!"

And then he heard the heavy, unyielding clump-clump of the boards of the front porch, seeming to move questioningly along the wall. The sphere of alien thoughts began to exert an irresistible centrifugal pressure. He felt his sanity being smothered between the assaults from within and without. Very deliberately he shaved off the ash of his cigarette against the edge of the tray.

"It was a picture of the roof of Estrey," he said casually. "Gunnison told me Hulda had taken a number of pictures of that sort. I wanted to see a sample."

"Some sort of creature in it, wasn't there?" Knots flickered into being and vanished with bewildering speed. It seemed to him suddenly that more than twine was being manipulated, and more than empty air tied and loosed. As if the knots were somehow creating an influence, as an electric current along a twisted wire creates a complex magnetic field.

"No," he said, and then made himself chuckle, "unless you count in a stray cement dragon or two." He watched the rippling twine. At times it seemed to glitter, as if there were a metal strand in it.

If ordinary cords and knots, magically employed, could control winds, what would a part-metal cord control? Lightning?

Thunder ripped and crashed deafeningly. Lightning might have struck in the neighborhood. Tansy did not move a muscle. "That was a Lulu," Norman started to say. Then, as the thunder crash trailed off in rumblings and there was a second's lull in the rain, he heard the sound of something leaping heavily down from the front porch toward the large low window, behind him.

He got to his feet and managed to take a few steps toward the window, as if to look out at the storm. As he passed Tansy's chair he saw that her rippling fingers were creating a strange knot resembling a flower, with seven loops for petals. She stared like a sleep walker. Then he was between her and the window, shielding her.

The next lightning flash showed him what he knew he must see. It crouched, facing the window. The head was still blank and crude as an unfinished skull.

In the ensuing surge of blackness, the sphere of alien thoughts expanded with instant swiftness, until it occupied his entire mind.

He glanced behind him. Tansy's hands were still. The strange seven-looped knot was poised between them.

Just as he was turning back, he saw the hands jerk apart and the loops whip in like a seven-fold snare—and hold.

And in that same moment of turning he saw the street brighten like day and a great ribbon of lightning split the tall elm opposite and fork into several streams which streaked across the street toward the window and the stony form upreared against it.

Then—blinding light, and a tingling electrical surge through his whole body.

But on his retina was burned the incandescent track of the lightning, whose multiple streams, racing toward the up-reared stony form, had converged upon it as if drawn together by a seven-fold knot.

The sphere of alien thoughts expanded beyond his skull at a dizzy rate, vanished.

His gasping, uncontrollable laughter rose above the dying reverberations of the titanic thunder blast. He dragged open the window, pulled a bridge lamp up to it, jerked the cover from the lamp so its light flooded outward.

"Look, Tansy!" he called, his words mixed with the manic laughter. "Look what those crazy students have done! Those frat men, I bet, I kidded in class. Look what they dragged down from campus and stuck in our front yard. Of all the crazy things—we'll have to call Buildings and Grounds to take it away tomorrow."

Rain splattered in his face. There was a sulphurous, metallic odor. Her hand touched his shoulder. She stared out blankly, her eyes still asleep.

It stood there, propped against the wall, solid and inert as only the inorganic can be. In some places the cement was darkened and fused.

"And of all mad coincidences," he gasped, "the lightning had to go and strike it."

On an impulse, he reached out his hand and touched it. At the feel of the rough, unyielding surface, still hot from the lightning flash, his laughter died.

"*Eppur si muove,*" he murmured to himself, so low that even Tansy, standing beside him, might not have heard. "*Eppur si muove.*"

X

Next day the appearance Norman presented to Hempnell was a close approximation of that of a soldier suffering from battle-fatigue. He had had a long and heavy sleep, but he looked as if he were stupefied by weariness and nervous strain. And he was. Even Harold Gunnison remarked on it.

"It's nothing," Norman replied. "I'm just lazy."

Gunnison smiled skeptically. "You've been working too hard. It butchers efficiency. Better ration your hours of work. Your jobs won't go hungry if you feed them eight hours a day.

"Trustees are queer cusses," he continued with apparent irrelevance. "And in some ways Pollard is more of a politician than an educator. But he brings in the money, and that's what college presidents are for."

Norman was grateful for Gunnison's tactful commiseration on his loss of the sociology chairmanship, especially since he knew it cost Harold an effort to criticize Pollard in any way. But he felt as far removed from Gunnison as from the hordes of gaily dressed students who filled the walks and socialized in clusters. As if there were a wall of faintly clouded glass between him and them. His only aim—and even that was blurred—was to prolong his present state of fatigued reaction from last night's events and to avoid all thoughts.

Thoughts are dangerous, he told himself, and thoughts against all science, all sanity, all civilized intelligence, are the most dangerous of all. He felt their presence here and there in his brain, like pockets of poison, harmless as long as you left them encysted and did not prick them.

One was more familiar than the others. It had been there last night at the height of the storm. He felt vaguely thankful that he could no longer see inside of it.

Another thought-cyst was concerned with Tansy, and why she had seemed so cheerful and forgetful this morning.

Another—a very large one—was sunk so deeply in his mind that he could only perceive a small section of its globular surface. He knew it was connected with an unfamiliar, angry, destructive emotion that he had yesterday sensed in himself more than once, and he knew that it must under no circumstances be disturbed. He could feel it pulsate slowly and rhythmically, like a monster asleep in mud.

Another had to do with hands—hands in flannel gloves.

Another—tiny but prominent—was somehow concerned with cards.

And there were more, many more.

His situation was akin to that of the legendary hero who must travel through a long and narrow corridor, without once touching the morbidly enticing, poisoned walls.

He knew he could not avoid contact with the thought-cysts indefinitely, but in the meantime they might shrink and disappear.

The day fitted his superficially dull and lethargic mood. Instead of the cool spell that should have followed the storm, there was a foretaste of summer in the air. Student absences rose sharply. Those who came to class were inattentive and exhibited other symptoms of spring fever.

Only Bronstein seemed animated. He kept drawing Norman's other students aside by twos and threes, and whispering to them animatedly, heatedly. Norman found out that he was trying to get up a petition of protest on Sawtelle's appointment. Norman asked him to stop it. Bronstein refused, but in any case he seemed to be failing in the job of arousing the other students.

Norman's lectures were languid. He contented himself with transforming his notes into accurate verbal statements with a minimum of mental effort. He watched the pencils move methodically as notes were taken, or wander off into intricate doodles. Two girls were engrossed in sketching the handsome profile of the fraternity president in the second row. He watched foreheads wrinkle as they picked up the thread of his lecture, smooth out again as they dropped it.

And all the while his own mind was wandering off on side

tracks too dreamlike and irrational to be called thoughts. They consisted of mere trails of words, like a psychologist's association test.

One such trail began when he recalled the epigram about a lecture being a process of transferring the contents of the teacher's notebook into the notebooks of the students, without allowing it to pass through the minds of either. That made him think of mimeographing.

Mimeograph, it went on. Margaret Van Nice. Theodore Jennings. Gun. Windowpane. Galileo. Scroll—(Sheer away from that! Forbidden territory.)

The daydream backtracked and took a different turning. Jennings. Gunnison. Pollard. President. Emperor. Empress. Juggler. Tower. Hanged Man—(Hold on! Don't go any further.)

As the long dull day wore on, the daydreams gradually assumed a uniform coloration.

Gun. Knife. Sliver. Broken glass. Nail. Tetanus.

After his last class he retreated to his office and moped and fussed around on little jobs, so preoccupied that at times he forgot what he was doing. The daydreams still wouldn't let him alone.

War. Mangled bodies. Mayhem. Murder. Rope. Hangman. (Sheer off again!) Gas. Gun. Poison.

The coloration of blood and physical injury.

And ever more strongly he felt the slow-pulsing respiration of the monster in the depths of his mind, dreaming nightmares of carnage from which it would soon awaken and heave up out of the mud. And he powerless to stop it. It was as if a crusted-over swamp, swollen with underground water, were pushing up the seemingly healthy ground by imperceptible degrees—nearing the point when it would burst through in one vast slimy eruption.

Starting home, Norman fell in with Mr. Carr.

"Good evening, Norman," said the old gentleman, lifting his Panama hat to mop his forehead, which merged into an extensive bald area.

"Good evening, Linthicum," said Norman. But his mind

was occupied with speculating how, if a man let a thumbnail grow and then sharpened it carefully, he could cut the veins of his wrist and so bleed to death.

Mr. Carr wiped the handkerchief under his beard.

"I enjoyed the bridge thoroughly," he said. "Perhaps the four of us could have a game when the ladies are away at the faculty wives' meeting next Thursday? You and I could be partners and use the Culbertson slam conventions." His voice became wistful. "I'm tired of always having to play the Blackwood."

Norman nodded, but he was thinking of how men have learned to swallow their tongues, when the occasion came, and die of suffocation. He tried to check himself. These were speculations appropriate only to the concentration camp. Visions of death kept rising in his mind, replacing one another. He felt the pulsations of the thing below his thoughts become almost unendurably strong. Mr. Carr nodded pleasantly and turned off. Norman quickened his pace, as if the walls of the poisoned passageway were contracting on the legendary hero and, unless the end were soon reached, he would have to shove out against them wildly.

From the corner of his eye he saw one of his students. She was staring puzzledly, at him, or at something behind him. He brushed past her.

He reached the boulevard. The lights were against him. He paused on the curb. A large red truck was rumbling toward the intersection at a fair rate of speed.

And then he knew just what was going to happen, and that he would be unable to stop himself.

He was going to wait until the truck was very close and then he was going to throw himself under the wheels. End of the passageway.

That was the meaning of the fifth stick figure, the tarot diagram that had departed from tradition.

Empress—Juggler—The truck was very close. Tower—The light had started to change but the truck was not going to stop. Hanged man—

It was only when he leaned forward, tensing his leg muscles, that the small flat voice spoke into his ear, a voice that was a monotone and yet diabolically humorous, the voice of his dreams:

"Not for two weeks, at least. Not for two more weeks."

He regained his balance. The truck thundered by. He looked over his shoulder—first up, then around. No one but a small Negro boy and an elderly man, rather shabbily dressed, carrying a shopping bag. Neither of them near him. A shiver settled on his spine.

Hallucinations, of course, he told himself. That voice had been inside his head. Nevertheless his eyes shifted warily from side to side, probing the very air for hints of the unseen, as he crossed the street and proceeded home. As soon as he was inside, he poured himself a more than generous drink. Oddly, Tansy had set out soda and whiskey on the sideboard. He mixed the highball and gulped it down. Mixed himself another, took a gulp, then looked at the glass doubtfully.

Just then he heard a car stop and a moment later Tansy came in, carrying a bundle. Her face was smiling and a little flushed. With a sigh of relief she set down the bundle and pushed aside the dark bangs from her forehead.

"Whew! What a muggy day. I thought you'd be wanting a drink. Here, let me finish that one for you."

When she put down the glass there was only ice in it. "There, now we're blood brothers or something. Mix yourself another."

"That was my second," he told her.

"Oh, heck, I thought I was cheating you." She sat on the edge of the table and wagged a finger in his face. "Look, mister, you need a rest. Or some excitement. I'm not sure which. Maybe both. Now here's my plan. I make us a cold supper—sandwiches. Then, when it's dark we get in Oscar and drive to the Hill. We haven't done that for years. How about it, mister?"

He hesitated. Helped by the drink, his thoughts were veering. Half his mind was still agonizing over the hallucination he'd just experienced, with its unnerving suggestion of unsuspected suicidal impulses and . . . he wasn't sure what. The other half was coming under the spell of Tansy's gaiety.

She reached and pinched his nose. "How about it?"

"All right," he said.

"Hey, you're supposed to act interested!" She slid off the table, started for the kitchen, then added darkly over her shoulder. "But that will come later."

She looked provocatively pretty. He couldn't see any difference between now and fifteen years ago. He felt he was seeing her for the hundredth first time.

Feeling halfway relaxed at last, or at least diverted, he sat down in the easy chair. But as he did, he felt something hard and angular indent his thigh. He stood up quickly, stuck his hand in his trousers pocket, and drew out Theodore Jennings' revolver.

He stared at it frightenedly, unable to recall when he had taken it from the drawer at the office. Then, with a quick glance toward the kitchen, he hurried over to the sideboard, opened the bottom drawer, stuffed it under a pile of linen.

When the sandwiches came, he was reading the evening paper. He had just found a local-interest item at the bottom of the fifth page.

A practical joke is worth any amount of trouble and physical exertion. At least, that is the sentiment of a group of Hempnell College students, as yet unidentified. But we are wondering about the sentiments of Professor Norman Saylor, when he looked out the window this morning and saw a stone gargoyle weighing a good three hundred pounds sitting in the middle of his lawn. It had been removed from the roof of one of the college buildings. How the students managed to detach it, lower it from the roof, and transport it to Professor Saylor's residence, is still a mystery.

When President Randolph Pollard was asked about the pranksters, he laughingly replied, "I guess our physical education program must be providing our men with exceptional reserves of strength and energy."

When we spoke to President Pollard he was leaving to

address the Lions' Club on "The Greater Hempnell: College and Town." (For details of his address, see Page 1.)

Just what you might expect. The usual inaccuracies. It wasn't a gargoyle; gargoyles are ornamental rainspouts. And then no mention at all of the lightning. Probably the reporter had suppressed it because it didn't fit into any of the conventional patterns for supposedly unconventional news stories. Newspapers were supposed to love coincidences, but God, the weird ones they missed!

Finally, the familiar touch of turning the item into an advertisement for the physical-education department. You had to admit that the Hempnell publicity office had a kind of heavy-handed efficiency.

Tansy swept the paper out of his hands.

"The world can wait," she said. "Here, have a bite of my sandwich."

XI

It was quite dark when they started for the Hill. Norman drove carefully, taking his time at intersections. Tansy's gaiety still did no more than hold in check the other half of his thoughts.

She was smiling mysteriously. She had changed to a white sports dress. She looked like one of his students.

"I might be a witch," she said, "taking you to a hilltop rendezvous. Our own private Sabbat."

Norman started. Then he quickly reminded himself that when she said things like that, she was making a courageous mockery of her previous behavior. He must on no account let her see the other half of his thoughts.

It would never do to let her realize how badly worried he was about himself.

The lights of the town dropped behind. Half a mile out, he turned off sharply onto the road that wound up the Hill.

It was bumpier than he remembered from the last time—was it as much as ten years ago? And the trees were thicker, their twigs brushing the windshield.

When they emerged into the half acre of clearing on the top, the red moon, two days after full, was rising.

Tansy pointed to it and said, "Check! I timed it perfectly. But where are the others? There always used to be two or three cars up here. And on a night like this!"

He stopped the car close to the edge. "Fashions in lovers' lanes change like anything else," he told her. "We're traveling a disused folkway."

"Always the sociologist!"

"I guess so. Maybe Mrs. Carr found out about this place. And I suppose the students range farther afield nowadays."

She rested her head on his shoulder. He switched off the headlights, and the moon cast soft shadows.

"We used to do this at Gorham," Tansy murmured. "When I was taking your classes, and you were the serious young instructor. Until I found out you weren't any different from the college boys—only better. Remember?"

He nodded and took her hand. He looked down at the town, made out the campus, with its prominent floodlights designed to chase couples out of dark corners. Those garishly floodlighted Gothic buildings seemed for the moment to symbolize a whole world of barren intellectual competition and jealous traditionalism, a world which at the moment he felt to be infinitely alien.

"I wonder if this is why they hate us so?" he asked, almost without thinking.

"Whatever you are talking about?" But the question sounded lazy.

"I mean the rest of the faculty, or most of them. Is it because we can do things like this?"

She laughed. "So you're actually coming alive. We don't do things like this so very often, you know."

He kept on with his idea. "It's a devilishly competitive and jealous world. And competition in an institution can be nastier than any other kind, because it's so confined. Think so?"

"I've lived with it for years," said Tansy simply.

"Of course, it's all very petty. But petty feelings can come to outweigh big ones. Their size is better suited to the human mind."

He looked down at Hempnell and tried to visualize the amount of ill will and jealousy he had inevitably accumulated for himself. He felt a slight chill creeping on his skin. He realized where this train of thought was leading. The darker half of his mind loomed up.

"Here, philosopher," said Tansy, "have a slug."

She was offering him a small silver flask.

He recognized it. "I never dreamed you'd kept it all these years."

"Uh-huh. Remember when I first offered you a drink from it? You were a trifle shocked, I believe."

"I took the drink."

"Uh-huh. So take this one."

It tasted like fire and spice. There were memories in it, too, memories of those crazy prohibition years, and of Gorham and New England.

"Brandy?"

"Greek. Give me some."

The memories flooded over the darker half of his mind. It disappeared beneath their waves. He looked at Tansy's sleek hair and moon-glowing eyes. Of course she's a witch, he thought lightly. She's Lilith. Ishtar. He'd tell her so.

"Do you remember the time," he said, "we slid down the bank to get away from the night watchman at Gorham? There would have been a magnificent scandal if he'd caught us."

"Oh, yes, and the time—"

When they went down the hill, the moon was an hour higher. He drove slowly. No need to imitate the sillier practices of the prohibition era. A truck chugged past him. "Two more weeks." Rot! Who'd he think he was, hearing voices? Joan of Arc?

He felt hilarious. He wanted to tell Tansy all the ridiculous things he'd been imagining the last few days, so she could laugh at them, too. It would make a swell ghost story. There was a reason he shouldn't tell her, but now it seemed an insignificant reason—part and parcel of this cramped, warped, overcautious Hempnell life they ought to break away from more often. What was life worth, anyway, if you had to sit around remembering not to mention this, that, and the other thing because someone else might be upset?

So when they arrived in the living room and Tansy flopped down on the sofa, he began, "You know, Tansy, about this witch stuff. I want to tell you—"

He was caught completely off guard by whatever force, real or unreal, hit him. A moment later he was sitting in the easy chair, completely sober, with the outer world an ice pressure on his senses, the inner world a whirling sphere of alien thought, and the future a dark corridor two weeks long.

It was as if a very large, horny hand had been clapped roughly over his mouth, and as if another such hand had grasped him by the shoulder, shaken him, and slammed him down in the leather chair.

As if?

He looked around uneasily.

Maybe there had been hands.

Apparently Tansy had not noticed anything. Her face was a white oval in the gloom. She was still humming a snatch of song. She did not ask what he had started to say.

He got up, walked unsteadily into the dining room, and poured himself a drink from the sideboard. On the way he switched on the lights.

So he couldn't tell Tansy or anyone else about it, even if he wanted to? That was why you never heard from real witchcraft victims, he told himself, his thoughts for the moment quite out of hand. And why they never seemed able to escape, even if the means of escape were at hand. It wasn't weak will. They were *watched*. Like a gangster taken on a ride from an expensive night-club. He must excuse himself from the loud-mouthed crowd at his table and laugh heartily, and stop to chat with friends and throw a wink at the pretty girls, because right behind him are those white-scarfed trigger boys, hands in the pockets of their velvet-collared dress overcoats. No use dying now. Better play along. There might be a chance.

But that was thriller stuff, movie stuff.

So were the horny hands.

He nodded at himself in the glass above the sideboard.

"Meet Professor Saylor," he said, "the distinguished ethnologist and firm believer in real witchcraft."

But the face in the glass did not look so much disgusted as frightened.

He mixed himself another drink, and one for Tansy, and took them into the living room.

"Here's to wickedness," said Tansy. "Do you realize that you haven't been anywhere near drunk since Christmas?"

He grinned. Getting drunk was just what the movie gangster would do, to grab a moment of forgetfulness when the Big Boy had put him on the spot. And not a bad idea.

Slowly, and at first only in a melancholy minor key, the mood of the Hill returned. They talked, played old records, told jokes that were old enough to be young again. Tansy hammered at the piano and they sang a crazy assortment of songs, folk songs, hymns, national anthems, workers' and revolutionists' songs, blues, Brahms, Schubert—haltingly at first, later at the top of their voices.

They remembered.

And they kept on drinking.

But always, like a shimmering sphere of crystal, the alien thoughts spun in Norman's mind. The drink made it possible for him to regard them dispassionately, without constant revulsions in the name of common sense. With the singlemindedness of inebriation, his scholar's mind began to assemble world-wide evidence of witchcraft.

For instance, was it not likely that all self-destructive impulses were the result of witchcraft? Those universal impulses that were a direct contradiction to the laws of self-preservation and survival. To account for them, Poe had fancifully conceived an "Imp of the Perverse," and psychoanalysts had laboriously hypothesized a "death wish." How much simpler to attribute them to malign forces outside the individual, working by means as yet unanalyzed and therefore classified as supernatural.

His experiences during the past days could be divided into two categories. The first included those natural misfortunes and antagonisms from which Tansy's magic had screened him. The attack on his life by Theodore Jennings should probably be placed in this category. The chances were that Jennings was actually psychopathic. He would have made his murderous attack at an earlier date, had not Tansy's magic kept it from getting started. As soon as her protective screen was down, as soon as Norman burned the last hand, the idea had suddenly burgeoned in Jennings' mind like a hothouse flower. Jennings had himself admitted it. "I didn't realize it until this minute—"

Margaret Van Nice's accusation, Thompson's sudden burst of interest in his extracurricular activities, and Sawtelle's chance discovery of the Cunningham thesis probably belong in the same category.

In the second category—active and malign witchcraft, directed against himself.

"A penny for your thoughts," offered Tansy, looking over the rim of her glass.

"I was thinking of the party last Christmas," he replied smoothly, though in a somewhat blurred voice, "and of how Welby crawled around playing a St. Bernard, with the bearskin rug over his shoulders and the bottle of whiskey slung under his neck. And I was wondering why the best fun always seems so trite afterward. But I'd rather be trite than respectable." He felt a childish pride in his cunning at having avoided being trapped into admission. He simultaneously thought of Tansy as a genuine witch and as a potentially neurotic individual who had to be protected at all costs from dangerous suggestions. The liquor made his mind work by parts, and the parts had no check on each other.

Things began to happen by fits and starts. His consciousness began to black out, though in the intervals between, his thoughts went on with an exaggerated scholarly solemnity.

They were wailing, "St. James Infirmary."

He was thinking: "Why shouldn't the women be the witches? They're the intuitionalists, the traditionalists, the irrationalists. They're superstitious to start with. And like Tansy, most of them are probably never quite sure whether or not their witchcraft really works."

They had shoved back the carpet and were dancing to "Chloe." Sometime or other Tansy had changed to her rose dressing gown.

He was thinking: "In the second category, put the Estrey dragon. Animated by a human or nonhuman soul conjured into it by Mrs. Gunnison and controlled through photographs. Put also the obsidian knife, the obedient wind, and the obdurate truck."

They were playing a record of Ravel's "Bolero," and he was beating out the rhythm with his fist.

He was thinking: "Business men buy stocks on the advice of fortune-tellers, numerologists rule the careers of movie stars, half the world governs its actions by astrology, advertisements bleat constantly of magic and miracles, and most modern and all surrealist art is nothing but attempted witchcraft, borrowing its forms from the primitive witchdoctor and its ideas from the modern theosophist."

He was watching Tansy as she sang "St. Louis Blues" in a hoarsely throbbing voice. It was true, just as Welby had always maintained, that she had a genuine theatrical flair. Make a good chanteuse.

He was thinking: "Tansy stopped the Estrey dragon with the knots. But she'll have a hard time doing anything like that again because Mrs. Gunnison has her book of formulas and can figure out ways to circumvent her."

They were sharing a highball that would have burned his throat if his throat had not been numb, and he seemed to be getting most of it.

He was thinking: "The stick figure of the man and the truck is the key to a group of related sorceries. Cards began as instruments of magic, like art. These sorceries aim at finishing me off. The bull-roarer acts as an amplifier. The invisible thing standing behind me, with the flat voice and heavy hands, is a guardian, to see to it that I do not deviate from the path appointed. Narrow corridor. Two weeks more.''

The strange thing was that these thoughts were not altogether unpleasant. They had a wild, black, poisonous beauty of their own, a lovely, deadly shimmer. They possessed the fascination of the impossible, the incredible. They hinted at unimaginable vistas. Even while they terrorized, they did not lose that chillingly poignant beauty. They were like the visions conjured up by some forbidden drug. They had the lure of an unknown sin and an ultimate blasphemy. Norman could understand the force that compelled the practitioners of black magic to take any risk.

His drunkenness made him feel safe. It had broken his mind down into its ultimate particles, and those particles were incapable of fear because they could not be injured. Just as the atoms in a man are not slain by the bullet that slays him.

But now the particles were whirling crazily. Consciousness was wavering.

He and Tansy were in each other's arms.

Tansy was asking eagerly, coaxingly, ''All that's mine is yours? All that's yours is mine?''

The question awakened a suspicion in his mind, but he could not grasp it clearly. Something made him think that the words held a trap. But what trap? His thoughts stumbled.

She was saying—it sounded like the Bible—''And I have drunk from your cup and you have drunk from mine—''

Her face was a blurred oval, her eyes like misty jewels.

''Everything you have is mine? You give it to me without hindrance and of your own free choice?''

Somewhere a trap.

But the voice was irresistibly coaxing, like caressing fingers.

''All you have is mine? Just say it once, Norm, just once. For me.''

Of course he loved her. Better than anything in the world. He drew the blurred face toward him, tried to kiss the misty eyes.

''Yes . . . yes . . . everything—'' he heard himself saying.

And then his mind toppled and plunged down into a fathomless ocean of darkness and silence and peace.

XII

Sunlight made a bright, creamy design on the drawn blind. Filtered sunlight filled the bedroom, like a coolly glowing liquid. The birds were chirruping importantly. Norman closed his eyes again and stretched luxuriously.

Let's see, it was about time he got started on that article for *The American Anthropologist*. And there was still some work to do on the revision of his *Textbook of Ethnology*. Lots of time, but better get it out of the way. And he ought to have a serious talk with Bronstein about his thesis. That boy had some good ideas, but he needed a balance wheel. And then his address to the Off-campus Mothers. Might as well tell them something useful. . . .

Eyes still closed, he enjoyed that most pleasant of all sensations—the tug of work a man likes to do and is able to do well, yet that needn't be done immediately.

For today was certainly too good a day for golf to miss. Might see what Gunnison was doing. And then he and Tansy had not made an expedition into the country this whole spring. He'd talk to her about it, at breakfast. Saturday breakfast was an event. She must be getting it ready now. He felt as if a shower would make him very hungry. Must be late.

He opened one eye and focused on the bedroom clock. Twelve thirty-five? Say, just when had he got to bed last night? What had he been doing?

Memory of the past few days uncoiled like a spring, so swiftly that it started his heart pounding. Yet there was a difference now in his memories. From the very first moment they all seemed incredible and unreal. He had the sensation of reading the very detailed case-history of another person, a person with a lot of odd ideas about witchcraft, suicide, persecution, and what not else. His memories could not be made to fit with his present sense of well-being. What was stranger, they did not seriously disturb that sense of well-being.

He searched his mind diligently for traces of super-natural fear, of the sense of being watched and guarded, of that monstrous self-destructive impulse. He could not discover or even suggest to himself the slightest degree of such emotions. Whatever they had been, they were now part of the past, beyond the reach of everything except intellectual memory. "Spheres of alien thought!" Why, the very notion was bizarre. And yet somehow it had all happened. *Something* had happened.

His movements had automatically taken him under the shower. And now, as he soaped himself and the warm water cascaded down, he wondered if he ought not to talk it over with Holstrom of psychology or a good practicing psychiatrist. The mental contortions he'd gone through in the past few days would provide material for a whole treatise! But feeling as sound as he did this morning, it was impossible for him to entertain any ideas of serious mental derangement. No, what had happened was just one of those queer, inexplicable spasms of irrationality that can seize the sanest people, perhaps because they *are* so sane—a kind of discharge of long-inhibited morbidity. Too bad, though, that he had bothered Tansy with it, even though it was her own little witchcraft complex, now happily conquered, that had touched it off. Poor kid, she had been working hard to cheer him up last night. It ought to have been the other way around. Well, he would make it up to her.

He shaved leisurely and with enjoyment. The razor behaved perfectly.

As he finished dressing, a doubt struck him. Again he searched his mind, closing his eyes like a man listening for an almost inaudible sound.

Nothing. Not the faintest trace of any morbid fears.

He was whistling as he pushed into the kitchen.

There was no sign of breakfast. Beside the sink were some

unwashed glasses, empty bottles, and an ice tray filled with tepid water.

"Tansy!" he called. "Tansy!"

He walked through the house, with the vague apprehension that she might have passed out before getting to bed. They'd been drinking like fish. He went out to the garage and made sure that the car was still there. Maybe she'd walked to the grocer's to get something for breakfast. But he began to hurry as he went back into the house.

This time when he looked in the study he noticed the upset ink bottle, and the scrap of paper just beside it on the edge of the drying black pool. The message had come within an inch of being engulfed.

It was a hurried scrawl—twice the pen point had gouged through the paper—and it broke off in the middle of a sentence, but it was undeniably in Tansy's handwriting.

For a moment it isn't watching me. I didn't realize it would be too strong for me. Not two weeks—two days! Don't try to follow me. Only chance is to do exactly what I tell you. Take four four-inch white—

His eyes traced the smear going out from the black pool and ending in the indistinct print of a hand, and involuntarily his imagination created a scene. Tansy had been scribbling desperately, stealing quick glances over her shoulder. Then *it* had awakened to what she was doing and roughly struck the pen out of her hand, and shaken her. He recalled the grip of those huge horny hands, and winced. And then . . . then she had got together her things, very quietly although there was little chance of him awakening, and she had walked out of the house and down the street. And if she met anyone she knew, she had talked to them gayly, and laughed, because *it* was behind her, waiting for any false move, any attempt at escape.

So she had gone.

He wanted to run out into the street and shout her name.

But the pool of ink had dried to glistening black flakes all around the margin. It must have been spilled hours ago.

Where had she gone, in the night?

Anywhere. Wherever the narrow corridor ended for her, no longer two weeks but only two days long.

In a flash of insight he understood why. If he hadn't been drunk last night, he would have guessed.

One of the oldest and best-established types of conjuration in the world. Transference of evils. Like the medicine man who conjures sickness into a stone, or into an enemy, or into himself—because he is better able to combat it—she had taken his curse upon herself. Shared his drink last night, shared his food. Used a thousand devices to bring them together. It was all so obvious! He racked his brain to recover those last words she had said. "Everything you have is mine? All you have is mine?"

She had meant the doom that had been laid on him.

And he had said, "Yes."

Wait a minute! What the devil was he letting himself think? He raised his eyes to the shelves of soberly bound books. Why, here he was giving way to the same sort of rot he'd been weakly toying with the past few days—now when something serious was at stake. No, no, there was nothing supernatural in this—no *it*, no guardian except a figment of his and her neurotic nerves. What *had* happened was that he had *suggested* all this nonsense to her. He had forced upon her the products of his own morbid imagination. Undoubtedly he had babbled nonsense to her while he was drunk. All his childish fancies. And it had worked on her suggestible nature—she already believing in witchcraft—until she had got the idea of transferring his doom to herself, and had convinced herself that the transference had actually occurred. And then gone off, God knows where.

And that was bad enough.

He found himself looking again at the scrawled message. He automatically asked himself, "Now what the devil are 'four-inch whites'?"

There was a light chime from the front door. He extracted

a letter from the mailbox, ripped it open. It was addressed with a soft pencil and the graphite had smeared. But he knew the handwriting.

The message was so jerky and uneven that he was some time reading it. It began and ended in the middle of a sentence.

cords—and a length of gut, a bit of platinum or iridium, a piece of lodestone, a phonograph needle that has only played Scriabin's "Ninth Sonata." Then tie—

"Cords." Of course!

That was all. A continuation of the first message, with its bizarre formula. Had she really convinced herself that there was a guardian watching her, and that she could only communicate during the infrequent moments when she imagined its attention was elsewhere? He knew the answer. When you had an obsession you could convince yourself of anything.

He looked at the postmark. He recognized the name of a town several miles east of Hempnell. He could not think of a soul they knew there, or anything else about the town. His first impulse was to get out the car and rush over. But what could he do when he got there?

He looked again. The phone was ringing. It was Evelyn Sawtelle.

"Is that you, Norman? Please ask Tansy to come to the phone. I wish to speak to her."

"I'm sorry, but she isn't in."

Evelyn Sawtelle did not sound surprised at the answer—her second question came too quickly. "Where is she then? I must get in touch with her."

He thought. "She's out in the country," he said, "visiting some friends of ours. Is there something I can tell her?"

"No, I wish to speak to Tansy. What is your friend's number?"

"They don't have a phone!" he said angrily.

"No? Well, it's nothing of importance." She sounded oddly pleased, as if his anger had given her satisfaction. "I'll call again. I must hurry now. Hervey is so busy with his new responsibilities. Good-by."

He replaced the phone. Now, why the devil—Suddenly an explanation occurred to him. Perhaps Tansy had been seen leaving town, and Evelyn Sawtelle had scented the possibility of some sort of scandal and had wanted to check. Perhaps Tansy had been carrying a suitcase.

He looked in Tansy's dressing room. The small suitcase was gone. Drawers were open. It looked as if she had packed in a hurry. But what about money? He examined his billfold. It was empty. Forty-odd dollars missing.

You could go a long way on forty dollars. The jerky illegibility of the message suggested that it had been written on a train or bus.

The next few hours were very miserable ones for Norman. He checked schedules and found that several busses and trains passed through the town from which Tansy's letter had been sent. He drove to the stations and made guarded inquiries, with no success.

He wanted to do all the things you should do when someone disappears, but he held back. What could he say? "My wife, sir, has disappeared. She is suffering from the delusion that—" And what if she should be found and questioned in her present state of mind, examined by a doctor, before he could get to her?

No, this was something for him to handle alone. But if he did not soon get a clue to where she had gone, he would have no choice. He would have to go to the police, inventing some story to cover the facts.

She had written, "Two days." If she believed that she were doomed to die in two days, might not the belief be enough?

Toward evening he drove back to the house, repressing the chimerical hope that she had returned in his absence. The special-delivery man was just getting into his car. Norman pulled up alongside.

"Anything for Saylor?"

"Yes, sir. It's in the box."

The message was longer this time, but just as difficult to read.

> *At last its attention is somewhere else. If I control my emotions, it isn't so quick to notice my thoughts. But it was hard for me to post the last letter, Norman, you must do what I tell you. The two days end Sunday midnight. Then the Bay. You must follow all directions. Tie the four cords into a granny, a reef, a cat's-paw, and a carrick bend. Tie the gut in a bowline. Then add—*

He looked at the postmark. The place was two hundred miles east. Not on the railroad lines, as far as he could recall. That should narrow down the possibilities considerably.

One word from the letter was repeating itself in his mind, like a musical note struck again and again until it becomes unendurable.

Bay. Bay. Bay. Bay.

The memory came of a hot afternoon years ago. It was just before they were married. They were sitting on the edge of a ramshackle little pier. He remembered the salty, fish smell and the splintery, gray old planks.

"Funny," she had said, looking into the green water, "but I always used to think that I'd end up down there. Not that I'm afraid of it. I've always swum way out. But even when I was a little girl I'd look at the Bay—maybe green, maybe blue, maybe gray, covered with whitecaps, glittering with moonbeams or shrouded by fog—and I'd think, 'Tansy, the Bay is going to get you, but not for years and years.' Funny, isn't it?"

And he had laughed and put his arms around her tight, and the green water had gone on lapping at the piles trousered with seaweed.

He had been visiting with her family, when her father was still alive, at their home near Bayport on the southern shore of New York Bay.

The narrow corridor ended for her in the Bay, tomorrow night, midnight.

She must be headed for the Bay.

He made several calls—first bus lines, then railroad and air. It was impossible to get a reservation on the airlines, but tonight's train would get him into Jersey City an hour ahead of the bus she must be traveling on, according to the deductions he made from the place and time of the postmarks.

He knew he had ample time to pack a few things, cash a check on his way to the station.

He spread her three notes on the table—one in pen, the two in pencil. He reread the crazy incomplete formula.

He frowned. Would a scientist neglect the millionth-and-one possibility? Would the commander of a trapped army disdain a stratagem just because it was not in the books? This stuff looked like gibberish. Yesterday it might have meant something to him emotionally. Today it was just nonsense. But tomorrow night it might conceivably represent a fantastic last chance.

But to compromise with magic.

"Norman, you *must* do what I tell you." The words stared at him.

After all, he might need the junk to pacify her if he found her in a near-insane state.

He went into the kitchen and got a ball of white twine.

He rummaged in the closet for his squash racket and cut out the two center strings. That ought to do for gut.

The fireplace had not been cleaned since the stuff from Tansy's dressing table had been burned. He poked around the edges until he found a bit of blackened rock that attracted a needle. Lodestone.

He located the recording of Scriabin's "Ninth Sonata" and started the phonograph, putting in a new needle. He glanced at his wrist watch and paced the room restlessly. Gradually the music took hold of him. It was not pleasant music. There was something tantalizing and exasperating about it, with its droning melody and rocking figures in the bass and shakes in the treble and elaborate ornamentation that writhed up and down the piano keyboard. It rasped the nerves.

He began to remember things he had heard about it. Hadn't Tansy told him that Scriabin had called his "Ninth Sonata" a "Black Mass" and had developed an antipathy to playing it? Scriabin, who had conceived a color organ and tried to translate mysticism into music and died of a peculiar lip infection. An innocent-faced Russian with a huge curling mustache. Critical phrases Tansy had repeated to him floated through his mind. "The poisonous 'Ninth Sonata'—the most perfidious piece of music ever conceived—" Ridiculous! How could music be anything but an abstract pattern of tones?

And yet while listening to the thing, one could think differently.

Faster and faster it went. The lovely second theme became infected, was distorted into something raucous and discordant—a march of the damned—a dance of the damned—breaking off suddenly when it had reached an unendurable pitch. Then a repetition of the droning first theme, ending on a soft yet grating note low in the keyboard.

He removed the needle, sealed it in an envelope, and packed it along with the rest of his stuff. Only then did he ask himself why, if he were gathering this junk merely to pacify Tansy, he had bothered to play the "Ninth Sonata" with the needle. Certainly an unused needle would have done just as well. He shrugged his shoulders.

On an afterthought, he tore out of the big dictionary a page carrying an illustrated list of knots.

The telephone stopped him as he was going out.

"Oh, Professor Saylor, would you mind calling Tansy to the phone?" Mrs. Carr's voice was very amicable.

He repeated what he had told Mrs. Sawtelle.

"I'm glad she's having a rest in the country," said Mrs. Carr. "You know, Professor Saylor, I don't think that Tansy's been looking so well lately. I've been a little worried. You're sure she's all right?"

At just that moment, without any warning whatever, another voice cut in.

"What's the idea of checking up on me! Do you think I'm a child? I know what I'm doing!"

"Be quiet!" said Mrs. Carr, sharply. Then in her sweet voice, "I think someone must have cut in on us. Good-by, Professor Saylor."

The line went dead. Norman frowned. That second voice had sounded remarkably like Evelyn Sawtelle's.

He picked up his suitcase and walked out.

XIII

The bus driver they pointed out to Norman in Jersey City had thick shoulders and sleepy, competent-looking eyes. He was standing by the wall, smoking a cigarette.

"Sure, she must have been with me," he told Norman after thinking a moment. "A pretty woman, on the small side, in a gray dress, with a silver brooch like you mentioned. One suitcase. Light pigskin. I figured her out as going to see someone who was very sick or had been in an accident, maybe."

Norman curbed his impatience. If it had not been for the hour-and-a-half delay outside Jersey City, his train would have been here well ahead of the bus, instead of twenty minutes behind it.

He said, "I want, if possible, to get a line on where she went after she left your bus. The men at the desk can't help me."

The driver looked at Norman. But, he did not say, "Whatcha wanta know for?"—for which Norman was grateful. He seemed to decide that Norman was okay.

He said, "I can't be sure, mister, but there was a local bus going down the shore. I think she got on that."

"Would it stop at Bayport?"

The driver nodded.

"How long since it left?"

"About twenty minutes."

"Could I get to Bayport ahead of it? If I took a cab?"

"Just about. If you wanted to pay the bill there and back—

and maybe a little extra—I think Alec could take you.'' He waved casually at a man sitting in a cab just beyond the station. "Mind you, mister, I can't say for certain she got on the shore bus."

"That's all right. Thanks a lot."

In the glow of the street lamp Alec's foxy eyes were more openly curious than the bus driver's, but he did not make any comments.

"I can do it," he said cheerfully, "but we haven't any time to waste. Jump in."

The shore highway led through lonely stretches of marsh and wasteland. Occasionally Norman caught the sibilant rustle of the leagues of tall stiff seagrass, and amid the chemical stenches of industry, a brackish tang from the dark inlets crossed by long low bridges. The odor of the Bay.

Indistinctly he made out factories, oil refineries, and scattered houses.

They passed three of four buses without Alec making any comment. He was paying close attention to the road.

After a long while Alec said, "That should be her."

A constellation of red and green taillights was vanishing over the rise ahead.

"About three miles to Bayport," he continued. "What shall I do?"

"Just get to Bayport a little ahead of her, and stop at the bus station."

"Okay."

They overtook the bus and swung around it. The windows were too high for Norman to see any of the occupants. Besides, the interior lights were out.

As they drew ahead, Alec nodded confirmingly, "That's her, all right."

The bus station at Bayport was also the railway depot. Vaguely Norman remembered the loosely planked platform, the packed cinders between it and the railway tracks. The depot was smaller and dingier than he recalled, though it still boasted the grotesque ornamental carpentry of the days when Bayport had been a summer resort for New York's rich. The windows of the depot were dark but there were several cars and a long local cab drawn up and there were some men standing around talking in low voices and a couple of soldiers, from Fort Monmouth on nearby Sandy Hook, he supposed.

He had time to scent the salt air, with its faint and not unpleasant trace of fishiness. Then the bus pulled in.

Several passengers stepped down, looking around to spot the people waiting for them.

Tansy was the third. She was staring straight ahead. She was carrying the pigskin suitcase.

"Tansy," he said.

She did not look at him. He noted a large black stain on her right hand, and remembered the spilled ink on his study table.

"Tansy!" he said. "Tansy!"

She walked straight past him, so close that her sleeve brushed his.

"Tansy, what's the matter with you?"

He had turned and hurried after her. She was headed for the local cab. He was conscious of a silence and of curious unfriendly glances. They made him angry.

She did not slacken her pace. He grabbed her elbow and pulled her around. He heard a remonstratory murmur behind him.

"Tansy, stop acting this way! Tansy!"

Her face looked frozen. She stared past him without a hint of recognition in her eyes.

That infuriated him. He did not pause to think. Accumulated tensions prodded him into an explosion. He grabbed both elbows and shook her. She still looked past him, completely aloof—a perfect picture of an aristocratic woman enduring brutality. If she had yelled and fought him, the men might not have interfered.

He was jerked back.

"Lay off her!"

"Who do you think you are, anyway?"

She stood there, with maddening composure. He noticed

a scrap of paper flutter out of her hand. Then her eyes met his and he seemed to see fear in them; then he felt a slight, queer shock, as if something had passed from her eyes to his; simultaneously with that and with the pricking of his scalp, there seemed to rise up behind her, but for one moment only a shaggy black form twice her height, with hulking shoulders, outstretched massive hands, and dully glowing eyes.

For one moment only, though. When she turned away, she was alone. Though he did fancy that her shadow on the planking was swollen out and shot up to a size that the position of the street lamp would not account for. Then they swung him around and he could no longer see her.

In a queer sort of daze—for the kind of hallucination he had just experienced mixes badly with any other emotion— he listened to them jabber at him.

"I ought to take a crack at you," he finally heard someone say.

"All right," he replied in a flat voice. "They're holding my hands."

He heard Alec's voice. "Say, what's going on here?" Alec sounded cautious, but not unfriendly, as if he were thinking. "The guy's my fare, but I don't know anything about him."

One of the soldiers spoke. "Where's the lady? She doesn't seem to be making any complaint."

"Yeah, where is she?"

"She got in Jake's cab and drove off," someone volunteered.

"Maybe he had a good reason for what he did," said the soldier.

Norman felt the attitude of the crowd change.

One of the men holding him retorted, "Nobody's got a right to treat a lady that way." But the other slackened his grip and asked Norman, "How about it? Did you have a reason for doing that?"

"I did. But it's my business."

He heard a woman's voice, high-pitched, "A lot of fuss over nothing!" and a man's, richly sardonic. "Mix in family quarrels—!"

Grumbling, the two men let him go.

"But mind you," said the more belligerent one, "if she'd stuck around and complained, I'd sure have taken a crack at you."

"All right," said Norman, "in that case you would have." His eyes were searching for the scrap of paper.

"Can anyone tell me the address she gave the cab driver?" he asked at random.

One or two shook their heads. The others ignored the question. Their feelings toward him had not changed enough to make them cooperative. And very likely, in the excitement, no one had heard.

Silently the little crowd drifted apart. People waited until they got out of earshot before beginning to argue about what had happened. Most of the cars drove off. The two soldiers wandered over to the benches in front of the depot, so they could sit down while they waited for their bus or train. Norman was alone except for Alec.

He located the scrap of paper in one of the slots between the worn planks. It had almost slipped through.

He took it over to the cab and studied it.

He heard Alec say, "Well, where do we go now?" Alec sounded dubious.

He glanced at his watch. Ten thirty-five. Not quite an hour and a half until midnight. There were a lot of things he could do to try and find Tansy, but he could not do more than a couple of them in that time. He thoughts moved sluggishly, almost painfully, as if that awful thing he had seemed to see behind Tansy had hurt his brain.

He looked around at the dim buildings. The seaward halves of some of the street lamps still showed traces of black paint from the old wartime dimout. Up a side street there were signs of life. He looked at the scrap of paper.

He thought of Tansy. He thought hard. It was a question of what might help her most, of what his deepest loyalty to her must now direct him to do. Of course he could go chasing up and down along the shore, along the railroad tracks, though Lord knew to what point the taxi had taken her. He might be able to locate the old pier where they'd gone swimming and try waiting there. Or he could wait for the taxi she'd taken to come back. And he might go to the police, convince them if he could that his wife intended suicide, get them to help him search.

But he also thought of other things. He thought of her confession of witchcraft, of how he had burned the last "hand," of the sudden telephone calls from Theodore Jennings and Margaret Van Nice, of the flurry of ill-will and undesired revelations that had struck him at the college. He thought of Jennings' asinine attempt on his life, of the recordings of a bull-roarer, the photograph of a dragon, and the stick-figure of tarot cards. He thought of the death of Totem, of the seven-branched lightning bolt, of his sudden attack of accident-proneness and suicidal fancies. He thought of the hallucination he had had, while drunk, of something gripping his shoulder and shutting off his speech. He thought of the hallucination he had had just now of something behind Tansy. He thought hard.

He looked again at the scrap of paper.

He came to a decision.

"I think there's a hotel on the main street," he told Alec. "You can drive me there."

XIV

"Eagle Hotel," read the black-edged gold letters on the plateglass window, behind which the narrow lobby with its half-dozen empty chairs was nakedly revealed.

He told Alec to wait, and took a room for the night. The clerk was an old man in a shiny blue coat. Norman saw from the register that no one else had checked in recently. He carried his bag up to the room and immediately returned to the lobby.

"I haven't been here for ten years," he told the clerk. "I

believe there is a cemetery about five blocks down the street, away from the Bay?''

The old man's sleepy eyes blinked wide open.

''Bayport Cemetery? Just three blocks, and then a block and a half to the left. But—'' He made a vague questioning noise in his throat.

''Thank you,'' said Norman.

After a moment's thought, he paid off Alec, who took the money and with obvious relief kicked his cab into life. Norman walked down the main street, away from the Bay.

After the first block there were no more stores. In this direction, Bayport petered out quickly. Most of the houses were dark. And after he turned left there were no more street lights.

The gates of the cemetery were locked. He felt his way along the wall, behind the masking shrubbery, trying to make as little noise as possible, until he found a scrubby tree whose lowest branch could bear his weight. He got his hands on the top of the wall, scrambled up, and cautiously let himself down on the other side.

Behind the wall it was very dark. There was a sound, as if he had disturbed some small animal. More by feeling than sight he located a headstone. It was a thin one, worn, mossy toward the base, and tilted at an angle. Probably from the middle of last century. He dug into the earth with his hand, and filled an envelope he took from his pocket.

He got back over the wall, making what seemed a great deal of noise in the shrubbery. But the street was empty as before.

On his way back to the hotel he looked up at the sky, located the Pole Star, and calculated the orientation of his room.

As he crossed the lobby, he felt the curious gaze of the old clerk boring into him.

His room was in darkness. Chill salt air was pouring through the open window. He locked the door, shut the window, pulled down the blind, and switched on the light—a glaring overhead which revealed the room in all its dingy severity. A cradle phone struck the sole modern note.

He took the envelope out of his pocket and weighted it in his hand. His lips curled in a peculiarly bitter smile. Then he re-read the scrap of paper that had fluttered from Tansy's hand.

a small quantity of graveyard dirt and wrap all in a piece of flannel, wrapping widdershins. Tell it to stop me. Tell it to bring me to you.

Graveyard dirt. That was what he had found in Tansy's dressing table. It had been the beginning of all this. Now he was fetching it himself.

He looked at his watch. Eleven twenty.

He cleared the small table and set it in the center of the room, jabbing in his penknife to mark the edge facing east. "Widdershins," meant "against the sun"—from west to east.

He placed the necessary ingredients on the table, cutting a short strip of flannel from the hem of his bathrobe, and fitted together the four sections of Tansy's note. The distasteful, bitter smile did not leave his lips.

Taken together, the significant portions of the note read:

Take four lengths of four-inch white cord and a length a gut, a bit of platinum or iridium, a piece of lodestone, a phonograph needle that has only played Scriabin's "Ninth Sonata." Tie the four white cords into a granny, a reef, a cat's-paw, and a carrick bend. Tie the gut in a bowline. Add a small quantity of graveyard dirt, and wrap it all in a piece of flannel, wrapping widdershins. Tell it to stop me. Tell it to bring me to you.

In general outline, it was similar to a hundred recipes for Negro tricken-bags he had seen or been told about. The phonograph needle, the knots, and one or two other items were obvious "white" additions.

And it was all on the same level as the mental operations

of a child or neurotic adult who religiously steps on, or avoids, sidewalk cracks.

A clock outside bonged the half-hour.

Norman sat there looking at the stuff. It was hard for him to begin. It would have been different, he told himself, if he were doing it for a joke or a thrill, or if he were one of those people who dope up their minds with morbid supernaturalism—who like to play around with magic because it's medieval and because illuminated manuscripts look pretty. But to tackle it in dead seriousness, to open your mind deliberately to superstition—that was to join hands with the forces pushing the world back into the dark ages, to cancel the term "science" out of the equation.

But, behind Tansy, he had seen that thing. Of course it had been an hallucination. But when hallucinations start behaving like realities, with a score of coincidences to back them up, even a scientist has to face the possibility that he may have to treat them like realities. And when hallucinations begin to threaten you and yours in a direct physical way—

No, more than that. When you must keep faith with someone you love. He reached out for the first length of cord and tied the ends together in a granny.

When he came to the cat's-paw, he had to consult the page he had torn from the dictionary. After a couple of false starts he managed it.

But on the carrick bend he was all thumbs. It was a simple knot but no matter how he went about it, he could not get it to look like the illustration. Sweat broke out on his forehead. "Very close in the room," he told himself. "I'm still overheated from rushing about." The skin on his fingertips felt an inch thick. The ends of the cord kept eluding them. He remembered how Tansy's fingers had rippled through the knots.

Eleven forty-one. The phonograph needle started to roll off the table. He dropped the cord and laid the phonograph needle against his fountain pen, so it would not roll. Then he started again on the knot.

For a moment he thought he must have picked up the gut,

the cord seemed so stiff and unresponsive. Incredible what nervousness can do to you, he told himself. His mouth was dry. He swallowed with difficulty.

Finally, by keeping his eyes on the illustration and imitating it step by step, he managed to tie a carrick bend. All the while he felt as if there were more between his fingers than a cord, as if he were manipulating against a great inertia. Just as he finished, he felt a slight prickly chill, like the onset of fever, and the light overhead seemed to dim a trifle. Eyestrain.

The phonograph needle was rolling in the opposite direction, spinning faster and faster. He slapped his hand down on it, missed it, slapped again, caught it at the edge of the table.

Just like a Ouija board, he told himself. You try to keep your fingers, poised on the planchette, perfectly motionless. As a result, muscular tensions accumulate. They reach the breaking point. Seemingly without any volition on your part, the planchette begins to roll and skid about on its three little legs, traveling from letter to letter. Same thing here. Nervous and muscular tensions made it difficult for him to tie knots. Obeying a universal tendency, he projected the difficulty into the cord. And, by elbow and knee pressure, he had been doing some unconscious table tipping.

Between his fingers, the phonograph needle seemed to vibrate, as if it were a tiny part of a great machine. There was a very faint suggestion of electric shock. Unbidden, the torturesome, clangorous chords of the "Ninth Sonata" began to sound in his mind. Rot! One well-known symptom of extreme nervousness is a tingling in the fingers, often painfully intense. But his throat was dry and his snort of bitter contempt sounded choked.

He pinned the needle in the flannel for greater safety.

Eleven forty-seven. Reaching for the gut, his fingers felt shaky and weak as if he just climbed a hundred-foot rope hand over hand. The stuff looked normal, but it was slimy to the touch, as if it had just bee dragged from the beast's belly and twisted into shape. And for some moments he had been conscious of an acrid, almost metallic odor replacing the salt smell of the Bay. Tactual and olfactory hallucinations joining in with the visual and auditory, he told himself. He could still hear the "Ninth Sonata."

He knew how to tie a bowline backwards, and it should have been easier since the gut was not as stiff as it ought to be, but he felt there were other forces manipulating it or other mentalities trying to give orders to his fingers, so that the gut was trying to tie itself into a slip-knot, a reef, a half hitch—anything but a bowline. His fingers ached, his eyes were heavy with an abnormal fatigue. He was working against a mounting inertia, a crushing inertia. He remembered Tansy telling him that night when she had confessed her witchcraft to him: "There's a law of reaction in all conjuring—like the kick of a gun—" Eleven fifty-two.

With a great effort, he canalized his mental energy, focused his attention only on the knot. His numb fingers began to move in an odd rhythm, a rhythm of the "Ninth Sonata," *piu vivo*. The bowline was tied.

The overhead light dimmed markedly, throwing the whole room into sooty gloom. Hysterical blindness, he told himself—and small town power systems are always going on the blink. It was very cold now, so cold that he fancied he could see his breath. And silent, terribly silent. Against that silence he could feel and hear the rapid drumming of his heart, accelerating unendurably to the thundering, swirling rhythm of the music.

Then, in one instant of diabolic, paralyzing insight, he knew that *this* was sorcery. No mere puttering about with ridiculous medieval implements, no effortless sleight of hand, but a straining, back-breaking struggle to keep control of *forces summoned*, of which the objects he manipulated were only the symbols. Outside the walls of the room, outside the walls of his skull, outside the impalpable energy-walls of his mind, he felt those forces gathering, swelling up, dreadfully expectant, waiting for him to make a false move so that they could crush him.

He could not believe it. He did not believe it. Yet somehow he *had* to believe it.

The only question was—would he be able to stay in control?

Eleven fifty-seven. He started to gather the objects together on the flannel. The needle jumped to the lodestone, dragging the flannel with it, and clung. It shouldn't have; it had been a foot away. He took a pinch of graveyard dirt. Between finger and thumb, each separate particle seemed to crawl, like a tiny maggot. He sensed that something was missing. He could not remember what it was. He fumbled for the formula. A current of air was blowing the scraps of paper off the table. He sensed an eager, inward surge of the forces outside, as if they knew he was failing. He clutched at the papers, managed to pin them down. Bending close, he made out the words "platinum or iridium." He jabbed his fountain pen against the table, broke off the nib, and added it to the other objects.

He stood at the side of the table away from the knife that marked the east, trying to steady his shaking hands against the edge. His teeth were chattering. The room was utterly dark now except for the impossible bluish light that beat through the window shade. Surely the street light wasn't that mercury-vapor hue.

Abruptly the strip of flannel started to curl like a strip of heated gelatine, to roll itself up from east to west, *with* the sun.

He jerked forward, got his hand inside the flannel before it closed; drew it apart—in his numb hands it seemed like metal—and rolled it up against the sun, widdershins.

The silence was intensified. Even the sound of his beating heart was cut off. He knew that something was listening with a terrible intentness for his command, and that something was hoping with an even more terrible avidity that he would not be able to utter that command.

Somewhere a clock was booming—or was it not a clock, but the secret sound of time? Nine—ten—eleven—twelve.

His tongue stuck to the roof of his mouth. He kept on

choking soundlessly. It seemed to him that the walls of the room were closer to him than they had been a minute before.

Then, in a dry, croaking voice he managed: "Stop Tansy. Bring her here."

Norman felt the room shake, the floor buckle, and lift under his feet, as if an earthquake had visited New Jersey. Darkness became absolute. The table, or some force erupting from the table, seemed to rise and strike him. He felt himself flung back onto something soft.

Then the forces were gone. In all things, tension gave way to limpness. Sound and light returned. He was sprawled across the bed. On the table was a little flannel packet, no longer of any consequence.

He felt as if had been doped, or were waking after a debauch. There was no inclination to do anything. Emotion was absent.

Outwardly everything was the same. Even his mind, with automatic rationality, could wearily take up the thankless task of explaining his experiences on a scientific basis—weaving an elaborate web in which psychosis, hallucination, and improbable coincidences were the strands.

But inwardly something had changed, and would never change back.

Considerable time passed.

He heard steps mounting the stairs, then in the hall. They made a *squish-squish* sound, as if the shoes were soaking wet.

They stopped outside his door.

He crossed the room, turned the key in the lock, opened the door.

A strand of seaweed was caught in the silver brooch. The gray suit was dark now and heavy with water, except for one spot which had started to dry and was faintly dusted with salt. The odor of the Bay was intimate and close. There was another strand of seaweed clinging to one ankle against the wrinkled stockings.

Around the stained shoes, a little pool of water was forming.

His eyes traced the wet footprints down the hall. At the head of the stairs the old clerk was standing, one foot still on the last step. He was carrying a small pigskin suitcase, waterstained.

"What's this all about?" he quavered, when he saw that Norman was looking at him. "You didn't tell me you were expecting your wife. She looks like she'd thrown herself in the Bay. We don't want anything queer happening in this hotel—anything wrong."

"It's quite all right," said Norman, prolonging the moment before he would have to look in her face. "I'm sorry I forgot to tell you. May I have the bag?"

"—only last year we had a suicide,"—the old clerk did not seem to realize he was speaking his thoughts aloud—"bad for the hotel." His voice trailed off. He looked at Norman, gathered himself together, and came hesitatingly down the hall. When he was a few steps away, he stopped, reached out and put down the suitcase, turned, and walked rapidly away.

Unwillingly, Norman raised his eyes until they were on a level with hers.

The face was pale, very pale, and without expression. The lips were tinged with blue. Wet hair was plastered against the cheeks. A thick lock crossed one eye socket, like a curtain, and curled down toward the throat. One eye stared at him, without recognition. And no hand moved to brush the lock of hair away from the other.

From the hem of the skirt, water was dripping.

The lips parted. The voice had the monotonous murmur of water.

"You were too late," the voice said. "You were a minute too late."

XV

For a third time they had come back to the same question. Norman had the maddening sensation of following a robot that was walking in a huge endless circle and always treading on precisely the same blades of grass as it retraced its path.

With the hopeless conviction that he would not get any further this time, he asked the question again: "But how can you lack consciousness, and at the same time *know* that you lack consciousness? If your mind is blank, you cannot at the same time be aware that your mind is blank."

The hands of his watch were creeping toward three in the morning. The chill and sickliness of night's lowest ebb pervaded the dingy hotel room. Tansy sat stiffly, wearing Norman's bathrobe and fleece-lined slippers, with a blanket over her knees and a bath towel wrapped around her head. They should have made her look childlike and perhaps even artlessly attractive. They did not. If you were to unwind the towel you would find the top of the skull sawed off and the brains removed, an empty bowl—that was the illusion Norman experienced every time he made the mistake of looking into her eyes.

The pale lips parted. "I know nothing. I only speak. They have taken away my soul. But my voice is a function of my body."

You could not say the voice was patiently explanatory. It was too empty and colorless even for that. The words, clearly enunciated and evenly spaced, all sounded alike. They were like the noise of a machine.

The last thing he wanted to do was hammer questions at this stiff pitiful figure, but he felt that at all costs he must awaken some spark of feeling in the masklike face; he must find some intelligible starting point before his own mind could begin to work effectually.

"But Tansy, if you can talk about the present situation, you must be aware of it. You're here in this room with me!"

The toweled head shook once, like that of a mechanical doll.

"Nothing is here with you but a body. 'I' is not here."

His mind automatically corrected "is" to "am" before he realized that there had been no grammatical error. He trembled.

"You mean," he asked, "that you can see or hear nothing? That there is just a blackness?"

Again that simple mechanical headshake, which carried more absolute conviction than the most heated protestations.

"My body sees and hears perfectly. It has suffered no injury. It can function in all particulars. But there is nothing inside. There is not even a blackness."

His tired, fumbling mind jumped to the subject of behavioristic psychology and its fundamental assertion that human reactions can be explained completely and satisfactorily without once referring to consciousness—that it need not even be assumed that consciousness exists. Here was the perfect proof. And yet not so perfect, for the behavior of this body lacked every one of those little mannerisms whose sum is personality. The way Tansy used to squint when thinking through a difficult question. The familiar quirk at the corners of her mouth when she felt flattered or slyly amused. All gone. Even the quick triple headshake he knew so well, with the slight rabbity wrinkling of the nose, had become a robot's "No."

Her sensory organs still responded to stimuli. They sent impulses to the brain, where they traveled about and gave rise to impulses which activated glands and muscles, including the motor organs of speech. But that was all. None of those intangible flurries we call consciousness hovered around the webwork of nervous activity in the cortex. What had imparted style—Tansy's style, like no one else's—to every movement and utterance of the body, was gone. There was left only a physiological organism, without sign or indication of personality. Not even a mad or an idiot soul—yes! why not use that old term now that it had an obvious specific meaning?—peered from the gray-green eyes which winked at intervals with machine-like regularity, but only to lubricate the cornea, nothing more.

He felt a grim sort of relief go through him, now that he had been able to picture Tansy's condition in definite terms. But the picture itself—his mind veered to the memory of a newspaper story about an old man who had kept locked in his bedroom for years the body of a young woman whom he loved and who had died of an incurable disease. He had maintained the body in an astonishing state of preservation by wax and other means, they said, had talked to it every night and morning, had been convinced that he would some day reanimate it complete—until they found out and took it away from him and buried it.

He suddenly grimaced. Damn it all, he commented inwardly, why did he let his mind go off on these wild fancies, when it was obvious that Tansy was suffering from an unusual nervous condition, a strange self-delusion?

Obvious.

Wild fancies?

"Tansy," he asked, "when your soul went, why didn't you die?"

"Usually the soul lingers to the end, unable to escape, and vanishes or dies when the body dies," the voice answered, its words as evenly spaced as if timed to a metronome. "But He Who Walks Behind was tearing at mine. There was the weight of green water against my face. I knew it was midnight. I knew you had failed. In that moment of despair, He Who Walks Behind was able to draw forth my soul. In the same moment Your Agent's arms were about me, lifting me toward the air. My soul was close enough to know what had happened, yet not close enough to return. Its doubled anguish was the last memory it imprinted on my brain. Your Agent and He Who Walks Behind concluded that each had obtained the thing he had been sent for, so there was no struggle between them."

The picture created in Norman's mind was so shockingly

vivid that it seemed incredible that it could have been produced by the words of a mere physiological machine. And
yet only a physiological machine could have told the story
with such total restraint.

"Is there nothing that touches you?" he asked abruptly in
a loud voice, gripped by an intolerable spasm of anguish at
the emptiness of her eyes. "Haven't you a single emotion
left?"

"Yes. One." This time it was not a robot's headshake, but
a robot's nod. For the first time there was a stir of feeling, a
hint of motivation. The tip of a pallid tongue licked hungrily
around the pale lips. "I want my soul."

He caught his breath. Now that he had succeeded in awakening a feeling in her, he hated it. There was something so
animal about it, so like some light-sensitive worm greedily
wriggling toward the sunlight.

"I want my soul," the voice repeated mechanically, tearing at his emotions more than any plaintive or whining accents could have done. "At the last moment, although it could
not return, my soul implanted that one emotion in me. It
knew what awaited it. It knew there are things that can be
done to a soul. It was very much afraid."

He ground out the words between his teeth. "Where do
you think your soul is?"

"She has it. The woman with the small dull eyes."

He looked at her. Something began to pound inside him.
He knew it was rage, and for the moment he didn't care
whether it was sane rage or not.

"Evelyn Sawtelle?" he asked huskily.

"Yes. But it is not wise to speak of her by name."

His hand shot out for the phone. He had to do something
definite, or lose control of himself completely.

After a time he roused the night clerk and got the local
operator.

"Yes, sir," came the singsong voice. "Hempnell 1284.
You wish to make a person-to-person call to Evelyn Sawtelle—E-V-E-L-Y-N S-A-W-T-E-L-L-E, sir? . . . Will you

please hang up and wait? It will take considerable time to make a connection.''

"I want my soul. I want to go to that woman. I want to go to Hempnell." Now that he had touched off the blind hunger in the creature facing him, it persisted. He was reminded of a phonograph needle caught in the same groove, or a mechanical toy turned on to a new track by a little push.

"We'll go there all right." It was still hard for him to control his breathing. "We'll get it back."

"But I must start for Hempnell soon. My clothes are ruined by the water. I must have the maid clean and press them."

With a slow, even movement she got to her feet and started toward the phone.

"But, Tansy," he objected involuntarily, "it's three in the morning. You can't get a maid now."

"But my clothes must be cleaned and pressed. I must start for Hempnell soon."

The words might have been those of an obstinate woman, sulky and selfish. But they had less tone than a sleepwalker's. She kept on toward the phone. Although he did not anticipate that he would do it, he shrank out of her way, pressing close against the side of the bed.

"But even if there is a maid," he said, "she won't come at this hour."

The pallid face turned toward him incuriously.

"The maid will be a woman. She will come when she hears me."

Then she was talking to the night clerk. "Is there a maid in the hotel? . . . Send her to my room. . . . Then ring her. . . . I cannot wait until morning. . . . I need her at once. . . . I cannot tell you the reason. . . . Thank you."

There was a long wait while he heard faintly the repeated ringing at the other end of the line. He could imagine the sleepy, surly voice that finally answered.

"Is this the maid? . . . Come at once to Room 37." He could almost catch the indignant answer. Then—"Can't you hear my voice? Don't you realize my condition? . . . Yes. . . . Come at once.'' And she replaced the phone in its cradle.

"Tansy—" he began. His eyes were on her still and once again he found himself making a halting preamble, although he had not intended to. "You are able to hear and answer my questions?"

"I can answer questions. I have been answering questions for three hours."

But—logic prompted wearily—if she can remember what has been happening these last three hours, then surely—And yet, what is memory but a track worn in the nervous system? In order to explain memory you don't need to bring in consciousness.

Quit banging your head against that stone wall, you fool!— came another inward prompting. You've looked in her eyes, haven't you? Well, then, get on with it!

"Tansy," he asked, "when you say that Evelyn Sawtelle has your soul, what do you mean?"

"Just that."

"Don't you mean that she, and Mrs. Carr and Mrs. Gunnison too, have some sort of psychological power over you, that they hold you in a kind of emotional bondage?"

"No."

"But your soul—"

"—is my soul."

"Tansy." He hated to bring up this subject, but he felt he must. "Do you believe that Evelyn Sawtelle is a witch, that she is going through the motions of practicing witchcraft, just as you did?"

"Yes."

"And Mrs. Carr and Mrs. Gunnison?"

"They too."

"You mean you believe they're doing the same things that you did—laying spells and making charms, making use of their husbands' special knowledge, trying to protect their husbands and advance their careers?"

"They go further."

"What do you mean?"

"They use black magic as well as white. They don't care if they hurt or torment or kill."

"Why are they different in that way?"

"Witches are like people. There are the sanctimonious, self-worshipping, self-deceiving ones, the ones who believe their ends justify any means."

"Do you believe that all three of them are working together against you?"

"Yes."

"Why?"

"Because they hate me."

"Why?"

"Partly they hate me because of you and what your advancement might do to their husbands and themselves. But more than that, they hate me because they sense that my inmost standards are different from theirs. They sense that, though I conform on the surface, I do not really worship respectability. Witches, you see, are apt to have the same gods as people. They fear me because I do not bow down to Hempnell. Though Mrs. Carr, I think, has an additional reason."

"Tansy," he began and hesitated. "Tansy, how do you think it happens that these three women are witches?"

"It happens."

There was a silence in the room then, as Norman's thoughts dully revolved around the topic of paranoia. Then, "But Tansy," he said with an effort, "don't you see what that implies? The idea that all women are witches."

"Yes."

"But how can you ever—"

"Ssh." There was no more expression to the sound than an escape of steam from a radiator, but it shut up Norman. "She is coming."

"Who?"

"The maid. Hide, and I will show you something."

"Hide?"

"Yes." She came toward him and he involuntarily backed

away from her. His hand touched a door. "The closet?" he asked, wetting his lips.

"Yes. Hide there, and I will prove something to you."

Norman heard footsteps in the hall. He hesitated a moment, frowning, then did as she asked him.

"I'll leave the door a little ajar," he said. "See, like this."

The robot nod was his only answer.

There was a tapping at the door. Tansy's footsteps, the sound of the door opening.

"Y'ast for me, ma'am?" Contrary to his expectations, the voice was young. It sounded as if she had swallowed as she spoke.

"Yes. I want you to clean and press some things of mine. They've been in salt water. They're hanging on the edge of the bathtub. Go and get them."

The maid came into his line of vision. She would be fat in a few years, he thought, but she was handsome now, though puffed with sleep. She had pulled on a dress, but her feet were in slippers and her hair was snarly.

"Be careful with the suit. It's wool," came Tansy's voice, sounding just as toneless as when it had been directed at him. "And I want them within an hour."

Norman half expected to hear an objection to this unreasonable request, but there was none. The girl said, "All rightie, ma'am," and walked rapidly out of the bathroom, the damp clothes hurriedly slung over one arm, as if her one object were to get away before she was spoken to again.

"Wait a minute, girl. I want to ask you a question." The voice was somewhat louder this time. That was the only change, but it had a startling effect of command.

The girl hesitated, then swung around unwillingly, and Norman got a good look at her face. He could not see Tansy—the closet door just cut her off—but he could see the fear come to the surface of the girl's sleep-creased face.

"Yes, ma'am?" she managed.

There was a considerable pause. He could tell from the way the girl shrank, hugging the damp clothes tight to her body, that Tansy had lifted her eyes and was looking at her.

Finally: "You know The Easy Way to Do Things? The Ways to Get and Guard?"

Norman could have sworn that the girl gave a start at the second phrase. But she only shook her head quickly, and mumbled, "No, ma'am. I . . . I don't know what you're talking about."

"You mean you never learned How to Make Wishes Work? You don't conjure, or spell or hex? You don't know the Art?"

The time the "No" was almost inaudible. The girl was trying to look away and failing.

"I think you are lying."

The girl twisted, hands tightly clutching her overlapping arms. She looked so frightened that Norman wanted to go out and stop it, but curiosity held him rigid.

The girl's resistance broke. "Please, ma'am, we're not supposed to tell."

"You may tell me. What Procedures do you use?"

The girl's perplexity at the new word looked real.

"I don't know anything about that, ma'am. I don't do much. Like when my boyfriend was in the army, I did things to keep him from getting shot or hurt, and I've spelled him so that he'll keep away from other women. And I kin annernt with erl for sickness. Honest, I don't do much, ma'am. And it don't always work. And lots of things I can't get that way." Her words had begun to run away with her.

"Very well. Where did you learn to do this?"

"Some I learned form Ma when I was a kid. And some from Mrs. Neidel—she got spells against bullets from her grandmother who had a family in some European war way back. But most women won't tell you anything. And some spells I kind of figure out myself, and try different ways until they work. You won't tell on me, ma'am?"

"No. Look at me now. What has happened to me?"

"Honest, ma'am, I don't know. Please, don't make me say it." The girl's terror and reluctance were so obviously genuine that Norman felt a surge of anger at Tansy. Then he remembered that the thing beyond the door was incapable of either cruelty or kindness.

"I want you to tell me."

"I don't know how to say it, ma'am. But you're . . . you're *dead*." Suddenly she threw herself at Tansy's feet. "Oh, please, please, don't take my soul! Please!"

"I would not take your soul. You would get much the best of that bargain. You may go away now."

"Oh, thank you, thank you." The girl hastily gathered up the scattered clothes. "I'll have them all ready for you very soon. Really I will." And she hurried out.

Only when he moved, did Norman realize that his muscles were stiff and aching from those few taut minutes of peering. The robed and toweled figure was sitting in exactly the same position as when he had last seen it, hands loosely folded, eyes still directed toward where the girl had been standing.

"If you knew all this," he asked simply, his mind in a kind of trance from what he had witnessed, "why were you willing to stop last week when I asked you?"

"There are two sides to every woman." It might have been a mummy dispensing elder wisdom. "One is rational, like a man. The other knows. Men are artificially isolated creatures like islands in a sea of magic, protected by their rationality and by the devices of their women. Their isolation gives them greater forcefulness in thought and action, but the women know. Women might be able to rule the world openly, but they do not want the work or the responsibility. And men might learn to excel them in the Art. Even now there may still be male sorcerers, but very few.

"Last week I suspected much that I did not tell you. But the rational side is strong in me, and I wanted to be close to you in all ways. Like many women, I was not certain. And when I destroyed my charms and guards, I became temporarily blind to sorcery. Like a person used to large doses of a drug, I was uninfluenced by small doses. Rationality was dominant. I enjoyed a few days of false security. Then rationality itself proved to me that you were the victim of sorcery. And during my journey here I learned much, partly from what He Who Walks Behind let slip." She paused and added, with the blank innocent cunning of a child, "Shall we go back to Hempnell now?"

The phone rang. It was the night clerk, almost incoherent in his agitation, babbling threateningly about the police and eviction. To pacify him, Norman had to promise to come down at once.

The old man was waiting at the foot of the stairs.

"Look here, mister," he began, shaking a finger, "I want to know what's going on. Just now Sissy came down from your room white as a sheet. She wouldn't tell me anything, but she was trembling like all get-out. Sissy's my granddaughter. I got her this job, and I'm responsible for her.

"I know what hotels are. I've worked in 'em all my life. And I know the kind of people that come to them—sometimes men and women working together—and I know the kind of things they try to do to young girls.

"Now I'm not saying anything against you, mister. But it was mighty queer the way your wife came here. I thought when she asked me to call Sissy that she was sick or something. But if she's sick, why haven't you called a doctor? And what are you doing still up at four? Mrs. Thompson in the next room called to say there was talking in your room—not loud, but it scared her. I got a right to know what's going on."

Norman put on his best classroom manner and blandly dissected the old man's apprehensions until they began to look very unsubstantial. Dignity told. With a last show of grumbling the old man let himself be convinced. As Norman started upstairs, he was shuffling back to the switchboard.

On the second flight, Norman heard a phone ringing. As he was walking down the hall, it stopped.

He opened the door. Tansy was standing by the bed, speaking into the phone. Its dull blackness, curving from mouth to ear, emphasized the pallor of lips and cheeks and the whiteness of the toweling.

"This is Tansy Saylor," she was saying tonelessly. "I want my soul." A pause. "Can't you hear me, Evelyn? This is Tansy Saylor. I want my soul."

He had completely forgotten the call he had made in a moment of crazy anger. He no longer had any clear idea of what he had been going to say.

A low wailing was coming from the phone. Tansy was talking against it.

"This is Tansy Saylor. I want my soul."

He stepped forward. The wailing sound had swiftly risen to a squeal, but mixed with it was an intermittent windy whirring.

He reached out to take the phone. But at that instant Tansy jerked around and something seemed to happen to the phone.

When a lifeless object begins to act as if it has life, there is always the possibility of illusion. For instance, there is a trick of manipulating a pencil that makes it look as if it were being bent back and forth like a stick of rubber. And Tansy did have her hand to the phone and was twisting about so rapidly that it was hard to be sure of anything.

Nevertheless, to Norman it seemed that the phone suddenly became pliable and twisted about like a stumpy black worm, fastened itself tight to the skin, and dug into Tansy's chin and into her neck just below the ear, like a double-ended black paw. And with the squeal he seemed to hear a muffled sucking.

His reaction was immediate, involuntary, and startling. He dropped to his knees and ripped the phone cord from the wall. Violet sparks spat from the torn wire. The loose end whipped back with his jerk, seeming to writhe like a wounded snake, and wrapped itself around his forearm. To Norman it seemed that it tightened spasmodically, then relaxed. He tore it away with a panicky loathing, then stood up.

The phone had fallen to the floor. There seemed to be nothing out of the ordinary about it now. He gave it a little kick. There was a dull *plunk* and it slid solidly across the floor a few inches. He stooped and after hesitating a few moments gingerly touched it. It felt as hard and rigid as it should.

He looked at Tansy. She was standing in the same place. Not an atom of fear showed in her expression. With the unconcernedness of a machine, she had lifted a hand and was slowly massaging her cheek and neck. From the corner of her mouth a few drops of blood were trickling.

Of course, she could have bashed the phone against her teeth and cut her lip that way.

But he had seen—

Still, she might have shaken the phone rapidly, so that it only seemed to become pliable and bend.

But it hadn't looked that way. What he had seen . . . had been impossible.

But so many "impossible" things had been happening.

And it *had* been Evelyn Sawtelle at the other end of the phone. He *had* heard the sound of the bull-roarer coming over the phone. Nothing supernatural about that. If the recording of a bull-roarer had been played very loudly over the phone it would have sounded just like that. He *couldn't* have been mistaken about it. This was a fact and he must stick to it.

It gave him the emotional cue he needed. Anger. He was almost startled by the surge of hatred that went through him at the thought of that woman with the small dull eyes. For a moment he felt like an inquisitor confronted with evidence of malicious witchcraft. Visions of the rack and the wheel and the boot flitted through his mind. Then that phantasmagoria of the Middle Ages faded, but the anger remained, settling down to a steady pulse of detestation.

Whatever had happened to Tansy, he *knew* that Evelyn Sawtelle and Hulda Gunnison and Flora Carr were responsible. He had too much evidence in their own actions. That was another fact that he must stick to. Whether they were working on Tansy's mind by an incredibly subtle and diabolic campaign of suggestion, or by some unnamed means, they were responsible.

There was no way of getting at them by psychiatry or law. What had happened in the past few days was something that only he, of all the men in the world, could believe or understand. He must fight them himself, using their own weapons against them—that other unnamed means.

In every way he must act as if he believed in that other unnamed means.

Tansy stopped massaging her face. Her tongue licked the lip where the blood was drying.

"Shall we go back to Hempnell now?"

"Yes!"

XVI

The rhythmic rattle and clank of the train was a Machine Age lullaby. Norman could hear the engine snoring. The wide, heat-baked, green fields swinging past the window of the compartment drowsed in the noonday sun. The farms and cattle and horses dotting them here and there were entranced by the heat. He would have liked to doze too, but he knew he would not be able to. And as for—she apparently never slept.

"I want to run over some things," he said. "Interrupt me if you hear anything that sounds wrong or you don't understand."

From the corner of his eye he noted the figure sitting between him and the window nod once.

It occurred to him that there was something terrible about an adaptability that could familiarize him even to—her, so that now, after only a day and a half, he was using her as a kind of thinking machine, asking for her memories and reactions in the same way that a man might direct a servant to put a certain record on the phonograph.

At the same time he knew that he was able to make this close contact endurable only by carefully directing his thoughts and actions—like the trick he had acquired of never quite looking at her directly. And he was buoyed up a little by his hope that her present condition was only temporary. But if had once let himself start to think what it would mean to live a lifetime, to share bed and board, with that coldness, that inner blackness, that vacancy . . .

Other people noticed the difference, all right. Like those crowds he had to push through in New York yesterday. Somehow people always edged away, so they wouldn't have to touch her, and he caught more than one following glance, poised between curiosity and fear. And when that other woman started to scream—lucky they had been able to lose themselves in the crowd.

The brief stopover at New York had given him time for some vitally necessary thinking. But he had been glad last night when it was over. The Pullman compartment seemed a haven of privacy.

What was it those other people noticed? True, if you looked closely, the heavy cosmetics only provided a grotesque and garnish contrast to the underlying pallor, and powder did not wholly conceal the ugly dark bruise around the mouth. But the veil helped, and you had to look very closely—the cosmetics were practically a theatrical makeup. Was it her walk that they noticed, or the way her clothes hung? Her clothes always looked a little like a scarecrow's now, though you could not tell the reason. Or was there actually something to what the Bayport girl had said?

It occurred to him that he was letting his mind wander because he didn't want to get on with the distasteful task he had set himself, this task that was abhorrent to him because it was so false—or because it was so true.

"Magic is a practical science," he began quickly. He talked to the wall, as if dictating. "There is all the difference in the world between a formula in physics and a formula in magic, although they have the same name. The former describes, in terse mathematical symbol, cause-effect relationships of wide generality. But a formula in magic is a way of getting or accomplishing something. It always takes into account the motivation or desire of the person invoking the formula—be it greed, love, revenge, or what not. Whereas the experiment in physics is essentially independent of the experimenter. In short, there has been little or no pure magic, comparable to pure science.

"This distinction between physics and magic is only an

accident of history. Physics started out as a kind of magic, too—witness alchemy and the mystical mathematics of Pythagoras. And modern physics is ultimately as practical as magic, but it possesses a superstructure of theory that magic lacks. Magic could be given such a superstructure by research in pure magic and by the investigation and correlation of the magic formulas of different peoples and times, with a view to deriving basic formulas which could be expressed in mathematical symbols and which would have a wide application. Most persons practicing magic have been too interested in immediate results to bother about theory. But just as research in pure science has ultimately led, seemingly by accident, to results of vast practical importance, so research in pure magic might be expected to yield similar results.

"The work of Rhine at Duke, indeed, has been very close to pure magic, with its piling up of evidence for clairvoyance, prophecy, and telepathy; its investigation of the direct linkage between all minds, their ability to affect each other instantaneously, even when they are on opposite sides of the earth."

He waited a moment, then went on.

"The subject matter of magic is akin to that of physics, in that it deals with certain forces and materials, though these—"

"I believe it is more akin to psychology," the voice interrupted.

"How so?" He still looked at the wall.

"Because it concerns the control of other beings, the summoning of them, and the constraining of them to perform certain actions."

"Good. That is very suggestive. Fortunately, formulas may still hold good so long as their reference is clear, though we are ignorant of the precise nature of the entities to which they refer. For example, a physicist need not be able to give a visual description of an atom, even if the term visual appearance has any meaning when applied to an atom, which is doubtful. Similarly, a sorcerer need not be able to describe the appearance and nature of the entity he summons—hence the common references in the literature of magic to indescribable and nameless horrors. But the point is well taken. Many seemingly impersonal forces, when broken down sufficiently, become something very much like personality. It's not too far-fetched to say that it would take a science resembling psychology to describe the behavior of a single electron, with all its whims and impulses, though electrons in the aggregate obey relatively simple laws, just as human beings do when considered as crowds. The same holds true of the basic entities of magic, and to a much greater degree.

"It is partly for this reason that magical processes are so unreliable and dangerous, and why their working can be so readily impeded if the intended victim is on guard against them—as your formulas have to our knowledge been nullified since Mrs. Gunnison stole your notebook."

His words possessed for him an incredibly strange overtone. But it was only by maintaining a dry, scholarly manner that he could keep going. He knew that if he permitted himself to be casual, mental confusion would engulf him.

"There remains one all-important consideration," he went on swiftly. "Magic appears to be a science which markedly depends on its environment—that is, the situation of the world and the general conditions of the cosmos at any particular time. For example, Euclidean geometry is useful on Earth, but out in the great depths of space a non-Euclidean geometry is more practical. The same is true of magic, but to a more striking degree. The basic, unstated formulas of magic appear to change with the passage of time, requiring frequent restatement—though it might conceivably be possible to discover master-formulas governing that change. It has been speculated that the laws of physics show a similar evolutionary tendency—though if they do evolve, it is at a much less rapid rate than those of magic. For example, it is believed that the speed of light may slowly change with its age. It is natural that the laws of magic should evolve more swiftly, since magic depends on a contact between the material world and another level of being—and that contact is complex and may be shifting rapidly.

"Take astrology, for example. In the course of several thousand years, the precession of equinoxes has put the Sun into entirely different celestial houses—signs of the Zodiac—at the same times of year. A person born, say, on March 22nd, is still said to be born in Aries, though he is actually born when the Sun is in the constellation Pisces. A failure to take into consideration this change since the formulas of astrology were first discovered, has rendered the formulas obsolete and invalidated them for—"

"It is my belief," the voice broke in, like a phonograph suddenly starting, "that astrology has always been largely invalid. That it is one of the many pretended sciences which have been confused with true magic and used as a kind of window dressing. Such is my belief."

"I presume that may be the case, and it would help to explain why magic itself has been outwardly discredited as a science—which is the point I am getting at.

"Suppose the basic formulas of physics—such as Newton's three laws of motion—had changed several times in the last few thousand years. The discovery of any physical laws at any time would have been vastly difficult. The same experiments would give different results in different ages. But that is the case with magic, and explains why magic has been periodically discredited and become repugnant to the rational mind. It's like what old Carr was saying about the run of cards at bridge. After a few shuffles of a multitude of cosmic factors, the laws of magic change. A sharp eye can spot the changes, but continual experimentation, of the trial-and-error sort, is necessary to keep the crude practical formulas of magic in anything like working order, especially since the basic formulas and the master-formulas have never been discovered.

"Take a concrete example—the formula I used Sunday night. It shows signs of recent revision. For instance, what did the original, unrevised formula have in place of the phonograph needle?"

"A willow whistle of a certain shape, which had been blown only once," the voice told him.

"And the platinum or iridium?"

"The original formula mentioned silver, but a heavier

metal serves better. Lead, however, proved altogether ineffective. I tried it once. It was apparently too unlike silver in other respects."

"Precisely. Trial-and-error experimentation. Moreover, in the absence of thorough investigation, we cannot be sure that all the ingredients of a magic formula are essential in making it work. A comparison of the magic formulas of different countries and peoples would be helpful in this respect. It would show which ingredients are common to all formulas and therefore presumably essential, and which are not essential."

There was a discreet knock at the door. Norman spoke a few words, and the figure drew down its veil and turned toward the window, as if staring stolidly at the passing fields. Then he opened the door.

It was lunch, as long in coming as breakfast had been. And there was a new face—coffee-colored instead of ebony. Evidently the first waiter, who had shown growing nervousness in his previous trips to the compartment, had decided to let someone else get the big tip.

With a mixture of curiosity and impatience, Norman waited for the reactions of the newcomer. He was able to predict most of them. First a very quick inquisitive glance past him at the seated figure—Norman guessed they had become the major mystery of the train. Then a longer, sideways glance while setting up the folding table, ending with the eyes getting very wide; he could almost feel the coffee-colored flesh crawl. Only hurried, almost unwilling glances after that, with a growing uneasiness manifested in clumsy handling of the dishes and glassware. Then a too-pleasant smile and a hasty departure.

Only once Norman interfered—to place the knives and forks so they lay at right angles to their usual position.

The meal was a very simple one, almost ascetic. He did not look across the table as he ate. There was something worse than animal greediness about that methodical feeding. After the meal he settled back and started to light a cigarette, but—"Aren't you forgetting something?" the figure said. The question was uninflected.

He roused himself, got up and put the left-overs into a small cardboard box, covered them with a napkin he had used to wipe the dishes clean, and placed the box in his suitcase beside an envelope containing clippings from his own finger-nails. The sight of the clean breakfast dishes had been one of the things which had helped to disturb the first waiter, but Norman was determined to adhere strictly to all taboos that Tansy seemed to desire.

So he collected food fragments, saw to it that no knives or other sharp instruments pointed toward himself or his com-panion, had them sleep with their heads nearest the engine and their destination, and enforced a number of other minor regulations. Eating in private satisfied still another taboo, but there was more than one reason for that.

He glanced at his watch. Only half an hour until Hempnell. He had not realized they were so close. There was the faint sense of an almost physical resistance from the region ahead, as if the air were thickening. And his mind was tossing with a multitude of problems yet to be considered.

Deliberately turning his back, he said, "According to the myths, souls may be imprisoned in all sorts of ways—in boxes, in knots, in animals, in stones. Have you any ideas on this subject?"

As he feared, this particular question brought the usual response. The answering words had the same dull insistence as when he had first heard them.

"I want my soul."

His hands, clasped in his lap, tightened. This was why he had avoided the question until now. Yet he had to know more, if that were possible.

"But where exactly should we look for it?"

"I want my soul."

"Yes." It was hard for him to control his voice. "But how, precisely, might it be hidden? It would help if I knew."

There was rather a long pause. Then, in robot-imitativeness of his lecture manner: "The environment of the soul is the human brain. If it is free, it immediately seeks such an environment. It may be said that soul and body are two separate creatures, living together in a symbiotic relationship so intimate and tight that they normally seem to be only one creature. The closeness of this contact appears to have increased with the centuries. Indeed, when the body it is occupying dies, the soul is usually unable to escape and appears to die too. But by supernatural means the soul may sometimes be divorced from the body it is occupying. Then, if it is prevented from re-entering its own body, it is irresistibly drawn to another, whether or not that other body possesses a soul. And so the captive soul is unusually imprisoned in the brain of its captor and forced to view and feel, in complete intimacy, the workings of that soul. Therein lies perhaps its chief torment."

Beads of sweat prickled Norman's scalp and forehead.

His voice did not shake, but it was unnaturally heavy and sibilant as he asked, "What is Evelyn Sawtelle like?"

The answer sounded as if it were being read verbatim from the summary of a political dossier.

"She is dominated by a desire for social prestige. She spends most of her time in unsuccessfully attempting to be snobbish. She has romantic ideas about herself, but since they are too high-flown for any reasonable chance of satisfaction, she is prim and moralistic, with rigid standards of conduct. She believes she was cheated in her husband, and is always apprehensive that he will lose what ground she has gained for him. Being unsure of herself, she is given to acts of maliciousness and sudden cruelty. At present she is very frightened and constantly on guard. This is why she had her magic all ready when she received the telephone call."

Norman asked, "Mrs. Gunnison—what do you think of her?"

"She is a woman of abundant vigor and appetites. She is a good housewife and hostess, but those activities hardly take the edge off her energies. She should have been mistress of a feudal domain. She is a born tyrant and grows fat on it. Her appetites, many of them incapable of open satisfaction in our present society, nevertheless find devious outlets. Servant girls of the Gunnisons have told stories, but not often, and then guardedly, for she is ruthless against those who are disloyal to her or threaten her security.''

"And Mrs. Carr?''

"Little can be said of her. She is conventional, an indulgent ruler of her husband, and enjoys being thought sweet and saintly. Yet she hungers for youth. It is my belief that she became a witch in middle age and therefore feels a deep frustration. I am uncertain of her deeper motivations. Curiously little of her mind shows above the surface.''

Norman nodded. Then he nerved himself. "What,'' he asked quickly, "do you know of the formulas for regaining a stolen soul?''

"Very little. I had a large number of such formulas jotted down in the notebook Mrs. Gunnison stole. I had the shadowy idea of working out a safeguard against some possible attack. But I do not remember them and I doubt if any of them would work. I have never tried them, and in my experience formulas never work at the first attempt. They must always be refined by trial and error.''

"But if it were possible to compare them, to find the master formula underlying them all, then—?''

"Perhaps.''

There was a knock. It was the porter come for the bags.

"Be in Hempnell in five minutes, sir. Shall I brush you in the corridor?''

Norman tipped him, but declined the service. He also told him they would carry their own bags. The porter smiled jerkily and backed out.

Norman crossed to the window. For a moment there was only the giddily-whirring gravel wall of a gully and dark trees flashing indistinctly above. But then the gravel wall gave way to a wide panorama, as the tracks swung around and down the hillside.

There was more woodland than field in the valley. The trees seemed to encroach on the town, dwarfing it. From this particular point it looked quite tiny. But the college buildings stood out with a cold distinctness. He fancied he could make out the window of his office.

Those cold gray towers and darker roofs were like an intrusion from some other, older world, and his heart began to pound, as if he had suddenly sighted the fortress of the enemy.

XVII

Suppressing the impulse to slink, Norman rounded the corner of Morton, squared his shoulders, and forced himself to look across the campus. The thing that hit him hardest was simply the air of normality. True, he had not consciously expected Hempnell to manifest any physical stench of evil, any outward sign of poisonous inward neurosis—or whatever it was he was battling. But this abnormal, story-book wholesomeness—the little swarms of students trooping back to the dormitories and over to the soda fountain at Student Union, the file of girls in white bound for a tennis lesson, the friendly familiar look of the wide walks—it struck at the very core of his mind, as if deliberately trying to convict him of insanity.

"Don't fool yourself," his thoughts told him. "Some of those laughing girls are already infected, with something. Their very respectable mammas have given them delicate hints about all sorts of unusual ways of Making Wishes Work. They already know that there's more to neurosis than the psychiatry books tell and that the economics texts don't even scratch the surface of the Magic of Money. And it certainly isn't chemistry formulas they're memorizing when that faraway look comes into their eyes as they sip their cokes or chatter about their boy friends."

He turned into Morton and quickly mounted the stairs.

His capacity for surprise was not yet exhausted, however, as he realized when he saw a group of students emerging from the classroom at the other end of the third-floor corridor. He glanced at his watch and realized that it was one of his own classes dispersing after having waited ten minutes—the usual tardy professor's grace—for him to appear. That was right, he reminded himself, he was Professor Saylor, a man with classes, committee meetings, and appointments. He slipped around the bend in the corridor before he was noticed.

After standing in front of the door for a few minutes, he entered his office. Nothing seemed to have been disturbed, but he was careful in his movements and on the alert for unfamiliar objects. He did not put his hand into any drawer without closely inspecting it first.

One letter in the little pile of accumulated mail was important. It was from Pollard's office, ominously requesting him to appear at a meeting of the trustees later that week. He smiled with grim satisfaction at this evidence that his career was still skidding downhill.

He methodically removed certain sections from his files, stuffed his briefcases full, and made a package of the remainder.

After a last glance around, during which he noted that the Estrey dragon had not been restored to whatever had been its original position on the roof, he started downstairs.

Outside he met Mrs. Gunnison.

He was acutely conscious of the way his arms were encumbered. For a moment he did not seem able to see the woman clearly.

"Lucky I found you," she began immediately. "Harold's been trying every which way to get in touch with you. Where have you been?"

Suddenly she registered on him as her old, blunt, sloppy self. With a sense of mingled frustration and relief, he realized that the warfare in which he was engaged was a strictly undercover affair, and that outwardly all relationships were the same as ever. He found himself explaining how Tansy and he, week-ending with friends out in the country, had gotten a touch of food poisoning, and how his message to Hempnell must have gone astray. This lie, planned some time ago, had the advantage of providing a reason for Tansy's appearance if anyone should see her, and it would enable him to plead a recurrence of the attacks as an excuse for neglecting his academic duties.

He did not expect Mrs. Gunnison to believe the lie, still he ought to be consistent.

She accepted the story without comment, offered her sympathies and went on to say, "But be sure and get in touch with Harold. I believe it has to do with that meeting of the trustees you've been asked to attend. You know, Harold thinks a great deal of you. Good-by."

He watched her puzzledly as she tramped off. Odd, but at the last moment he fancied he caught a note of genuine friendliness in her manner, as if for a moment something that was not Mrs. Gunnison had appealed to him out of her eyes.

But there was work to do. Off campus, he hurried down a side street to where his car was parked. With hardly a sidewise glance at the motionless figure in the front seat, he stepped in and drove to Sawtelle's.

The house was bigger than they needed, and the front lawn was very formal. But the grass was yellow in patches, and the soldierlike rows of flowers looked neglected.

"Wait here," he said. "Don't get out of the car under any circumstances."

To his surprise, Hervey met him at the door. There were circles under Hervey's always-worried eyes, and his fidgetiness was more than usually apparent.

"I'm so glad you've come," he said pulling Norman inside. "I don't know what I'm going to do with all these departmental responsibilities on my shoulders. Classes having to be dismissed. Stopgap instructors to be obtained. And the deadline on next year's catalogue tomorrow! Here, come into my study." And he pushed Norman through a huge living room, expensively but stiffly furnished, into a dingy, book-lined cubby-hole with one small window.

"I'm almost going out of my mind. I haven't dared stir out of the house since Evelyn was attacked Saturday night."

"What!"

"Haven't you heard?" He stopped and looked at Norman

in surprise. Even here he had been trying to pace up and down, although there was not room enough. "Why, it was in the papers. I wondered why you didn't come over or call up. I kept trying to get you at your home and the office, but no one could locate you. Evelyn's been in bed since Sunday, and she gets hysterical if I even speak of going out of the house. Just now she's asleep, thank heavens."

Hastily Norman related his trumped-up excuse. He wanted to get back to what had happened Saturday night. As he glibly mouthed his lie about food poisoning, his mind jumped to Bayport and the telephone call to Evelyn Sawtelle that had occurred late on that same Saturday night. Only then Evelyn had seemed to be attacking, not attacked. He had come here to confront her. But now—

"Just my luck!" Sawtelle exclaimed tragically when Norman had finished. "The whole department falling apart the very first week I'm in charge of it—not that it's your fault of course. And young Stackpole laid up with the 'flu.' "

"We'll manage," said Norman. "Sit down and tell me about Evelyn."

Unwillingly, Sawtelle cleared a space so he could perch on the cluttered desk. He groaned when his eyes chanced to light on papers presumably concerned with urgent business.

"It happened about four o'clock Sunday morning," he began, aimlessly fiddling with the papers. "I was awakened by a terrible scream. Evelyn's bed was empty. It was pitch dark out in the hall. But I could hear some sort of struggle going on downstairs. A bumping and threshing around—"

Suddenly he jerked up his head. "What was that? I thought I heard footsteps out in the front hall." Before Norman could say anything he went on. "Oh, it's just my nerves. They've been acting up ever since.

"Well, I picked up something—a vase—and went downstairs. About that time the sounds stopped. I switched on the lights and went through all the rooms. In the sewing room I found Evelyn stretched unconscious on the floor with some ghastly bruises beginning to show around her neck and mouth. Beside her lay the phone—we have it there because

Evelyn has so many occasions to use it. I nearly went frantic. I called a doctor and the police. When Evelyn regained consciousness, she was able to tell us about it, although she was terribly shaken up. It seems the phone had rung. She went downstairs in the dark without waking me. Just as she was picking up the phone, a man jumped out of the corner and attacked her. She fought him off—oh, it drives me mad to think of it!—but he overpowered her and choked her unconscious.''

In his excitement Sawtelle crumpled a paper he was holding, saw what he had done, and hastily smoothed it out.

"Thank heavens I came downstairs when I did! That must have been what frightened him off. The doctor found that, except for bruises, there weren't any other injuries. Even the doctor was shocked at those bruises, though. He said he had never seen any quite like them.

"The police think that after the man got in the house he called Central and asked them to ring this phone—pretending he thought the bell was out of order or something—in order to lure someone downstairs. They were puzzled as to how he got inside, though, for all the windows and doors were shut fast. Probably I forgot to lock the front door when we went to bed—one of my pieces of unforgivable carelessness!

"The police think he was a burglar or sex offender, but I believe he must have been a real madman besides. Because there was a silver plate on the floor, and two of our silver forks jammed together strangely, and other odds and ends. And he must have been playing the phonograph in the sewing room, because it was open and the turntable was going and on the floor was one of Evelyn's speech records, smashed to bits.''

Norman stared at his jittery departmental superior, but behind the stupidity of his gaze, his thoughts were working wildly. The first idea that stayed with him was that here was physical confirmation that he had heard a bull-roarer over the Bayport phone—what else could the smashed record mean?—and that Evelyn Sawtelle was going through the motions of practicing magic as much as Tansy ever had—else what was the significance of silver plate and forks and "other odds and ends"? Also, Evelyn, must have been expecting a call and been prepared for it, else why would she have had the things ready?

But then his thoughts scurried on to what Sawtelle had said about his wife's injuries—those bruises that sounded identical with the ones Tansy had inflicted on herself with, or somehow received from, a phone. The same bruises, the same possible instruments, suggested a shadow world in which black magic, thwarted, returned on its sender, or in which schemes to frighten by the pretense of black magic struck back at the guilty and psychotic mind of their originator.

"It's all my fault," Sawtelle was repeating mournfully, tugging at his necktie. Norman remembered that Sawtelle always assumed that he was guilty whenever anything hurt or merely upset Evelyn. "I should have awakened! I should have been the one to go down to the phone. When I think of that delicate creature feeling her way through the dark, and lurking just ahead of her that—Oh, and the department! I tell you I am going out of my mind. Poor Evelyn has been in such a pitifully frightened state ever since, you wouldn't believe it!" And he tugged at his necktie so strongly that it started to choke him and he had to undo it quickly.

"I tell you, I haven't slept a wink," he continued when he got his breath. "If Mrs. Gunnison hadn't been kind enough to spend a couple of hours with Evelyn yesterday morning, I don't know how I'd have managed. Even then she was too frightened to let me stir. . . . My God! . . . Evelyn!"

But Norman couldn't identify the agonized scream, and he seriously doubted whether Sawtelle could, except that it had come from the upper part of the house. Crying out, "I knew I heard footsteps! He's come back!" Sawtelle ran full tilt out of the study. Norman was just behind him, suddenly conscious of a very different fear. It was confirmed by a glance through the living-room window at his empty car.

He beat Sawtelle up the stairs and was the first to reach the bedroom door. He stopped. Sawtelle, almost gibbering with anxiety and guilt, ran into him.

It was not at all what Norman expected.

The pink silk coverlet clutched around her, Evelyn Sawtelle had retreated to the side of the bed nearest the wall. Her teeth were chattering, her face was a dirty white.

Beside the bed stood Tansy. For a moment Norman felt a great, sudden hope. Then he saw her eyes, and the hope shot away with sickening swiftness. She was not wearing the veil. In that heavy make-up with those rouged cheeks and thickly carmined lips, she looked like some indecently daubed statue, impossibly grotesque against a background of ridiculous pink silk hangings. But a hungry statue.

Sawtelle scrambled past him, shouting. "What's happened? What's happened?" He saw Tansy. "I didn't know you were here. When did you come in?" Then, "You frightened her!"

The statue spoke, and its quiet accents hushed him.

"Oh, no, I didn't frighten her. Did I, Evelyn?"

Evelyn Sawtelle was staring at Tansy in abject, wide-eyed terror, and her jaw was still working. But when she spoke, it was to say, "No, Tansy didn't . . . frighten me. We were talking together . . . and then . . . I . . . I thought I heard a noise."

"Just a noise, dear?" Sawtelle said.

"Yes . . . like footsteps . . . very quiet footsteps in the hall." She did not take her eyes off Tansy, who nodded once when she had finished.

Norman accompanied Sawtelle on a futile but highly melodramatic search of the top floor. When they came back, Evelyn was alone.

"Tansy's gone out to the car," she told Norman weakly. "I'm sure I just imagined those footsteps."

But her eyes were still full of fear when he left her and she seemed quite unaware of her husband, although he was fussing about straightening the coverlet and shaking out the pillows.

Tansy was sitting in the car, staring ahead. Norman could see the body was still dominated by its one emotion. He had to ask a question.

"She does not have my soul," was the answer. "I questioned her at length. As a final and certain test I embraced her. That was when she screamed. She is very much afraid of the dead."

"What did she tell you?"

"She said that someone came and took my soul from her. Someone who did not trust her very much. Someone who desired my soul, to keep as a hostage and for other reasons. Mrs. Gunnison."

The knuckles of Norman's hands were white on the steering wheel. He was thinking of that puzzling look of appeal that Mrs. Gunnison had given him.

XVIII

Professor Carr's office seemed an attempt to reduce the lusty material world to the virginal purity of geometry. The narrow walls displayed three framed prints of conic sections. Atop the bookcase filled with slim, gold-stamped mathematical books, were two models of complex curved surfaces executed in German silver and fine wire. The half-furled umbrella in the corner might have been another such model. And the surface of the small desk between Carr himself and Norman was bare except for five sheets of paper covered with symbols. Carr's thin, pale finger touched the top sheet.

"Yes," he said, "these are allowable questions in symbolic logic."

Norman had been pretty sure they were, but he was glad to hear a mathematician say so. The hurried reference he had made to *Principia Mathematica* had not altogether satisfied him.

"The capitals stand for classes of entities, the lower case letters for relationships," he said helpfully.

"Ah, yes." Carr tugged at the dark skin of his chin beneath the white Vandyke. "But what sort of entities and relationships are they?"

"You could perform operations on the equations, couldn't you, without knowing the reference of the individual symbols?" Norman countered.

"Most certainly. And the results of the operations would be valid whether the entities referred to were apples, battleships, poetic ideas, or signs of the zodiac. Always providing, of course, that the original references between entity and symbol had been made correctly."

"Then here's my problem," Norman went on hastily. "There are seventeen equations on that first sheet. As they stand, they seem to differ a great deal. Now I'm wondering if one simple, underlying equation doesn't appear in each of the seventeen, jumbled up with a lot of nonessential terms and procedures. Each of the other sheets presents a similar problem."

"Hm-m-m—" Professor Carr began to finger a pencil, and his eyes started to go back to the first sheet, but he checked the movement. "I must confess I'm rather curious about the entities referred to," he said, and added innocently, "I wasn't aware that there had been attempts to apply symbolic logic to sociology."

Norman was prepared for this. "I'll be frank with you, Linthicum," he said. "I have a pretty wild, off-trail theory, and I've promised myself I won't discuss it until I have a better idea of whether or not there's anything to it."

Carr's face broke into a reminiscent smile. "I think I understand your sentiments," he said. "I can still recall the disastrous consequences of my announcement that I had trisected the angle.

"Of course, I was only in seventh grade at the time," he added hastily.

"Though I did give my teacher a bad half-hour," he finished with a touch of pride.

When he next spoke, it was with a return to his mood of boyishly sly curiosity. "Nevertheless, I'm very much piqued by those symbols. As it stands they might refer to . . . hm-m-m . . . anything."

"I'm sorry," said Norman. "I know I'm asking a lot of you."

"Not at all. Not at all." Twiddling the pencil Carr glanced again at the sheet. Something caught his eye. "Hm-m-m . . . this is very interesting," he said. "I hadn't noticed this before." And his pencil began to fly about the sheet, deftly striking out terms, neatly inscribing new equations. The single vertical furrow between his gray eyebrows deepened. In a moment he was wholly absorbed.

With an unbreathed sigh of relief, Norman leaned back. He felt dog-tired, and his eyes hurt. Those five sheets represented twenty hours of uninterrupted work. Tuesday night, Wednesday morning, part of Wednesday afternoon. Even at that he couldn't have done it without Tansy to take notes from his dictation. He had come to trust absolutely her present mindless, machinelike accuracy.

Half hypnotized, he watched the agile old fingers half fill a fresh sheet of paper with derived equations. Their swift, orderly movements intensified the serene, monastic quiet of the small office.

What strangeness pressing on the heels of strangeness it was, Norman thought dreamily, not only to pretend to believe in black magic in order to overawe three superstitious, psychotic women who had a hold on his wife's mental life, but even to invoke the modern science of symbolic logic in the service of that pretended belief. Symbolic logic used to disentangle the contradictions and ambiguities of witchcraft formulas! What wouldn't old Carr say if he were really told "the entities referred to"!

And yet it had only been by invoking the superior prestige of higher mathematics that he had been able to convince Tansy that he could make strong enough magic to work against her enemies. And that was all in the best traditions of sorcery, when you came to think of it. Sorcerers always tried to incorporate the latest bits of information and wisdom into their systems, for prestige purposes. What was sorcery but a battle for prestige in the realms of mysticism, and what was a sorcerer but someone who had gotten an illegitimate mental jump on his fellows?

What a ludicrous picture it was, though (everything was beginning to seem hysterically laughable to his weary mind): a woman who half believed in witchcraft driven mad by three women who perhaps believed fully in witchcraft or perhaps not at all, their schemes opposed by a husband who believed not at all, but pretended to believe to the full—and was determined to act in every way in accord with that belief.

Or, he thought (his dreaminess verging toward slumber and the sweet mathematical simplicity of his surroundings wooing his mind toward visions of absolute space in which infinity was before his eyes), why not drop all these stuffy rationalizations and admit that Tansy had something called a soul and that it had been stolen by the thin witch Evelyn Sawtelle, and then stolen from her by the fat witch Hulda Gunnison, and that he was even now seeking the magic that would—

He jerked himself resolutely awake and back to the world of rationalizations again. Carr had shoved a paper toward him and had immediately started to work on another of the five sheets Norman had given him.

"You've already found the first underlying equations?" Norman asked incredulously.

Carr seemed annoyed at the interruption. "Surely. Of course." His pencil had already started to dart about again, when he stopped and looked at Norman oddly. "Yes," he said. "It's the last equation there, the short one. To tell the truth, I wasn't sure I'd find one when I started, but your entities and relationships seem to have some sense to them, whatever they are." And then he and his pencil were off again.

Norman shivered, staring at the brief ultimate equation, wondering what its meaning might be. He could not tell without referring to his code and he certainly didn't want to get that out here.

"Sorry to be making all this work for you," he said dully.

Carr spared him a glance. "Not at all, I enjoy it. I always did have a peculiar knack for these things."

The afternoon shadows deepened. Norman switched on the overhead light, and Carr thanked him with a quick preoccupied nod. The pencil flew. Three more sheets had been shoved across to Norman, and Carr was finishing the last one, when the door opened.

"Linthicum!" came the sweet voice, with hardly a trace of reproachfulness. "Whatever's keeping you? I've waited downstairs half an hour."

"I'm sorry, dear," said the old man, looking at his watch and his wife. "But I had become so absorbed—"

She saw Norman. "Oh, I didn't know you had a visitor. *Whatever* will Professor Saylor *think*! I'm afraid I've given him the impression that I tyrannize over you."

And she accompanied the words with such a quaint smile that Norman found himself echoing Carr's "Not at all."

"Professor Saylor looks *dead* tired," she said, peering at Norman anxiously. "I hope you haven't been wearing him out, Linthicum."

"Oh, no, my dear, I've been doing all the work," her husband told her.

She walked around the desk and looked over his shoulder. "What is it?" she asked, pleasantly.

"I don't know," he said. He straightened up and, winking at Norman, went on, "I believe that, behind these symbols, Professor Saylor is revolutionizing the science of sociology. But it's a great secret. And in any case I haven't the slightest idea of what the symbols refer to. I'm just being a sort of electronic brain."

With a polite, by-your-leave nod toward Norman, Mrs. Carr picked up one of the sheets and studied it through her thick glasses. But apparently at sight of the massed rows of symbols, she put it down.

"Mathematics is not my forte," she explained. "I was *such* a poor scholar."

"Nonsense, Flora," said Carr. "Whenever we go to the

market, you're much quicker at totaling the bill than I am. And I try to beat you, too.''

"But that's such a *little* thing," said Mrs. Carr delightedly.

"I'll only be a moment more," said her husband, returning to his calculations.

Mrs. Carr spoke across to Norman in a half-whisper. "Oh, Professor Saylor, would you be so kind as to convey a message to Tansy? I want to invite her for bridge tomorrow night—that's Thursday—with Hulda Gunnison and Evelyn Sawtelle. Linthicum has a *meeting*."

"I'll be glad to," said Norman quickly. "But I'm afraid she might not be up to it." And he explained about the food poisoning.

"How too, too *terrible*!" observed Mrs. Carr. "Couldn't I come over and help her?"

"Thank you," Norman lied, "but we have someone staying with her."

"How *wise*," said Mrs. Carr, and she looked at Norman intently, as if to spy out the source of that wisdom. Her steady gaze made him feel uncomfortable, it seemed at once so predatory and so naive. It somehow wouldn't have surprised him in one of his students, one of his girl students, but in this old woman—

Carr put down his pencil. "There," he said. "I'm done."

With further expression of thanks, Norman gathered up the sheets.

"Really no trouble at all," Carr assured him. "You gave me a very exciting afternoon. I must confess you've aroused my curiosity."

"Linthicum dotes on anything mathematical, especially when it's like a puzzle," Mrs. Carr told him. "Why, once," she continued, with a kind of roguish indulgence, "he made all sorts of tabulation on *horse races*."

"Er . . . yes . . . but only as a concrete example of the calculus of probabilities," Carr interposed quickly. But his smile was equally indulgent.

Her hand was on his shoulder, and he had reached up his

own to cover hers. Frail, yet somehow hearty, withered, yet somehow fresh, they seemed like the perfect aged couple.

"I promise you," Norman told him, "that if I revolutionize the science of sociology, you'll be the first to hear of it. Good evening." And he bowed out.

As soon as he could hurry home he got out the code. "W" was the identifying letter at the top of the first sheet. He thought he remembered what that meant, but he looked it up just to be sure.

"W—To conjure out the soul."

Yes, that was it. He turned to the supplementary sheet covered with Carr's calculations, and carefully decoded the final equation. "C—Notched strip of copper." He nodded. "T—Twirl sunwise." He frowned. He could have expected that to cancel out. Good thing he'd gotten a mathematician's help in simplifying the seventeen equations, each representing a different people's formula for conjuring out the soul— Arabian, Zulu, Polynesian, American Negro, American Indian, and so on; the most recent formulas available, and ones that had known actual use.

"A—Deadly amanita." Bother! He'd been certain that one would cancel out. It would be a bit of time and trouble getting a deathcup mushroom. Well, he could manage without that formula if he had to. He took up two other sheets: "V—To control the soul of another," "Z—To cause the dwellers in a house to sleep" and set to work on one of them. In a few minutes he had assured himself that the ingredients presented no special difficulties, save that Z required a Hand of Glory to be used as well as graveyard dirt to be thrown onto the roof of the house in which sleep was to be enforced. But he ought to have little difficulty in filching a suitable severed hand from the anatomy lab. And then if—

Conscious of a sudden weariness and of a revulsion from these formulas, which persisted in seeming more obscene than ridiculous, he pushed back his chair. For the first time since had had come into the house, he looked at the figure by the window. It sat in the rocking chair, face turned toward the drawn curtains. When it started rocking, he did not know.

But the muscles of its body automatically continued the rhythmical movement, once it had begun.

With the suddenness of a blow, longing for Tansy struck him. Her intonations, her gestures, her mannerisms, her funny fancies—all the little things that go to make a person real and human and loved—he wanted them all instantly; and the presence of this dead-alive imitation, this husk of Tansy, only made the longing less bearable. And what sort of a man was he, to be puttering around with occult formulas, while all the time—"There are things that can be done to a soul," she had said. "Servant girls of the Gunnisons have told stories—" He ought to go straight to the Gunnisons, confront Hulda, and force the issue!

With a quick effort he subdued his anger. Any such action on his part might ruin everything. How could you use open force against someone who held the mentality, the very consciousness, of your dearest possession as a hostage? No, he had been all over this before and his course was set. He might fight those women with their own weapons; these repugnant occult formulas were his best hope and he had gotten his usual punishment for making the mistake of looking at its face. Deliberately he moved to the other side of the table, so his back was toward the rocking chair.

But he was restless, his muscles itching with fatigue poisons, and for the moment he could not get back to work.

Suddenly he spoke. "Why do you suppose everything has become violent and deadly so abruptly?"

"The Balance was upset," was the answer. There was no interruption in the steady rocking.

"How was that?" He started to look over the back of his chair, but checked himself in time.

"It happened when I ceased to practice magic." The rocking was a grating monotony.

"But why should that lead to violence?"

"It upset the Balance."

"Yes, but how can that explain the abruptness of the shift from relatively trivial attacks to a deadly maliciousness?"

The rocking had stopped. There was no answer. But, as

he told himself, he knew the answer already that was shaping in that mindless mind behind him. This witches' warfare it believed in was very much like trench warfare or a battle between fortified lines—a state of siege. Just as reinforced concrete or armor plating nullified the shells, so counter-charms and protective procedures rendered relatively futile the most violent onslaughts. But once the armor and concrete were gone, and the witch who had foresworn witchcraft was out in a kind of no man's land—

Then, too, fear of the savage counterattacks that could be launched from such highly fortified positions, was a potent factor in discouraging direct assaults. The natural thing would be to sit pat, snipe away, and only attack if the enemy exposed himself recklessly. Besides, there were probably all sorts of unsuspected hostages and secret agreements, all putting a damper on violence.

This idea also seemed to explain why Tansy's apparently pacific action had upset the Balance. What would any country think, if in the midst of a war, its enemy scuttled all his battleships and dismantled all his aircraft, apparently laying himself wide open to attack? For the realistic mind, there could be only one likely answer. Namely, that the enemy had discovered a weapon far more potent than battleships or aircraft, and was planning to ask for a peace that would turn out to be a trap. The only thing would be to strike instantly and hard, before the secret weapon could be brought into play.

"I think—" he started to say.

Then something—perhaps a faint *whish* in the air or a slight creaking of the floor under the heavy carpet, or some less tangible sensation—caused him to glance around.

With a writhing jerk sideways, he managed—just managed—to get his head out of the path of that descending metal flail, which was all he saw at first. With a shocking *swish* it crashed downward against the heavy back of the chair and its force was broken. But his shoulder, which took only the broken blow, went numb.

Clawing at the table with his good hand, he threw himself forward against the table and whirled around.

He recoiled from the sight as from another blow, throwing back his good hand to save himself from overbalancing.

It was poised in the center of the room, having sprung back catlike after the first blow failed. Almost stiff-legged, but with the weight forward. In stocking feet—the slippers that might have made a noise were laid by the rocking chair. In its hand was the steel poker, stealthily lifted from the stand by the fireplace.

There was life in the face now. But it was life that champed the teeth and drooled, life that pinched and flared the nostrils with every breath, life that switched hair from the eyes with quick, angry flirts, life that glared redly and steadily.

With a low snarl it lifted the poker and struck, not at him, but at the chandelier overhead. Pitch darkness flooded the room he had curtained tightly against prying eyes.

There was a rush of soft footsteps. He ducked to one side. Nevertheless, the *swish* came perilously close. There was a sound as if it had dived or rolled across the table after he eluded the headlong rush—he could hear the slur of papers skidding and the faint crackle as some drifted to the floor. Then silence, except for the rapid *snuff-snuff* of animal breathing.

He crouched on the carpet, trying not to move a muscle, straining his ears to catch the direction of that breathing. Abominable, he thought, how inefficient the human auditory system is at localizing a sound. First the snuffing sound came from one direction, then another, although he could not hear the slightest rustle of intervening movement—until he began to lose his sense of direction in the room. He tried to remember his exact movements in springing away from the table. As he had hit the carpet, he had spun around. But how far? Was he facing toward or away from the wall? In his zeal to avoid the possibility of anyone spying on them, he had blacked out this room and the bedroom, and the blackout was effective. No discernible atom of light filtered through from the night outside. He was somewhere on what was beginning to seem an endless expanse of carpet, a low-ceilinged, wall-less infinity.

And somewhere else on that expanse, it was. Could it see and hear more than he? Could it discern form in retinal patterns that were only blackness to Tansy's soul? What was it waiting for? He strained his ears, but the rapid breathing was no longer audible.

This might be the darkness of some jungle floor, roofed by yards of matted creepers. Civilization is a thing of light. When light goes, civilization is snuffed out. Norman was rapidly being reduced to *its* level. Perhaps it had counted on that when it smashed the lights. This might be the inner chamber of some primeval cave, and he some cloudy-minded primitive huddled in abject terror of his mate, into whose beloved form a demon had been conjured up by the witch woman—the brawny, fat witch woman with the sullen lip and brutish eyes, and copper ornaments twisted in matted red hair. Should he grope for his ax and seek to smash the demon from the skull where it was hiding? Or should he seek out the witch woman and throttle her until she called off her demon? But how could he constrain his wife meanwhile? If the tribe found her, they would slay her instantly—it was the law. And even now the demon in her was seeking to slay him.

With thoughts almost as murky and confused as those of that ghostly primitive forerunner, Norman sought to grapple with the problem, until he suddenly realized what it was waiting for.

Already his muscles were aching. He was getting twinges of pain from his shoulder as the numbness went out of it. Soon he would make an involuntary movement. And in that instant it would be upon him.

Cautiously he stretched out his hand. Slowly—very slowly—he swung it around until it touched a small table and located a large book. Clamping thumb and finger around the book where it projected from the table edge, he lifted it and drew it to him. His muscles began to shake a little from the effort to maintain absolute quiet.

With a slow movement he launched the book toward the center of the room, so that it hit the carpet a few feet from him. The sound drew the instant response he had hoped for. Waiting a second he dove forward, seeking to pin it to the floor. But its cunning was greater than he had guessed. His arms closed on a heavy cushion that it had hurled toward the book, and only luck saved him as the poker thudded savagely against the carpet close by his head.

Clutching out blindly, his hands closed on the cold metal. There was a moment of straining as it sought to break his grip. Then he was sprawling backward, the poker in his hand, and the footsteps were retreating toward the rear of the house.

He followed it to the kitchen. A drawer, jerked out too far, fell to the floor, and he heard the chilling clatter and scrape of cutlery.

But there was enough light in the kitchen to show him its silhouette. He lunged at the upraised hand holding the long knife, caught the wrist. Then it threw itself against him, and they dropped to the floor.

He felt the warm body against his, murderously animated to the last limits of its strength. For a moment he felt the coldness of the flat of the knife against his cheek, then he had forced the weapon away. He doubled up his legs to protect himself from its knees. It surged convulsively down on him and he felt jaws clamp the arm with which he held away the knife. Teeth sawed sideways trying to penetrate the fabric of his coat. Cloth ripped as he sought with his free hand to drag the body away from him. Then he found the hair and forced back the head so the teeth lost their grip. It dropped the knife and clawed at his face. He seized the fingers seeking his eyes and nostrils; it snarled and spat at him. Steadily he forced the arms, twisting them behind it, and with a sudden effort got to his knees. Strangled sounds of fury came from its throat.

Only too keenly aware of how close his muscles were to the trembling weakness of exhaustion, he shifted his grip so that with one hand he held the straining wrists. With the other he groped sideways, jerked open the lower door of the cabinet, found a length of cord.

XIX

"It's pretty serious this time, Norm," said Harold Gunnison. "Fenner and Liddell want your scalp."

Norman drew his chair closer, as if the discussion were the real reason for his visit to Gunnison's office this morning.

Gunnison went on. "I think they're planning to rake up that Margaret Van Nice business and start yelping that where there's smoke there must be fire. And they may try to use Theodore Jennings against you, Claim that his 'nervous breakdown' was aggravated by unfairness and undue severity on your part, et cetera. Of course we have the strongest defense for you in both cases, still just talking about such matters is bound to have an unfavorable effect on the other trustees. And then this talk on sex you're going to give the Off-campus Mothers, and those theatrical friends of yours you've invited to the college. I have no personal objections, Norm, but you did pick a bad time."

Norman nodded, dutifully, Mrs. Gunnison ought to be here soon. The maid had told him over the phone that she had just left for her husband's office.

"Of course, such matters aren't enough in themselves." Gunnison looked unusually heavy-eyed and grave. "But as I say, they have a bad taste, and they can be used as an entering wedge. The real danger will come from a restrained but concerted attack on your conduct of classes, your public utterances, and perhaps even trivial details of your social life, followed by talk about the need for retrenchment where it is expeditious—you know what I mean." He paused. "What really bothers me is that Pollard's cooled toward you. I told him just what I thought of Sawtelle's appointment, but he said the trustees had overruled him. He's a good man, but he's a politician." And Gunnison shrugged, as if it were common knowledge that the distinction between politicians and professors went back to the Ice Age.

Norman roused himself. "I'm afraid I insulted him last week. We had a long talk and I blew up."

Gunnison shook his head. "That wouldn't explain it. He can absorb insults. If he sides against you, it will be because he feels it necessary or at least expeditious (I hate that word) on the grounds of public opinion. You know his way of running the college. Every couple of years he throws someone to the wolves."

Norman hardly heard him. He was thinking of Tansy's body as he had left it—the trussed-up limbs, the lolling jaw, the hoarse heavy breathing from the whiskey he had finally made it guzzle. He was taking a long chance, but he couldn't see any other way. At one time last night he had almost decided to call a doctor and perhaps have it placed in a sanitarium. But if he did that he might lose forever his chance to restore Tansy's rightful self. What psychiatrist would believe the morbid plot he knew existed against his wife's sanity? For similar reasons there was no friend he could call on for help. No, the only way was to strike swiftly at Mrs. Gunnison. But it was not pleasant to think of such headlines as: "PROFESSOR'S WIFE A TORTURE VICTIM, FOUND TRUSSED IN CLOSET BY MATE."

"It's really serious, Norm," Gunnison was repeating. "My wife thinks so, and she's smart about these things. She knows people."

His wife! Obediently, Norman nodded.

"Hard luck it had to come to a head now," Gunnison continued, "when you've been having more than your share of troubles with sickness and what-not." Norman could see that Gunnison was looking with a faint shade of inquisitiveness at the strip of surgical tape close to the corner of his left eye and the other one just below his nostrils. But he attempted no explanation. Gunnison shifted about and resettled himself in his chair. "Norm," he said, "I've got the feeling that something's gone wrong. Ordinarily I'd say you could weather this blow all right—you're one of our two-three best men—but I've got the feeling that something's gone wrong all the way down the line.''

The offer his words conveyed was obvious enough, and Norman knew it was made in good faith. But only for a moment did he consider telling Gunnison even a fraction of the truth. It would be like taking his troubles into the law courts, and he could imagine—with the sharp, almost hallucinatory vividness of extreme fatigue—what that would be like.

Imagine putting Tansy in the witness box even in her earlier non-violent condition. ''You say, Mrs. Saylor, that your soul was stolen from your body?'' ''Yes.'' ''You are conscious of the absence of your soul?'' ''No, I'm not conscious, of anything.'' ''Not conscious? You surely don't mean that you are unconscious?'' ''But I do. I can neither see nor hear.'' ''You mean that you can neither see nor hear me?'' ''That is correct.'' ''How then—'' Bang of the judge's gavel. ''If this tittering does not cease immediately, I will clear the court!'' Or Mrs. Gunnison called to the witness box and he himself bursting out with an impassioned plea to the jury. ''Gentlemen, look at her eyes! Watch them closely, I implore you. My wife's soul is there, if you would only see it!''

''What's the matter, Norm?'' he heard Gunnison ask. The genuine sympathy of the voice tugged at him confusedly. Groggy with sudden sleepiness he tried to rally himself to answer.

Mrs. Gunnison walked in.

''Hullo,'' she said. ''I'm glad you two finally got together.'' Almost patronizingly she looked Norman over. ''I don't think you've slept for the last two nights,'' she announced brusquely. ''And what's happened to your face? Did that cat of yours finally scratch it?''

Gunnison laughed, as he usually did, at his wife's frankness. ''What a woman. Loves dogs. Hates cats. But she's right about your needing sleep, Norm.''

The sight of her and the sound of her voice stung Norman into an icy wakefulness. She looked as if she had been sleeping ten hours a night for some time. An expensive green suit set off her red hair and gave her a kind of buxom beauty. Her slip showed and the coat was buttoned in a disorderly way, but now it conveyed to Norman the effect of the privileged carelessness of some all-powerful ruler who is above ordinary standards of neatness. For once she was not carrying the bulging purse. His heart leaped.

He did not trust himself to look into her eyes. He started to get up.

"Don't go yet, Norm," Gunnison told him. "There's a lot we should talk about."

"Yes, why don't you stay?" Mrs. Gunnison seconded.

"Sorry," said Norman. "I'll come around this afternoon if you can spare the time. Or tomorrow morning, at the latest."

"Be sure and do that," said Gunnison seriously. "The trustees are meeting tomorrow afternoon."

Mrs. Gunnison sat down in the chair he had vacated.

"My regards to Tansy," she said. "I'll be seeing her tonight at the Carrs'—that is, if she's recovered sufficiently." Norman nodded. Then he walked out rapidly and shut the door behind him.

While his hand was still on the knob, he saw Mrs. Gunnison's green purse lying on the table in the outer office. It was just this side of the display case of Prince Rupert drops and similar oddities. His heart jumped again.

There was one girl in the outer office—a student employee. He went to her desk.

"Miss Miller," he said, "would you be so kind as to get me the grade sheets of the following students?" And he rattled off half a dozen names.

"The sheets are in the Recorder's Office, Professor Saylor," she said, a little doubtfully.

"I know. But you tell them I sent you. Dr. Gunnison and I want to look them over."

Obediently she took down the names.

As the door closed behind her he pulled out the top drawer of her desk, where he knew the key for the display case would be.

A few minutes later Mrs. Gunnison came out.

"I thought I heard you go out," she exclaimed sharply. Then in her usual blunt manner, "Are you waiting for me to leave, so you can talk to Harold alone?"

He did not answer. He glanced at her nose.

She picked up her purse. "There's really no point in trying to make a secret of it," she said. "I know as much about your troubles here as he does—in fact, considerably more. And, to be honest, they're pretty bad." Her voice had begun to assume the arrogance of the victor. She smiled at him.

He continued to look at her nose.

"And you needn't pretend you're not worried," she went on, her voice reacting irritably to his silence. "Because I know you are. And tomorrow Pollard will ask for your resignation." Then, "What are you staring at?"

"Nothing," he answered, hastily, averting his glance.

With an incredulous sniff, she took out her mirror, glanced at it puzzledly for a moment, then held it up for a detailed inspection of her face.

To Norman the second hand of the wall clock seemed to stand still.

Very softly, but swiftly, and in a most casual voice, which did not even cause Mrs. Gunnison to look around he said, "I know you've stolen my wife's soul, Mrs. Gunnison, and I know how you've stolen it. I know a bit about stealing souls myself; for instance, if you're in a room with someone whose soul you want, and they happen to be looking into a mirror, and the mirror breaks while their reflection is still in it, then—"

With a swift, tinkling crack, not very loud, the mirror in Mrs. Gunnison's hand puffed into a little cloud of iridescent dust.

Instantly it seemed to Norman that a weight added itself to his mind, a tangible darkness pressed down upon his thoughts.

The gasp of astonishment or fear that issued from Mrs. Gunnison's lips was cut short. What seemed a loose, stupid look flowed slowly over her face, but it was only because the muscles of her face had quite relaxed.

Norman stepped up to Mrs. Gunnison and took her arm.

For a moment she stared at him, emptily, then her body lurched, she took a slow step, then another, as he said, "Come with me. It's your best chance."

He trembled, hardly able to credit his success, as she followed him into the hall. Near the stairs they met Miss Miller returning with a handful of large cards.

"I'm very sorry to have put you to the trouble," he told her. "But it turned out that we don't need them. You had better return them to the Recorder's Office."

The girl nodded with a polite but somewhat wry smile. "Professors!"

As Norman steered the uncharacteristically docile Mrs. Gunnison out of the Administration Building, the queer darkness still pressed upon his thoughts. It was like nothing he had ever before experienced.

Suddenly then the darkness parted, as storm clouds might part at sunset, letting through a narrow beam of crimson light. Only the storm clouds were inside his mind and the crimson light was impotent red rage and obscene anger. And yet it was not wholly unfamiliar.

From it, Norman's mind cringed. The campus ahead seemed to wobble and waver, tinged by a faint red glare.

He thought: "If there were such a thing as split personality, and if a crack appeared in the wall between those separate consciousnesses . . ."

But that was insanity.

Abruptly another memory buffeted him—words that had issued from Tansy's lips in the Pullman compartment: "The environment of the soul is the human brain."

Again: "If it is prevented from re-entering its own body, it is irresistibly drawn to another, whether or not that other body possesses a soul. And so the captive soul is usually imprisoned in the brain of its captor."

Just then, through the slit in the darkness, riding a wave in the pounding red anger that hurled it to the center of his mind, came an intelligible thought. The thought was simple, "Stupid man, how did you do it?" but it, like the red rage, was so utterly *like* Mrs. Gunnison that he accepted (whether or not it meant he was crazy, whether or not it meant witchcraft was true) that the mind of Mrs. Gunnison was inside his skull, talking with his mind.

For a moment he glanced at the slack-featured face of the hulking female body he was piloting across the campus.

For a moment he quailed at the idea of touching, with his mind, naked personality.

But only for a moment. Then (whether or not it meant he was crazy) his acceptance was complete. He walked across campus, talking inside his head with Mrs. Gunnison.

The questioning thought was repeated: "How did you do it?"

Before he realized it, his own thoughts had answered:

"It was the Prince Rupert mirror from the display case. The warmth of your fingers shattered it. I held it in the folds of my handkerchief while transferring it to your pocketbook. According to primitive belief, your reflection is your soul, or a vehicle for your soul. If a mirror breaks when your reflection is in it, your soul is trapped outside your body." All this, without the machinery of speech to delay it, flashed in an instant.

Instantly too, Mrs. Gunnison's next thought came through the slit in the darkness. "Where are you taking my body?"

"To our house."

"What do you want?"

"My wife's soul."

There was a long pause. The slit in the darkness closed, then opened again.

"You cannot take it. I hold it, as you hold my soul. But my soul hides it from you. And my soul holds it."

"I cannot take it. But I can hold your soul until you return my wife's soul to her body."

"What if I refuse?"

"Your husband is a realist. He will not believe what your body tells him. He will consult the best alienists. He will be very much grieved. But in the end he will commit your body to an asylum."

He could sense defeat and submission—and a kind of panic,

too—in the texture of the answering thought. But defeat and submission were not yet admitted directly.

"You will not be able to hold my soul. You hate it. It fills you with abhorrence. Your mind will not be able to endure it."

Then, in immediate substantiation of this statement, there came through the slit a nasty trickle growing swiftly to a spate. His chief detestations were quickly spied out and rasped upon. He began to hurry his steps, so that the mindless bulk beside him breathed hard.

"There was Ann," came Mrs. Gunnison's thoughts, not in words but in the complete fullness of memory. "Ann came to work for me eight years ago. A frail-looking little blonde, but able to get through a hard day's work for all that. She was very submissive, and a prey to fear. Do you know that it is possible to rule people through fear alone, without an atom of direct force? A sharp word, a stern look—it's the implications that do it, not what's said directly. Gradually I gathered about myself all the grim prestige that father, teacher, and preacher had had for Ann. I could make her cry by looking at her in a certain way. I could make her writhe with fright just by standing outside the door of her bedroom. I could make her hold hot dishes without a whimper while serving us at dinner, and make her wait while I talked to Harold. I've looked at her hands afterward."

Similarly he lived through the stories of Clara and Milly, Mary and Ermengarde. He could not shut his own mind from hers, nor could he close the slit, though it was within his power to widen it. Like some foul medusa, or some pulpy carnivorous plant, her soul unfolded and clung to his, until it seemed almost that his was the prisoner.

"And there was Trudie. Trudie worshipped me. She was a big girl, slow and a little stupid. She had come from a farm. She used to spend hours on my clothes. I encouraged her in various ways, until everything about me became sacred to Trudie. She lived for my little signs of favor. In the end she would do anything for me, which was very amusing, because she was very easily embarrassed and never lost her painfully acute sense of shame.''

But now he was at the door of his house, and the unclean trickle of thoughts ceased. The slit narrowed to the tiniest watchful crack.

He shepherded Mrs. Gunnison's body to the door of Tansy's dressing room. He pointed at the bound form huddled on the blanket he had thrown across the floor. It lay as he had left it, eyes closed, jaw lolling, breathing heavily. The sight seemed to add a second crushing pressure to his mind, pressing on it from below, through its eye-sockets.

''Take away what you have conjured into it,'' he heard himself command.

There was a pause. A black spider crawled off Tansy's skirt and scuttled across the blanket. Even as there came the thought, ''That is it,'' he lunged out and cracked it under his heel as it escaped onto the flooring. He was aware of a half-cloaked comment, ''Its soul sought the nearest body. Now faithful King will go on no more errands for me. No more will he animate human flesh or wood or stone. I will have to find another dog.''

''Return to it what you have taken,'' he commanded.

This time there was a longer pause. The slit closed entirely.

The bound figure stirred, as if seeking to roll over. The lips moved. The slack jaw tightened. Conscious only of the black weight against his mind, and of a sensory awareness so acute that he believed he could hear the very beating of the heart in Tansy's body, he stooped and cut the lashings, removed the carefully arranged paddings from wrists and ankles.

The head rolled restlessly from side to side. The lips seemed to be saying, ''Norman. . . . '' The eyelids fluttered and he felt a shiver go over the body. And then, in one sudden glorious flood, like some flower blooming miraculously in an instant, expression surged into the face, the limp hands caught at his shoulders, and from the wide-open eyes a lucid, sane, fearless human soul peered up at him.

An instant later the repellent darkness that had been pressing against his mind, lifted.

With one venomous, beaten glance, Mrs. Gunnison turned away. He could hear her footsteps trail off, the front door open. Then his arms were around Tansy, his mouth against hers.

XX

The front door closed. As if that were a signal, Tansy pushed him away while her lips were still returning his kiss.

"We daren't be happy, Norman," she said. "We daren't be happy for one single moment."

A disturbed and apprehensive look clouded the longing in her eyes, as if she were looking at a great wall that shut out the sunlight. When she answered his bewildered question, it was almost in a whisper, as if even to mention the name might be dangerous.

"Mrs. Carr—"

Her hands tightened on his arms as though to convey to him the immediacy of danger.

"Norman, I'm frightened. I'm *terribly* frightened. For both of us. My soul has learned so much. Things are different from what I thought. They're much worse. And Mrs. Carr—"

Norman's mind felt suddenly foggy and tired. It seemed to him almost unendurable that his feeling of relief should be broken. The desire to pretend at least for a while that things were rational and ordinary had become an almost overwhelming hunger. He stared at Tansy groggily, as if she were a figure in an opium dream.

"You're safe," he told her with a kind of harshness in his voice. "I've fought for you. I've got you back, and I'm going to hold you. They can never touch you again, not one of them."

"Oh, Norman," she began, dropping her eyes. "I know how brave and clever you've been. I know the risks you've run, the sacrifices you've made for me—wrenching your whole life away from rationality in the bare space of a week, enduring the beastliness of that woman's naked thoughts. And you have beaten Evelyn Sawtelle and Mrs. Gunnison *fairly* and at their own game. But Mrs. Carr—'' Her hands transmitted her trembling to him. ''Oh, Norman, she only *let* you beat them. She wanted to give them a fright, and she preferred to let you do it for her. But now she'll take a hand herself.''

''No, Tansy, no,'' he said with a dull insistence, but unable to summon up any argument to support his negative.

''You poor dear, you're tired,'' she said, becoming suddenly solicitous. ''I'll fetch you a drink.''

It seemed to him hat he did nothing but rub his eyes and blink them, and shake his head, until she came back with the bottle.

''I want to change,'' she said, looking down at her torn and creased dress. ''Then we must talk.''

He downed a stiff drink, poured himself another. But there was no stimulation. They didn't seem to be getting rid of his opium-dream mood, instead deepened it. After a while he got up and sluggishly made his way to the bedroom.

Tansy had put on a white wool dress, one which he had always liked very much, but which she had not worn for some time. He remembered she had told him that it had shrunk and become too small for her. But now he sensed that, in the joy of her return, she took a naive pride in her youthful body and wanted to show it to best advantage.

''It's like coming into a new house,'' she told him, with a quick little smile that momentarily cut across her apprehensive look. ''Or rather like coming home after you've been away for a long time. You're very happy, but everything is a little strange. It takes you a while to get used to it.''

Now that she mentioned it, he realized that there was a kind of uncertainty about her movements, gestures and expressions, like a person convalescent after a long sickness and just now able to get up and about.

She had combed out her hair so that it fell to her shoulders, and she was still in her bare feet, giving her a diminutive and girlish appearance that he found attractive even in his stupid-headed, nightmarish state of mind.

He had brought her a drink, but she merely sipped it and put it aside.

"No, Norman," she said, "we must talk. There is a great deal I have to tell you, and there may not be much time."

He looked around the bedroom. For a while his glance rested on the creamy door of Tansy's dressing-room. Then he nodded heavily and sat down on the bed. The opium-dream feeling was stronger than ever and Tansy's oddly brisk voice and brittle manner seemed part of it.

"Back of everything is Mrs. Carr," she began. "It was she who brought Mrs. Gunnison and Evelyn Sawtelle together, and that one act speaks volumes. Women are invariably secret about their magic. They work alone. A little knowledge is passed from the elder to the younger ones, especially from mother to daughter, but even that is done grudgingly and with suspicion. This is the only case Mrs. Gunnison knew of—I learned most of this from watching her soul—in which three women actually cooperated. It is an event of revolutionary importance, betokening heaven knows what for the future. Even now, I have only an inkling of Mrs. Carr's ambitions, but they involve vast augmentations of her present powers. For almost three quarters of a century she had been weaving her plans."

Norman torpidly absorbed these grotesque statements. He took a swallow of his second drink.

"She seems an innocent and rather foolish old lady, strait-laced yet ineffectual, girlish but prudish," she continued. Norman started for he fancied he caught in her voice a note of secret glee. It was so jarringly incongruous that he decided it must be his imagination. When she resumed, it was gone. "But that's only part of a disguise, along with her sweet voice and jolly manners. She's the cleverest actress imaginable. Underneath she's hard as nails—cold where Mrs. Gunnison would be hot, ascetic where Mrs. Gunnison would be a slave to appetites. But she has her own deeply hidden hungers, nevertheless. She is a great admirer of Puritan Massachusetts. Sometimes I have the queerest feeling that she is planning by some unimaginable means, to re-establish that witch-ridden, so-called theocratic community in this present day and age.

"She rules the other two by fear. In a way they are little more than her apprentices. You know something of Mrs. Gunnison, so you will understand what it means when I say that I have seen Mrs. Gunnison's thoughts go weak with terror because she was afraid that she had slightly offended Mrs. Carr."

Norman finished his drink. His mind was slipping away from this new menace, instead of grasping it firmly. He must whip himself awake, he told himself unwillingly. Tansy pushed her drink over toward him.

"And Mrs. Gunnison's fear is justified, for Mrs. Carr has powers so deadly that she has never had to use them except as a threat. Her eyes are the worst. Those thick glasses of hers—she possesses that most feared of supernatural weapons, against which half the protective charms in recorded magic are intended. That weapon whose name is so well known throughout the whole world that it has become the laughing-stock of skeptics. The evil eye. With it, she can blight and wither. With it, she can seize control of another's soul at a single glance.

"So far she has held back, because she wanted the other two punished for certain trifling disobediences, and put into a position where they would have to beg her help. But now she will act quickly. She recognizes in you and your work a danger to herself." Tansy's voice had become so breathlessly rapid that Norman realized she must be talking against time. "Besides that, she has another motive buried in the darkness of her mind. I hardly dare mention it, but sometimes I have caught her studying my every movement and expression with the strangest avidity—"

Suddenly she broke off and her face went white.

"I can feel her now. . . . I can feel her seeking me out. . . . She is breaking through—No!" Tansy screamed.

"No, you can't make me do it! . . . *I won't!* . . . *I won't!*"
Before he knew it, she was on her knees, clinging to him,
clutching at his hands. "Don't let her *touch* me, Norman,"
she was babbling like a terrified child. "Don't let her come
near me."

"I won't," he said sharply, suddenly stung awake.

"Oh . . . but you can't stop her. . . . She's coming *here*,
she says, in her own body, that's how much she's afraid of
you! She's going to take my soul away again. I can't tell you
what she wants. It's too repulsive."

He gripped her shoulders. "You must tell me," he said.
"What is it?"

Slowly she lifted up her white, frightened face, until her
eyes were looking into his. And she never once looked away
as she whispered. "You know how Mrs. Carr loves youth,
Norman. You know her ridiculous youthful manner. You
know how she always wants to have young people around
her, how she feeds on their feelings and innocence and en-
thusiasms. Norman, hunger for youth has been Mrs. Carr's
ruling passion for decades. She's fought off age and death for
a long time, longer than you think, she's nearer ninety than
seventy, but they're relentlessly closing in. It isn't so much
that she's afraid of death, but she'd do anything, anything,
Norman, to have a young body.

"Don't you see, Norman? The others wanted my soul, but
she wants my body. Haven't you ever noticed the way she
looks at you, Norman? She desires you, Norman, that foul
old woman desires you, and she wants to love you in my
body. She wants to possess my body and to leave my soul
trapped in that withered old walking-stick body of hers, leave
my soul to die in her *filthy* flesh. And she's coming here *now*
to do it, she's coming here *now*."

He stared in dull horror at her terrified, unwinking, almost
hypnotic eyes.

"You must *stop* her, Norman, you must stop her in the
only way she can be stopped." And without taking her eyes
off his, Tansy rose and backed out of the room.

And perhaps there was something truly hypnotic about her

eyes, some queer effect of her own terror, for it seemed to Norman that she had no sooner left the room than she was back at his side, pressing something very angular and cold into his hand.

"You must be very *quick*," she was saying. "If you hesitate for the tiniest *instant*, if you give her the slightest opportunity to fix you with her eyes, you'll be lost—and I'll be lost forever. You know the cobra that spits venom at its victim's eyes—it's like that. Get ready, Norman. She's very close."

There were hurried steps on the walk outside. He heard the front door open. Suddenly Tansy pushed her body against his so that he felt her breasts. Her moist lips felt for his own. Almost brutally he returned her kiss. She whispered into his lips, "Only be quick, darling." Then she slipped away.

There were steps in the hall. Norman lifted the gun. He realized that it was unnaturally dark in the bedroom—Tansy had pulled the shades. The bedroom door was pushed inward. A thin form in gray silk was silhouetted against the light from the hall. Beyond the sight of the gun he saw the faded face, the thick glasses. His finger tightened on the trigger.

The silver-haired head gave a little shake.

"Quick, Norman, *quick*!" The voice from behind him rose nervously.

The gray figure in the doorway did not move. The gun wavered, then swung suddenly around until it pointed at the figure beside him.

"Norman!"

XXI

Small restless breezes stirred the leaves of the oak standing like some burly guard beside the narrow house of the Carrs. Through the overlapping darkness gleamed the white of the walls—such a spotless, pristine white that neighbors laughingly vowed that the old lady herself came out after everyone had gone to sleep and washed them down with a long-handled mop. Everywhere was the impression of neatly tended, wholesome old age. It even had an odor—like some old chest in which a clipper captain had brought back elegant spices from his voyages in the China Trade.

The house faced the campus. The girls could see it, going to classes, and it called to their minds afternoons they had spent there, sitting in straight-backed chairs, all on their best behavior, while a wood fire burned merrily on the shining brass andirons in the white fireplace. Mrs. Carr was such a strait-laced innocent old dear! But her innocence was all to the good—it was no trouble at all to pull the wool over her eyes. And she did tell the quaintest stories with the most screamingly funny, completely unconscious points. And she did serve the nicest gingerbread with her cinnamon tea.

A light came on in the hall, casting a barred pattern through the fanlight onto the old wooden scrollwork of the porch. The six-paneled white door below the fanlight opened.

"I'm going, Flora," Professor Carr called. "Your bridge partners are a bit tardy, aren't they?"

"They'll be here soon." The silvery voice floated down the hall. "Good-by, Linthicum."

Professor Carr closed the door. Too bad he had to miss the bridge. But the paper young Rayford was going to read on the Theory of Primes would undoubtedly be interesting, and one couldn't have everything. His footsteps sounded on the pebbly walk with its edging of tiny white flowers, like old lace. Then they reached the concrete and slowly died away.

Somewhere at the rear of the house a car drew up. There was the sound of something being lifted; then heavy, plodding footsteps. A door at the back of the house opened, and for a moment against the oblong of light a man could be seen carrying slung over his shoulder a limp and bulky bundle that might have been a muffled-up woman, except that such mysterious and suspicious goings-on were unthinkable at the Carrs', as any neighbor would have assured you. Then that door closed, too, and for a while longer there was silence, while the breezes played with the oak leaves.

With thriftless waste of rubber a black Studebaker jerked to a stop in front. Mrs. Gunnison stepped out.

"Hurry up, Evelyn," she said. "You've made us late again. You know she hates that."

"I'm coming as fast as I can," replied her companion plaintively.

As soon as the six-paneled door swung open, the faded spicy odor became more apparent.

"You're late, dears," came the silvery, laughing voice. "But I'll forgive you this once, because I've a surprise for you. Come with me."

They followed the frail figure in faintly hissing silk into the living room. Just beyond the bridge table, with its embroidered cover and two cut-glass dishes of sweets, stood Norman Saylor. In the mingled lamplight and firelight, his face was expressionless.

"Since Tansy is unable to come," said Mrs. Carr, "he's agreed to make a fourth. Isn't that a nice surprise? And isn't it very nice of Professor Saylor?"

Mrs. Gunnison seemed to be gathering her courage. "I'm not altogether sure that I like the arrangement," she said finally.

"Since when did it matter whether you liked something or not?" came the sharp answer. Mrs. Carr was standing very straight. "Sit down, all of you!"

When they had taken their places around the bridge table, Mrs. Carr ran through a deck, flipping out certain cards. When she spoke, her voice was as sweet and silvery as ever.

"Here are you two, my dear," she said placing the queens of diamonds and clubs side by side. "And here is Professor Saylor." She added the king of hearts to the group. "And here am I." She placed the queen of spades so that it overlapped all three. "Off here to the side is the queen of hearts—Tansy Saylor. Now what I intend to do is this." She moved the queen of hearts so that it covered the queen of spades. "You don't understand? Well, it isn't what it looks like and neither of you is especially bright. You'll understand in a moment. Professor Saylor and I have just had ever so interesting a talk," she went on. "All about his work. Haven't we, Professor Saylor?" He nodded. "He's made some of the most fascinating discoveries. It seems there are laws governing the things that we women have been puttering with. Men are so clever in some ways, don't you think?

"He's been good enough to tell all those laws to me. You'd never dream how much easier and safer it makes everything—and more efficient. Efficiency is so very important these days. Why, already Professor Saylor has made something for me—I won't tell you what it is, but there's one for each of you and one for someone else. They aren't presents, because I'll keep them all. And if one of you should do something naughty, they'll make it ever so easy for me to whisk part of you away—you know what part.

"And now something is going to happen that will enable Professor Saylor and me to work together closely in the future—how closely you could never imagine. You're to help. That's why you're here. Open the dining-room door, Norman."

It was an old-fashioned sliding door, gleaming white. Slowly he pushed it aside.

"There," said Mrs. Carr. "I'm full of surprises tonight."

The body was lashed to the chair. From over the gag, the eyes of Tansy Saylor glared at them with impotent hate.

Evelyn Sawtelle half rose, stifling a scream.

"You needn't get hysterics, Evelyn," said Mrs. Carr sharply. "It's got a soul in it now."

Evelyn Sawtelle sank back, lips trembling.

Mrs. Gunnison's face had grown pale, but she set her jaw firmly and put her elbows on the table. "I don't like it," she said. "It's too risky."

"I am able to take chances I wouldn't have taken a week ago, dear," Mrs. Carr said sweetly. "In this matter your aid and Evelyn's is essential to me. Of course, you're perfectly welcome not to help if you don't want to. Only I do hope you understand the consequences."

Mrs. Gunnison dropped her eyes. "All right," she said. "But let's be quick about it."

"I am a very old woman," began Mrs. Carr with tantalizing slowness, "and I am very fond of life. It has been a little dispiriting for me to think that mine is drawing to a close. And, for reasons I think you understand, I have something more to fear in death than most persons.

"But now it seems that I am once more going to experience all those things that an old woman looks upon as forever lost. The unusual circumstances of the last two weeks have helped a great deal in preparing the ground. Professor Saylor has helped too. And you, my dears, are going to help. You see, it's necessary to build a certain kind of tension, and only people with the right background can do that, and it takes at least four of them. Professor Saylor—he has such a brilliant mind!—tells me that it's very much like building up electrical tension, so that a spark will be able to jump a gap. Only in this case the gap will be from where I am sitting to there"— and she pointed at the bound figure. "And there will be two sparks. And then, when it's over, the queen of hearts will exactly cover the queen of spades. Also, the queen of spades will exactly cover the queen of hearts. You see, tonight, dears, we're positively fourth-dimensional. But it's the things you can't see that are always the most important, don't you think?"

"You can't do it!" said Mrs. Gunnison. "You won't be able to keep the truth hidden!"

"You think not? On the contrary, I won't have to make an effort. Let me ask you what would happen if old Mrs. Carr claimed that she were young Tansy Saylor. I think you know very well what would happen to that dear, sweet, innocent old lady. There are times when the laws and beliefs of a skeptical society can be so very convenient.

"You can begin with the fire, Norman. I'll tell the others exactly what they are to do."

He tossed a handful of powder on the fire. It flared up greenly, and a pungent, cloying aroma filled the room.

And then—who knows?—there may have been a stirring at

the heart of the world and movement of soundless currents in the black void. Upon the dark side of the planet, a million women moved restlessly in their sleep, and a few woke trembling with unnamed fears. Upon the light side, a million more grew nervous, and unaccustomed daydreams chased unpleasantly through their minds; some made mistakes at their work and had to add again a column of figures, or attach a different wire to a different tube, or send a misdrilled piece of metal to salvage, or re-mix the baby's formula; a few found strange suspicion growing mushroomlike among their thoughts. And perhaps a certain ponderous point began to work closer and closer to the end of the massive surface supporting it, not unlike a top slowly wobbling toward the edge of a table, and certain creatures who were nearby saw what was happening and skittered away terrified through the darkness. Then, at the very edge, the weird top paused. The irregularity went out of its movement, and it rode steady and true once more. And perhaps one might say that the currents ceased to trouble the void, and that the Balance had been restored. . . .

Norman Saylor opened the windows at top and bottom so the breeze might fan out the remnants of pungent vapor. Then he cut the lashings of the bound figure and loosened the gag from its mouth. In a little while she rose, and without a word they started from the room.

All this while, none of the others had spoken. The figure in the gray silk dress sat with head bowed, shoulders hunched, frail hands dropped limply at her side.

In the doorway the woman whom Norman Saylor had loosed turned back.

"I have only one more thing to say to you. All that I told you earlier this evening was completely true, with one exception—"

Mrs. Gunnison looked up. Evelyn Sawtelle half turned in her chair. The third did not move.

"The soul of Mrs. Carr was not transferred to the body of Tansy Saylor this evening. That happened much earlier—when Mrs. Carr stole Tansy Saylor's soul from Mrs. Gunnison and then occupied Tansy Saylor's bound and empty-brained body, leaving the captive soul of Tansy Saylor trapped in her own aged body—and doomed to be murdered by her own husband in accord with Mrs. Carr's plan. For Mrs. Carr knew that Tansy Saylor would have only one panic-stricken thought—to run home to her husband. And Mrs. Carr was very sure that she could persuade Norman Saylor to kill the body housing the soul of his wife, under the impression that he was killing Mrs. Carr. And that would have been the end of Tansy Saylor's soul.

"You knew, Mrs. Gunnison, that Mrs. Carr had taken Tansy Saylor's soul from you, just as you had taken it from Evelyn Sawtelle, and for similar reasons. But you dared not reveal that fact to Norman Saylor because you would have lost your one bargaining point. This evening you half suspected that something was different from what it seemed, but you did not dare make a stand.

"And now as a result of what we have done this evening with your help, the soul of Mrs. Carr is once more in the body of Mrs. Carr, and the soul of Tansy Saylor is in the body of Tansy Saylor. My body. Good night, Evelyn. Good night, Hulda. Good night, Flora, dear."

The six-paneled door closed behind them. The pebbly path crunched under their feet.

"How did you know?" was Tansy's first question. "When I stood there in the doorway, blinking through those awful spectacles, gasping after the way I'd hurried with only the blind thought of finding you—how did you know?"

"Partly," he said reflectively, "because she gave herself away toward the end. She began to emphasize words in that exaggerated way of hers. But that wouldn't have been enough in itself. She was too good an actress. And after seeing how well you played her part tonight, with hardly any preparation, I wonder I ever did see through her."

"Then how did you?"

"It was partly the way you hurried up the walk—it didn't sound like Mrs. Carr. And partly something about the way you held yourself. But mainly it was that headshake you gave—that quick, triple headshake. I couldn't fail to recognize it. After that, I realized all the other things."

"Do you think," said Tansy softly, "that after this you'll every begin to wonder if I am really I?"

"I suppose I will," he said seriously. "But I'll always be able to conquer my doubts."

There were footsteps, then a friendly greeting from the shadows ahead.

"Hello, you two," called Mr. Gunnison. "Bridge game over? I thought I'd walk back with Linthicum and then drive home with Hulda. Say, Norman, Pollard dropped in to speak to me after the paper had been read. He's had a sudden change of heart on that matter we were talking about. On his advice the trustees have cancelled their meeting."

"It was a very interesting paper," Mr. Carr informed them, "and I had the satisfaction of asking the speaker a very tricky question. Which I am happy to say he answered excellently, after I'd cleared up a couple of minor points. But I'm sorry I missed the bridge. Oh, well, I don't suppose I'll ever notice any difference."

"And the funny thing," Tansy told Norman after they had walked on, "is that he really *won't*." And she laughed, the intoxicating, mischievous laugh of utter relief.

"Oh, my darling," she said, "do you honestly believe all this, or are you once more just pretending to believe for my sake? Do you believe that tonight you rescued your wife's soul from another woman's body? Or has your scientific mind already explained to you that you've been spending the last week pretending to believe in witchcraft to cure your wife and three other psychotic old ladies of the delusion of being each other and heaven knows what else?"

"I don't know," said Norman softly and as seriously as before. "I don't really know."

OUR LADY OF DARKNESS

But the third Sister, who is also the youngest—! Hush! whisper whilst we talk of *her*! Her kingdom is not large, or else no flesh should live; but within that kingdom all power is hers. Her head, turreted like that of Cybele, rises almost beyond the reach of sight. She droops not; and her eyes, rising so high, *might* be hidden by distance. But, being what they are, they cannot be hidden; through the treble veil of crape which she wears the fierce light of a blazing misery, that rests not for matins or for vespers, for noon of day or noon of night, for ebbing or for flowing tide, may be read from the very ground. She is the defier of God. She also is the mother of lunacies, and the suggestress of suicides. Deep lie the roots of her power; but narrow is the nation that she rules. For she can approach only those in whom a profound nature has been upheaved by central convulsions; in whom the heart trembles and the brain rocks under conspiracies of tempest from without and tempest from within. Madonna moves with uncertain steps, fast or slow, but still with tragic grace. Our Lady of Sighs creeps timidly and stealthily. But this youngest Sister moves with incalculable motions, bounding, and with tiger's leaps. She carries no key; for, though coming rarely amongst men, she storms all doors at which she is permitted to enter at all. And *her* name is *Mater Tenebrarum*—our Lady of Darkness.

—Thomas De Quincey
"Levana and Our Three Ladies of Sorrow"
Suspiria de Profundis

I

The solitary, steep hill called Corona Heights was black as pitch and very silent, like the heart of the unknown. It looked steadily downward and northeast away at the nervous, bright lights of downtown San Francisco as if it were a great predatory beast of night surveying its territory in patient search of prey.

The waxing gibbous moon had set, and the stars at the top of the black heavens were still diamond sharp. To the west lay a low bank of fog. But to the east, beyond the city's business center and the fog-surfaced Bay, the narrow ghostly ribbon of the dawn's earliest light lay along the tops of the low hills behind Berkeley, Oakland, and Alameda, and still more distant Devil's Mountain—Mount Diablo.

On every side of Corona Heights the street and house lights of San Francisco, weakest at end of night, hemmed it in apprehensively, as if it were indeed a dangerous animal. But on the hill itself there was not a single light. An observer below would have found it almost impossible to make out its jagged spine and the weird crags crowning its top (which even the gulls avoided); and breaking out here and there from its raw, barren sides, which although sometimes touched by fog, had not known the pelting of rain for months.

Someday the hill might be bulldozed down, when greed had grown even greater than it is today and awe of primeval nature even less, but now it could still awaken panic terror.

Too savage and cantankerous for a park, it was inadequately designated as a playground. True, there were some tennis courts and limited fields of grass and low buildings and little stands of thick pine around its base; but above those it rose rough, naked, and contemptuously aloof.

And now something seemed to stir in the massed darkness there. (Hard to tell what.) Perhaps one or more of the city's wild dogs, homeless for generations, yet able to pass as tame. (In a big city, if you see a dog going about his business, menacing no one, fawning on no one, fussing at no one—in fact, behaving like a good citizen with work to do and no time for nonsense—and if that dog lacks tag or collar, then you may be sure he hasn't a neglectful owner, but is wild—and well adjusted.) Perhaps some wilder and more secret animal that had never submitted to man's rule, yet lived almost unglimpsed amongst him. Perhaps, conceivably, a man (or woman) so sunk in savagery or psychosis that he (or she) didn't need light. Or perhaps only the wind.

And now the eastern ribbon grew dark red, the whole sky lightened from the east toward the west, the stars were fading, and Corona Heights began to show its raw, dry, pale brown surface.

Yet the impression lingered that the hill had grown restless, having at last decided on its victim.

II

Two hours later, Franz Westen looked out of his open casement window at the 1,000-foot TV tower rising bright red and white in the morning sunlight out of the snowy fog that still masked Sutro Crest and Twin Peaks three miles away and against which Corona Heights stood out, humped and pale brown. The TV tower—San Francisco's Eiffel, you could call it—was broad-shouldered, slender-waisted, and long-legged like a beautiful and stylish woman—or demigoddess. It mediated between Franz and the universe these days, just as man is supposed to mediate between the atoms and the stars. Looking at it, admiring, almost reverencing it, was his regular morning greeting to the universe, his affirmation that they were in touch, before making coffee and settling back into bed with clipboard and pad for the day's work of writing supernatural horror stories and especially (his bread and butter) novelizing the TV program "Weird Underground," so that the mob of viewers could also read, if they wanted to, something like the mélange of witchcraft, Watergate, and puppy love they watched on the tube. A year or so ago he would have been focusing inward on his miseries at this hour and worrying about the day's first drink—whether he still had it or had drunk up everything last night—but that was in the past, another matter.

Faint, dismal foghorns cautioned each other in the distance. Franz's mind darted briefly two miles behind him to where more fog would be blanketing San Francisco Bay except for the four tops thrusting from it of the first span of the bridge to Oakland. Under that frosty-looking surface there would be the ribbons of impatient, fuming cars, the talking ships, and coming from far below the water and the mucky bottom, but heard by fishermen in little boats, the eerie roar of the BART (Bay Area Rapid Transit) trains rocketing through the tube as they carried the main body of commuters to their jobs.

Dancing up the sea air into his room there came the gay, sweet notes of a Telemann minuet blown by Cal from her recorder two floors below. She meant them for him, he told himself, even though he was twenty years older. He looked at the oil portrait of his dead wife Daisy over the studio bed, beside a drawing of the TV tower in spidery black lines on the large oblong of fluorescent red cardboard, and felt no guilt. Three years of drunken grief—a record wake!—had worked that all away, ending almost exactly a year ago.

His gaze dropped to the studio bed; still half-unmade. On the undisturbed half, nearest the wall, there stretched out a long, colorful scatter of magazines, science-fiction paperbacks, a few hardcover detective novels still in their wrappers, a few bright napkins taken home from restaurants, and a half-dozen of those shiny little *Golden Guides* and *Knowledge Through Color* books—his recreational reading as opposed to his working materials and references arranged on the coffee table beside the bed. They'd been his chief—almost his sole—companions during the three years he'd laid sodden there stupidly goggling at the TV across the room; but always fingering them and stupefiedly studying their bright, easy pages from time to time. Only a month ago it had suddenly occurred to him that their gay casual scatter added up to a slender, carefree woman lying beside him on top of the covers—that was why he never put them on the floor; why he contented himself with half the bed; why he unconsciously arranged them in a female form with long, long legs. They were a "scholar's mistress," he decided, on the analogy of "Dutch wife," that long, slender bolster sleepers clutch to soak up sweat in tropical countries—a very secret playmate, a dashing but studious call girl, a slim, incestuous sister, eternal comrade of his writing work.

With an affectionate glance toward his oil-painted dead wife and a keen, warm thought toward Cal still sending up pirouetting notes on the air, he said softly with a conspiratorial smile to the slender cubist form occupying all the inside of the bed, "Don't worry, dear, you'll always be my best girl, though we'll have to keep it a deep secret from the others," and turned back to the window.

It was the TV tower standing way out there so modern-tall on Sutro Crest, its three long legs still deep in fog, that had first gotten him hooked on reality again after his long escape in drunken dream. At the beginning the tower had seemed unbelievably cheap and garish to him, an intrusion worse than the high rises in what had been the most romantic of cities, an obscene embodiment of the blatant world of sales and advertising—even, with its great red and white limbs against blue sky (as now, above the fog), an emblazonment of the American flag in its worst aspects: barberpole stripes; fat, flashy, regimented stars. But then it had begun to impress him against his will with its winking red lights at night—so many of them! he had counted nineteen: thirteen steadies and six winkers—and then it had subtly led his interest to the other distances in the cityscape and also in the real stars so far beyond, and on lucky nights the moon, until he had got passionately interested in all real things again, no matter what. And the process had never stopped; it still kept on. Until Saul had said to him, only the other day, "I don't know about welcoming in every new reality. You could run into a bad customer."

"That's fine talk, coming from a nurse in a psychiatric ward," Gunnar had said, while Franz had responded instantly, "Taken for granted. Concentration camps. Germs of plague."

"I don't mean things like those exactly," Saul had said. "I guess I mean the sort of things some of my guys run into at the hospital."

"But those would be hallucinations, projections, archetypes, and so on, wouldn't they?" Franz had observed, a little wonderingly. "Parts of *inner* reality, of course."

"Sometimes I'm not so sure," Saul had said slowly. "Who's going to know what's what if a crazy says he's just seen a ghost? Inner or outer reality? Who's to tell then? What do you say, Gunnar, when one of your computers starts giving readouts it shouldn't?"

"That it's got overheated," Gun had answered with conviction. "Remember, my computers are normal people to start out with, not weirdos and psychotics like your guys."

"Normal—what's that?" Saul had countered.

Franz had smiled at his two friends who occupied two apartments on the floor between his and Cal's. Cal had smiled, too, though not so much.

Now he looked out the window again. Just outside it, the

six-story drop went down past Cal's window—a narrow shaft between this building and the next, the flat roof of which was about level with his floor. Just beyond that, framing his view to either side, were the bone-white, rain-stained back walls— mostly windowless—of two high rises that went up and up.

It was a rather narrow slot between them, but through it he could see all of reality he needed to keep in touch. And if he wanted more he could always go up two stories to the roof, which he often did these days and nights.

From this building low on Nob Hill the sea of roofs went down and down, then up and up again, tinying with distance, to the bank of fog now masking the dark green slope of Sutro Crest and the bottom of the tripod TV tower. But in the middle distance a shape like a crouching beast, pale brown in the morning sunlight, rose from the sea of roofs. The map called it just Corona Heights. It had been teasing Franz's curiosity for several weeks. Now he focused his small seven-power Nikon binoculars on its bare earth slopes and humped spine, which stood out sharply against the white fog. He wondered why it hadn't been built up. Big cities certainly had some strange intrusions in them. This one was like a raw remnant of upthrust from the earthquake of 1906, he told himself, smiling at the unscientific fancy. Could it be called Corona Heights from the crown of irregularly clumped big rocks on its top, he asked himself, as he rotated the knurled knob a little more, and they came out momentarily sharp and clear against the fog.

A rather thin, pale brown rock detached itself from the others and waved at him. Damn the way these glasses jiggled with his heartbeat! A person who expected to see neat, steady pictures through them just hadn't used binoculars. Or could it be a floater in his vision, a microscopic speck in the eye's fluid? No, there he had it again! Just as he'd thought, it was some tall person in a long raincoat or drab robe moving about almost as if dancing. You couldn't see human figures in any detail at two miles even with sevenfold magnification; you just got a general impression of movements and attitude. They were simplified. This skinny figure on Corona Heights was moving around rather rapidly, all right, maybe dancing with arms waving high, but that was the most you could tell.

As he lowered the binoculars he smiled broadly at the thought of some hippie type greeting the morning sun with ritual prancings on a mid-city hilltop newly emerged from fog. And with chantings too, no doubt, if one could hear—unpleasant wailing ululations like the yelping siren he heard now in the distance, the sort that was frantic-making when heard too close. Someone from the Haight-Ashbury, likely, it was out that way. A stoned priest of a modern sun god dancing around an accidental high-set Stonehenge. The thing had given him a start, at first, but now he found it very amusing.

A sudden wind blew in. Should he shut the window? No, for now the air was quiet again. It had just been a freakish gust.

He set down the binoculars on his desk beside two thin old books. The topmost, bound in dirty gray, was open at its title page, which read in a utilitarian typeface and layout marking it as last century's—a grimy job by a grimy printer with no thought of artistry: *Megapolisomancy: A New Science of Cities*, by Thibaut de Castries. Now that was a funny coincidence! He wondered if a drug-crazed priest in earthen robes—or a dancing rock, for that matter!—would have been recognized by that strange old crackpot Thibaut as one of the "secret occurrences" he had predicted for big cities in the solemnly straight-faced book he'd written back in the 1890s. Franz told himself that he must read some more in it, and in the other book, too.

But not right now, he told himself suddenly, looking back at the coffee table where there reposed, on top of a large and heavy manila envelope already stamped and addressed to his New York agent, the typed manuscript of his newest novelization—*Weird Underground #7: Towers of Treason*—all ready to go except for one final descriptive touch he'd hankered to check on and put in; he liked to give his readers their money's worth, even though this series was the flimsiest of escape reading, secondary creativity on his part at best.

But this time, he told himself, he'd send the novelization off without the final touch and declare today a holiday—he was beginning to get an idea of what he wanted to do with it. With only a flicker of guilt at the thought of cheating his readers of a trifle, he got dressed and made himself a cup of coffee to carry down to Cal's, and as afterthoughts the two thin old books under his arm (he wanted to show them to Cal) and the binoculars in his jacket pocket—just in case he was tempted to check up again on Corona Heights and its freaky rock god.

III

In the hall, Franz passed the black knobless door of the disused broom closet and the smaller padlocked one of an old laundry chute or dumbwaiter (no one remembered which) and the big gilded one of the elevator with the strange black window beside it, and he descended the red-carpeted stairs, which between each floor went in right-angling flights of six and three and six steps around the oblong stair well beneath the dingy skylight two stories up from his floor. He didn't stop at Gun's and Saul's floor—the next, the fifth—though he glanced at both their doors, which were diagonally opposite each other near the stairs, but kept on to the fourth.

At each landing he glimpsed more of the strange black windows that couldn't be opened and a few more black doors without knobs in the empty red-carpeted halls. It was odd how old buildings had secret spaces in them that weren't really hidden but were never noticed; like this one's five airshafts, the windows to which had been painted black at some time to hide their dinginess, and the disused broom closets, which had lost their function with the passing of cheap maid service, and in the baseboard the tightly snap-capped round openings of a vacuum system which surely hadn't been used for decades. He doubted anyone in the building ever consciously saw them, except himself, newly aroused to reality by the tower and all. Today they made him think for a moment of the old times when this building had probably been a small hotel with monkey-faced bellboys and maids whom his fancy pictured as French with short skirts and naughty low laughs (dour slatterns more likely, reason commented). He knocked at 407.

It was one of those times when Cal looked like a serious schoolgirl of seventeen, lightly wrapped in dreams, and not ten years older, her actual age. Long, dark hair, blue eyes, a quiet smile. They'd been to bed together twice, but didn't kiss now—it might have seemed presumptuous on his part, she didn't quite offer to, and in any case he wasn't sure how far he wanted to commit himself. She invited him in to the breakfast she was making. Though a duplicate of his, her room looked much nicer—too good for the building—she had redecorated it completely with help from Gunnar and Saul. Only it didn't have a view. There was a music stand by the window and an electronic piano that was mostly keyboard and black box and that had earphones for silent practicing, as well as speaker.

"I came down because I heard you blowing the Telemann," Franz said.

"Perhaps I did it to summon you," Cal replied offhandedly from where she was busy with the hot plates and toaster. "There's magic in music, you know."

"You're thinking of *The Magic Flute*?" he asked. "You make a recorder sound like one."

"There's magic in all woodwinds," she assured him. "Mozart's supposed to have changed the plot of *The Magic Flute* midway so that it wouldn't be too close to that of a rival opera, *The Enchanted Bassoon*."

He laughed, then went on. "Musical notes do have at least one supernatural power. They can levitate, fly up through the air. Of course words can do that, too, but not as well."

"How do you figure that?" she asked over her shoulder.

"From cartoons and comic strips," he told her. "Words need balloons to hold them up, but notes just come flying out of the piano or whatever."

"They have those little black wings," she said, "at least the eighth and shorter ones. But it's all true. Music can fly—it's all release—and it has the power to release other things and make them fly and swirl."

He nodded. "I wish you'd release the notes of this piano, though, and let them swirl out when you practice harpsichord," he said, looking at the electronic instrument, "instead of keeping them shut up inside the earphones."

"You'd be the only one who'd like it," she informed him.

"There's Gun and Saul," he said.

"Their rooms aren't on this shaft. Besides, you'd get sick of scales and arpeggios yourself."

"I'm not so sure," he said, then teased, "But maybe harpsichord notes are too tinkly to make magic."

"I hate that word," she said, "but you're still wrong. Tinkly (ugh!) notes can make magic too. Remember Papageno's bells—there's more than one kind of magic music in *The Flute*."

They ate toast, juice, and eggs. Franz told Cal of his decision to send the manuscript of *Towers of Treason* off just as it was.

He finished, "So my readers won't find out just what a document-shredding machine sounds like when it works—what difference does that make? I actually saw that program on the tube, but when the Satanist wizard fed in the rune, they had smoke come out—which seemed stupid."

"I'm glad to hear you say that," she said sharply. "You put too much effort into rationalizing that silly program." Her expression changed. "Still, I don't know. It's partly that you always try to do your best, whatever at, that makes me think of you as a professional." She smiled.

He felt another faint twinge of guilt but fought it down easily.

While she was pouring him more coffee, he said, "I've got a great idea. Let's go to Corona Heights today. I think there'd be a great view of Downtown and the Inner Bay. We could take the Muni most of the way, and there shouldn't be too much climbing."

"You forget I've got to practice for the concert tomorrow night and couldn't risk my hands, in any case," she said a shade reproachfully. "But don't let that stop you," she added with a smile that asked his pardon. "Why not ask Gun or Saul—I think they're off today. Gun's great on climbing. Where is Corona Heights?"

He told her, remembering that her interest in Frisco was neither as new nor as passionate as his—he had a convert's zeal.

"That must be close to Buena Vista Park," she said. "Now don't go wandering in there, please. There've been some murders there quite recently. Drug related. The other side of Buena Vista is right up against the Haight."

"I don't intend to," he said, "though maybe you're a little too uptight about the Haight. It's quieted down a lot the last few years. Why, I got these two books there in one of those really fabulous secondhand stores."

"Oh, yes, you were going to show them to me," she said.

He handed her the one that had been open, saying, "That's just about the most fascinating book of pseudo-science I've ever seen—it has some genuine insights mixed with the hokum. No date, but printed about 1900, I'd judge."

" 'Megapolisomancy,' " she pronounced carefully. "Now what would that be? Telling the future from . . . from cities?"

"From *big* cities," he said, nodding.

"Oh, yes, the *mega*."

He went on. "Telling the future and all other sorts of things. And apparently making magic, too, from that knowledge. Though de Castries calls it a 'new science,' as if he were a second Galileo. Anyhow, this de Castries is very much concerned about the 'vast amounts' of steel and paper that are being accumulated in big cities. And coal oil (kerosene) and natural gas. And electricity, too, if you can believe it— he carefully figures out just how much electricity is in how many thousands of miles of wire, how many tons of illuminating gas in tanks, how much steel in the new skyscrapers, how much paper for government records and yellow journalism, and so on.''

''My-oh-my,'' Cal commented. ''I wonder what he'd think if he were alive today.''

''His direct predictions vindicated, no doubt. He *did* speculate about the growing menace of automobiles and gasoline, but especially electric cars carrying buckets of direct electricity around in batteries. He came so close to anticipating our modern concern about pollution—he even talks of 'the vast congeries of gigantic fuming vats' of sulphuric acid needed to manufacture steel. But what he was most agitated about was the psychological or spiritual (he calls them 'paramental') effects of all that stuff accumulating in big cities, its sheer liquid and solid mass.''

''A real proto-hippie,'' Cal put in. ''What sort of man was he? Where did he live? What else did he do?''

''There's absolutely no indication in the book of any of those things,'' Franz told her, ''and I've never turned up another reference to him. In his books he refers to New England and eastern Canada quite a bit, and New York City, but only in a general way. He also mentioned Paris (he had it in for the Eiffel Tower) and France a few times. And Egypt.''

Cal nodded. ''What's with the other book?''

''Something quite interesting,'' Franz said, passing it over. ''As you can see, it's not a regular book at all but a journal of blank rice-paper pages, as thin as onionskin but more opaque, bound in ribbed silk that was tea rose, I'd say, before it faded. The entries, in violet ink with a fine-point fountain pen, I'd guess, hardly go a quarter of the way through. The rest of the pages are blank. Now when I bought these books they were tied together with an old piece of string. They looked as if they'd been joined for decades—you can still see the marks.''

''Uh-huh,'' Cal agreed. ''Since 1900 or so? A very charming diary book—I'd like to have one like it.''

''Yes, isn't it? No, just since 1928. A couple of the entries are dated, and they all seem to have been made in the space of a few weeks.''

"Was he a poet?" Cal asked. "I see groups of indented lines. Who was he, anyway? Old de Castries?''

"No, not de Castries, though someone who had read his book and knew him. But I do think he was a poet. In fact, I think I have identified the writer, though it's not easy to prove since he nowhere signs himself. I think he was Clark Ashton Smith.''

"I've heard that name," Cal said.

"Probably from me," Franz told her. "He was another supernatural horror writer. Very rich, doomful stuff: Arabian Nights chinoiserie. A mood like Beddoes's *Death's Jest-Book*. He lived near San Francisco and knew the old artistic crew, he visited George Sterling at Carmel, and he could easily have been here in San Francisco in 1928 when he'd just begun to write his finest stories. I've given a photocopy of that journal to Jaime Donaldus Byers, who's an authority on Smith and who lives here on Beaver Street (which is just by Corona Heights, by the way, the map shows it), and he showed it to de Camp (who thinks it's Smith for sure) and to Roy Squires (who's as sure it isn't). Byers himself just can't decide, says there's no evidence for an extended San Francisco trip by Smith then, and that although the writing looks like Smith's, it's more agitated than any he's ever seen. But I have reasons to think Smith would have kept the trip secret and have had cause to be supremely agitated.''

"Oh, my," Cal said. "You've gone to a lot of trouble and thought about it. But I can see why. It's *très romantique*, just the feel of this ribbed silk and rice paper.''

"I had a special reason," Franz said, unconsciously dropping his voice a little. "I bought the books four years ago, you see, before I moved here, and I read a lot in the journal. The violet-ink person (whoever, *I* think Smith) keeps writing about 'visiting Tiberius at 607 Rhodes.' In fact, the journal is entirely—or chiefly—an account of a series of such interviews. That '607 Rhodes' stuck in my mind, so that when I went hunting a cheaper place to live and was shown the room here—''

"Of course, it's your apartment number, 607," Cal interrupted.

Franz nodded. "I got the idea it was predestined, or prearranged in some mysterious way. As if I'd had to look for the '607 Rhodes' and had found it. I had a lot of mysterious drunken ideas in those days and didn't always know what I was doing or where I was—for instance, I've forgotten exactly where the fabulous store was where I bought these books, and its name, if it had one. In fact, I was pretty drunk most of the time—period."

"You certainly were," Cal agreed, "though in a quiet way. Saul and Gun and I wondered about you and we pumped Dorotea Luque and Bonita," she added, referring to the Peruvian apartment manager and her thirteen-year-old daughter. "Even then you didn't seem an ordinary lush. Dorotea said you wrote '*ficción* to scare, about *espectros y fantasmas de los muertos y las muertas*,' but that she thought you were a gentleman."

Franz laughed. "Specters and phantoms of dead men and dead ladies. How very Spanish! Still, I'll bet you never thought—" he began and stopped.

"That I'd some day get into bed with you?" Cal finished for him. "Don't be too sure. I've always had erotic fantasies about older men. But tell me—how did your weird then-brain fit in the Rhodes part?"

"It never did," Franz confessed. "Though I still think the violet-ink person had some definite place in mind, besides the obvious reference to Tiberius's exile by Augustus to the island of Rhodes, where the Roman emperor-to-be studied oratory along with sexual perversion and a spot of witchcraft. The violet-ink person doesn't always say Tiberius, incidentally. It's sometimes Theobald and sometimes Tybalt, and once it's Thrasyllus, who was Tiberius's personal fortune-teller and sorcerer. But always there's that '607 Rhodes.' And once it's Theudebaldo and once Dietbold, but three times Thibaut, which is what makes me sure, besides all the other things, it must have been de Castries that Smith was visiting almost every day and writing about.''

''Franz,'' Cal said, ''all this is perfectly fascinating, but I've just got to start practicing. Working up harpsichord on a dinky electronic piano is hard enough, and tomorrow night's not just anything, it's the Fifth Brandenburg Concerto.''

''I know, I'm sorry I forgot about it. It was inconsiderate of me, a male chauvinist—'' Franz began, getting to his feet.

''Now, don't get tragic,'' Cal said briskly. ''I enjoyed every minute, really, but now I've got to work. Here, take your cup—and for heaven's sake, these books—or I'll be peeking into them when I should be practicing. Cheer up—at least you're not a male chauvinist pig, you only ate one piece of toast.

''And—Franz,'' she called. He turned with his things at the door. ''Do be careful up there around Beaver and Buena Vista. Take Gun or Saul. And remember—'' Instead of saying what, she kissed two fingers and held them out toward him a moment, looking quite solemnly into his eyes.

He smiled, nodded twice, and went out feeling happy and excited. But as he closed the door behind him he decided that whether or not he went to Corona Heights, he wouldn't ask either of the two men on the next floor up to go with him— it was a question of courage, or at least independence. No, today would be his own adventure. Damn the torpedoes! Full speed ahead!

IV

The hall outside Cal's door duplicated all the features of the one on Franz's floor: black-painted airshaft window, knobless door to disused broom closet, drab golden elevator door, and low-set, snap-capped vacuum outlet—a relic of the days when the motor for a building's vacuum system was in the basement and the maid handled only a long hose and a brush. But before Franz, starting down the hall, had passed any of these, he heard from ahead an intimate, giggly laugh that made him remember the one he'd imagined for the imaginary maids. Then some words he couldn't catch in a man's voice: low, rapid, and jocular. Saul's?—it did seem to come from above. Then the feminine or girlish laughter again, louder and a little explosive, almost as if someone were being tickled. Then a rush of light footsteps coming down the stairs.

He reached them just in time to get a glimpse, down and across the stairwell, of a shadowy slender figure disappearing around the last visible angle—just the suggestion of black hair and clothing and slim white wrists and ankles, all in swift movement. He moved to the well and looked down it, struck by how the successive floors below were like the series of reflections you saw when you stood between two mirrors. The rapid footsteps continued their spiraling descent all the way down, but whoever was making them was keeping to the wall and away from the rail lining the well, as if driven by centrifugal force, so he got no further glimpse.

As he peered down that long, narrow tube dimly lit from the skylight above, still thinking of the black-clad limbs and laughter, a murky memory rose in his mind and for a few moments possessed him utterly. Although it refused to come wholly clear, it gripped him with the authority of a very unpleasant dream or bad drunk. He was standing upright in a dark, claustrophobically narrow, crowded, musty space. Through the fabric of his trousers he felt a small hand laid on his genitals and he heard a low, wicked laugh. He looked down in his memory and saw the foreshortened, ghostly, featureless oval of a small face and the laugh was repeated, mockingly. Somehow it seemed there were black tendrils all around him. He felt a weight of sick excitement and guilt and, almost, fear.

The murky memory lifted as Franz realized the figure on the stairs had to have been that of Bonita Luque wearing the black pajamas and robe and feathered black mules she'd been handed down from her mother and already outgrown, but sometimes still wore as she darted around the building on her mother's early-morning errands. He smiled disparagingly at the thought that he was almost sorry (not really!) he was no longer drunk and so able to nurse various kinky excitements.

He started up the stairs, but stopped almost at once when he heard Gun's and Saul's voices from the floor above. He did not want to see either of them now, at first simply from a reluctance to share today's mood and plans with anyone but Cal, but as he listened to the clear and sharpening voices his motive became more complicated.

Gun asked, "What was that all about?"

Saul answered, "Her mother sent the kid up to check if either of us had lost a cassette player-recorder. She thinks her kleptomaniac on the second floor has one that doesn't belong to her."

Gun remarked, "That's a big word for Mrs. Luque."

Saul said, "Oh, I suppose she said 'e-stealer.' I told the kid that no, I still had mine."

Gun asked, "Why didn't Bonita check with me?"

Saul answered, "Because I told her you didn't have a cassette player to start with. What's the matter? Feeling left out?"

"No!"

During this interchange Gun's voice had grown increasingly nagging, Saul's progressively cooler yet also teasing. Franz had listened to mild speculation about the degree of homosexuality in Gun's and Saul's friendship, but this was the first time he found himself really wondering about it. No, he definitely didn't want to barge in now.

Saul persisted, "Then what's the matter? Hell, Gun, you know I always horse around with Bonny."

Gun's voice was almost waspish as he said, "I know I'm a puritanized North European, but I'd like to know just how far liberation from Anglo-Saxon body-contact taboos is supposed to go."

And Saul's voice was almost taunting as he replied, "Why, just as far as you both think proper, I suppose."

There was the sound of a door closing very deliberately. It was repeated. Then silence. Franz breathed his relief, continued softly up—and as he emerged into the fifth-floor hall found himself almost face to face with Gun, who was standing in front of the shut door to his room, glaring across at Saul's. Set on the floor beside him was a knee-high rectangular object with a chrome carrying handle protruding from its gray fabric cover.

Gunnar Nordgren was a tall, slim man, ashen blond, a fined-down Viking. Right now he had shifted his gaze and was looking at Franz with a growing embarrassment that matched Franz's own feelings. Abruptly Gun's usual amiability flooded back into his face, and he said, "Say, I'm glad you came by. A couple of nights ago you were wondering about document-shredding machines. Here's one I had here from the office overnight."

He whipped off the cover, revealing a tall blue and silvery box with a foot-wide maw on top and a red button. The maw fed down into a deep basket which Franz, coming closer, could see was one-quarter filled with a dirty snow of paper diamonds less than a quarter inch across.

The uncomfortable feelings of a moment before were gone. Looking up, Franz said, "I know you're going to work and all, but could I hear it in operation once?"

"Of course." Gun unlocked the door behind him and led Franz into a neat, rather sparely furnished room, the first features of which to strike the eye were large astronomical photographs in color and skiing equipment. As Gun unrolled the electric cord and plugged it in, he said lightheartedly, "This is a Shredbasket put out by Destroyit. Properly dire names, eh? Costs only five hundred dollars or so. Larger models go up to two thousand. A set of circular knives cuts the paper to ribbons; then another set cuts the ribbons across. Believe it or not, these machines were developed from ones for making confetti. I like that—it suggests that mankind first thinks of making frivolous things and only later puts them to serious use—if you can call this serious. Games before guilt."

The words poured out of him in such an excess of excitement or relief that Franz forgot his wonder as to why Gun should have brought such a machine home—what he'd been destroying. Gun continued, "The ingenious Italians—what was it Shakespeare said? Supersubtle Venetians?—lead the world, you know, in inventing machines for food and fun. Ice-cream makers, pasta extruders, espresso coffee machines, set-piece fireworks, hurdy-gurdies . . . and confetti. Well, here goes.''

Franz had taken out a small notebook and ballpoint pen. As Gun's finger moved toward the red button, he leaned close, rather cautiously, expecting some rather loud sound.

Instead, there came a faint, breathy buzzing, as if Time were clearing her throat.

Delightedly Franz jotted down just that.

Gun fed in a pastel sheet. Pale blue snow showered down upon the dirty white. The sound barely thickened a little.

Franz thanked Gun and left him coiling up the cord. Mounting past his own floor and the seventh toward the roof, he felt pleased. Getting that scrap of observed fact had been just the bit of luck he'd needed to start the day perfectly.

V

The cubical room housing the elevator's hoist was like a wizard's den atop a tower: skylight thickly filmed with dust, electric motor like a broad-shouldered dwarf in greasy green armor, and old-fashioned relays in the form of eight black cast-iron arms that writhed when in use like those of a chained-down giant spider—and with big copper switches that clashed loudly as they opened and closed whenever a button was pushed below, like such a spider's jaws.

Franz stepped out into sunlight on the flat, low-walled roof. Tar-embedded gravel gritted faintly under his shoes. The cool breeze was welcome.

To the east and north bulked the huge downtown buildings and whatever secret spaces they contained, blocking off the Bay. How old Thibaut would have scowled at the Transamerica Pyramid and the purple-brown Bank of America monster! Even at the new Hilton and St. Francis towers. The words came into his head, "The ancient Egyptians only buried people in their pyramids. We are living in ours." Now where had he read that? Why, in *Megapolisomancy*, of course. How apt! And did the modern pyramids have in them secret markings foretelling the future and crypts for sorcery?

He walked past the low-walled rectangular openings of the narrow airshafts lined with gray sheet-iron, to the back of the roof and looked up between the nearby high rises (modest compared with those downtown) at the TV tower and Corona Heights. The fog was gone, but the pale irregular hump of the latter still stood out sharply in the morning sunlight. He looked through his binoculars, not very hopefully, but—yes, by God!—there was that crazy, drably robed worshiper, or what-not, still busy with his ritual, or whatever. If these glasses would just settle down! Now the fellow had run to a slightly lower clump of rocks and seemed to be peering furtively over it. Franz followed the apparent direction of his gaze down the crest and almost immediately came to its probable object: two hikers trudging up. Because of their colorful shorts and shirts, it was easier to make them out. Yet despite their flamboyant garb they somehow struck Franz as more respectable characters than the lurker at the summit. He wondered what would happen when they met at the top. Would the robed hierophant try to convert them? Or solemnly warn them off? Or stop them like the Ancient Mariner and tell them an eerie story with a moral? Franz looked back, but now the fellow (or could it have been a woman?) was gone. A shy type, evidently. He searched the rocks, trying to spot him hiding, and even followed the plodding hikers until they reached the top and disappeared on the other side, hoping for a surprise encounter, but none came.

Nevertheless, when he shoved the binoculars back in his pocket, he had made up his mind. He'd visit Corona Heights. It was too good a day to stay indoors.

"If you won't come to me, then I will come to you," he said aloud, quoting an eerie bit from a Montague Rhodes James ghost story and humorously applying it both to Corona

Heights and to its lurker. The mountain came to Mohammed, he thought, but he had all those jinn.

VI

An hour afterward Franz was climbing Beaver Street, taking deep breaths to avoid panting later. He had added the bit about Time clearing her throat to *Weird Underground #7*, sealed the manuscript in its envelope, and mailed it. When he'd started, he'd had his binoculars hanging around his neck on their strap like a storybook adventurer's, so that Dorotea Luque, waiting in the lobby with a couple of elderly tenants for the mailman, had observed merrily, "You go to look for the e-scary thing to write e-stories about, no?" and he had replied. *"Sí, Señora Luque. Espectros y fantasmas,"* in what he hoped was equally cockeyed Spanish. But then a block or so back, a bit after getting off the Muni car on the Market, he'd wedged them into his pocket again, alongside the street guide he'd brought. This seemed a nice enough neighborhood, quite safe-looking really; still there was no point in displaying advertisements of affluence, and Franz judged binoculars would be that even more than a camera. Too bad big cities had become—or were thought to have become—such perilous places. He'd almost chided Cal for being uptight about muggers and nuts, and look at him now. Still, he was glad he'd come alone. Exploring places he'd first studied from his window was a natural new stage in his reality trip, but a very personal one.

Actually there were relatively few people in the streets this morning. At the moment he couldn't see a single one. His mind toyed briefly with the notion of a big, modern city suddenly completely deserted, like the barque *Marie Celeste* or the *luxe* resort hotel in that disquietingly brilliant film *Last Year at Marienbad*.

He went by Jaime Donaldus Byers's place, a narrow-fronted piece of carpenter Gothic now painted olive with gold trim, very Old San Francisco. Perhaps he'd chance ringing the bell coming back.

From here he couldn't see Corona Heights at all. Nearby stuff masked it (and the TV tower, too). Conspicuous at a distance—he'd got a fine view of its jagged crest at Market and Duboce—it had hidden itself like a pale brown tiger on his approach, so that he had to get out his street guide and spread its map to make sure he hadn't got off the track.

Beyond Castro the way got very steep, so that he stopped twice to even out his breathing.

At last he came out on a short dead-end cross street behind some new apartments. At its other end a sedan was parked with two people sitting in the front seats—then he saw that he'd mistaken headrests for heads. They did look so like dark little tombstones!

On the other side of the cross street were no more buildings, but green and brown terraces going up to an irregular crest against blue sky. He saw he'd finally reached Corona Heights, somewhat on the far side from his apartment.

After a leisurely cigarette, he mounted steadily past some tennis courts and lawn and up a fenced and winding hillside ramp and emerged on another dead-end street—or road, rather. He felt very good, really, in the outdoors. Gazing back the way he'd come, he saw the TV tower looking enormous (and handsomer than ever) less than a mile away, yet somehow just the right size. After a moment he realized that was because it was now the same size his binoculars magnified it to from his apartment.

Strolling to the dead end of the road, he passed a long, rambling one-story brick building with generous parking space that modestly identified itself as the Josephine Randall Junior Museum. There was a panel truck with the homely label "Sidewalk Astronomer." He recalled hearing of it from Dorotea Luque's daughter Bonita as the place where children could bring pet tame squirrels and snakes and brindled Japanese rats (and bats?) when for some reason they could no longer keep them. He also realized he'd seen its low roofs from his window.

From the dead end, a short path led him to the foot of the crest, and there on the other side was all the eastern half of San Francisco and the Bay beyond and both the bridges spread out before him.

Resolutely resisting the urge to scan in detail, he set himself to mounting the ridge by the hard gravelly path near its crest. This soon became rather tiresome. He had to pause more than once for breath and set his feet carefully to keep from slipping.

When he'd about reached the spot where he'd first seen the hikers, he suddenly realized that he'd grown rather childishly apprehensive. He almost wished he had brought Gun and Saul, or run into other climbers of the solid, respectable sort, no matter how colorfully clad or otherwise loud and noisy. At the moment he wouldn't even object to a transistor radio blatting. He was pausing now not so much for breath as to scan very carefully each rock clump before circling by it, for if he thrust his head too trustingly around one, what face or no-face might he not see?

This really was too childish of him, he told himself. Didn't he want to meet the character on the summit and find out just what sort of an oddball he was? A gentle soul, most likely, from his simple garb and timidity and love of solitude. Though of course he most likely had departed by now.

Nevertheless Franz kept using his eyes systematically as he mounted the last of the slope, gentler now, to its top.

The ultimate outcropping of rocks (the Corona? the crown?) was more extensive and higher than the others. After holding back a bit (to spy out the best route, he told himself), he mounted by three ledges, each of which required a leg-stretching step, to the very top, where he at last stood up (though rather carefully, bracing his feet wide—there was a lot of wind from the Pacific up here) with all of Corona Heights beneath him.

He slowly turned around in a full circle, tracing the horizon but scanning very thoroughly all the clumps of rock and all the brown and green slopes immediately below him, familiarizing himself with his new surroundings and incidentally ascertaining that there wasn't another being besides himself anywhere on Corona Heights.

Then he went down a couple of ledges and settled himself comfortably in a natural rock seat facing east, completely out of the wind. He felt very much at ease and remarkably secure in this eyrie, especially with the sense of the mighty TV tower rising behind him like a protective goddess. While smoking another leisurely cigarette, he surveyed with un-aided eyes the great spread of the city and Bay with its great ships tinier than toys, from the faintly greenish thin pillow of smog over San Jose in the south to the dim little pyramid of Mount Diablo beyond Berkeley and on to the red towers of the Golden Gate Bridge in the north with Mount Tamalpais beyond them. It was interesting how landmarks shifted with this new vantage point. Compared with his view from the roof, some of the downtown buildings had shot up, while others seemed trying to hide behind their neighbors.

After another cigarette he got out his binoculars and put their strap around his neck and began to study this and that. They were quite steady now, not like this morning. He chuc-klingly spelled out a few big billboards south of Market on the Embarcadero in the Mission, mostly ads for cigarettes and beer and vodka—that Black Velvet theme!—and a couple of the larger topless spots for the tourists.

After a survey of the steely, gleaming inner waters and following the Bay Bridge all the way to Oakland, he set in seriously on the downtown buildings and soon discovered to his embarrassment that they were quite hard to identify from here. Distance and perspective had subtly altered their hues and arrangement. And then contemporary skyscrapers were so very anonymous—no signs or names, no pinnacle statues or weathercocks or crosses, no distinctive facades and cor-nices, no architectural ornament at all: just huge blank slabs of featureless stone, or concrete or glass that was either sleekly bright with sun or dark with shadow. Really, they might well be the "gargantuan tombs or monstrous vertical coffins of living humanity, a breeding ground for the worst of paramental entities'' that old de Castries had kept ranting about in his book.

After another stretch of telescopic study in which he managed to identify a couple of the shifty skyscrapers, at last, he let his binoculars hang and got out from his other pocket the meat sandwich he'd made himself. As he unwrapped and slowly ate it, he thought of what a fortunate person he really was. A year ago he'd been a mess, but now—

He heard a *scrutch* of gravel, then another. He looked around but didn't see anything. He couldn't decide from what direction the faint sounds had come. The sandwich was dry in his mouth.

With an effort he swallowed and continued eating, and recaptured his train of thought. Yes, now he had friends like Gun and Saul . . . and Cal . . . and his health was a damn sight better, and best of all, his work was going well, his precious stories (well, precious to him) and even that terrible *Weird Underground* stuff—

Another *scrutch*, louder, and with it an odd little high-pitched laugh. He tensed himself and looked around quickly, sandwich and thoughts forgotten.

There came the laugh again, mounting toward a shrill shriek, and from behind the rocks there came dashing, along the path just below, two little girls in dark blue playclothes. The one caught the other and they spun around, squealing happily, in a whirl of sun-browned limbs and fair hair.

Franz had barely time to think what a refutation this was of Cal's (and his own) worries about this area, and for the afterthought that still it didn't seem right for parents to let such small, attractive girls (they couldn't be more than seven or eight) ramble in such a lonely place, when there came loping from behind the rocks a shaggy Saint Bernard, whom the girls at once pulled into their whirling game. But after only a little more of that, they ran on along the path by which Franz had come up, their large protector close behind. They'd either not seen Franz at all or else, after the way of little girls, they'd pretended not to notice him. He smiled at how the incident had demonstrated his unsuspected residual nervousness. His sandwich no longer tasted dry.

He crumpled the wax paper into a ball and stuck it in his pocket. The sun was already westering and striking the distant tall walls confronting him. His trip and climb had taken longer than he'd realized, and he'd been sitting here longer too. What was that epitaph Dorothy Sayers had seen on an old tombstone and thought the acme of all grue? Oh, yes: "It is later than you think." They'd made a popular song of that just before World War Two: "Enjoy yourself, enjoy yourself, it's later than you think." There was shivery irony for you. But he had lots of time.

He got busy with his binoculars again, studying the medieval greenish brown cap of the Mark Hopkins Hotel housing the restaurant-bar Top of the Mark. Grace Cathedral atop Nob Hill was masked by the high rises there, but the modernistic cylinder of St. Mary's Cathedral stood out plainly on newly named Cathedral Hill. An obviously pleasant task occurred to him: to spot his own seven-story apartment house. From his window he could see Corona Heights. Ergo, from Corona Heights he could see his window. It would be in a narrow slot between two high rises, he reminded himself, but the sun would be striking into that slot by now, giving good illumination.

To his chagrin, it proved extremely difficult. From here the lesser roofs were almost a trackless sea, literally, and such a foreshortened one that it was very hard to trace the line of streets—a checkerboard viewed from the edge. The job preoccupied him so that he became oblivious of his immediate surroundings. If the little girls had returned now and stared up at him, he probably wouldn't have noticed them. Yet the silly little problem he'd set himself was so puzzling that more than once he almost gave it up.

Really, a city's roofs were a whole dark alien world of their own, unsuspected by the myriad dwellers below, and with their own inhabitants, no doubt, their own ghosts and "paramental entities."

But he rose to the challenge and with the help of a couple

of familiar watertanks he knew to be on roofs close to his and of a sign BEDFORD HOTEL painted in big black letters high on the side wall of that nearby building, he at last identified his apartment house.

He was wholly engrossed in his task.

Yes, there was the slot, by God! and there was his own window, the second from the top, very tiny but distinct in the sunlight. Lucky he'd spotted it now—the shadow traveling across the wall would soon obscure it.

And then his hands were suddenly shaking so that he'd dropped his binoculars. Only his strap kept them from crashing on the rocks.

A pale brown shape had leaned out of his window and waved at him.

What was going through his head was a couple of lines from that bit of silly folk doggerel which begins:

> *Taffy was a Welshman, Taffy was a thief.*
> *Taffy came to my house and stole a piece of beef.*

But it was the ending that was repeating itself in his head:

> *I went to Taffy's house, Taffy wasn't home.*
> *Taffy went to my house and stole a marrowbone.*

Now for God's sake don't get so excited, he told himself, taking hold of the dangling binoculars and raising them again. And stop breathing so hard—you haven't been running.

He was some time locating his building and the slot again—damn the dark sea of roofs!—but when he did, there was the shape again in his window. Pale brown, like old bones—now don't get morbid! It could be the drapes, he told himself, half blown out of his window by the wind—he'd left it open. There were freakish winds among high buildings. His drapes were green, of course, but their lining was a nondescript hue like this. And the figure wasn't waving to him now—its dancing was that of the binoculars—but rather regarding him thoughtfully as if saying, ''You chose to visit my place, Mr. Westen, so I decided to make use of that opportunity to have a quiet look at yours.'' Quit it! he told himself. The last thing we need now is a writer's imagination.

He lowered his binoculars to give his heartbeat a chance to settle down and to work his cramped fingers. Suddenly anger filled him. In his fantasizing he'd lost sight of the plain fact that someone was mucking about in his room! But who? Dorotea Luque had a master key, of course, but she was never a bit sneaky, nor her grave brother Fernando, who did the janitor work and had hardly any English at all but played a remarkably strong game of chess. Franz had give his own duplicate key to Gun a week ago—a matter of a parcel to be delivered when he was out—and hadn't got it back. Which meant that either Gun or Saul—or Cal, for that matter—might have it now. Cal had a big old faded bathrobe she sometimes mucked around in—

But no, it was ridiculous to suspect any of them. But what about what he'd overheard from Saul on the stairs?—the 'e-stealer' Dorotea Luque had been worried about. That made more sense. Face up to it, he told himself: while he was gadding about out here, satisfying obscure aesthetic curiosities, some sneak-thief, probably on hard drugs, had somehow got into his apartment and was ripping him off.

He took up the binoculars again in a hard fury and found his apartment at once, but this time he was too late. While he'd been steadying his nerves and wildly speculating, the sun had moved on, the slot had filled with shadow, so that he could no longer make out his window, let alone any figure in it.

His anger faded. He realized it had been mostly reaction to his little shock at what he'd seen, or thought he'd seen . . . no, he'd seen something, but as to exactly what, who could be sure?

He stood up on his rocky seat, rather slowly, for his legs were a bit numb from sitting and his back was stiff, and he stepped carefully up into the wind again. He felt depressed— and no wonder, for streamers of fog were blowing in from the west, around the TV tower and half masking it; there were shadows everywhere. Corona Heights had lost its magic for him; he just wanted to get off it as soon as possible (and back to check his room), so after a quick look at his map, he headed straight down the far side, as the hikers had. Really, he couldn't get home too soon.

VII

The far side of Corona Heights, which faced Buena Vista Park and turned its back on the central city, was steeper than it looked. Several times Franz had to restrain his impulse to hurry and make himself move carefully. Then, halfway down, a couple of big dogs came to circle and snarl at him, not Saint Bernards but those black Dobermans that always made one think of the SS. Their owner down below took his time calling them off, too. Franz almost ran across the green field at the hill's base and through the small door in the high wire fence.

He thought of phoning Mrs. Luque or even Cal, and asking them to check out his room, but hesitated to expose them to possible danger—or upset Cal while she was practicing—while as for Gun and Saul, they'd be out.

Besides, he was no longer certain what he most suspected and in any case liked to handle things alone.

Soon—but not too soon for him, by any means—he was hurrying along Buena Vista Drive East. The park it closely skirted—another elevation, but a wooded one—mounted up from beside him dark green and full of shadows. In his present mood it looked anything but a ''good view'' to him, rather an ideal spot for heroin intrigues and sordid murders. The sun was altogether gone by now, and ragged arms of fog came curving after him. When he got to Duboce, he wanted to rush down, but the sidewalks were too steep—as steep as any he'd seen on any of San Francisco's more than seven hills—and once again he had to grit his teeth and place his feet with care and take his time. The neighborhood seemed quite as safe as Beaver Street, but there were few people out in the chilly change of weather, and once more he stuffed his binoculars back into his pocket.

He caught the N-Judah car where it comes out of the tunnel under Buena Vista Park (Frisco's hills were honeycombed with 'em, he thought) and rode it down Market to the Civic Center. Among the crowders boarding a 19-Polk there, a hulking drab shape lurching up behind him gave him a start, but it was only a blank-eyed workman powdered with pale dust from some demolition job.

He got off the 19 at Geary. In the lobby of 811 Geary there was only Fernando vacuuming, a sound as gray and hollow as the day had grown outside. He would have liked to chat, but the short man, blocky and somber as a Peruvian idol, had less English than his sister and was additionally rather deaf. They bowed gravely to each other, exchanged a "Senyor Loókay" and a "meestair Juestón," Fernando's rendering of "Westen."

He rode the creaking elevator up to six. He had the impulse to stop at Cal's or the boys' first, but it was a matter of—well, courage—not to. The hall was dark (a ceiling globe was out) and the shaft-window and knobless closet door next to his room darker. As he approached his own door, he realized his heart was thumping. Feeling both foolish and apprehensive, he slipped his key into the lock, and clutching his binoculars in his other hand as an impromptu weapon, he thrust the door swiftly open and quickly switched on the ceiling light inside.

The 200-watt glare showed his room empty and undisturbed. From the inside of the still-tousled bed, his colorful "scholar's mistress" seemed to wink at him humorously. Nevertheless, he didn't feel secure until he'd rather shamefacedly peered in the bathroom and then opened the closet and the tall clothes cabinet and glanced inside.

He switched off the top light then and went to the open window. The green drapes were lined with a sun-faded tan, all right, but if they'd been blown halfway out the window at some point, a chance of wind had blown them neatly back into place afterward. The serrated hump of Corona Heights showed up dimly through the advancing high fog. The TV tower was wholly veiled. He looked down and saw that the windowsill and his narrow desk abutting it and the carpet at his feet were all strewn with crumbles of brownish paper that reminded him of Gun's paper-shredding machine. He recalled that he'd been handling some old pulp magazines here yesterday, tearing out pages he wanted to save. Had he thrown the magazines away afterward? He couldn't remember, but probably—they weren't lying around anywhere nearby, at any rate, only a neat little stack of ones he hadn't looted yet. Well, a thief who stole only gutted old pulp magazines was hardly a serious menace—more like a trashman, a helpful scavenger.

The tension that had been knotting him departed at last. He realized he was very thirsty. He got a split of ginger ale from the small refrigerator and drank it eagerly. While he made coffee on the hot plate, he sketchily straightened the disordered half of the bed and turned on the shaded light at its head. He carried over his coffee and the two books he'd shown Cal that morning, and settled himself comfortably, and read around in them and speculated.

When he realized it was getting darker outside, he poured himself more coffee and carried it down to Cal's. The door was ajar. Inside, Cal's shoulders were lifting rhythmically as she played with furious precision, her ears covered with large padded phones. Franz couldn't be sure whether he heard the ghost of a concerto, or only the very faint thuds of the keys.

Saul and Gun were talking quietly on the couch, Gun with a green bottle beside him. Remembering this morning's bitter words he'd overheard, Franz looked for signs of strain, but all seemed harmony. Perhaps he'd read too much into their words.

Saul Rosenzweig, a thin man with dark hair shoulder-length and dark-circled eyes, quirked a smile and said, "Hello, Calvina asked us down to keep her company while she practices, though you'd think a couple of window dummies could do the job as well. But Calvina's a romantic puritan at heart. Deep inside she wants to frustrate us.''

Cal had taken off her headphones and stood up. Without a word or a look at anyone, or anything apparently, she picked up some clothes and vanished like a sleepwalker into the bathroom, whence there came presently the sound of showering.

Gun grinned at Franz and said, ''Greetings. Sit down and join the devotees of silence. How goes the writer's life?''

They talked inconsequentially and lazily of this and that. Saul carefully made a long thin cigarette. Its piney smoke was pleasant, but Franz and Gun smilingly declined to share, Gun tilting his green bottle for a long swallow.

Cal reappeared in a surprisingly short time, looking fresh and demure in a dark brown dress. She poured herself a tall thin glass of orange juice from the fridge and sat down.

''Saul,'' she said quietly, ''you know my long name is not Calvina, but Calpurina—the minor Roman Cassandra who kept warning Caesar. I may be a puritan, but I wasn't named for Calvin. My parents were both born Presbyterians, it's true, but my father early progressed into Unitarianism and died a devout Ethical Culturist. He used to pray to Emerson and swear by Robert Ingersoll. While my mother was, rather frivolously, into Bahai. And I don't own a couple of window dummies, or I might use them. No, no pot, thank you. I have to hold myself intact until tomorrow night. Gun, thanks for humoring me. It does help to have people in the room, even when I'm incommunicada. It helps especially when evening begins to close in. That ale smells wonderful, but alas . . . same reason as no pot. Franz, you're looking quietly prodigious. What happened at Corona Heights?''

Pleased that she had been thinking about him and observing him so closely and accurately, Franz told the story of his adventure. He was struck by how in the telling it became rather trivial-seeming and less frightening, though paradoxically more entertaining—the writer's curse and blessing.

Gun happily summed up. ''So you go to investigate this apparition or what-not, and find it's pulled the big switch and is thumbing its nose at you from your own window two miles away. 'Taffy went to my house'—that's neat.''

Saul said, "Your Taffy story reminds me of my Mr. Edwards. He gets the idea that two enemies in a parked car across the street from the hospital have got a pain-ray projector trained on him. We wheel him over there so he can see for himself there ain't no one in any of the cars. He's very much relieved and keeps thanking us, but when we get him back to his room, he lets out a sudden squeal of agony. Seems his enemies have taken advantage of his absence to plant a pain-ray projector somewhere in the walls.''

"Oh, Saul," Cal said in mildly scathing tones, "we're not all of us your hospital people—at least yet. Franz, I wonder if those two innocent-seeming little girls may not have been involved. You said they were running around and dancing, like your pale brown thing. I'm sure that if there's such a thing as psychic energy, little girls have lots of it.''

"I'd say you have a good artistic imagination. That angle hadn't even occurred to me," Franz told her, acutely aware that he was beginning to disparage the whole incident, but unable to help himself. "Saul, I may very well have been projecting—at least in part—but if so, what? Also, the figure was nondescript, remember, and wasn't doing anything objectively sinister.''

Saul said, "Look, I wasn't suggesting any parallel. That's your idea, and Cal's. I was just reminded of another weird incident.''

Gun guffawed. "Saul doesn't think we're all completely crazy. Just fringe-psychotic.''

There was a knock and then the door opened as Dorotea Luque let herself in. She sniffed and looked at Saul. She was a slender version of her brother, with a beautiful Inca profile and jet-black hair. She had a small parcel-post package of books for Franz.

"I wondered you'd be down here, and then I heard you talk," she explained. "Did you find the e-scary things to write about with your . . . how you say . . . ?" She made binoculars of her hands and held them to her eyes, and then looked questioningly around when they all laughed.

While Cal got her a glass of wine, Franz hastened to explain. To his surprise, she took the figure in the window very seriously.

"But are you e-sure you weren't ripped off?" she demanded anxiously. "We had an e-stealer on the second floor, I think."

"My portable TV and tape recorder were there," he told her. "A thief would take those first."

"But how about your marrowbone?" Saul put in. "Taffy get that?"

"And did you close your transom and double-lock your door?" Dorotea persisted, illustrating with a vigorous twist of her wrist. "Is double-lock now?"

"I always double-lock it," Franz assured her. "I used to think it was only in detective stories they slipped locks with a plastic card. But then I found I could slip my own with a photograph. The transom, no. I like it open for ventilation."

"Should always close the transom, too, when you go out," she pronounced. "All of you, you hear me? Is thin people can get through transoms, you better believe. Well, I am glad you weren't ripped off. *Gracias*," she added, nodding to Cal as she sipped her wine.

Cal smiled and said to Saul and Gun, "Why shouldn't a modern city have its special ghosts, like castles and graveyards and big old manor houses once had?"

Saul said, "My Mrs. Willis thinks the skyscrapers are out to get her. At night they make themselves still skinnier, she says, and come sneaking down the streets after her."

Gun said, "I once heard lightning whistle over Chicago. There was a thunderstorm over the Loop, and I was on the South Side at the university, right near the site of the first atomic pile. There'd be a flash on the northern horizon and then, seven seconds later, not thunder, but this high-pitched moaning scream. I had the idea that all the elevated tracks were audio-resonating a radio component of the flash."

Cal said eagerly, "Why mightn't the sheer mass of all that steel—? Franz, tell them about the book."

He repeated what he'd told her this morning about *Megapolisomancy* and a little besides.

Gun broke in. "And he says our modern cities are our Egyptian pyramids? That's beautiful. Just imagine how, when we've all been killed off by pollution (nuclear, chemical, smothered in unbiodegradable plastic, red tides of dying microlife, the nasty climax of our climax culture), an archaeological expedition arrives by spaceship from another solar system and starts to explore us like a bunch of goddamn Egyptologists! They'd use roving robot probes to spy through our utterly empty cities, which would be too dangerously radioactive for anything else, as dead and deadly as our poisoned seas. What would they make of the World Trade Center in New York City and the Empire State Building? Or the Sears Building in Chicago? Or even the Transamerica Pyramid here? Or that space-launch assembly building at Canaveral that's so big you can fly light planes around inside? They'd probably decide they were all built for religious and occult purposes, like Stonehenge. They'd never imagine people lived and worked there. No question, our cities will be the eeriest ruins ever. Franz, this de Castries had a sound idea—the sheer amount of stuff there is in cities. That's heavy, heavy."

Saul put in, "Mrs. Willis says the skyscrapers get very heavy at night when they—excuse me—screw her."

Dorotea Luque's eyes grew large, then she exploded in giggles. "Oh, that's naughty," she reproved him merrily, wagging a finger.

Saul's eyes got a faraway look like a mad poet's, and he embroidered his remark with, "Can't you imagine their tall gray skinny forms sneaking sideways down the streets, one flying buttress erected for a stony phallus?" and there was more sputtery laughter from Mrs. Luque. Gun got her more wine and himself another bottle of ale.

VIII

Cal said, "Franz, I've been thinking on and off all day, in the corner of my mind that wasn't Brandenburging, about that '607 Rhodes' that drew you to move here. Was it a definite place? And if so, where?"

"607 Rhodes—what's that all about?" Saul asked.

Franz explained again about the rice-paper journal and the violet-ink person who might have been Clark Ashton Smith and his possible interviews with de Castries. Then he said, "The 607 can't be a street address—like 811 Geary here, say. There's no such street as Rhodes in 'Frisco. I've checked. The nearest to it is a Rhode Island Street, but that's way over in the Potrero, and it's clear from the entries that the 607 place is here downtown, within easy walking distance of Union Square. And once the journal-keeper describes looking out the window at Corona Heights and Mount Sutro—of course, there wasn't any TV tower then—"

"Hell, in 1928 there weren't even the Bay and Golden Gate Bridges," Gun put in.

"—and at Twin Peaks," Franz went on. "And then he says that Thibaut always referred to Twin Peaks as Cleopatra's Breasts."

"I wonder if skyscrapers ever have breasts," Saul said. "I must ask Mrs. Willis about that."

Dorotea bugged her eyes again, indicated her bosom, said, "Oh, no!" and once more burst into laughter.

Cal said, "Maybe Rhodes is the name of a building or hotel. You know, the Rhodes Building."

"Not unless the name's been changed since 1928," Franz told her. "There's nothing like that now that I've heard of. The name Rhodes strike a bell with any of you?"

It didn't.

Gun speculated, "I wonder if *this* building ever had a name, the poor old raddled dear."

"You know," Cal said, "I'd like to know that too."

Dorotea shook her head. "Is just 811 Geary. Was once hotel maybe—you know, night clerk and maids. But I don't know."

"Buildings Anonymous," Saul remarked without looking up from the reefer he was making.

"Now we do close transom," said Dorotea, suiting actions to words. "Okay smoke pot. But do not—how you say?—advertise."

Heads nodded wisely.

After a bit they all decided that they were hungry and should eat together at the German Cook's around the corner because it was his night for sauerbraten. Dorotea was persuaded to join them. On the way she picked up her daughter Bonita and the taciturn Fernando, who now beamed.

Walking together behind the others, Cal asked Franz, "Taffy is something more serious than you're making out, isn't it?"

He had to agree, though he was becoming curiously uncertain of some of the things that had happened today—the usual not-unpleasant evening fog settling around his mind like a ghost of the old alcoholic one. High in the sky, the lopsided circle of the gibbous moon challenged the street lights.

He said, "When I thought I saw that thing in my window, I strained for all sorts of explanations, to avoid having to accept a . . . well, supernatural one. I even thought it might have been you in your old bathrobe."

"Well, it could have been me, except it wasn't," she said calmly. "I've still got your key, you know. Gun gave it to me that day your big package was coming and Dorotea was out. I'll give it to you after dinner."

"No hurry," he said.

"I wish we could figure out that 607 Rhodes," she said, "and the name of our own building, if it ever had one."

"I'll try to think of a way," he said. "Cal, did your father actually swear by Robert Ingersoll?"

"Oh, yes—'In the name of . . .' and so on—and by William James, too, and Felix Adler, the man who founded Ethical Culture. His rather atheistic coreligionists thought it odd of him, but he liked the ring of sacerdotal language. He thought of science as a sacrament."

Inside the friendly little restaurant, Gun and Saul were shoving two tables together with the smiling approval of blonde and red-cheeked Rose, the waitress. The way they ended up, Saul sat between Dorotea and Bonita with Gun on Bonita's other side. Bonita had her mother's black hair, but was already a half-head taller and otherwise looked quite Anglo—the narrow-bodied and -faced North European type; nor was there any trace of Spanish in her American schoolgirl voice. He recalled hearing that her divorced and now nameless father had been black Irish. Though pleasingly slim in sweater and slacks, she looked somewhat gawky—very far from the shadowy, hurrying shape that had briefly excited him this morning and awakened an unpleasant memory.

He sat beside Gun with Cal between himself and Fernando, who was next to his sister. Rose took their orders.

Gun switched to a dark beer. Saul ordered a bottle of red wine for himself and the Luques. The sauerbraten was delicious, the potato pancakes with applesauce out of this world. Bela, the gleaming-faced German Cook (Hungarian, actually) had outdone himself.

In a lull in the conversation, Gun said to Franz, "That was really a very strange thing that happened to you on Corona Heights. As near as you can get today to what you'd call the supernatural."

Saul heard and said at once, "Hey, what's a materialist scientist like you doing talking about the supernatural?"

"Come off it, Saul," Gun answered with a chuckle. "I deal with matter, sure. But what is that? Invisible particles, waves, and force fields. Nothing solid at all. Don't teach your grandmother to suck eggs."

"You're right," Saul grinned, sucking his. "There's no reality but the individual's immediate sensations, his awareness. All else is inference. Even the individuals are inference."

Cal said, "I think the only reality is number . . . and music, which comes to the same thing. They are both real and they both have power."

"My computers agree with you, all the way down the line," Gun told her. "Number is all they know. Music?—well, they could learn that."

Franz said, "I'm glad to hear you all talk that way. You see, supernatural horror is my bread and butter, both that *Weird Underground* trash—"

Bonita protested, "No!"

"—and the more serious junk, but sometimes people tell me there's no such thing as supernatural horror anymore—that science has solved, or can solve, all mysteries, that religion is just another name for social service, and that modern people are too sophisticated and knowledgeable to be scared of ghosts even for kicks."

"Don't make me laugh," Gun said. "Science has only increased the area of the unknown. And if there is a god, her name is Mystery."

Saul said, "Refer those brave erudite skeptics to my Mr. Edwards or Mrs. Willis, or simply to their own inevitable buried fears. Or refer 'em to me, and I'll tell 'em the story of the Invisible Nurse who terrorized the locked ward at St. Luke's. And then there was . . ." He hesitated, glancing toward Cal. "No, that's too long a story to tell now."

Bonita looked disappointed. Her mother said eagerly, "But are e-strange things. In Lima. This city too. *Brujas*—how you say?—witches!" She shuddered happily.

Her brother beamed his understanding and lifted a hand to preface one of his rare remarks. *"Hay hechicería,"* he said vehemently, with a great air of making himself clear. *"Hechicería ocultada en murallas."* He crouched a little, looking up. *"Murallas muy altas."*

Everyone nodded pleasantly as if they understood.

Franz asked Cal in a low voice, "What's that *hechi*?"

She whispered, "Witchcraft, I think. Witchcraft hidden in the walls. Very high walls." She shrugged.

Franz murmured, "Where in the walls, I wonder? Like Mr. Edwards' pain-ray projector?"

Gun said, "There's one thing, though, Franz, I do wonder about—whether you really identified your own window correctly from Corona. You said the roofs were like a sea on edge. It reminds me of difficulties I've run into in identifying localities in photographs of stars, or pictures of the earth taken from satellites. The sort of trouble every amateur astronomer runs into—the pros, too. So many times you come across two or more localities that are almost identical."

"I've thought of that myself," Franz said. "I'll check it out."

Leaning back, Saul said, "Say, here's a good idea, let's all of us some day soon go for a picnic to Corona Heights. You and I, Gun, could bring our ladies—they'd like it. How does that grab you, Bonny?"

"Oh, yes," Bonita replied eagerly.

On that note they broke up.

Dorotea said, "We thank you for the wine. But remember, double-lock doors and close transoms when go out."

Cal said, "Now with any luck I'll sleep twelve hours. Franz, I'll give you your key some other time." Saul glanced at her.

Franz smiled and asked Fernando if he cared to play chess later that evening. The Peruvian smiled agreeably.

Bela Szlawik, sweating from his labors, himself made change as they paid their checks, while Rose fluttered about and held the door for them.

As they collected on the sidewalk outside, Saul looked toward Franz and Cal and said, "How about drifting back with Gun to my room before you play chess? I'd sort of like to tell you that story."

Franz nodded. Cal said, "Not me. Straight off to bed." Saul nodded that he understood her.

Bonita had heard. "You're going to tell him the story of the Invisible Nurse," she said accusingly. "I want to hear that, too."

"No, it is time for bed," her mother asserted, not too commandingly or confidently. "See, Cal goes bed."

"I don't care," Bonita said, pushing up against Saul closely, invading his space. "Please? Please?" she coaxed insistently.

Saul grabbed her suddenly, hugged her tight, and blew down her neck with a great raspberry sound. She squealed loudly and happily. Franz, glancing almost automatically toward Gun, saw him start to wince, then control it, but his lips were thin. Dorotea smiled almost as happily as if it were her own neck being blown down. Fernando frowned slightly and held himself with a somewhat military dignity.

As suddenly Saul held the girl away from him and said to her matter-of-factly, "Now look here, Bonny, this is another story I want to tell Franz—a very dull one of interest only to writers. There is no Story of the Invisible Nurse. I just made that up because I needed something to illustrate my point."

"I don't believe you," Bonita said, looking him straight in the eye.

"Okay, you're right," he said abruptly, dropping his hands away from her and standing back. "There *is* a Story of the Invisible Nurse Who Terrorized the Locked Ward at St. Luke's, and the reason I didn't tell it was not that it's too long—it's quite short—but simply too horrible. But now you've brought it down upon yourself and all these other good people. So gather round, all of you."

As he stood in the dark street with the light of the gibbous moon shining on his flashing eyes, sallow face, and elf-locked, long dark hair, he looked very much like a gypsy, Franz thought.

"Her name was Wortly," Saul began, dropping his voice. "Olga Wortly, R.N.—(Registered Nurse). That's not her real name—this became a police case and they're still looking for her—but it has the flavor of the real one. Well, Olga Wortly, R.N., was in charge of the swing shift (the four to midnight) in the locked ward at St. Luke's. And there was no terror then. In fact, she ran what was in a way the happiest and certainly the quietest swing shift ever, because she was very generous with her sleeping potions, so that the graveyard shift never had any trouble with wakeful patients and the day shift sometimes had difficulty getting some of them waked up for lunch, let alone breakfast.

"She didn't trust her L.V.N. (Licensed Vocational Nurse) to dispense her goodies. And she favored mixtures, whenever she could shade or stretch the doctor's order to allow them, because she thought two drugs were always surer than one— Librium *with* the Thorazine (she doted on Tuinal because it's *two* barbiturates: red Seconal with blue Amytal), chloral hydrate *with* the phenobarbital, paraldehyde *with* the yellow Nembutal—in fact, you could always tell when she was coming (our fairy snooze mother, our dark goddess of slumber) because the paralyzing stench of the paraldehyde always preceded her; she always managed to have at least one patient on paraldehyde. It's a superaromatic, superalcohol, you know, that tickles the top of your sinuses, and it smells like God-knows-what—super banana oil; some nurses call it gasoline— and you give it with fruit juice for a chaser and you dispense it in a glass shot-glass because it'll melt a plastic one, and its molecules travel through the air ahead of it faster than light!"

Saul had his audience well in hand, Franz noted. Dorotea was listening with as rapt delight as Bonita; Cal and Gun were smiling indulgently; even Fernando had caught the spirit and was grinning at the long drug names. For the moment the sidewalk in front of the German Cook's was a moonlit gypsy encampment, lacking only the dancing flames of an open fire.

"Every night, two hours after supper, Olga would make her druggy-wug rounds. Sometimes she'd have the L.V.N. or an aide carry the tray, sometimes she'd carry it herself.

" 'Sleepy-bye time, Mrs. Binks,' she'd say. 'Here's your pass to dreamland. That's a good little girl. And now this lovely yellow one. Good evening, Miss Cheeseley, I've got your trip to Hawaii for you—blue for the deep blue ocean, red for the sunset skies. And now a sip of the bitter to wash it down—think of the dark salt waves. Hold out your tongue,

Mr. Finelli, I've something to make you wise. Whoever'd think, Mr. Wong, they could put nine hours and maybe ten of good, good darkness into such a tiny time-capsule, a gelatin spaceship bound for the stars. You smelled us coming, didn't you, Mr. Auerbach? Grape juice chaser tonight!' And so on and so on.

"And so Olga Wortly, R.N., our mistress of oblivion, our queen of dreams, kept the locked ward happy," Saul continued, "and even won high praise—for everyone likes a quiet ward—until one night she went just a little too far and the next morning every last patient had O.D.'ed (overdosed) and was D.O.A. (that's Dead on Arrival, Bonny) with a beatific smile on his or her face. And Olga Wortly was gone, never to be seen again.

"Somehow they managed to hush it up—I think they blamed it on an epidemic of galloping hepatitis or malignant eczema—and they're still looking for Olga Wortly."

"That's about all there is to it," he said with a shrug, relaxing, "except"—he held up a finger dramatically, and his voice went low and eerie—"except they say that on nights when there's a lot of moonlight, just like this now, and it's sleepy-bye time, and the L.V.N. is about to start out with her tray of night medicines in their cute little paper favor cups, you get a whiff of paraldehyde at the nurses' station (although they *never* use that drug there now) and it travels from room to room and from bed to bed, not missing one, that unmistakable whiff does—the Invisible Nurse making her rounds!"

And with more or less appropriate oohs, ahs, and chuckles, they set out for home in a body. Bonita seemed satisfied. Dorotea said extravagantly, "Oh, I am frightened! When I wake up tonight, I think nurse coming I can't see make me swallow that parry-alley stuff."

"Par-al-de-hyde," Fernando said slowly, but with surprising accuracy.

IX

There was so much stuff in Saul's room and such a variety of it, apparently unorganized (in this respect it was the antithesis of Gun's), that you wondered why it wasn't a mess—until you realized that nothing in it looked thrown away or tossed aside, everything looked loved: the stark and unglamorized photographs of people, mostly elderly (they turned out to be patients at the hospital, Saul pointed out Mr. Edwards and Mrs. Willis); books from Merck's Manual to Colette, *The Family of Man* to Henry Miller, Edgar Rice to William S. Burroughs to George Borrow (*The Gypsies in Spain*, *Wild Wales*, and *The Zincali*); a copy of Nostig's *The Subliminal Occult* (that really startled Franz); a lot of hippie, Indian, and American Indian beadwork; hash-smoking accessories; a beer stein filled with fresh flowers; an eye chart; a map of Asia; and a number of paintings and drawings from childish to mathematical to wild, including a striking acrylic abstraction on black cardboard that teemed with squirming shapes and jewel and insect colors and seemed to reproduce in miniature the room's beloved confusion.

Saul indicated it, saying, "I did that the one time I took cocaine. If there is a drug (which I doubt) that adds something to the mind instead of just taking away, then it's cocaine. If I ever went the drug route again, that'd be my choice."

"Again?" Gun asked quizzically, indicating the pot paraphernalia.

"Pot is a plaything," Saul averred, "a frivolity, a social lubricant to be classed with tobacco, coffee, and the other tea. When Anslinger got Congress to classify it as—for all practical purposes—a hard drug, he really loused up the development of American society and the mobility of its classes."

"As much as that?" Gun began skeptically.

"It's certainly not in the same league as alcohol," Franz agreed, "which mostly has the community's blessing, at least the advertising half of it: Drink booze and you will be sexy, healthy, and wealthy, the ads say, especially those Black Velvet ones. You know, Saul, it was funny you should bring paraldehyde into your story. The last time I was 'separated' from alcohol—to use that oh-so-delicate medical expression—I got a little paraldehyde for three nights running. It really was delightful—the same effect as alcohol when I first drank it—a sensation I thought I'd never experience again, that warm, rosy glow."

Saul nodded. "It does the same job as alcohol, without so much immediate wear and tear on the chemical systems. So the person who's worn out with drinking ordinary booze responds to it nicely. But of course it can become addictive, too, as I'm sure you know. Say, how about more coffee? I've only got the freeze-dried, of course."

As he quickly set water to boil and measured brown crystals into colorful mugs, Gun ventured, "But wouldn't you say that alcohol is mankind's natural drug, with thousands of years of use and expertise behind it—learning its ways, becoming seasoned to it."

"Time enough, at any rate," Saul commented, "for it to kill off all the Italians, Greeks, Jews, and other Mediterraneans with an extreme genetic weakness in respect to it. The American Indians and Eskimos aren't so lucky. They're still going through that. But hemp and peyote and the poppy and the mushroom have pretty long histories, too."

"Yes, but there you get into the psychedelic, consciousness-distorting (I'd say, instead of -enlarging) sort of thing," Gun protested, "while alcohol has a more straightforward effect."

"I've had hallucinations from alcohol, too," Franz volunteered in partial contradiction, "though not so extreme as those you get from acid, from what they tell me. But only during withdrawal, oddly, the first three days. In closets and dark corners and under tables—never in very bright light—I'd see these black and sometimes red wires, about the thickness of telephone cords, vibrating, whipping around. Made me think of giant spiders' legs and such. I'd know they were hallucinations—they were manageable, thank God. Bright light would always wipe them out.''

"Withdrawal's a funny and sometimes touch-and-go business,'' Saul observed as he poured boiling water. "That's when drinkers get delirium tremens, not when they're drinking—I'm sure you know that, too. But the perils and agonies of withdrawal from the hard drugs have ben vastly exaggerated—it's part of the mythos. I learned that when I was a paramedical worker in the great days of the Haight-Ashbury, before I became a nurse, running around and giving Thorazine to hippies who'd O.D.'d or thought they had.''

"Is that true?'' Franz asked, accepting his coffee. "I've always heard that quitting heroin cold turkey was about the worst.''

"Part of the mythos,'' Saul assured Franz, shaking his long-haired head as he handed Gun his coffee and began to sip his own. "The mythos that Anslinger did so much to create back in the thirties (when all the boys who'd been big in Prohibition enforcement were trying to build themselves equal narcotics jobs) when he went to Washington with a couple of veterinary doctors who knew about doping race horses and a satchel of sensational Mexican and Central American newspaper clippings about murders and rapes and such committed by peons supposedly crazed with marijuana.''

"A lot of writers jumped on that bandwagon,'' Franz put in. "The hero would take one drag of a strange cigarette and instantly start having weird hallucinations, mostly along the lines of sex and bloodshed. Say, maybe I could suggest a 'Weird Underground' episode bringing in the Narcotics Bureau,'' he added thoughtfully, more to himself than them. "It's a thought.''

"And the agonies of cold-turkey withdrawal were part of that mythos picture,'' Saul took up, "so that when the beats and hippies and such began taking drugs as a gesture of rebellion against the establishment and their parents' generation, they started having all the dreadful hallucinations and withdrawal agonies the cop-invented mythos told them they would.'' He smiled crookedly, ''You know, I've sometimes thought it was very similar to the long-range effects of war propaganda on the Germans. In World War Two they committed all the atrocities, and more, that they were accused of, mostly falsely, in World War One. I hate to say it, but people are always trying to live up to worst expectations.''

Gun added, ''The hippie-era analogue to the SS Nazis being the Manson Family.''

''At any rate,'' Saul resumed, ''that's what I learned when I was rushing around the Hashbury at dead of night, giving Thorazine to flipping flower children *per anum*. I couldn't use a hypodermic needle because I wasn't a real nurse yet.''

Gun put in reflectively, ''That's how Saul and I met.''

''But it wasn't to Gun I was giving the rectal Thorazine,'' Saul amended. ''—that would have been just too romantic— but to a friend of his, who'd O.D.'ed, then called him up, so he called us. That's how we met.''

''My friend recovered very nicely,'' Gun put in.

''How did you both meet Cal?'' Franz asked.

''When she moved here,'' Gun said.

''At first it was only as if a silence had descended on us,'' Saul said thoughtfully. ''For the previous occupant of her room had been exceptionally noisy, even for this building.''

Gun said, ''And then it was as if a very quiet but musical mouse had joined the population. Because we became aware of hearing flute music, we thought it was, but so soft we couldn't be sure we weren't imagining it.''

''At the same time,'' Saul said, ''we began to notice this attractive, uncommunicative, very polite young woman who'd get on or off at four, always alone and always opening and closing the elevator gates very gently.''

Gun said, ''And then one evening we went to hear some Beethoven quarters at the Veterans Building. She was in the audience and we introduced ourselves.''

''All three of us taking the initiative,'' Saul added. ''By the end of the concert we were pals.''

"And the next weekend we were helping her redecorate her apartment," Gun finished. "It was as if we'd known each other for years."

"Or at least as if she'd known us for years," Saul qualified. "We were a lot longer learning about her—what an incredibly overprotected life she'd led, her difficulties with her mother . . ."

"How hard her father's death hit her . . ." Gun threw in.

"And how determined she was to make a go of things on her own and"—Saul shrugged—"and learn about life." He looked at Franz. "We were even longer discovering just how sensitive she was under that cool and competent exterior of hers, and also about her abilities in addition to the musical."

Franz nodded, then asked Saul, "And now are you going to tell me the story about her you've been saving?"

"How did you know it was going to be about her?" the other inquired.

"Because you glanced at her before you decided not to tell it at the restaurant," Franz told him, "and because you didn't really invite me over until you were sure she wouldn't be coming."

"You writers are pretty sharp," Saul observed. "Well, this happens to be a writer's story, in a way. Your sort of writer— the supernatural horror sort. Your Corona Heights thing made me want to tell it. The same realm of the unknown, but a different country in it."

Franz wanted to say, "I had rather anticipated that, too," but he refrained.

X

Saul lit a cigarette and settled himself back against the wall. Gun occupied the other end of the couch. Franz was in the armchair facing them.

"Early on," Saul began, "I realized that Cal was very interested in my people at the hospital. Not that she'd ask questions, but from the way she'd hold still whenever I mentioned them. They were one more thing in the tremendous outside world she was starting to explore that she felt compelled to learn about and sympathize with or steel herself against—with her it seems to be a combination of the two.

"Well, in those days I was pretty interested in my people myself. I'd been on the evening shift for a year and pretty well in charge of it for a couple of months, and so I had a lot of ideas about changes I wanted to make and was making. One thing, the nurse who'd been running the ward ahead of me had been overdoing the sedation, I felt." He grinned. "You see, that story I told for Bonny and Dora tonight wasn't all invented. Anyway, I'd been cutting most of them down to the point where I could communicate and work with them and they weren't still comatose at breakfast time. Of course, it makes for a livelier and sometimes more troublesome ward, but I was fresh and feisty and up to handling that."

He chuckled. "I suppose that's something almost every new person in charge does at first: cuts down on the barbiturates—until he or she gets tired and maybe a bit frazzled and decides that peace is worth a little sedation.

"But I was getting to know my people pretty well, or thought I was, what stage of their cycles each was in, and so be able to anticipate their antics and keep the ward in hand. There was this young Mr. Sloan, for instance, who had epilepsy—the *petit mal* kind—along with extreme depression. He was well educated, had showed artistic talent. As he'd approach the climax of his cycle, he'd begin to have his *petit mal* attacks—you know, brief loss of consciousness, being 'not there' for a few seconds, he'd sway a little—closer and closer together, every twenty minutes or so, then even closer. You know, I've often thought that epilepsy is very much like the brain trying to give itself electroshock. At any rate, my young Mr. Sloan would climax with a seizure approximating or mimicking *grand mal* in which he'd fall to the floor and writhe and make a great racket and perform automatic acts and lose control of all his bodily functions—psychic epilepsy, thye used to call it. Then his *petit mal* attacks would space themselves way out and he'd be better for a week, about. He seemed to time all this very exactly and put a lot of creative effort into it—I told you he had artistic talent. You know, all insanity is a form of artistic expression, I often think. Only the person has nothing but himself to work with—he can't get at outside materials to manipulate them—so he puts all his art into his behavior.

"Well, as I've said, I knew that Cal was getting very curious about my people, she'd even been hinting that she'd like to see them, so one night when everything was going very smoothly—all my people at a quiet stage in their cycles—I had her come over. Of course by now I was bending the hospital rules quite a bit, as you'd expect. There wasn't any moon either that night—new moon or near it—moonlight does excite people, especially the crazies—I don't know how, but it does."

"Hey, you never told me about this before," Gun interjected. "I mean, about having Cal at the hospital."

"So?" Saul said, and shrugged. "Well, she arrived about an hour after the day shift left, looking somewhat pale and apprehensive but excited . . . and almost immediately everything in the ward started to get out of hand and go wacko. Mrs. Willis began to whine and wail about her terrible misfortunes—she wasn't due to do that for a week, I'd figured, it's really heartrending to hear—and that set off Miss Craig, who's good at screaming. Mr. Schmidt, who'd been very well behaved for over a month, managed to get his pants down and unload a pile of shit before we could stop him in front of Mr. Bugatti's door, who's his 'enemy' from time to time— and we hadn't had *that* sort of thing happening on the ward since the previous year. Meanwhile, Mrs. Gutmayer had overturned her dinner tray and was vomiting, and Mr. Stowacki had somehow managed to break a plate and cut himself—and Mrs. Harper was screaming at the sight of blood (there wasn't much) and that made two of them (two screamers—not in Fay Wray's class, but good).

"Well, naturally I had to abandon Cal to her own devices while we dealt with all this, though of course I was wondering what she must be thinking and kicking myself for having invited her over at all and for being such a megalomaniac about my ability to predict and forestall disasters.

"By the time I got back to her, Cal had gone or retreated to the recreation room with young Mr. Sloan and a couple of others, and she'd discovered our piano and was quietly trying it out—horribly out of tune, of course, it must have been, at least to her ears.

"She listened to the hurried rundown I gave her on things— excuses, I suppose—we didn't usually have shit out in the halls, etcetera—and from time to time she'd nod, but she kept on working steadily at the piano at the same time, as if she were hunting for the keys that were least discordant (afterward she confirmed that that was exactly what she had been doing). She was paying attention to me, all right, but she was doing this piano thing, too.

"About then I became aware that the excitement was building up behind me in the ward again and that Harry's (young Sloan's) *petit mal* seizures were coming much closer together than they ought to, while he was pacing restlessly in a circle around the recreation room. By my count he wasn't due to climax until the next night, but now he'd unaccountably speeded up his cycle so he'd throw his *grand mal* fit tonight for sure—in a very short time, in fact.

"I started to warn Cal about what was likely to happen, but just then she sat back and screwed up her face a little, like she sometimes does when she's starting a concert, and then she began to play something very catchy of Mozart's— Cherubino's Song from *The Marriage of Figaro*, it turned out to be—but in what seemed to be the most discordant key of all on that banged-up old upright (afterward she confirmed this, too).

"Next thing, she was modulating the music into another key that was only a shade less discordant than the first, and so on and so on. Believe it or not, in her fooling around she'd worked out a succession of the keys from the most to the least discordant on that old out-of-tune loonies' piano, and now she was playing that Mozart air in all of them in the same order, least to most harmonious—Cherubino's Song, the words to which go something like (in English) 'We who love's power surely do feel—why should it ever through my heart steal?' And then there's something about 'in my sorrow lingers delight.'

"Meanwhile, I could feel the tensions building up around me and I could actually *see* young Harry's *petit mal* attacks coming faster and faster as he shuffled around, and I knew he was going to have his big one the next minute, and I began to wonder if I shouldn't stop Cal by grabbing her wrists as if she were some sort of witch making black magic with music—the ward had gone crazy at her arrival, and now she was doing the same damn thing with her Mozart, which was getting louder and louder.

"But just then she modulated triumphantly into the least discordant key and by contrast it sounded like perfect pitch, incredibly right, and at that instant young Harry launched, not into his *grand mal* attack, but into *a weirdly graceful, leaping dance* in perfect time to Cherubino's Song, and almost before I knew what I was doing I'd taken hold of Miss Craig (whose mouth was open to scream but she wasn't screaming) and was waltzing her around after young Harry— and I could feel the tension in the whole ward around us vanish like smoke. Somehow Cal had *melted* that tension, loosened and unbound it just as she had young Harry's depression, getting him over the hump into safety without his throwing a big fit. It seemed to me at the time to be the nearest thing to magic I've ever seen in my life—witchcraft, all right, but white witchcraft."

At the words "loosened and unbound," Franz recalled Cal's words that morning about music having "the power to release other things and make them fly and swirl."

Gun asked, "What happened then?"

"Nothing much, really," Saul said. "Cal kept playing the same tune over and over in the same triumphant key, and we kept on dancing and I think a couple of the others joined in, but she played it a little more softly each time, until it was like music for mice, and then she stopped it and very quietly closed the piano, and we stopped dancing and were smiling at each other, and that was that—except that all of us were in a different place from where we'd started. And a little later she went home without waiting through the shift, as though taking it for granted that what she'd done was something that couldn't possibly be repeated. And we never talked about it much afterwards, she and I. I remember thinking: 'Magic is a one-time thing.' ''

"Say, I like that," Gun said. "I mean the idea of magic—and miracles, too, like those of Jesus, say—and art, too, and history of course—simply being phenomena that *cannot* be repeated. Unlike science, which is all about phenomena that *can* be repeated."

Franz mused, "Tension *melted* . . . depression loosened and unbound . . . the notes fly upward like the sparks. . . . You know, Gun, that somehow makes me think of what your Shredbasket does that you showed me this morning."

"Shredbasket?" Saul queried.

Franz briefly explained.

Saul said to Gun, "You never told me about that."

"So?" Gun smiled and shrugged.

"Of course," Franz said, almost regretfully, "the idea of music being good for lunatics and smoothing troubled souls goes way back."

"At least as far as Pythagoras," Gun put in, agreeing. "That's two and a half thousand years."

Saul shook his head decidedly. "This thing Cal did went farther than that."

There was a sharp double knock at the door. Gun opened it.

Fernando looked around the room, bowing politely, then beamed at Franz and said, "E-chess?"

XI

Fernando was a strong player. In Lima he'd had an expert's rating. In Franz's room they divided two rather long, hard-fought games, which were just the thing to occupy fully Franz's dulled evening mind, and during them he became aware of how physically tired his climbing had left him.

From time to time he mused fleetingly about Cal's "white witchcraft" (if it could be called anything like that) and the black sort (even less likely) he'd intruded on at Corona Heights. He wished he'd discussed both incidents at greater length with Saul and Gun, yet doubted they'd have got any further. Oh, well, he'd see them both at the concert tomorrow night—their last words had been of that, asking him to hold seats for them if he came early.

As Fernando departed, the Peruvian pointed at the board and asked, *"Mañana por la noche?"*

That much Spanish Franz understood. He smiled and nodded. If he couldn't play chess again tomorrow night, he could always let Dorotea know.

He slept like the dead and without any remembered dreams.

He awoke completely refreshed, his mind clear and sharp and very calm, his thoughts measured and sure—a good sleep's benison. All of the evening dullness and uncertainty were gone. He remembered each of yesterday's events just as it had happened, but without the emotional overtones of excitement and fear.

The constellation of Orion was shouldering into his window, telling him dawn was near. Its nine brightest stars made an angular, tilted hourglass, challenging the smaller, slenderer one made by the nineteen winking red lights of the TV tower.

He made himself a small, quick cup of coffee with the very hot water from the tap, then put on slippers and robe and took up his binoculars and went very quietly to the roof. All his sensations were sharp. The black windows of the shafts and the black knobless doors of the disused closets stood out as distinctly as the doors of the occupied rooms and the old banisters, many times repainted, he touched as he climbed.

In the room on the roof his small flashlight showed the gleaming cables, the dark, hunched electric motor, and the coldly bunched small, silent iron arms of the relays that would wake violently, and make a great sudden noise, swinging and snapping, if someone pressed an electric button below. The green dwarf and the spider.

Outside, the night wind was bracing. Passing a shaft, he paused and on an impulse dropped a grain of gravel down it. The small sharp sound with its faint hollow overtones from the sheet-iron lining was almost three seconds, he judged, in coming back to him from the bottom. About eighty feet, that was right. There was satisfaction in thinking of how he was awake and clearheaded while so many were still dead asleep.

He looked up at the stars studding the dark dome of night like tiny silver nails. For San Francisco with its fogs and mists, and the invasive smog from Oakland and San Jose, it was a good night for seeing. The gibbous moon had set. He studied lovingly the superconstellation of very bright stars he called the Shield, a sky-spanning hexagon with its corners marked by Capella toward the north, bright Pollux (with Castor near and these years Saturn, too), Procyon the little dogstar, Sirius brightest of all, Bluish Rigel in Orion, and (swinging north again) red-gold Aldebaran. Bringing his binoculars into play, he scanned the golden swarm of the Hyades about that last and then quite close beside the Shield, the tiny bluish-white dipper of the Pleiades.

The sure and steady stars fitted the mood of his morning mind and reinforced it. He looked again at tilted Orion, then dropped his gaze to the red-flashing TV tower. Below it, Corona Heights was a black hump amongst the city's lights.

The memory came to him (a crystal-clear drop, as memories came to him these days in the hour after waking) of how when he'd first seen the TV tower at night, he'd thought of a line from Lovecraft's story, "The Haunter of the Dark," where the watcher of another ill-omened hill (Federal, in Providence) sees "the red Industrial Trust beacon had blazed up to make the night grotesque." When he'd first seen the tower he'd thought it worse than grotesque, but now—how strange!—it had become almost as reassuring to him as starry Orion.

"The Haunter of the Dark!" he thought with a quiet laugh. Yesterday he had lived through a section of a story that might fittingly be called "The Lurker at the Summit." How very strange!

Before returning to his room he briefly surveyed the dark rectangles and skinny pyramid of the downtown sky-scrapers—old Thibaut's bugaboos!—the tallest of them with their own warning red lights.

He made himself more coffee, this time using the hot plate and adding sugar and half-and-half. Then he settled himself in bed, determined to use his morning mind to clarify matters that had grown cloudy last evening. Thibaut's drab book and the washed-out tea-rose journal already made the head of his colorful Scholar's Mistress lying beside him on the inside. To them he added the thick black rectangles of Lovecraft's *The Outsider* and the *Collected Ghost Stories* of Montague Rhodes James, and also several yellowed old copies of *Weird Tales* (some puritan had torn their lurid covers off) containing stories by Clark Ashton Smith, shifting some bright magazines to the floor to make room, and the colorful napkins with them.

"You're fading, dear," he told her gaily in his thoughts, "putting on somber hues. Are you getting dressed for a funeral?"

Then for a space he read more systematically in *Megapolisomancy*. My God, the old boy certainly could do a sort of scholarly-flamboyant thing quite well. Consider:

At any particular time of history there have always been one or two cities of the monstrous sort—*viz.*, Babel or Babylon, Ur-Lhassa, Nineveh, Syracuse, Rome, Samarkand, Tenochtitlan, Peking—but we live in the

Megapolitan (or Necropolitan) Age, when such disastrous blights are manifold and threaten to conjoin and enshroud the world with funebral yet multipotent city-stuff. We need a Black Pythagoras to spy out the evil lay of our monstrous cities and their foul shrieking songs, even as the White Pythagoras spied out the lay of the heavenly spheres and their crystalline symphonies, two and a half millennia ago.

Or, adding thereto more of his own brand of the occult:

Since we modern city-men already dwell in tombs, inured after a fashion to mortality, the possibility arises of the indefinite prolongation of this life-in-death. Yet, although quite practicable, it would be a most morbid and dejected existence, without vitality or even thought, but only paramentation, our chief companions paramental entities of azoic origin more vicious than spiders or weasels.

Now what would paramentation be like? Franz wondered. Trance? Opium dreams? Dark, writhing phantoms born of sensory deprivation? Or something entirely different?
Or:

The electro-mephitic city-stuff whereof I speak has potencies for achieving vast effects at distant times and localities, even in the far future and on other orbs, but of the manipulations required for the production and control of such I do not intend to discourse in these pages.

As the overworked yet vigorous current exclamation had it, *wow!* Franz picked up one of the old crumble-edged pulps and was tempted to read Smith's marvelous fantasy, "The City of the Singing Flame," in which great looming metropolises move about and give battle to each other, but he resolutely set it aside for the journal.

Smith (he was sure it was he) had certainly been greatly impressed by de Castries (must be he also), as well he might have been almost fifty years ago. And he had clearly read *Megapolisomancy*, too. It occurred to Franz that this copy was most likely Smith's. Here was a typical passage in the journal:

Three hours today at 607 Rhodes with the furious Tybalt. All I could take. Half the time railing at his fallen-off acolytes, the other half contemptuously tossing me scraps of paranatural truth. But what scraps! That bit about the significance of diagonal streets! How that old devil sees into cities and their invisible sicknesses—a new Pasteur, but of the dead-alive.

He says his book is kindergarten stuff, but the new thing—the core and why of it and how to work it—he keeps only in his mind and in the Grand Cipher he's so sly about. He sometimes calls it (the Cipher) his Fifty-Book, that is, if I'm right and they are the same. Why fifty?

I should write Howard about it, he'd be astounded and—yes!—transfigured, it so agrees with and *illuminates* the decadent and putrescent horror he finds in New York City and Boston and even Providence (not Levantines and Mediterraneans, but half-sensed paramentals!). But I'm not sure he could take it. For that matter, I'm not sure how much more of it I can take myself. And if I so much as hint to old Tiberius at sharing his paranatural knowledge with other kindred spirits, he grows as ugly as his namesake in his last Caprian days and goes back to excoriating those whom he feels failed and betrayed him in the Hermetic Order he created.

I should get out myself—I've all that I can use as there are stories crying to be written. But can I give up the ultimate ecstasy of knowing each day I'll hear from the very lips of Black Pythagoras some new paranatural truth?

It's like a drug I have to have. Who can give up such fantasy?—especially when—*the fantasy is the truth*.

The paranatural, only a word—*but what it signifies*! The supernatural—a dream of grandmothers and priest and horror writers. But the *paranatural*! Yet how much can I take? Could I stand full contact with a paramental entity and not crack up?

Coming back today, I felt that my senses were metamorphosing. San Francisco was a meganecropolis vibrant with paramentals on the verge of vision and of audition, each block a surreal cenotaph that would bury Dali, and I one of the living dead aware of everything with cold delight. But now I am afraid of this room's walls!

Franz glanced with a chuckle at the drab wall next to the inside of the bed and below the spiderwebby drawing of the TV tower on fluorescent red, remarking to his Scholar's Mistress lying between them, "He certainly was worked up about it, wasn't he, dear?"

Then his face grew intent again. The "Howard" in the entry had to be Howard Phillips Lovecraft, that twentieth-century puritanic Poe from Providence, with his regrettable but undeniable loathing of the immigrant swarms he felt were threatening the traditions and monuments of his beloved New England and the whole Eastern seaboard. (And hadn't Lovecraft done some ghost-writing for a man with a name like Castries? Catser? Carswell?) He and Smith had been close friends by correspondence. While the mention of a Black Pythagoras was pretty well enough by itself to prove that the keeper of the journal had read de Castries's book. And those references to a Hermetic Order and a Grand Cipher (or Fifty-Book) teased the imagination. But Smith (who else?) had clearly been as much terrified as fascinated by the ramblings of his crabbed mentor. It showed up even more strikingly in a later entry.

Hated what gloating Tiberius hinted today about the disappearance of Bierce and the deaths of Sterling and

Jack London. Not only that they were suicides (which I categorically deny, particularly in the case of Sterling!) but that there were other elements in their deaths—elements for which the old devil appears *to take credit*.

He positively sniggered as he said, ''You can be sure of one thing, my dear boy, that all of them had a very rough time *paramentally* before they were snuffed out, or shuffled off to their gray paranatural hells. Very distressing, but it's the common fate of Judases—and little busybodies,'' he added, glaring at me from under his tangled white eyebrows.

Could he be hypnotising me?

Why do I linger on, now that the menaces outweigh the revelations? That disjointed stuff about techniques of giving paramental entities the scent—clearly a threat.

Franz frowned. He knew quite a bit about the brilliant literary group centered in San Francisco at the turn of the century and of the strangely large number of them who had come to tragic ends—among those, the macabre writer Ambrose Bierce vanishing in revolution-torn Mexico in 1913, London dying of uremia and morphine poisoning a little later, and the fantasy poet Sterling perishing of poison in the 1920s. He reminded himself to ask Jaime Donaldus Byers more about the whole business at the first opportunity.

The final diary entry, which broke off in the middle of a sentence, was in the same vein:

Today surprised Tiberius making entries in black ink in a ledger of the sort used for bookkeeping. His Fifty-Book? The Grand Cipher? I glimpsed a solid page of what looked like astronomical and astrological symbols (Could there be fifty such?) before he snapped it shut and accused me of spying. I tried to get him off the topic, but he would talk of nothing else.

Why do I stay? The man is a genius (paragenius?) but he's also a paranoiac!

He shook the ledger at me, cackling, "Perhaps you should sneak in some night on those quiet little feet of yours and steal it! Yes, why not do that? It would merely mean your finish, paramentally speaking! That wouldn't hurt. Or would it?"

Yes, by God, it is time I

Franz riffled through the next few pages, all blank, and then gazed over them at the window, which from the bed showed only the equally blank wall of the nearer of the two high rises. It occurred to him what an eerie fantasia of *buildings* all this was: de Castries's ominous theories about them, Smith seeing San Francisco as a . . . yes, mega-necropolis, Lovecraft's horror of the swarming towers of New York, the downtown skyscrapers seen from the roof here, the sea of roofs he'd scanned from Corona Heights, and this beaten old building itself, with its dark halls and yawning lobby, strange shafts and closets, black windows and hiding holes.

XII

Franz made himself more coffee—it had been full daylight now for some time—and lugged back to bed with him an armful of books from the shelves by his desk. To make room for them, more of the colorful recreational reading had to go on the floor. He joked with his Scholar's Mistress, "You're growing darker and more intellectual, my dear, but not a day older and as slim as ever. How do you manage it?"

The new books were a fair sampling of what he thought of as his reference library of the really eerie. Mostly not the new occult stuff, which tended to be the work of charlatans and hacks out for the buck, or naive self-deceivers innocent even of scholarship—flotsam and froth on the rising tide of witchcraft (which Franz was also skeptical about)—but books which approached the weird obliquely yet from far firmer footings. He leafed about in them swiftly, intently, quite delightedly, as he sipped his steaming coffee. There was Prof. D.M. Nostig's *The Subliminal Occult*, that curious, intensely skeptical book which rigorously disposes of all claims of the learned parapsychologists and still finds a residue of the inexplicable; Montague's witty and profound monograph *White Tape*, with its thesis that civilization is being asphyxiated, mummy-wrapped by its own records, bureaucratic and otherwise, and by its infinitely recessive self-observations; precious, dingy copies of those two extremely rare, slim books thought spurious by many critics—*Ames et Fantômes de Douleur* by the Marquis de Sade and *Knochenmädchen in Pelze (mit Peitsche)* by Sacher-Masoch; Oscar Wilde's *De Profundis* and *Suspiria de Profundis* (with its Three Ladies of Sorrow) by Thomas De Quincey, that old opium-eater and metaphysician, both commonplace books but strangely linked by more than their titles; *The Mauritzius Case* by Jacob Wasserman; *Journey to the End of the Night* by Céline; several copies of Bonewits's periodical *Gnostica*; *The Spider Glyph in Time* by Mauricio Santos-Lobos; and the monumental *Sex, Death and Supernatural Dread* by Ms. Frances D. Lettland, Ph.B.

For a long space his morning mind darted about happily in the eerie wonder-world evoked and buttressed by these books and de Castries's and the journal and by clear-cut memories of yesterday's rather strange experiences. Truly, modern cities were the world's supreme mysteries, and skyscrapers their secular cathedrals.

Scanning the "Ladies of Sorrow" prose poem in *Suspiria*, he wondered not for the first time, whether those creations of De Quincey had anything to do with Christianity. True, *Mater Lachrymarum*, Our Lady of Tears, the eldest sister, did remind one of *Mater Dolorosa*, a name of the Virgin; and the second sister too, *Mater Suspiriorum*, Our Lady of Sighs—and even the terrible and youngest sister, *Mater Tenebrarum*, Our Lady of Darkness. (De Quincey had intended to write a whole book about her, *The Kingdom of Darkness*, but apparently never had—*that* would have been something, now!) But no, their antecedents were in the classical world (they paralleled the three Fates and the three Furies) and in the labyrinths of the English laudanum-drinker's drug-widened awareness.

Meanwhile his intentions were firming as to how he'd spend this day, which promised to be a beauty, too. First, start pinning down that elusive 607 Rhodes, beginning by getting the history of this anonymous building, 811 Geary. It would make an excellent test case—and Cal, as well as Gun, had wanted to know. Next, go to Corona Heights again to check out whether he'd really seen his own window from there. Sometime in the afternoon visit Jaime Donaldus Byers. (Call him first.) Tonight, of course, Cal's concert.

He blinked and looked around. Despite the open window, the room was full of smoke. With a sorry laugh he carefully stubbed out his cigarette on the edge of the heaped ashtray.

The phone rang. It was Cal, inviting him down to late breakfast. He showered and shaved and dressed and went.

XIII

In the doorway Cal looked so sweet and young in a green dress, her hair in a long pony tail, that he wanted to grab and kiss her. But she also still had on her rapt, meditative look— "Keep intact for Bach."

She said, "Hello, dear. I actually slept those twelve hours I threatened to in my pride. God is merciful. Do you mind eggs again? It's really brunchtime. Pour yourself coffee."

"Any more practice today?" he asked, glancing toward the electronic keyboard.

"Yes, but not with that. This afternoon I'll have three or four hours with the concert harpsichord. And I'll be tuning it."

He drank creamed coffee and watched the poetry of motion as she dreamily broke eggs, an unconscious ballet of white ovoids and slender key-flattened fingertips. He found himself comparing her to Daisy, and, to his amusement, to his Scholar's Mistress. Cal and the latter were both slender, somewhat intellectual, rather silent types, touched with the White Goddess definitely, dreamy but disciplined. Daisy had been touched with the White Goddess too, a poet, and also disciplined, keeping herself intact . . . for brain cancer. He veered off from that.

But White was certainly Cal's adjective; all right, no Lady of Darkness, but a Lady of Light and in eternal opposition to the other, yang to its yin, Ormadz to its Ahriman—yes, by Robert Ingersoll!

And she really did look such a schoolgirl, her face a mask of gay innocence and good behavior. But then he remembered her as she had launched into the first piece of a concert. He'd been sitting up close and a little to one side so that he had seen her full profile. As if by some swift magic, she had become someone he'd never seen before and wasn't sure for a moment he wanted to. Her chin had tucked down into her neck, her nostril had flared, her eye had become all-seeing and merciless, her lips had pressed together and turned down at the corners quite nastily, like a savage schoolmistress, and it had been as if she had been saying, "Now hear me, all you strings, and *Mister* Chopin. You behave perfectly now, or else!" It had been the look of the young professional.

"Eat them while they're hot," Cal murmured, slipping his plate in front of him. "Here's the toast. Buttered, somehow."

After a while she asked, "How did you sleep?"

He told her about the stars.

She said, "I'm glad you worship."

"Yes, that's true in a way," he had to admit. "Saint Copernicus, at any rate, and Isaac Newton."

"My father used to swear by them, too," she told him. "Even, I remember once, by Einstein. I started to do it myself too, but Mother gently discouraged me. She thought it tomboyish."

Franz smiled. He didn't bring up this morning's reading or yesterday's events; they seemed wrong topics for now.

It was she who said, "I thought Saul was quite cute last night. I like the way he flirts with Dorotea."

"He loves to pretend to shock her," Franz said.

"And she loves to pretend to be shocked," Cal agreed. "I think I'll give her a fan for Christmas, just to have the delight of watching her manage it. I'm not sure I'd trust him with Bonita, though."

"What, our Saul?" he asked, in only half-pretended astonishment. The memory came, vividly and uncomfortably, of laughter overheard on the stairs yesterday morning, a laughter alive with touching and tickling.

"People have unexpected sides," she observed placidly. "You're very brisk and brimming with energy this morning. Almost bumptious, except you're being considerate for my mood. But underneath you're thoughtful. What are your plans for today?"

He told her.

"That sounds good," she said. "I've heard Byers's place is quite spooky. Or maybe they meant exotic. And I'd really like to find out about 607 Rhodes. You know—peer over the shoulder of 'stout Cortez' and see it there, whatever it is, 'silent upon a peak in Darien.' And just find out the history of this building, like Gun was wondering. That would be fascinating. Well, I should be getting ready."

"Will I see you before? Take you there?" he asked as he got up.

"No, not before, I think," she said thoughtfully. "But afterward." She smiled at him. "I'm relieved to hear you'll be there. Take care, Franz."

"You take care too, Cal," he told her.

"On concert days I wrap myself in wool. No, wait."

She came toward him, head lifted, continuing to smile. He got his arms around her before they kissed. Her lips were soft and cool.

XIV

An hour later, a pleasantly grave young man in the Recorder's Office at City Hall informed Franz that 811 Geary Street was designated Block 320, Lot 23 in his province.

"For anything about the lot's previous history," he said, "you'd have to go to the Assessor's Office. They would know because they handle taxes."

Franz crossed the wide, echoing marble corridor with its ceiling two stories high to the Assessor's Office, which flanked the main entrance to City Hall on the other side. The two great civic guards and idols, he thought, papers and moneys.

A worried woman with graying red hair told him, "Your next step is to go to the Office of Building Permits in the City Hall Annex across the street to your left when you go out, and find when a permit to build on the lot was applied for. When you bring us that information, we can help you. It should be easy. They won't have to go back far. Everything in that area went down in 1906."

Franz obeyed, thinking that all this was becoming not just a fantasia but a ballet of buildings. Investigating just one modest building had led him into what you could call this Courtly Minuet of the Runaround. Doubtless the bothersome public was supposed to get bored and give up at this point, but he'd fool 'em! The brimming spirits Cal had noticed in him were still high.

Yes, a national ballet of all buildings great and small, skyscrapers and shacks, all going up and haunting our streets and cross streets for a while and then eventually coming down, whether helped by earthquakes or not, to the tune of ownership, money, and records, with a symphony orchestra of millions of clerks and bureaucrats, papermen all, each intently reading and obediently tootling his scrap of the infinite score, which itself would all be fed, as the buildings tumbled, into the document-shredding machines, ranks upon ranks of them like banks of violins, not Stradivariuses but Shredmasters. And over everything the paper snow.

In the annex, a businesslike building with low ceilings, Franz was pleasantly surprised (but his cynicism rather dashed) when a portly young Chinaperson, upon being properly supplicated with the ritual formula of numbered block and lot, within two minutes handed him a folded old printed form filled in with ink that had turned brown and which began "Application for Permit to erect a 7-story Brick Building with Steel Frame on the south side of Geary Street 25 feet west of Hyde Street at Estimated Cost of $74,870.00 for Use as a Hotel," and ended with "Filed Jul 15, 1925."

His first thought was that Cal and the others would be relieved to hear that the building apparently had a steel frame—a point they'd wondered about during earthquake speculations and to which they'd never been able to get a satisfactory answer. His second was that the date made the building almost disappointingly recent—the San Francisco of Dashiell Hammett . . . and Clark Ashton Smith. Still, the big bridges hadn't been built then; ferries did all their work. Fifty years was a respectable age.

He copied out most of the brown-ink stuff, returned the application to the stout young man (who smiled, hardly inscrutably), and footed it back to the Assessor's Office, swinging his briefcase jauntily. The red-haired woman was worrying elsewhere, and two ancient men who both limped received his information dubiously, but finally deigned to consult a computer, joking together as to whether it would work, but clearly reverent for all their humor.

One of them pushed some buttons and read off from a screen invisible to the public, "Yep, permit granted September nine, 1925, and built in '26. Construction completed Jun—June."

"They said it was for a use as a hotel," Franz asked. "Could you tell me what name?"

"For that you'd have to consult a city directory for the year. Ours don't go back that far. Try in the public library across the square."

Franz dutifully crossed the wide gray expanse, dark green with little segregated trees and bright with small gushing fountains and two long pools rippling in the wind. On all four sides the civic buildings stood pompously, most of them blocky and nondescript, but City Hall behind him with its greenish dome and classic cupola and the main public library ahead somewhat more decorated, the latter with names of great thinkers and American writers, which (score one for our side) included Poe. While a block north the darkly severe and wholly modern (all glass) Federal Building loomed up like a watchful elder brother.

Feeling ebullient and now a bit lucky, too, Franz hurried. He still had much to do today and the high sun said it was getting on. Inside the swinging doors he angled through the press of harsh young women with glasses, children, belted hippies, and cranky old men (typical readers all), returned two books, and without waiting for an okay, he took the elevator to the empty corridor of the third floor. In the hushed, rather elegant San Francisco Room a slightly precious lady whispered to him that her city directories went up only to 1918, the later (more common?) ones were in the main catalog room on the second floor with the phone books.

Feeling slightly deflated and a bit run-around again, but not much, Franz descended to the big, fantastically high-ceilinged familiar room. In the last century and the early years of this, libraries had been built in the same spirit as banks and railroad stations—all pomp and pride. In a corner partitioned off by high, packed shelves, he found the rows of books he wanted. His hand went toward the 1926, then shifted to the 1927—that would be sure to list the hotel, if there had been one. Now for some fun—looking up the addresses of everyone mentioned in the application and finding the hotel itself, of course, though that last would take some hunting, have to check the addresses (which might be given by cross streets rather than numbers) of all the hotels—and maybe of the apartment hotels, too.

Before seating himself he glanced at his wristwatch. My God, it was later than he'd thought. If he didn't make up some time, he'd arrive at Corona Heights after the sun had left the slot and so too late for the experiment he intended. And books like this didn't circulate.

He took only a couple of seconds coming to a decision. After a casual but searing look all around to make sure no one was watching him at the moment, he thrust the directory into his deep briefcase and marched out of the catalog room, picking up a couple of paperbacks at random from one of the revolving wire stands set here and there. Then he tramped softly and measuredly down the great marble stairs that were wide and lofty and long and broad-stepped enough for a triumph in a Roman film epic, feeling all eyes upon him but hardly believing that. He stopped at the desk to check out the two paperbacks and drop them ostentatiously into his briefcase, and then walked out of the building without a glance at the guard, who never did look into briefcases and bags (so far as Franz had noticed) provided he'd seen you check out some books at the desk.

Franz seldom did that sort of thing, but today's promise seemed to make it worth taking little risks.

There was a 19-Polk coming outside. He caught it, thinking somewhat complacently that now he had successfully become one of Saul's kleptomaniacs. Heigh-ho for the compulsive life!

XV

At 811 Franz glanced at his mail (nothing worth opening right away) and then looked around the room. He'd left the transom open. Dorotea was right—a thin, athletic person could crawl through it. He shut it. Then he leaned out the open casement window and checked each way—to either side and up (one window like his, then the roof) and down (Cal's two below and, three below that, the shaft's grimy bottom, a cul-de-sac, scattered with junk fallen over the years). There was no way anyone could reach this window short of using ladders. But he noticed that his bathroom window was only a short step away from the window of the next apartment on this floor. He made sure it was locked.

Then he took off the wall the big spidery black sketch of the TV tower that was almost entirely bright fluorescent red background and securely wedged and thumbtacked it, red side out, in the open casement window, using drawing pins. There! that would show up unmistakably from Corona in the sunlight when it came.

Next he put on a light sweater under his coat (it seemed a bit chillier than yesterday) and stuck an extra pack of cigarettes in his pocket. He didn't pause to make himself a sandwich (after all, he'd had *two* pieces of toast this morning at Cal's). At the last minute he remembered to stuff his binoculars and map into his pocket, *and* Smith's journal; he might want to refer to it at Byers's. (He'd called the man up earlier and gotten a typically effusive but somewhat listless invitation to drop in any time after the middle of the afternoon and stay if he liked for the little party coming up in the evening. Some of the guests would be in costume, but costume was not mandatory.)

As a final touch he placed the 1927 city directory where his Scholar's Mistress's rump would be, and giving it a quick intimate caress, said flippantly, "There, my dear, I've made you a receiver of stolen property; but don't worry, you're going to give it back."

Then without further leavetaking, or any send-off at all, he double-locked the door behind him and was away into the wind and sunlight.

At the corner there was no bus coming, so he started to walk the eight short blocks to Market, striding briskly. At Ellis he deliberately devoted a few seconds to looking at (worshiping?) his favorite tree in San Francisco: a six-story candlestick pine, guyed by some thin strong wires, waving its green fingers over a brown wooden wall trimmed with yellow between two taller buildings in a narrow lot the high-rise moguls had somehow overlooked. Inefficient bastards!

A block farther on, the bus overtook him and he got

aboard—it would save a minute. Transferring to the N-Judah car at Market, he got a start (and had to sidestep swiftly) when a pallid drunk in a shapeless, dirty pale gray suit (but no shirt) came staggering diagonally from nowhere (and apparently bound for the same place). He thought, "There but for the grace of God, et cetera," and veered off from those thoughts, as he had at Cal's from the memories of Daisy's mortal disease.

In fact, he banished all dark stuff so well from his mind that the creaking car seemed to mount Market and then Duboce in the bright sunlight like the victorious general's chariot in a Roman triumph. (Should he be painted red and have a slave at his elbow reminding him continuously in a low voice that he was mortal?—a charming fancy!) He swung off at the tunnel's mouth and climbed dizzying Duboce, breathing deeply. It seemed not quite so steep today, or else he was fresher. (And always easier to climb up than down—if you had wind enough!—the mountaineering experts said.) The neighborhood looked particularly neat and friendly.

At the top a young couple hand in hand (lovers, quite obviously) were entering the dappling shades and green glooms of Buena Vista Park. Why had the place seemed so sinister yesterday? Some other day he'd follow in their path to the park's pleasantly wooded summit and then stroll leisurely down the other side into the festive Haight, that overrated menace! With Cal and perhaps the others—the picnic Saul'd suggested.

But today his was another voyage—he had other business. Pressing business, too. He glanced at his wristwatch and stepped along smartly, barely pausing for the fine view of the Heights' jaggedy crest from the top of Park Hill. Soon he was going through the little gate in the high wire fence and across the green field back of the brown-sloped Heights with their rocky crown. To his right, two little girls were supervising a sort of dolls' tea party on the grass. Why, they were the girls he'd seen running yesterday. And just beyond them their Saint Bernard was stretched out beside a young woman in faded blue denim, who was kneading his loose, thickly furred mane as she combed her own long blonde hair.

While to the left, two Dobermans—the same two, by God!—were stretched out and yawning beside another young couple lying close together though not embracing. As Franz smiled at them, the man smiled back and waved a casual greeting. It really was the poet's cliché, "an idyllic scene." Nothing at all like yesterday. Now Cal's suggestion about the dark psionic powers of little girls seemed quite overwrought, even if charming.

He would have lingered, but time was wasting. Got to go to Taffy's house, he thought with a chuckle. He mounted the ragged, gravelly slope—it wasn't all that steep!—with just one breather. Over his shoulder the TV tower stood tall, her colors bright, as fresh and gussied-up and elegant as a brand-new whore (Your pardon, Goddess). He felt fey.

When he got to the corona, he noticed something he hadn't yesterday. Several of the rock surfaces—at least on his side—had been scrawled on at past times with dark and pale and various colored paints from spray cans, most of it rather weathered now. There weren't so many names and dates as simple figures. Lopsided five- and six-pointed stars, a sunburst, crescents, triangles and squares. And there a rather modest phallus with a sign beside it like two parentheses joined—yoni as well as lingam. He thought of—of all things!—de Castries's Grand Cipher. Yes, he noted with a grin, there were symbols here that could be taken as astronom-and/or astrological. Those circles with crosses and arrows—Venus and Mars. While that horned disk might be Taurus.

You certainly have odd tastes in interior decoration, Taffy, he told himself. Now to check if you're stealing my marrow-bone.

Well, spray-painting signs on rocky eminences was standard practice these progressive youth-oriented days—the graffiti of the heights. Though he recalled how at the beginning of the century the black magician Aleister Crowley had spent a summer painting in huge red capitals on the Hudson Palisades DO WHAT THOU WILT IS THE ONLY COM-

MANDMENT and EVERY MAN AND WOMAN IS A STAR to shock and instruct New Yorkers on riverboats. He perversely wondered what gay sprayed graffiti would have done to the eerie rock-crowned hills in Lovecraft's "Whisperer in Darkness" and "Dunwich Horror" or "At the Mountains of Madness," where the hills were Everests, or Leiber's "A Bit of the Dark World," for that matter.

He found his stone seat of yesterday and then made himself smoke a cigarette to give himself time to steady his nerves and breathing, and relax, although he was impatient to make sure he'd kept ahead of the sun. Actually he knew he had, though by a rather slender margin. His wristwatch assured him of that.

If anything, it was clearer and sunnier than yesterday. The strong west wind was sweeping the air, making itself felt even in San Jose, which now had no visible pillow of smog over it. The distant little peaks beyond the East Bay cities and north in Marin County stood out quite sharply. The bridges were bright.

Even the sea of roofs itself seemed friendly and calm today. He found himself thinking of the incredible number of lives it sheltered, some seven hundred thousand, while a slightly larger number even than that were employed beneath those roofs—a measure of the vast companies of people brought into San Francisco each day from the metropolitan area by the bridges and the other freeways and by BART under the waters of the Bay.

With unaided eyes he located what he thought was the slot in which his window was—it was full of sun, at any rate—and then got out his binoculars. He didn't bother to string them around his neck—his grip was firm today. Yes, there was the fluorescent red, all right, seeming to fill the whole window, the scarlet stood out so, but then you could tell it just occupied the lower left-hand quarter. Why, he could almost make out the drawing . . . no, that would be too much, those thin black lines.

So much for Gun's (and his own) doubts as to whether he'd located the right window yesterday! It was funny, though, how the human mind would cast doubt even on itself in order to explain away unusual and unconventional things it had seen vividly and unmistakably. It left you in the middle, the human mind did.

But the seeing was certainly exceptionally fine today. How clearly pale yellow Coit Tower on Telegraph Hill, once Frisco's tallest structure, now a trifle, stood out against the blue Bay. And the pale blue gilded globe of Columbus Tower—a perfect antique gem against the ordered window slits of the Transamerica Pyramid that were like perforations in a punch-card. And the high rounded windows of the shipshaped old Hobart Building's stern, that was like the lofty, richly encrusted admiral's cabin of a galleon, against the stark, vertical aluminum lines of the new Wells Fargo Building towering over it like a space-to-space interstellar freighter waiting to blast. He roved the binoculars around, effortlessly refining the focus. Why, he'd been wrong about Grace Cathedral with its darkly suggestive, richly colorful modern stained glass inside. Beside the unimaginative contemporary bulk of Cathedral Apartments you could see its slim, crocketed spire stabbing up like a saw-edged stiletto that carried on its point a small gilded cross.

He took another look into his window slot before the shadow swallowed it. Perhaps he *could* see the drawing if he 'fined the focus. . . .

Even as he watched, the oblong of fluorescent cardboard was jerked out of sight. From his window there thrust itself a pale brown thing that wildly waved its long, uplifted arms at him. While low between them he could see its face stretched toward him, a mask as narrow as a ferret's, a pale brown, utterly blank triangle, two points above that might mean eyes or ears, and one ending below in a tapered chin . . . no, snout . . . no, very short trunk—*a questing mouth that looked as if it were for sucking marrow. Then the paramental entity reached through the glasses at his eyes.*

XVI

In his next instant of awareness, Franz heard a hollow *chunk*
and a faint tinkling, and he was searching the dark sea of
roofs with his naked eyes to try to locate anywhere a swift
pale brown thing stalking him across them and taking advantage of every bit of cover: a chimney and its cap, a cupola,
a water tank, a penthouse large or tiny, a thick standpipe, a
wind scoop, a ventilator hood, hood of a garbage chute, a
skylight, a roof's low walls, the low walls of an airshaft. His
heart was pounding and his breathing fast.

His frantic thoughts took another turn and he was scanning
the slopes before and beside him, and the cover their rocks
and dry bushes afforded. Who knew how fast a paramental
traveled? as a cheetah? as sound? as light? It could well be
back here on the heights already. He saw his binoculars below the rock against which he'd unintentionally hurled them
when he'd thrust out his hands convulsively to keep the thing
out of his eyes.

He scrambled to the top. From the green field below the
little girls were gone, and their chaperone and the other couple and the three animals. But even as he was noticing that,
a large dog (one of the Dobermans? or something else?) loped
across it toward him and disappeared behind a clump of rocks
at the base of the slope. He'd thought of running down that
way, but not if that dog (and what others? and what else?)
were on the prowl. There was too much cover on this side of
Corona Heights.

He stepped quickly down and stood on his stone seat and
made himself hold still and look out squintingly until he found
the slot where his window was. It was full of darkness, so
that even with his binoculars he wouldn't have been able to
see anything.

He dropped down to the path, taking advantage of hand-
holds, and while shooting rapid looks around, picked up his

broken binoculars and jammed them in his pocket, though he didn't like the way the loose glass in them tinkled a little—or the gravel grated under his careful feet, for that matter. Such small sounds could give away a person's whereabouts.

One instant of awareness couldn't change your life this much, could it? But it had.

He tried to straighten out his reality, while not letting down his guard. To begin with, there were no such things as paramental entities, they were just part of de Castries's 1890s pseudoscience. But he had *seen* one, and as Saul had said, there was no reality except an individual's immediate sensations—vision, hearing, pain, those were real. Deny your mind, deny your sensations, and you deny reality. Even to try to rationalize was to deny. But of course there were false sensations, optical and other illusions. . . . Really, now! Try telling a tiger springing upon you he's an illusion. Which left exactly hallucination and, to be sure, insanity. Parts of inner reality . . . and who was to say how far inner reality went? As Saul had also said, "Who's going to believe a crazy if he says he's just seen a ghost? Inner or outer reality? Who's to tell then?" In any case, Franz told himself, he must keep firmly in mind that he might now be crazy—without letting down his guard one bit on that account either!

All the while that he was thinking these thoughts, he was moving watchfully, carefully, and yet quite rapidly down the slope, keeping a little off the gravel path so as to make less noise, ready to leap aside if something rushed him. He kept darting glances to either side and over his shoulder, noting points of concealment and the distances to them. He got the impression that something of considerable size was following him, something that was wonderfully clever in making its swift moves from one bit of cover to the next, something of which he saw (or thought he saw) only the edges. One of the dogs? Or more than one? Perhaps urged on by rapt-faced, fleet-footed little girls. Or . . . ? He found himself picturing the dogs as spiders as furry and as big. Once in bed, her limbs and breasts pale in the dawn's first light, Cal had told him a dream in which two big borzois following her had changed into two equally large and elegant creamy-furred spiders.

What if there were an earthquake now (he must be ready for *anything*) and the brown ground opened in smoking cracks and swallowed his pursuers up? And himself, too?

He reached the foot of the crest and soon was circling past the Josephine Randall Junior Museum. His sense of being pursued grew less—or rather of being pursued at such close distance. It was good to be close to human habitations again, even if seemingly empty ones, and even though buildings were objects that things could hide behind. This was the place where they taught the boys and girls not to be afraid of rats and bats and giant tarantulas and other entities. Where were the children anyhow? Had some wise Pied Piper led them all away from this menaced locality? Or had they piled into the "Sidewalk Astronomer" panel truck and taken off for other stars? What with earthquakes and eruptions of large pale spiders and less wholesome entities, San Francisco was no longer very safe. On, you fool, watch! watch!

As he left the low building behind him and descended the hillside ramp and went past the tennis courts and finally reached the short dead-end cross street that was the boundary of Corona Heights, his nerves quieted down somewhat and his whirling thoughts, too, though he got a dreadful start when he heard from somewhere a sharp squeal of rubber on asphalt and thought for a moment the parked car at the other end of the cross street had started for him, steered by its two little tombstone headrests.

Approaching Beaver Street by way of a narrow public stairway between two buildings, he had another quick vision of a local quake behind him and of Corona Heights convulsed but intact, and then lifting up its great brown shoulders and rocky head, and shaking the Josephine Randall Junior Museum off its back, preparatory to stalking down into the city.

As he descended Beaver Street, he began to encounter people at last; not many, but a few. He remembered as if from another lifetime his intention to visit Byers (he'd even phoned) and debated whether to go through with it. He'd never been here before, his previous meetings in San Francisco with the man had been at a mutual friend's apartment in the Haight. Cal had said someone had told her it was a spooky place, but it didn't look that from the outside with its fresh olive-green paint and thin gold trim.

His mind was made up for him when an ambulance on Castro, which he'd just crossed, let loose with its yelping siren on approaching Beaver, and the foul nerve-twanging sound growing suddenly unendurably loud as the vehicle crossed Beaver, fairly catapulted Franz up the steps to the faintly gold-arabesqued olive door and set him pounding the bronze knocker that was in the shape of a merman.

He realized that the idea of going somewhere other than home appealed to him. Home was as dangerous as—perhaps more dangerous than—Corona Heights.

After a maddeningly long pause the polished brass knob turned, the door began to open, and a voice grandiloquent as that of Vincent Price at his fruitiest said, "Here's a knocking indeed. Why, it's Franz Westen. Come in, come in. But you look shaken, my dear Franz, as if that ambulance had delivered you. What have the wicked, unpredictable streets done now?"

As soon as Franz was reasonably sure that the neatly bearded, rather theatric visage was Byers's, he pressed past him, saying, "Shut the door. I *am* shaken," while he scanned the richly furnished entry and the large, glamorous room opening from it and the thickly carpeted stairs ahead going up to a landing mellow with light that had come through stained glass, and the dark hall beyond the stairs.

Behind him, Byers was saying, "All in good time. There, it's locked, and I've even thrown a bolt, if that makes you feel better. And now some wine? Fortified, your condition would seem to call for. But tell me at once if I should call a doctor, so we won't have that fretting us."

They were facing each other now. Jaime Donaldus Byers was about Franz's age, somewhere in the mid-forties, medium tall, with the easy, proud carriage of an actor. He wore a pale green Nehru jacket faintly embroidered in gold, similar trousers, leather sandals, and a long, pale violet dressing gown, open but belted with a narrow sash. His well-combed auburn hair hung to his shoulders. His Vandyke beard and narrow moustache were neatly trimmed. His palely sallow complexion, noble brow, and large liquid eyes were Elizabethan, suggesting Edmund Spenser. And he was clearly aware of all this.

Franz, whose attention was still chiefly elsewhere, said, "No, no doctor. And no alcohol, this time, Donaldus. But if I could have some coffee, black . . ."

"My dear Franz, at once. Just come with me into the living room. Everything's there. But what is it that has shaken you? What's *chasing* you?"

"I am afraid," Franz said curtly and then added quickly, "of paramentals."

"Oh, is that what they're calling the big menace these days?" Byers said lightly, but his eyes had narrowed sharply first. "I'd always thought it was the Mafia. Or the CIA? Or something from your own 'Weird Underground,' some novelty? And there's always reliable Russia. I am up to date only sporadically. I live *firmly* in the world of art, where reality and fantasy are one."

And he turned and led the way into the living room, beckoning Franz to follow. As he stepped forward, Franz became aware of a melange of scents: freshly brewed coffee, wines and liqueurs, a heavy incense and some sharper perfume. He thought fleetingly of Saul's story of the Invisible Nurse and glanced toward the stairs and back hall, now behind him.

Byers motioned Franz to select a seat, while he busied himself at a heavy table on which stood slender bottles and two small steaming silver urns. Franz recalled Peter Viereck's poetry line, "Art, like the bartender, is never drunk," and briefly recalled the years when bars had been places of refuge for him from the terrors and agonies of the outside world. But this time fear had come inside with him.

XVII

The room was furnished sybaritically, and while not specifically Arabian, held much more ornamentation than depiction. The wallpaper was of a creamy hue, on which faint gold lines made a pattern of arabesques featuring mazes. Franz chose a larger hassock that was set against a wall and from which he had an easy view of the hall, the rear archway, and the windows, whose faintly glittering curtains transmitted yellowed sunlight and blurred, dully gilded pictures of the outdoors. Silver gleamed from two black shelves beside the hassock and Franz's gaze was briefly held against his will (his fear) by a collection of small statuettes of modish young persons engaged with great hauteur in various sexual activities, chiefly perverse—the style between Art Deco and Pompeiian. Under any other circumstances he would have given them more than a passing scrutiny. They looked incredibly detailed and devilishly expensive. Byers, he knew, came of a wealthy family and produced a sizable volume of exquisite poetry and prose sketches every three or four years.

Now that fortunate person set a thin, large white cup half-filled with steaming coffee and also a steaming silver pot upon a firm low stand by Franz that additionally held an obsidian ashtray. Then he settled himself in a convenient low chair, sipped the pale yellow wine he'd brought, and said, "You said you had some questions when you phoned. About that journal you attribute to Smith and of which you sent me a photocopy."

Franz answered, his gaze still roving systematically. "That's right. I do have some questions for you. But first I've got to tell you what happened to me just now."

"Of course. By all means. I'm most eager to know."

Franz tried to condense his narrative, but soon found he couldn't do much of that without losing significance, and ended by giving a quite full and chronological account of the events of the past thirty hours. As a result, and with some help from the coffee, which he'd needed, and from his cigarettes, which he'd forgotten to smoke for nearly an hour, he began after a while to feel a considerable catharsis. His nerves settled down a great deal. He didn't find himself changing his mind about what had happened or its vital importance, but having a human companion and sympathetic listener certainly did make a great difference emotionally.

For Byers paid close attention, helping him on by little nods and eye-narrowings and pursing of lips and voiced brief agreements and comments—at least they were mostly brief. True, those last weren't so much practical as aesthetic—even a shade frivolous—but that didn't bother Franz at all, at first, he was so intent on his story; while Byers, even when frivolous, seemed deeply impressed and far more than politely credulous about all Franz told him.

When Franz briefly mentioned the bureaucratic runaround he'd gotten, Byers caught the humor at once, putting in, "Dance of the clarks, how quaint!" And when he heard about Cal's musical accomplishments, he observed, "Franz, you have a sure taste in girls. A harpsichordist! What could be more perfect? My current dear-friend-secretary-playfellow-cohousekeeper-cum-moon-goddess is North Chinese, supremely erudite, and works in precious metal—she did those deliciously vile silvers, cast by the lost-wax process of Cellini. She'd have served you your coffee except it's one of our personal days, when we recreate ourselves apart. I call her Fa Lo Suee (the Daughter of Fu Manchu—it's one of our semi-private jokes) because she gives the delightfully sinister impression of being able to take over the world if ever she chose. You'll meet her if you stay this evening. Excuse me, please go on." And when Franz mentioned the astrological graffiti on Corona Heights, he whistled softly and said, "How *very* appropriate!" with such emphasis that Franz asked him, "Why?" but he responded, "Nothing. I mean the sheer *range* of our tireless defacers. Next: a pyramid of beer cans on Shasta's mystic top. This pear wine is delightful—you should taste it—a supreme creation of the San Martin winery on Santa Clara Valley's sun-kissed slopes. Pray continue.''

But when Franz mentioned *Megapolisomancy* a third or fourth time and even quoted from it, he lifted a hand in interruption and went to a tall bookcase and unlocked it and took from behind the darkly clouded glass a thin book bound in black leather beautifully tooled with silver arabesques and handed it to Franz, who opened it.

It was a copy of de Castries's gracelessly printed book, identical with his own copy, as far as he could tell, save for the binding. He looked up questioningly.

Byers explained, ''Until this afternoon I never dreamed you owned a copy, my dear Franz. You showed me only the violet-ink journal, you'll recall, that evening in the Haight, and later sent me a photocopy of the written-on pages. You never mentioned buying another book along with it. And on that evening you were, well . . . rather tiddly.''

''In those days I was drunk all of the time,'' Franz said flatly.

''I understand . . . poor Daisy . . . say no more. The point is this: *Megapolisomancy* happens to be not only a rare book, but also, literally, a very secret one. In his last years, de Castries had a change of mind about it and tried to hunt down every single copy and burn them all. And did! Almost. He was known to have behaved vindictively toward persons who refused to yield up their copies. He was, in fact, a very nasty and, I would say (except I abhor moral judgments) evil old man. At any rate, I saw no point at the time in telling you that I possessed what I thought then to be the sole surviving copy of the book.''

Franz said, ''Thank God! I was hoping you knew something about de Castries.''

Byers said, ''I know quite a bit. But first, finish your story. You were on Corona Heights, today's visit, and had just looked through your binoculars at the Transamerica Pyramid, which made you quote de Castries on 'our modern pyramids . . .' ''

''I will,'' Franz said, and did it quite quickly, but it was the worst part; it brought vividly back to him his sight of the triangular pale brown muzzle and his flight down Corona Heights, and by the time he was done he was sweating and darting his glance about again.

Byers let out a sigh, then said with relish, "And so you came to me, pursued by paramentals to the very door!" And he turned in his chair to look somewhat dubiously at the blurry golden windows behind him.

"Donaldus!" Franz said angrily, "I'm telling you things that happened, not some damn weird tale I've made up for your entertainment. I know it all hangs on a figure I saw several times at a distance of two miles with seven-power binoculars, and so anyone's free to talk about optical illusions and instrumental defects and the power of suggestion, but I know something about psychology and optics, and it was none of those! I went pretty deeply into the flying-saucer business, and I never once saw or heard of a single UFO that was really convincing—and I've seen haloed highlights on aircraft that were oval-shaped and glowed and pulsed exactly like the ones in half the saucer sightings. But I have no doubts of that sort about what I saw today and yesterday."

But even as he was pouring that out and still uneasily checking the windows and doors and glooms himself, Franz realized that deep down inside he *was* beginning to doubt his memories of what he'd seen—perhaps the human mind was incapable of holding a fear like his for more than about an hour unless it were reinforced by repetition—but he was damned if he'd tell Donaldus so!

He finished icily, "Of course, it's quite possible I've gone insane, temporarily or permanently, and am 'seeing things,' but until I'm sure of that I'm not going to behave like a reckless idiot—or a hilarious one."

Donaldus, who had been making protesting and imploring faces at him all the while, now said injuredly and placatingly, "My *dear* Franz, I never for a moment doubted your seriousness or had the faintest suspicion that you were psychotic. Why, I've been inclined to believe in paramental entities ever since I read de Castries's book, and especially after hearing several circumstantial, very peculiar stories about him, and now your truly shocking eyewitness narrative has swept my last doubts away. But I've not seen one yet—if I did, I'm sure I'd feel all the terror you do and more—but until then, and perhaps in any case, and despite the proper horror they evoke in us, they are most *fascinating* entities, don't you agree? Now as for thinking your account a tale or story, my dear Franz, to be a good story is to me the highest test of the truth of anything. I make no distinction whatever between reality and fantasy, or the objective and the subjective. All life and all awareness are ultimately one, including intensest pain and death itself. Not all the play need please us, and ends are never comforting. Some things fit together harmoniously and beautifully and startlingly with thrilling discords—those are true—and some do not, and those are merely bad art. Don't you see?''

Franz had no immediate comment. He certainly hadn't given de Castries's book the least credence by itself, but . . . He nodded thoughtfully, though hardly in answer to the question. He wished for the sharp minds of Gun and Saul . . . and Cal.

"And now to tell you *my* story," Donaldus said, quite satisfied. "But first a touch of brandy—that seems called for. And you? Well, some hot coffee then, I'll fetch it. And a few biscuits? Yes."

Franz had begun to feel headachy and slightly nauseated. The plain arrowroot cookies, barely sweet, seemed to help. He poured himself coffee from the fresh pot, adding some of the cream and sugar his host had thoughtfully brought this time. It helped, too. He didn't relax his watchfulness, but he began to feel more comfortable in it, as if the awareness of danger were becoming a way of life.

XVIII

Donaldus lifted a finger with a ring of silver filigree on it and said, "You have to keep in mind de Castries died when I (and you) were infants. Almost all my information comes from a couple of the not-so-close and hardly well-beloved friends of de Castries's last declining years: George Ricker, who was a locksmith and played *go* with him, and Herman Klaas, who ran a secondhand bookstore on Turk Street and was a sort of romantic anarchist and for a while a Technocrat. And a bit from Clark Ashton Smith. Ah, that interests you, doesn't it? It was only a bit—Clark didn't like to talk about de Castries. I think it was because of de Castries and his theories that Clark stayed away from big cities, even San Francisco, and became the hermit of Auburn and Pacific Grove. And I've got some data from old letters and clippings, but not much. People didn't like to write down things about de Castries, and they had reasons, and in the end the man himself made secrecy a way of life. Which is odd, considering that he began his chief career by writing and publishing a sensational book. Incidentally, I got my copy from Klaas when he died, and he may have found it among de Castries's things after de Castries died—I was never sure.

"Also," Donaldus continued, "I'll probably tell the story—at least in spots—in a somewhat poetic style. Don't let that put you off. It merely helps me organize my thoughts and select the significant items. I won't be straying in the least from the strict truth as I've discovered it; though there may be traces of paramentals in my story, I suppose, and certainly one ghost. I think all modern cities, especially the crass, newly built, highly industrial ones, should have ghosts. They are a civilizing influence."

XIX

Donaldus took a generous sip of brandy, rolled it around on his tongue appreciatively, and settled back in his chair.

"In 1900, as the century turned," he began dramatically, "Thibaut de Castries came to sunny, lusty San Francisco like a dark portent from realms of cold and coal smoke in the

East that pulsed with Edison's electricity and from which thrust Sullivan's steel-framed skyscrapers. Madame Curie had just proclaimed radioactivity to the world, and Marconi radio spanning the seas. Madame Blavatsky had brought eerie theosophy from the Himalayas and passed on the occult torch to Annie Besant. The Scottish Astronomer-Royal Piazzi Smith had discovered the history of the world and its ominous future in the Grand Gallery of the Great Pyramid of Egypt. While in the law courts, Mary Baker Eddy and her chief female acolytes were hurling accusations of witchcraft and black magic at each other. Spencer preached science. Ingersoll thundered against superstition. Freud and Jung were plunging into the limitless dark of the subconscious. Wonders undreamed had been unveiled at the Universal Exhibition in Paris, for which the Eiffel tower had been built, and the World's Columbian Exposition in Chicago. New York was digging her subways. In South Africa the Boers were firing at the British Krupp's field guns of unburstable steel. In far Cathay the Boxers raged, deeming themselves invulnerable to bullets by their magic. Count von Zeppelin was launching his first dirigible airship, while the Wright Brothers were readying for their first flight.

"De Castries brought with him only a large black Gladstone bag stuffed with copies of his ill-printed book that he could no more sell than Melville his *Moby Dick*, and a skull teeming with galvanic, darkly illuminating ideas, and (some insist) a large black panther on a leash of German silver links. And, according to still others, he was also accompanied or else pursued by a mysterious, tall, slender woman who always wore a black veil and loose dark dresses that were more like robes, and had a way of appearing and disappearing suddenly. In any case, de Castries was a wiry, tireless, rather small black eagle of a man, with piercing eyes and sardonic mouth, who wore his glamour like an opera cape.

"There were a dozen legends of his origins. Some said he improvised a new one each night, and some that they were all invented by others solely on the inspiration of his darkly magnetic appearance. The one that Klaas and Ricker most favored was moderately spectacular: that as a boy of thirteen during the Franco-Prussian War he had escaped from be-sieged Paris by hydrogen balloon along with his mortally wounded father, who was an explorer of darkest Africa; his father's beautiful and learned young Polish mistress; and a black panther (an earlier one) which his father had originally captured in the Congo and which they had just rescued from the zoological gardens, where the starving Parisians were slaughtering the wild animals for food. (Of course, another legend had it that at that time he was a boy aide-de-camp to Garibaldi in Sicily and his father the most darkly feared of the Carbonari.)

"Rapidly travelling southeast across the Mediterranean, the balloon encountered at midnight an electrical tempest which added to its velocity but also forced it down nearer and nearer to the white-fanged waves. Picture the scene as revealed by almost continuous lightning flashes in the frail and over-weighted gondola. The panther crouched back into one side, snarling and spitting, lashing his tail, his claws dug deeply into the wickerwork with a strength that threatened to rend it. The faces of the dying father (an old hawk), the earnest and flashing-eyed boy (already a young eagle), and the proud, intellectual, fiercely loyal, brooding girl—all of them desper-ate and pale as death in the lightning's bluish glare. While thunder resounded deafeningly, as if the black atmosphere were being ripped, or great artillery pieces let off at their ears. Suddenly the rain tasted salt on their wet lips—spray from the hungry waves.

"The dying father grasped the right hands of the two oth-ers, joined them together, gripped them briefly with his own, gasped a few words (they were lost in the gale) and with a final convulsive burst of strength hurled himself overboard.

"The balloon leaped upward out of the storm and raced on southeast. The chilled, terrorized, but undaunted young people huddled together in each other's arms. From across the gondola the black panther, subsiding, stared at them with enigmatic green eyes. While in the southeast, toward which they were speeding, the horned moon appeared above the clouds, like the witch-crown of the Queen of Night, setting her seal upon the scene.

"The balloon landing in the Egyptian desert near Cairo, young de Castries plunged at once into a study of the Great Pyramid, assisted by his father's young Polish mistress (now his own), and by the fact that he was maternally descended from Champollion, decipherer of the Rosetta Stone. He made all Piazzi Smith's discoveries (and a few more besides, which he kept secret) ten years in advance and laid the basis for his new science of supercities (and also his Grand Cipher) before leaving Egypt to investigate mega-structures and crypto-glyphics (he called it) and paramentality throughout the world.

"You know, that link with Egypt fascinates me," Byers said parenthetically as he poured himself more brandy. "It makes me think of Lovecraft's Nyarlathotep, who came out of Egypt to deliver pseudoscientific lectures heralding the crumbling away of the world."

Mention of Lovecraft reminded Franz of something. He interjected, "Say, didn't Lovecraft have a revision client with a name like Thibaut de Castries?"

Byers's eyes widened. "He did indeed. Adolphe De Castro."

"That much alike! You don't suppose . . . ?"

". . . that they were the same person?" Byers smiled. "The possibility has occurred to me, my dear Franz, and there is this additionally to be said for the idea: that Lovecraft variously referred to Adolphe De Castro as 'an amiable charlatan' and 'an unctuous old hypocrite' (he paid Lovecraft for rewriting them completely less than one-tenth of the price he got for his stories), but no"—he sighed, fading his smile—"no, De Castro was still alive pestering Lovecraft and visiting him in Providence after de Castries's death.

"To resume about de Castries; we don't know if his young Polish mistress accompanied him and possibly was the mysterious veiled lady who some said turned up at the same time he did in San Francisco. Ricker thought so. Klaas was inclined to doubt it. Ricker tended to romance about the Pole. He pictured her as a brilliant pianist (they're apt to say that about most Poles, aren't they? Chopin has much to answer for) who had totally suppressed that talent in order to put all her amazing command of languages and her profound secretarial skills—and all the solaces of her fierce young body—at the disposal and in the service of the still younger genius whom she adored even more devotedly than she had his adventurer father.''

''What was her name?'' Franz asked.

''I could never learn,'' Byers replied. ''Either Klaas and Ricker had forgotten, or else—more likely—it was one of the points on which the old boy went secretive on them. Besides, there's something so satisfying about just that one phrase 'his father's young Polish mistress'—what could be more exotic or alluring?—it makes one think of harpsichords and oceans of lace, champagne, and pistols! For, under her cool and learned mask, she seethed with temperament and with temper, too, as Ricker pictured her; so that she'd almost seem to fly apart or on the verge of it when in her rages, like an explosive rag doll. The fellahin feared her, thought she was a witch. It was during those years in Egypt that she began to go veiled, Ricker said.

''At still other times she'd be incredibly seductive, the epitome of Continental femininity, initiating de Castries into the most voluptuous erotic practices and greatly deepening and broadening his grasp of culture and art.

''At all events, de Castries had acquired a lot of dark, satanic charm from somewhere by the time he arrived at the City by the Golden Gate. He was, I'd guess, quite a bit like the Satanist Anton La Vey (who kept a more-or-less tame lion for a while, did you know?), except that he had no desire for the usual sort of publicity. He was looking, rather, for an elite of scintillating, freewheeling folk with a zest for life at its wildest—and if they had a lot of money, that wouldn't hurt a bit.

''And of course he found them! Promethean (and Dionysian) Jack London. George Sterling, fantasy poet and romantic idol, favorite of the wealthy Bohemian Club set. Their friend, the brilliant defense attorney Earl Rogers, who later defended Clarence Darrow and saved his career. Ambrose Bierce, a bitter, becaped old eagle of a man himself with his *Devil's Dictionary* and matchlessly tense horror tales. The poetess Nora May French. That mountain lioness of a woman, Charmian London. Gertrude Atherton, somewhere close by. And those were only the more vital ones.

"And of course they fell upon de Castries with delight. He was just the sort of human curiosity they (and especially Jack London) loved. Mysterious cosmopolitan background, Munchausen anecdotes, weird and alarming scientific theories, a strong anti-industrial and (we'd say) antiestablishment bias, the apocalyptic touch, the note of doom, hints of dark powers—he had them all! For quite a while he was their darling, their favorite guru of the left-hand path, almost (and I imagine he thought this himself) their new god. They even bought copies of his new book and sat still (and drank) while he read from it. Prize egotists like Bierce put up with him, and London let him have stage center for a while—he could afford to. And they were all quite ready to go along (in theory) with his dream of a utopia in which megapolitan buildings were forbidden (had been destroyed or somehow tamed) and paramentality put to benign use, with themselves the aristocratic elite and he the master spirit over all.

"Of course most of the ladies were quite taken with him romantically and several, I gather, eager to go to bed with him and not above taking the initiative in the matter—these were dramatic and liberated females for their day, remember—and yet there's no evidence that he had an affair with any one of them. The opposite, rather. Apparently, when things got to that point, he'd say something like, 'My dear, there's nothing I'd like better, truly, but I must tell you that I have a very savage and jealous mistress who if I so much as dallied with you, would cut my throat in bed or stab me in my bath (he *was* quite a bit like Marat, you know, Franz, and grew to be more so in his later years), besides dashing acid across your lovely cheeks and lips, my dear, or driving a hatpin into those bewitching eyes. She's learned beyond measure in the weird, yet a tigress.'

"He'd really build this (imaginary?) creature up to them, I'm told, until sometimes it wasn't clear whether it was a real woman, or a goddess, or some sort of metaphorical entity that he was talking about. 'She is all merciless night animal,' he would say, 'yet with a wisdom that goes back to Egypt and beyond—and which is invaluable to me. For she is my spy on buildings, you see, my intelligencer on metropolitan megastructures. She knows their secrets and their secret weaknesses, their ponderous rhythms and dark songs. And she herself is secret as their shadows. She is my Queen of Night, Our Lady of Darkness.' "

As Byers dramatized those last words of de Castries, Franz flashed that Our Lady of Darkness was one of De Quincey's Ladies of Sorrow, the third and youngest sister, who always went veiled in black crape. Had de Castries known that? And was his Queen of Night Mozart's?—all-powerful save for the magic flute and Papageno's bells? But Byers continued:

"For you see, Franz, there were these continuing reports, flouted by some, of de Castries being visited or pestered by a veiled lady who wore flowing dresses and either a turban or a wide floppy-brimmed hat, yet was very swift in her movements. They'd be glimpsed together across a busy street or on the Embarcadero or in a park or at the other end of a crowded theater lobby, generally walking rapidly and gesticulating excitedly or angrily at each other; but when you caught up with him, she would be gone. Or if, as on a few claimed occasions, she were still there, he would never introduce her or speak to her or act in any way as if he knew her. Except he would seem irritable and—one or two said—frightened."

"What was *her* name?" Franz pressed.

Byers quirked a smile. "As I just told you, my dear Franz, he'd never introduce her. At most he'd refer to her as 'that woman' or sometimes, oddly, 'that headstrong and pestiferous girl.' Perhaps, despite all his dark charms and tyrannies and S-M aura, he was afraid of women and she somehow stood for or embodied that fear.

"Reactions to this mysterious figure varied. The men tended to be indulgent, intrigued, and speculative, even

wildly so—it was suggested at various times that she was
Isadora Duncan, Eleanora Duse, and Sarah Bernhardt, though
they would have been, respectively, about twenty, forty, and
sixty at that time. But true glamour is ageless, they say; consider
Marlene Dietrich, Louise Brooks, or Arletty, or that doyenne
of them all—Cleopatra. There was always the disguising black
veil, you see, though sometimes it carried an array of black
polka dots, like ranked beauty marks, 'or as if she'd had the
black smallpox,' one lady is said to have said nastily.

"All the women, for that matter, uniformly loathed her.

"Of course, all this is probably somewhat distorted by my
getting it mostly as filtered through Klaas and Ricker. Ricker,
making a lot of the references to Egyptian wisdom and
learnedness, thought the mystery lady was still the Polish
mistress, gone mad through love, and he was somewhat critical of de Castries for his treatment of her.

"And of course all this left the way open for endless speculations about de Castries's sex life. Some said he was a
homosexual. Even in those days 'the cool, gray city of
love,' as Sterling epitomized it, had its homophiles—'cool,
gay city?' Others, that he was very kinky in an S-M way—
bondage and discipline of the direst sort. (Quite a few chaps
have accidentally strangled themselves that way, you know.)
Almost in one breath it was said he was a pederast, a pervert,
a fetishist, utterly asexual, or else that only slim little girls
could satisfy his Tiberian lusts—I'm sorry if I offend you,
Franz, but truly all the lefthand paths and their typical guides
or conductresses were mentioned.

"However, all this is really by-the-by. The important consideration is that for a while de Castries seemed to have his
chosen group just where he wanted them."

XX

Donaldus continued. "The high point of Thibaut de Castries's San Francisco adventure came when with much hush-

hush and weedings out and secret messages and some rare private occult pomps and ceremonies, I suppose, he organized the Hermetic Order—''

''Is that the Hermetic Order that Smith, or the journal, mentions?'' Franz interrupted. He had been listening with a mixture of fascination, irritation, and wry amusement, with at least half his attention clearly elsewhere, but he had grown more attentive at mention of the Grand Cipher.

''It is,'' Byers nodded, ''I'll explain. In England at that time there was the Hermetic Order of the Golden Dawn, an occult society with members like the mystic poet Yeats, who talked with vegetables and bees and lakes, and Dion Fortune and George Russell—A.E.—and your beloved Arthur Machen—you know, Franz, I've always thought that in his *The Great God Pan* the sexually sinister *femme fatale* Helen Vaughan was based on the real-life Satanist Diana Vaughan, even though *her* memoirs—and perhaps she herself—were a hoax perpetrated by the French journalist, Gabriel Jogand . . .''

Franz nodded impatiently, restraining his impulse to say, ''Get on with it, Donaldus!''

The other got the point. ''Well, anyhow,'' he continued, ''in 1898 Aleister Crowley managed to join the Gilded Dayspringers (neat, eh?) and almost broke up the society by his demands for Satanistic rituals, black magic, and other real tough stuff.

''In imitation, but also as a sardonic challenge, de Castries called *his* society the Hermetic Order of the Onyx Dusk. He is said to have worn a large black ring of *pietra dura* work with a bezel of mosaicked onyx, obsidian, ebony, and black opal polished flat, depicting a predatory black bird, perhaps a raven.

''It was at this point that things began to go wrong for de Castries and that the atmosphere became, by degrees, very nasty. Unfortunately, it's also the period for which I've had the most difficulty getting information that's at all reliable—or even any information at all, for reasons which are, or will become, very obvious.

''As nearly as I can reconstruct it, this is what happened.

As soon as his secret society had been constituted, Thibaut revealed to its double handful of highly select members that his utopia was not a far-off dream, but an immediate prospect, and that it was to be achieved by violent revolution, both material and spiritual (that is, paramental) and the chief and at first the sole instrument of that revolution was to be the Hermetic Order of the Onyx Dusk.

"This violent revolution was to begin with acts of terrorism somewhat resembling those the Nihilists were carrying out in Russia at that time (just before the abortive Revolution of 1905), but with a lot of a new sort of black magic (his megapolisomancy) thrown in. Demoralization rather than slaughter was to be the aim, at least at first. Black-powder bombs were to be set off in public places and on the roofs of big buildings during the deserted hours of the night. Other big buildings were to be plunged into darkness by locating and throwing their main switches. Anonymous letters and phone calls would heighten the hysteria.

"But more important would be the megapolisomantic operations, which would cause 'buildings to crumple to rubble, people to go screaming mad, until every last soul is in panic flight from San Francisco, choking the roads and foundering the ferries'—at least that's what Klaas said de Castries confided to him many years later while in a rare communicative mood. Say, Franz, did you know that Nicola Tesla, America's other electrical wizard, claimed in his last years to have invented or at least envisaged a device small enough to be smuggled into a building in a dispatch case and left there to shake the building to pieces at a preset time by sympathetic vibrations? Herman Klaas told me that too. But I digress.

"These magical or pseudoscientific acts (which would you call them?) would require absolute obedience on the part of Thibaut's assistants—which was the next demand Thibaut seems to have made on every last one of his acolytes in the Hermetic Order of the Onyx Dusk. One of them would be ordered to go to a specific address in San Francisco at a specified time and simply stand there for two hours, blanking his (or her) mind, or else trying to hold one thought. Or he'd be directed to take a bar of copper or a small box of coal or a toy balloon filled with hydrogen to a certain floor in a certain big building and simply leave it there (the balloon against the ceiling), again at a specified time. Apparently the elements were supposed to act as catalysts. Or two or three of them would be commanded to meet in a certain hotel lobby or at a certain park bench and just sit there together without speaking for half an hour. And everyone would be expected to obey every order unquestioningly and unhesitatingly, in exact detail, or else there would be (I suppose) various chilling Carbonari-style penalties and reprisals.

"Big buildings were always the main targets of his megapolisomancy—he claimed they were the chief concentration-points for city-stuff that poisoned great metropolises or weighed them down intolerably. Ten years earlier, according to one story, he had joined other Parisians in opposing the erection of the Eiffel Tower. A professor of mathematics had calculated that the structure would collapse when it reached the height of seven hundred feet, but Thibaut had simply claimed that all that naked steel looking down upon the city from the sky would drive Paris mad. (And considering subsequent events, Franz, I've sometimes thought that a case could be made out that it did just that. World Wars One and Two brought on like locust plagues by overly concentrated populations due to a rash or fever of high buildings—is that so fabulous?) But since he had found he couldn't stop the erection of such buildings, Thibaut had turned to the problem of their control. In some ways, you know, he had the mentality of an animal trainer—inherited from his Africa-traveled father, perhaps?

"Thibaut seems to have thought that there was—or that he had invented—a kind of mathematics whereby minds and big buildings (and paramental entities?) could be manipulated. Neo-Pythagorean metageometry, he called it. It was all a question of knowing the right times and *spots* (he'd quote Archimedes: 'Give me a place to stand and I will move the world') and then conveying there the right person (and mind) or material object. He also seemed to have believed that a limited clairvoyance and clairaudience and prescience existed at certain *places* in mega-cities for certain people. Once he started to outline in detail to Klaas a single act of megapolisomancy—give him the formula for it, so to speak—but then he got suspicious.

"Though there *is* one other anecdote about the megamagic thing, I'm inclined to doubt its authenticity, but it *is* attractive. It seems that Thibaut proposed to give a warning shake to the Hobart Building, or at any rate one of those early flatiron structures on Market—whether it would actually fall down would depend on the integrity of the builder, the old boy's supposed to have said. In this case his four volunteers or conscripts were (improbably?) Jack London, George Sterling, an octoroon ragtime singer named Olive Church, who was a protégée of that old voodoo queen, etcetera, Mammy Pleasant, and a man named Fenner.

"You know Lotta's Fountain there on Market?—gift to the city of Lotta Crabtree, 'the toast of the goldfields,' who was taught dancing (and related arts?) by Lola Montez (she of the spider dance and Ludwig of Bavaria and all). Well, the four acolytes were supposed to approach the fountain by streets that would trace the four arms of a counterclockwise swastika centering on the fountain while concentrating in their mind on the four points of the compass and bearing objects representing the four elements—Olive a potted lily for earth, Fenner a magnum of champagne for fluid, Sterling a rather large toy hydrogen-filled balloon for the gaseous, and Jack a long cigar for fire.

"They were supposed to arrive simultaneously and introduce their burdens into the fountain, George bubbling his hydrogen through its water and Jack extinguishing his cigar in the same.

"Olive and Fenner arrived first, Fenner somewhat drunk—perhaps he had been sampling his offering and we may assume that all four of them were at least somewhat 'elevated.' Well, apparently Fenner had been nursing a lech for Olive and she'd been turning him down, and now he wanted her to drink champagne with him and she wouldn't and he tried to force it on her and succeeded in sloshing it over her bosom *and* the potted lily she was holding and down her dress.

"While they were struggling that way at the fountain's edge, George came up protesting and tried to control Fenner without letting go of his balloon, with Olive shrieking and laughing at them while they were scuffling and while she still hugged the potted lily to her wet breasts.

"At this point Jack came up behind them, drunkest of all, and getting an irresistible inspiration thrust out his cigar at arm's length and touched off the balloon with its glowing tip.

"There was quite a loud, flaming explosion. Eyebrows were singed. Fenner, who thought Sterling had shot him, fell flat on his back in the fountain, letting go the magnum, which shattered on the sidewalk. Olive dropped her pot and went into hysterics. George was livid with fury at Jack, who was laughing like a demented god—while Thibaut was doubtless cursing them blackly from the sidelines somewhere.

"The next day they all discovered that almost exactly at the same time that night a small brick warehouse behind Rincon Hill had collapsed into a pile of masonry. Age and structural inadequacy were given as the causes, but of course Thibaut claimed it was his mega-magic misfiring because of their general frivolousness and Jack's idiot prank.

"I don't know if there's any truth to that whole story—at best probably distorted in the telling for comedy's sake. Still, it does give an idea, a sort of atmosphere at least.

"Well, in any case you can imagine how those prima donnas that he'd recruited reacted to Thibaut's demands. Conceivably Jack London and George Sterling might have gone through with things like the light-switch business for a lark, if they'd been drunk enough when Thibaut asked them. And even crotchety old Bierce might have enjoyed a little black-powder thunder, if someone else did all the work and set it off. But when he asked them to do *boring* things he wouldn't explain, it was too much. A dashing and eccentric society lady who was a great beauty (and an acolyte) is supposed to have said, "If only he'd asked me to do something *challenging*, such as seduce President Roosevelt (she'd have meant

Teddy, Franz) or appear naked in the rotunda of the City of Paris and then swim out to the Seal Rocks and chain myself to them like Andromeda. But just to stand in front of the public library with seven rather large steel ball bearings in my brassiere, thinking of the South Pole and saying nothing for an hour and twenty minutes—I *ask* you, darling!''

''When it got down to cases, you see, they must simply have refused to take him seriously—either his revolution or his new black magic. Jack London was a Marxist socialist from way back and had written his way through a violent class war in his science-fiction novel *The Iron Heel*. He could and would have poked holes in both the theory and the practice of Thibaut's Reign of Terror. And he'd have known that the first city to elect a Union Labor Party government was hardly the place to start a counterrevolution. He also was a Darwinian materialist and knew his science. He'd have been able to show up Thibaut's 'new black science' as a pseudo-scientific travesty and just another name for magic, with all the unexplained action at a distance.

''At any rate, they all refused to help him make even a test-run of his mega-magic. Or perhaps a few of them went along with it once or twice—the Lotta's Fountain sort of thing—and nothing happened.

''I suppose that at this point he lost his temper and began to thunder orders and invoke penalties. And they just laughed at him—and when he wouldn't see that the game was over and kept up with it, simply walked away from him.

''Or taken more active measures. I can imagine someone like London simply picking up the furious, spluttering little man by his coat collar and the seat of his pants and pitching him out.''

Byers's eyebrows lifted. ''Which reminds me, Franz, that Lovecraft's client De Castro knew Ambrose Bierce and claimed to have collaborated with him, but at their last meeting Bierce sped De Castro's departure by breaking a walking stick over his head. Really quite similar to what I was hy-pothesizing for de Castries. Such an attractive theory—that they were the same! But no, for De Castro was at Lovecraft to rewrite his memoirs of Bierce after de Castries's death.''

He sighed, then recovered swiftly with, "At any rate, something like that could have completed the transformation of Thibaut de Castries from a fascinating freak whom one humored into an unpleasant old bore, troublemaker, borrower, *and blackmailer*, against whom one protected oneself by whatever measures were necessary. Yes, Franz, there's the persistent rumor that he tried to and in some cases did blackmail his former disciples by threatening to reveal scandals he had learned about in the days when they were free with each other, or simply that they had been members of a terrorist organization—his own! Twice at this time he seems to have disappeared completely for several months, very likely because he was serving jail sentences—something several of his ex-acolytes were powerful enough to have managed easily, though I've never been able to track down an instance; so many records were destroyed in the quake.

"But some of the old dark glamour must have lingered about him for quite a while in the eyes of his ex-acolytes—the feeling that he was a being with sinister, paranatural powers—for when the earthquake did come very early in the morning of April eighteenth, 1906, thundering up Market in brick and concrete waves from the west and killing its hundreds, one of his lapsed acolytes, probably recalling his intimations of a magic that would topple skyscrapers, is supposed to have said, 'He's done it! The old devil's done it!'

"And there's the suggestion that Thibaut tried to use the earthquake in his blackmailing—you know, 'I've done it once. I can do it again.' Apparently he'd use anything that occurred to him to try to frighten people. In a couple of instances he's supposed to have threatened people with his Queen of Night, his Lady of Darkness (his old mystery lady or girl)—that if they didn't fork up, he'd send his Black Tigress after them.

"But mostly my information for this period is very sketchy and one-sided. The people who'd known him best were all trying to forget him (suppress him, you might say), while my two chief informants, Klaas and Ricker, knew him only as an old man in the 1920s and had heard only his side (or sides!) of the story. Ricker, who was nonpolitical, thought of him as a great scholar and metaphysician, who had been promised money and support by a group of wealthy, frivolous people and then cruelly disappointed, abandoned. He never seriously believed the revolution part. Klaas did, and viewed de Castries as a failed great rebel, a modern John Brown or Sam Adams or Marat, who'd been betrayed by wealthy, pseudoartistic, thrill-seeking backers who'd then gotten cold feet. They both indignantly rejected the blackmail stories.''

Franz interposed, ''What about his mystery lady—was she still around? What did Klaas and Ricker have to say about her?''

Byers shook his head. ''She was completely vanished by the 1920s—if she ever had any real existence in the first place. To Ricker and Klaas she was just one more story—one more of the endlessly fascinating stories they teased out of the old man from time to time. Or else (not so fascinating!) endured in repetition. According to them, he enjoyed no female society whatever while they knew him. Except Klaas once let slip the thought the old man occasionally hired a prostitute—refused to talk about it further when I pressed him, said it was the old man's business, no one else's. While Ricker said the old boy had a sentimental interest in ('a soft spot in his heart for') little girls—all most innocent, a modern Lewis Carroll, he insisted. Both of them vehemently denied any suggestion of a kinky sex life on the old man's part, just as they had denied the blackmail stories and the even nastier rumors that came later on: that de Castries was devoting his declining years to getting revenge on his betrayers by somehow doing them to death or suicide by black magic.''

''I know about some of those cases,'' Franz said, ''at least the ones I imagine you're going to mention. What happened to Nora May French?''

''She was the first to go. In 1907, just a year after the quake. A clear case of suicide. She died most painfully by poison—very tragic.''

"And when did Sterling die?"

"November seventeenth, 1926."

Franz said thoughtfully, though still not lost in thought, "There certainly seems to have been a suicidal drive at work, though operating over a period of twenty years. A good case can be made out that it was a death wish drove Bierce to go to Mexico when he did—a war-haunted life, so why not such a death?—and probably attach himself to Pancho Villa's rebels as a sort of unofficial revolution-correspondent and most likely get himself shot as an uppity old gringo who wouldn't stay silent for the devil himself. While Sterling was known to have carried a vial of cyanide in his vest pocket for years, whether he finally took it by accident (pretty far-fetched) or by intention. And then there was that time (Rogers's daughter tells about it in her book) when Jack London disappeared on a five-day spree and then came home when Charmian and Rogers's daughter and several other worried people were gathered, and with the mischievous, icy logic of a man who'd drunk himself sober, challenged George Sterling and Rogers *not to sit up with the corpse*. Though I'd think alcohol was enough villain there, without bringing in any of de Castries's black magic, or its power of suggestion."

"What'd London mean by that?" Byers asked, squinting as he carefully measured out for himself more brandy.

"That when they felt life losing its zest, their powers starting to fail, they take the Noseless One by the arm without waiting to be asked, and exit laughing."

"The Noseless One?"

"Why, simply, London's sobriquet for Death himself—the skull beneath the skin. The nose is all cartilage and so the skull—"

Byers's eyes widened and he suddenly shot a finger toward his guest.

"Franz!" he asked excitedly. "That paramental you saw—wasn't it noseless?"

As if he'd just received a posthypnotic command, Franz's eyes shut tight, he jerked back his face a little, and started to throw his hands in front of it. Byers's words had brought the pale brown, blank, triangular muzzle vividly back to his mind's eye.

"Don't"—he said carefully—"say things like that again without warning. Yes, it was noseless."

"My dear Franz, I will not. Please excuse me. I did not fully realize until now what effect the sight of it must have upon a person."

"All right, all right," Franz said quietly. "So four acolytes died somewhat ahead of their time (except perhaps for Bierce), victims of their rampant psyches . . . or of something else."

"And at least an equal number of less prominent acolytes," Byers took up again quite smoothly. "You know, Franz, I've always been impressed by how in London's last great novel, *The Star Rover*, mind triumphs completely over matter. By frightfully intense self-discipline, a lifer at San Quentin is enabled to escape in spirit through the thick walls of his prison house and move at will through the world and relive his past reincarnations, redie his deaths. Somehow that makes me think of old de Castries in the 1920s, living alone in downtown cheap hotels and brooding, brooding, brooding about past hopes and glories and disasters. And (dreaming meanwhile of foul, unending tortures) about the wrongs done him and about revenge (whether or not he actually worked something there) and about . . . who knows what else? Sending his mind upon . . . who knows what journeys?"

XXI

"And now," Byers said, dropping his voice, "I must tell you of Thibaut de Castries's last acolyte and final end. Remember that during this period we must picture him as a bent old man, taciturn most of the time, always depressed, and getting paranoid. For instance, now, he had a thing about never touching metal surfaces and fixtures, because his enemies were trying to electrocute him. Sometimes he was afraid they were poisoning his tap water in the pipes. He seldom would go out, for fear a car would jump the curb and get him, and he was no longer spry enough to dodge, or an enemy would shatter his skull with a brick or tile dropped from a high roof. At the same time he was frequently changing his hotel, to throw them off his trail. Now his only contacts with former associates were his dogged attempts to get back and burn all copies of his book, though there may still have been some blackmailing and plain begging. Ricker and Klaas witnessed one such book burning. Grotesque affair!—he burned two copies in his bathtub. They remembered opening the windows and fanning out the smoke. With one or two exceptions, they were his only visitors—lonely and eccentric types themselves, and already failed men like himself although they were only in their thirties at the time.

"Then Clark Ashton Smith came—the same age, but brimming with poetry and imagination and creative energy. Clark had been hard hit by George Sterling's nasty death and had felt driven to look up such friends and acquaintances of his poetic mentor as he could find. De Castries felt old fires stir. Here was another of the brilliant, vital ones he'd always sought. He was tempted (finally yielding entirely) to exert his formidable charm for a last time, to tell his fabulous tales, to expound compellingly his eerie theories, and to weave his spells.

"And Clark Ashton, a lover of the weird and of its beauty, highly intelligent, yet in some ways still a naive small-town youth, emotionally turbulent, made a most gratifying audience. For several weeks Clark delayed his return to Auburn, fearfully reveling in the ominous, wonder-shot, strangely *real* world that old Tiberius, the scarecrow emperor of terror and mysteries, painted for him afresh each day—a San Francisco of spectral though rock-solid megabuildings and invisible paramental entities more real than life. It's easy to see why the Tiberius metaphor caught Clark's fancy. At one point he wrote—hold on for a moment, Franz, while I get that photocopy—"

"There's no need," Franz said, dragging the journal itself

out of his side pocket. The binoculars came out with it and dropped to the thickly carpeted floor with a shivery little clash of the broken glass inside.

Byers's eyes followed them with morbid curiosity. "So those are the glasses that (Take warning, Franz!) several times saw a paramental entity and were in the end destroyed by it." His gaze shifted to the journal. "Franz, you sly dog! You came prepared for at least part of this discussion before you ever went to Corona Heights today!"

Franz picked up the binoculars and put them on the low table beside his overflowing ashtray, meanwhile glancing rapidly around the room and at its windows, where the gold had darkened a little. He said quietly, "It seems to me, Donaldus, you've been holding out, too. You take for granted now that Smith wrote the journal, but in the Haight and even in the letters we exchanged afterwards, you said you were uncertain."

"You've got me," Byers admitted with a rather odd little smile, perhaps ashamed. "But it really seemed *wise*, Franz, to let as few people in on it as possible. Now of course you know as much as I do, or will in a few minutes, but . . . The most camp of clichés is 'There are some things man was not meant to know,' but there are times when I believe it really applies to Thibaut de Castries and the paranatural. Might I see the journal?"

Franz flipped it across. Byers caught it as if it were made of eggshell, and with an aggrieved look at his guest carefully opened it and as carefully turned a couple of pages. "Yes, here it is. 'Three hours today at 607 Rhodes. What a locus for genius! How prosaick?—as Howard would spell it. And yet Tiberius is Tiberius indeed, miserly doling out his dark Thrasyllus-secrets in this canyoned, cavernous Capri called San Francisco to his frightened young heir (God, no! Not I!) Caligula. And wondering how soon I, too, will go mad.'"

As he finished reading aloud, Byers began to turn the next pages, one at a time, and kept it up even when he came to the blank ones. Now and then he'd took up at Franz, but he examined each page minutely with fingers and eyes before he turned it.

He said conversationally, "Clark did think of San Francisco as a modern Rome, you know, both cities with their seven hills. From Auburn he'd seen George Sterling and the rest living as if all life were a Roman holiday. With Carmel perhaps analogous to Capri, which was simply Tiberius's Little Rome, for the more advanced fun and games. Fishermen brought fresh-caught lobsters to the goatish old emperor; Sterling dove for giant abalone with his knife. Of course, Rhodes was the Capri of Tiberius's early middle years. No, I can see why Clark would not have wanted to be Caligula. 'Art, like the bartender, is never drunk'—or really schiz. Hello, what's this?"

His fingernails were gently teasing at the edge of a page. "It's clear you're not a bibliophile, dear Franz. I should have gone ahead and stolen the book from you that evening in the Haight, as at one point I fully intended to, except that something gallant in your drunken manner touched my conscience, which is *never* a good guide to follow. There!"

With the ghostliest of cracklings the page came apart into two, revealing writing hidden between.

He reported, "It's black as new—India ink, for certain—but done very lightly so as not to groove the paper in the slightest. Then a few tiny drops of gum arabic, not enough to wrinkle, and hey presto!—it's hidden quite neatly. The obscurity of the obvious. 'Upon their vestments is a writing no man may see . . .' *Oh dear me, no!*"

He resolutely averted his eyes, which had been reading while he spoke. Then he stood up and holding the journal at arm's length came over and squatted on his hams, so close beside Franz that his brandy breath was obvious, and held the newly liberated page spread before their faces. Only the right-hand one was written upon, in very black yet spider-fine characters very neatly drawn and not remotely like Smith's handwriting.

"Thank you," Franz said. "This is weird. I riffled through those pages a dozen times."

"But you did not examine each one minutely with the true bibliophile's profound mistrust. The signatory initials indicate it was written by old Tiberius himself. And I'm sharing this with you not so much out of courtesy, as fear. Glancing at the opening, I got the feeling this was something I did not want to read all by myself. This way feels safer—at least it spread the danger."

Together they silently read the following:

A CURSE upon Master Clark Ashton Smith and all his heirs, who thought to pick my brain and slip away, false fleeting agent of my old enemies. Upon him the Long Death, the paramental agony! when he strays back as all men do. The fulcrum (0) and the Cipher (A) shall be here, at his *beloved* 607 Rhodes. I'll be at rest in my appointed spot (1) under the Bishop's Seat, the heaviest ashes that he ever felt. Then when the weights are on at Sutro Mount (4) and Monkey Clay (5) [(4) + (1) = (5)] *BE his Life Squeezed Away*. Committed to Cipher in my 50-Book (A). Go out, my little book (B) into the world, and lie in wait in stalls and lurk on shelves for the unwary purchaser. Go out, my little book, and break some necks!

TdC

As he finished reading it, Franz's mind was whirling with so many names of places and things both familiar and strange that he had to prod himself to remind himself to check visually the windows and doors and corners of Byers's gorgeous living room, now filling with shadows. That business about "when the weights are on"—he couldn't imagine what it meant, but taken together with "heaviest ashes," it made him think of the old man pressed to death with heavy stones on a plank on his chest for refusing to testify at the Salem witchcraft trial of 1692, as if a confession could be forced out like a last breath.

"Monkey Clay," Byers muttered puzzledly. "Ape of clay? Poor suffering Man, molded of dust?"

Franz shook his head. And in the midst of all, he thought, that damnably puzzling 607 Rhodes! which kept turning up again and again, and had in a way touched all this off.

And to think he'd had this book for years and not spotted the secret. It made a person suspect and distrust all things closest to him, his most familiar possessions. What might not be hidden inside the lining of your clothes, or in your right-hand trousers pocket (or for a woman, in her handbag or bra), or in the cake of soap with which you washed (which might have a razor blade inside).

Also to think that he was looking at last at de Castries's own handwriting, so neatly drawn and yet so crabbed for all that.

One detail puzzled him differently. "Donaldus," he said, "how would de Castries ever have got hold of Smith's journal?"

Byers let out a long alcohol-laden sigh, massaged his face with his hands (Franz clutched the journal to keep it from falling), and said, "Oh, that. Klaas and Ricker both told me that de Castries was quite worried and hurt when Clark went back to Auburn (it turned out) without warning, after visiting the old man every day for a month or so. De Castries was so bothered, they said, that he went over to Clark's cheap roominghouse and convinced them he was Clark's uncle, so that they gave him some things Clark had left behind when he'd checked out in a great tearing hurry. 'I'll keep them for little Clark,' he told Klaas and Ricker and then later (after they'd heard from Clark) he added, 'I've shipped him back his things.' They never suspected that the old man ever entertained any hard feelings about Clark."

Franz nodded. "But then how did the journal (now with the curse in it) get from de Castries to wherever I bought it?"

Byers said wearily, "Who knows? The curse, though, does remind me of another side of de Castries's character that I haven't mentioned: his fondness for rather cruel practical jokes. Despite his morbid fear of electricity, he had a chair Ricker helped rig for him to give the sitter an electric shock through the cushion that he kept for salesmen and salesladies, children, and other stray visitors. He nearly got into police trouble through that too. Some young lady looking for typing work got her bottom burned. Come to think of it, that has an S-M feeling, don't you think?—the genuine sadomasochistic touch. Electricity—bringer of thrills and pain. Don't writers speak of electric kisses? Ah, the evil that lurks in the hearts of men,'' Byers finished sententiously and stood up, leaving the journal in Franz's hands, and went back to his place. Franz looked at him questioningly, holding out the journal toward him a little, but his host said, pouring himself more brandy, ''No, you keep it. It's yours. After all, you were—are—the purchaser. Only for Heaven's sake take better care of it! It's a *very* rare item.''

''But what do you think of it, Donaldus?'' Franz asked.

Donaldus shrugged as he began to sip. ''A shivery document indeed,'' he said, smiling at Franz as if he were very glad the latter had it. ''And it really did lie in wait in stalls and lurk on shelves for many years, apparently. Franz, don't you recall *anything* about where you bought it?''

''I've tried and tried,'' Franz said tormentedly. ''The place was in the Haight, I'm fairly sure of that. Called . . . the In Group? The Black Spot? The Black Dog? The Grey Cockatoo? No, none of those, and I've tried hundreds of names. I think that 'black' was in it, but I believe the proprietor was a white man. And there was a little girl—maybe his daughter—helping him. Not so little, really—she was into puberty, I seem to recall, and well aware of it. Pushing herself at me—all this is very vague. I also seem to recall (I was drunk of course) being attracted to her,'' he confessed somewhat ashamedly.

''My dear Franz, aren't we all?'' Byers observed. ''The little darlings, barely kissed by sex, but don't they know it! Who can resist? Do you recall what you paid for the books?''

''Something pretty high, I think. But now I'm beginning to guess and imagine.''

''You could search through the Haight, street by street, of course.''

"I suppose I could, if it's still there and hasn't changed its name. Why don't you get on with your story, Donaldus?"

"Very well. There's not much more of it. You know, Franz, there's one indication that that . . . er . . . curse isn't particularly efficacious. Clark lived a long and productive life, thirty-three more years. Reassuring, don't you think?"

"He didn't stray back to San Francisco," Franz said shortly. "At least not very often."

"That's true. Well, after Clark left, de Castries remained . . . just a lonely and gloomy old man. He once told George Ricker at about this time a very unromantic story of his past: that he was French-Canadian and had grown up in northern Vermont, his father by turns a small-town printer and a farmer, always a failure, and he a lonely and unhappy child. It has the ring of truth, don't you think? And it makes one wonder what the sex life of such a person would have been. No mistresses at all, I'd say, let alone intellectual, mysterious, and foreign ones. Well, anyhow, now he'd had his last fling (with Clark) at playing the omnipotent sinister sorcerer, and it had turned out as bitterly as it had the first time in *fin de siècle* San Francisco (if that was the first). Gloomy and lonely. He had only one other literary acquaintance at that time—or friend of any sort, for that matter. Klaas and Ricker both vouch for it. Dashiell Hammett, who was living in San Francisco in an apartment at Post and Hyde, and writing *The Maltese Falcon*. Those bookstore names you were trying out reminded me of it—the Black Dog and a cockatoo. You see, the fabulously jeweled gold falcon enameled black (and finally proven a fake) is sometimes called the Black Bird in Hammett's detective story. He and de Castries talked a lot about black treasures, Klaas and Ricker told me. And about the historical background of Hammett's book—the Knights Hospitalers (later of Malta) who created the falcon and how they'd once been the Knights of Rhodes—"

"Rhodes turning up again!" Franz interjected. "That damn 607 Rhodes!"

"Yes," Byers agreed. "First Tiberius, then the Hospitalers. They held the island for two hundred years and were finally driven out of it by the sultan Sulayman I in 1522. But about the Black Bird—you'll recall what I told you of de Castries's *pietra dura* ring of mosaicked black semiprecious stuff depicting a black bird? Klaas claimed it was the inspiration for *The Maltese Falcon*! One needn't go that far, of course, but just the same it's all very odd indeed, don't you think? De Castries and Hammett. The black magician and the tough detective."

"Not so odd as all that when you think about it," Franz countered, his eyes on one of their roving trips again. "Besides being one of America's few great novelists, Hammett was a rather lonely and taciturn man himself, with an almost fabulous integrity. He elected to serve a sentence in a federal prison rather than betray a trust. And he enlisted in World War II when he didn't have to and served it out in the cold Aleutians and finally toughed out a long last illness. No, he'd have been interested in a queer old duck like de Castries and showed a hard, unsentimental compassion toward his loneliness and bitterness and failures. Go on, Donaldus."

"There's really nothing more," Donaldus said, but his eyes were flashing. "De Castries died of a coronary occlusion in 1929 after two weeks in the City Hospital. It happened in the summertime—I remember Klaas saying the old man didn't even live to see the stock market crash and the beginnings of the Great Depression, 'which would have been a comfort to him because it would have confirmed his theories that because of the self-abuse of megacities, the world was going to hell in a handbasket.'

"So that was that. De Castries was cremated, as he'd wished, which took his last cash. Ricker and Klaas split his few possessions. There were of course no relatives."

"I'm glad of that," Franz said. "I mean, that he was cremated. Oh, I know he died—had to be dead after all these years—but just the same, along with all the rest today, I've had this picture of de Castries, a very old man, but wiry and somehow very fast, still slipping around San Francisco. Hearing that he not only died in a hospital but was cremated makes his death more final."

"In a way," Byers agreed, giving him an odd look. "Klaas had the ashes sitting just inside his front door for a while in a cheap canister the crematory had furnished, until he and Ricker figured out what to do with them. They finally decided to follow de Castries's wish there too, although it meant an illegal burial and doing it all secretly at night. Ricker carried a post-digger packaged in newspaper, and Klaas a small spade, similarly wrapped.

"There were two other persons in the funeral party. Dashiell Hammett—he decided a question for them, as it happened. They'd been arguing as to whether de Castries's black ring (Klaas had it) should be buried with the ashes, so they put it up to Hammett, and he said, 'Of course.' "

"That figures," Franz said, nodding. "But how very strange."

"Yes, wasn't it?" Byers agreed. "They bound it to the neck of the canister with heavy copper wire. The fourth person—he even carried the ashes—was Clark. I thought that would surprise you. They'd got in touch with him in Auburn and he'd come back just for that night. It shows, come to think of it, that Clark couldn't have known about the curse—or does it? Anyhow, the little burial detail set forth from Klaas's place just after dark. It was a clear night and the moon was gibbous, a few days before full—which was a good thing, as they had some climbing to do where there were no street lights."

"Just the four of them, eh?" Franz prompted when Byers paused.

"Odd you should ask that," Byers said. "After it was all over, Hammett asked Ricker, 'Who the devil was that woman who stayed in the background?—some old flame of his? I expected her to drop out when we got to the rocks, or else join us, but she kept her distance all the way.' It gave Ricker quite a turn—for he, as it happened, hadn't glimpsed anyone. Nor had Klaas or Smith. But Hammett stuck to his story."

Byers looked at Franz with a sort of relish and finished rapidly. "The burial went off without a hitch, though they needed the post-digger—the ground was hard. The only thing

lacking was the TV tower—that fantastic cross between a
dressmaker's dummy and a Burmese pagoda in a feast of red
lanterns—to lean down through the night and give a cryptic
blessing. The spot was just below a natural rock séat that de
Castries had called the Bishop's Seat after the one in Poe's
'Gold Bug' story, and just at the base of that big rock outcropping that is the summit of Corona Heights. Oh, incidentally, another of his whims they gratified—he was burned
wearing a bathrobe he'd worn to tatters—a pale old brown
one with a cowl.''

XXII

Franz's eyes, engaged in one of their roving all-inspections,
got the command to check the glooms and shadows not only
for a pale, blank, triangular face with restless snout, but also
for the thin, hawkish, ghostly one, tormented and torment-
ing, murder-bent, of a hyperactive old man looking like
something out of Doré's illustrations of Dante's *Inferno*. Since
he'd never seen a photograph of de Castries, if any existed,
that would have to do.

His mind was busy assimilating the thought that Corona
Heights was literally impregnated with Thibaut de Castries.
That both yesterday and today he had occupied for rather
long periods of time what must also certainly be the Bishop's
Seat of the curse, while only a few yards below in the hard
ground were the essential dusts (salts?) and the black ring.
How did that go in the cipher in Poe's tale? "Take a good
glass in the Bishop's Seat . . ." His glasses were broken, but
then he hardly needed them for this short-range work. Which
were worse—ghosts or paramentals?—or were they, conceivably, the same? When one was simply on watch for the approach of both or either, that was a rather academic question,
no matter how many interesting problems it posed about different levels of reality. Somewhere, deep down, he was aware
of being angry, or perhaps only argumentative.

"Turn on some lights, Donaldus," he said in a flat voice.

"I must say you're taking it very coolly," his host said in slightly aggrieved, slightly awed tones.

"What do you expect me to do, panic? Run out in the street and get shot?—or crushed by falling walls? or cut by flying glass? I suppose, Donaldus, that you delayed revealing the exact location of de Castries's grave so that it would have a greater dramatic impact, and so be truer, in line with your theory of the identity of reality and art?"

"Exactly! You *do* understand, and I *did* tell you there would be a ghost and how appropriately the astrological graffiti served as Thibaut's epitaph, or tomb decor. But isn't it all so very *amazing*, Franz? To think that when you first looked from your window at Corona Heights, Thibaut de Castries's mortal remains unknown to you—"

"Turn on some lights," Franz repeated. "What I find amazing, Donaldus, is that you've known about paramental entities for many years, and about the highly sinister activities of de Castries and the suggestive circumstances of his burial, and yet take no more precautions against them than you do. You're like a soldier dancing the light fantastic in no-man's-land. Always remembering that I, or you, or both of us may at this moment be totally insane. Of course, you learned about the curse only just now, if I can trust you. And you did bolt the door after I came in. Turn on some lights!"

Byers complied at last. A dull gold refulgence streamed from the large globular shade suspended above them. He moved to the front hall, somewhat reluctantly, it appeared, and flicked a switch, then to the back of the living room, where he did the same and then busied himself opening another bottle of brandy. The windows became dark rectangles netted with gold. Full night had fallen. But at least the shadows inside had been banished.

All this while he was saying in a voice that had grown rather listless and dispirited now that his tale had been told, "Of course you can trust me, Franz. It was out of consideration for your own safety that I didn't tell you about de Castries. Until today, when it became clear you were into the business, like it or not. I don't go babbling about it all, believe me. If I've learned one thing over the years, it's that it's a mercy *not* to tell anyone about the darker side of de Castries and his theories. That's why I've never even *considered* publishing a monograph about the man. What other reason could I have for that?—such a book would be brilliant. Fa Lo Suee knows all—one can't hide anything from a serious lover—but she has a very strong mind, as I've suggested. In fact, after you called this morning, I suggested to her as she was going out that if she had some spare time she have another look for the bookstore where you bought the journal—she has a talent for such problems. She smiled and said that, as it happened, she'd been planning to do just that.

"Also," he went on, "you say I take no precautions against them, but I do, I do! According to Klaas and Ricker the old man once mentioned three protections against 'undesirable influences': *silver*, old antidote to werewolfry (another reason I've encouraged Fa Lo Suee in her art), *abstract designs*, those old attention-trappers (hopefully the attention of paramentals too—hence all the mazelike arabesques you see about you), and *stars*, the primal pentagram—it was I, going there on several cold dawns, when I'd be sure of privacy, who sprayed most of those astrologic graffiti on Corona Heights!"

"Donaldus," Franz said sharply, "you've been a lot deeper and more steadily into this all along than you've told me—and your girlfriend too, apparently."

"Companion," Byers corrected. "Or, if you will, lover. Yes, that's right—it's been one of my chief secondary concerns (primary now) for quite a few years. But what was I saying? Oh, yes, that Fa Lo Suee knows all. So did a couple of her predecessors—a famous interior decorator and a tennis star who was also an actor. Clark, Klaas, and Ricker knew—they were my source—but they're all dead. So you see I do try to shield others—and myself up to a point. I regard paramental entities as very real and present dangers, about midway in nature between the atomic bomb and the archetypes of the collective unconscious, which include several highly dangerous characters, as you know. Or between a Charles

Manson or Zodiac killer and kappa phenomena as defined by Meleta Denning in *Gnostica*. Or between muggers and elementals, or hepatitis viruses and incubi. They're all of them things any sane man is on guard against.

"But mark this, Franz," he emphasized, pouring out brandy, "despite all my previous knowledge, so much more extensive and of such longer standing than your own, I've never actually *seen* a paramental entity. You have the advantage of me there. And it seems to be *quite* an advantage." And he looked at Franz with a mixture of avidity and dread.

Franz stood up. "Perhaps it is," he said shortly, "at least in making a person stay on guard. You say you're trying to protect yourself, but you don't act that way. Right now—excuse me, Donaldus—you're getting so drunk that you'd be helpless if a paramental entity—"

Byers's eyebrows went up. "You think you could defend yourself against them, resist them, fight them, destroy them, once they're around?" he asked incredulously, his voice strengthening. "Can you stop an atomic missile headed for San Francisco at this moment through the ionosphere? Can you command the germs of cholera? Can you abolish your Anima or your Shadow? Can you say to the poltergeist, 'Don't knock'? or to the Queen of the Night, 'Stay outside'? You can't stand guard twenty-four hours a day for months, for years. Believe me, I know. A soldier crouched in a dugout can't try to figure out if the next shell will be a direct hit or not. He'd go crazy if he tried. No, Franz, all you can do is to lock the doors and windows, turn on all the lights, and hope they pass you by. And try to forget them. Eat, drink and be merry. Recreate yourself. Here, have a drink."

He came toward Franz carrying in each hand a glass half-full of brandy.

"No, thank you," Franz said harshly, jamming the journal into his coat pocket, to Byers's fleeting distress. Then he picked up the tinkling binoculars and jammed them in the other side pocket, thinking in a flash of the binoculars in James's ghost story "A View from a Hill" that had been magicked to see the past by being filled with a black fluid from boiled bones that had oozed out nastily when they were broken. Could his own binoculars have been somehow doctored or gimmicked so that they saw things that weren't there? A wildly farfetched notion, and anyhow his own binoculars were broken, too.

"I'm sorry, Donaldus, but I've got to go," he said, heading for the hall. He knew that if he stayed he *would* take a drink, starting the old cycle, and the idea of becoming unconscious *and incapable of being roused* was very repellent.

Byers hurried after him. His haste and his gyrations to keep the brandy from spilling would have been comic under other circumstances and if he hadn't been saying in a horrified, plaintive, pleading voice, "You can't go out, it's dark. You can't go out with that old devil or his paramental slipping around. Here, have a drink and stay the night. At least stay for the party. If you're going to stand on guard, you're going to need some rest and recreation. I'm sure you'll find an agreeable and pleasing partner—they'll all be swingers, but intelligent. And if you're afraid of liquor dulling your mind, I've got some cocaine, the purest crystal." He drained one glass and set it down on the hall table. "Look, Franz, I'm frightened, too—and you've been pale ever since I told you where the old devil's dust is laid. Stay for the party. And have just one drink—enough to relax a little. In the end, there's no other way, believe me. You'd just get too tired, trying to watch forever." He swayed a little, wheedling, smiling his pleasantest.

A weight of weariness descended on Franz. He reached toward the glass, but just as he touched it he jerked his fingers away as if they'd been burned.

"Shh," he cautioned as Byers started to speak and he warningly gripped him by the elbow.

In the silence they heard a tiny, faintly grating, sliding metallic sound ending in a soft snap, as of a key being rotated in a lock. Their eyes went to the front door. They saw the brass inner knob revolve.

"It's Fa Lo Suee," Byers said. "I'll have to unbolt the door." He moved to do so.

"Wait!" Franz whispered urgently. "Listen!"

They heard a steady scratching sound that didn't end, as if some intelligent beast was drawing a horny claw round and round on the other side of the painted wood. There rose unbidden in Franz's imagination the paralyzing image of a large black panther crouched close against the other side of the gold-traced white opacity, a green-eyed, gleamingly black panther that was beginning to metamorphose into something more terrible.

"Up to her tricks," Byers muttered and drew the bolt before Franz could move to hinder him.

The door pressed halfway open, and around it came two pale gray, triangular flat feline faces that flittered at the edges and were screeching "Aiii-eee!" it sounded.

Both men recoiled, Franz flinching aside with eyes involuntarily slitted from two pale gray gleaming shapes, a taller and a slenderer one, that whirled past him as they shot menacingly at Byers, who was bent half double in his retreat, one arm thrown shieldingly across his eyes, the other across his groin, while the gleaming wineglass and the small sheet of amber fluid it had contained still sailed through the air from the point where his hand had abandoned them.

Incongruously, Franz's mind registered the odors of brandy, burnt hemp, and a spicy perfume.

The gray shapes converged on Byers, clutching at his groin, and as he gasped and gabbled inarticulately, weakly trying to fend them off, the taller was saying in a husky contralto voice with great enjoyment, "In China, Mr. Nayland Smith, we have ways to make men talk."

Then the brandy was on the pale green wallpaper, the unbroken wineglass on the golden-brown carpet, and the stoned, handsome Chinese woman and equally mind-blown urchin-faced girl had snatched off their gray cat-masks, though laughing wildly and continuing to grope and tickle Byers vigorously, and Franz realized they had both been screeching "Jaime," his host's first name, at the top of their voices.

His extreme fear had left Franz, but not its paralysis. The latter extended to his vocal cords, so that from the moment of the strange eruption of the two gray-clad females to the moment when he left the house on Beaver Street he never spoke a word but only stood beside the dark rectangle of the open door and observed the busy tableau farther down the hall with a rather cold detachment.

Fa Lo Suee had a spare, somewhat angular figure, a flat face with strong, bony structure, dark eyes that were paradoxically both bright and dull with marijuana (and whatever) and straight dull black hair. Her dark red lips were thin. She wore silver-gray stockings and gloves and a closely fitting dress (of ribbed silver-gray silk) and of the Chinese sort that always looks modern. Her left hand threatened Byers in his midst, her right lay loosely low around the slender waist of her companion.

The latter was a head shorter, almost but not quite skinny, and had sexy little breasts. Her face was actually catlike: receding chin, pouty lips, a snub nose, protuberant blue eyes and low forehead, from which straight blonde hair fell to one side. She looked about seventeen, bratty and worldly wise. She plinked a note in Franz's memory. She wore a pale gray leotard, silver-gray gloves, and a gray cloak of some light material that now hung to one side like her hair. Both of her hands mischievously groped Byers. She had a pink ear and a vicious giggle.

The two cat-masks, cast on the hall table now, were edged with silver sequins and had a few stiff whiskers, but they retained the nasty triangular snouty appearance which had been so unnerving coming around the door.

Donaldus (or Jaime) spoke no really intelligible word himself during this period before Franz's departure, except perhaps "Don't!" but he gasped and squealed and babbled a lot, with breathless little laughs thrown in. He stayed bent half-double and twisting from side to side, his hands constantly but rather ineffectually fending off the clutching ones. His pale violet dressing gown, unbelted, swished as he twisted.

It was the women who did all the talking and at first only Fa Lo Suee. "We reallly scared you, didn't we?" she said rapidly. "Jaime scares easily, Shirl, especially when he's drunk. That was my key scratching the door. Go on, Shirl, give it to him!'' Then resuming her Fu Manchu voice, "What have you and Dr. Petrie there been up to? In Honan, Mr. Nayland Smith, we have an infallible Chinese test for homophilia. Or is it possible you're AC-DC? We have the ancient wisdom of the East, all the dark lore that Mao Tse-tung's forgotten. Combined with western science, it's devastating. (That's it, girl, hurt him!) Remember my thugs and dacoits, Mr. Smith, my golden scorpions and red six-inch centipedes, my black spiders with diamond eyes that wait in the dark, then leap! How would you like one of those dropped down your pants? Repeat—what have you and Dr. Petrie been doing? Be careful what you say. My assistant, Miss Shirley Soames (Keep it up, Shirl!) has a rat-trap memory. No lie will go unnoticed.''

Franz, frozen, felt rather as if he were watching crayfish and sea anemones scuttling and grasping, fronds questing, pincers and flower-mouths opening and closing, in a rock pool. The endless play of life.

"Oh, by the way, Jaime, I've solved the problem of the Smith journal,'' Fa Lo Suee said in a bright casual voice while her own hands became more active. "This is Shirl Soames, Jaime (you're getting to him, girl!), who for years and years has been her father's assistant at the Gray's Inn bookstore in the Haight. And she remembers the whole transaction, although it was four years ago, because she has a *rat-trap* memory.''

The name "Gray's Inn'' lit up like neon in Franz's mind. How had he kept missing it?

"Oh, traps distress you, do they, Nayland Smith?'' Fa Lo Suee went on. "They're cruel to animals, are they? Western sentimentality! I will have you know, for your information, that Shirl Soames here can *bite*, as well as nip exquisitely.''

As she was saying that, she was sliding her silk-gloved right hand down the girl's rump and inward, until the tip of her middle finger appeared to be resting on the spot midway between the outer orifices of the reproductive and digestive systems. The girl appreciatively jogged her hips from side to side through a very short arc.

Franz took coldly clinical note of those actions and of the inward fact that under other circumstances it would have been an exciting gesture, making him want to do so himself to Shirley Soames, and so be done by. But why her in particular? Memories stirred.

Fa Lo Suee noticed Franz and turned her head. Giving him a very civilized glassy-eyed smile, she said politely, "Ah, you must be Franz Westen, the writer, who phoned Jaime this morning. So you as well as he will be interested in what Shirley has to say.

"Shirl, leave off excruciating Jaime. He's had enough punishment. Is this the gentleman?" and without removing her hand she gently swung the girl around until she faced Franz.

Behind them Byers, still bent over, was taking deep breaths mixed with dying chuckles as he began to recover from the working over he's been given.

With amphetamine-bright eyes the girl looked Franz up and down. While he was realizing that he knew that feline, foxy little face (face of a cat, presently licking cream), though on a body skinnier still and another head shorter.

"That's him, all right," she said in a rapid, sharp voice that still had something of a brat's "yah! yah!" in it. "Correct, mister? Four years ago, you bought two old books tied together out of a lot that had been around for years that my father'd bought that belonged to a George Ricker. You were squiffed, really skew-iffed! We were together in the stacks and I touched you and you looked so queer. You paid twenty-five dollars for those old books. I thought you thought you were paying for a chance to feel me up. Were you? So many of the older men wanted to." She read something in Franz's expression, her eyes brightened, and she gave a hoarse little laugh. "No, I got it! You paid all that money because you were feeling guilty because you were so drunk you thought—what a laugh!—you'd been molesting me, whereas in my sweet girlish way, I'd been molesting you! I was very good at molesting, it was the first thing dear Daddy taught me. I learnt on him.

And I was Daddy's star attraction at the store, and didn't he know it! But I'd already found out girls were nicer.''

All this while she'd continued to jog her little hips lasciviously, leaning back a little, and now she slipped her own right hand behind her, presumably to rest it on Fa Lo Suee's.

Franz looked at Shirley Soames and at the two others, and he knew that all that she had said was true, and he also knew that this was how Jaime Donaldus Byers escaped from his fears (and Fa Lo Suee from hers?). And without a word or any change in his rather stupid expression he turned and walked out the open door.

He had a sharp pang—"I am abandoning Donaldus!"— and two fleeting thoughts—"Shirl Soames and her touchings were the dark, musty, tendriled memory I had on the stairs yesterday morning" and "Would Fa Lo Suee immortalize the exquisite moment in slim silver, perhaps titling it 'The Loving Goose'?"—but nothing made him pause or reconsider. As he started down the steps, light from the doorway spilling around him, his eyes were already systematically checking the darkness ahead for hostile presences—each corner, each yawning areaway, each shadowy rooftop, each coign of vantage. As he reached the street, the soft light around him vanished as the door behind him was silently shut. That relieved him—it made him less of a target in the full onyx dusk that had now closed once more on San Francisco.

XXIII

As Franz moved cautiously down Beaver Street, his eyes checking the glooms between the rather few lights, he thought of how de Castries had ceased to be a mere parochial devil haunting the lonely hump of Corona Heights (and Franz's own room at 811 Geary?), but a ubiquitous demon, ghost, or paramental inhabiting the whole city with its scattered humping hills. For that matter, to keep it all materialistic, were not some of the atoms shed from de Castries's body during his life and during his burial forty years ago around Franz here at this very moment and in the very air that he was discreetly sniffing in?—atoms being so vastly tiny and infinity-numerous. As were the atoms, too, of Francis Drake (sailing past San Francisco Bay-to-be in the *Golden Hind*) and of Shakespeare and Socrates and Solomon (and of Dashiell Hammett and Clark Ashton Smith). And for that matter, too, had not the atoms that were to become Thibaut de Castries been circulating around the world before the pyramids were built, slowly converging on the spot (in Vermont? in France?) where the old devil would be born? And before that, had not those Thibaut atoms been swiftly vectoring from the violent birthplace of all the universe to the space-time spot where earth would be born and all its weird Pandora woes?

Blocks off, a siren yelped. Nearby, a dark cat darted into a black slit between walls set too close for human passage. It made Franz think of how big buildings had been threatening to crush man ever since the first megacity had been built. Really Saul's crazy (?) Mrs. Willis wasn't so far off the track, nor Lovecraft (and Smith?) with his fascinated dread of vast rooms with ceilings that were indoor skies and far walls that were horizons, in buildings vaster still. San Francisco was carbuncled with the latter, and each month new ones grew. Were the signs of the universe written into them? Whose wandering atoms didn't they hold? And were paramentals their personification of their vermin or their natural predators? In any case, it all transpired as logically and ineluctably as the rice-paper journal had passed from Smith, who wrote in purple ink; to de Castries, who added a deadly, secret black; to Ricker, who was a locksmith, not a bibliophile; to Soames, who had a precociously sexy daughter; to Westen, who was susceptible to weird and sexy things.

A dark blue taxi coasting slowly and silently downhill ghosted by Franz, and drew up at the opposite curb.

No wonder Donaldus had wanted Franz to keep the journal and its newfound curse! Byers was an old campaigner against paramentals, with his defense in depth of locks and lights and stars and signs and mazes, and liquor, drugs and sex, and outré sex—Fa Lo Suee had brought Shirley Soames for him as well as for herself; the humorously hostile groping had been to cheer him. Very resourceful, truly. A person had to sleep. Maybe he'd learn, Franz told himself, to use the Byers method himself some day, minus the liquor, but not tonight, no, not until he had to.

The headlights of an unseen car on Noe illuminated the corner ahead at the foot of Beaver. While Franz scanned for shapes that might have been hiding in the dark and now revealed, he thought of Donaldus's inner defense perimeter, meaning his aesthetic approach to life; his theory that art and reality, fiction and nonfiction, were all one, so that one needn't waste energy distinguishing them.

But wasn't even that defense a rationalization, Franz asked himself, an attempt to escape facing the overwhelming question that you're led to: *Are paramentals real?*

Yet how could you answer that question when you were on the run and getting weary and wearier?

And then Franz suddenly saw how he could escape for now, at least buy time in which to think in safety. And it did not involve liquor, drugs, or sex, or diminishing watchfulness in any way. He touched his pocketbook and felt inside it—yes, there was the ticket. He struck a match and glanced at his watch—not yet quite eight, still time enough if he moved swiftly. He turned. The dark blue cab, having discharged its passenger, was coming down Beaver with its hire light on. He stepped into the street and waved it down. He started to get in, then hesitated. A searching glance told him that the dusky, lustrous interior was empty. He got inside and slammed the door, noting approvingly that the windows were closed.

"The Civic Center," he directed. "The Veterans Building. There is a concert there."

"Oh, one of those," the driver said, an older man. "If you don't mind, I won't take Market; it's too torn up. Going around, we'll get there quicker."

"That's fine," Franz said, settling back as the cab turned north on Noe and speeded up. He knew—or had been assuming—that ordinary physical laws didn't apply to paramentals, even if they were real, and so that being in a swiftly moving vehicle didn't make his situation any safer, but it felt that way—it helped.

The familiar drama of a cab ride took hold of him a little— the dark houses and storefronts shooting past, the slowings at the bright corners, the red-green race with the stop lights. But he still kept scanning, regularly swinging his head to look behind, now to the left, now to the right.

"When I was a kid here," the driver said, "they didn't use to tear up Market so much. But now they do it all the time. That BART. And other streets too. All those damn high rises. We'd be better off without them."

"I'm with you there," Franz said.

"You and me both," the driver confirmed. "The driving'd sure be easier. Watch it, you bastard."

The last rather mildly spoken remark was intended for a car that was trying to edge into the right lane on McAllister, though hardly for the ears of its driver. Down a side street Franz saw a huge orange globe aloft like a Jupiter that was all one Red Spot—advertisement of a Union 76 gas station. They turned on Van Ness and immediately drew up at the curb. Franz paid his fare, adding a generous tip and crossed the wide sidewalk to the Veterans Building and through its wide glass door into its lofty lobby set with eight-inch-diameter tubular modernistic sculptures like giant metal worms at war.

With a few other latecoming concertgoers he hurried to the elevator at the back, feeling both claustrophobia and relief as the slow doors closed. On the fourth floor they joined the press of last-minute folk in the foyer giving up their tickets and taking their programs before entering the medium-size high, bone-white concert hall with its checkered ceiling and its rows of folding chairs, now mostly occupied, judging from here.

At first the press of people in the foyer bothered Franz (anyone might be, or hide, anything) but rather swiftly began to reassure him by their concert-normality: the mostly conservative clothes, whether establishment or hippie; the scatter of elven folk in arty garb suitable for rarefied artistic experiences; the elderly groups, the ladies in sober evening dresses with a touch of silver, the gentlemen rather fussily clad at collars and cuffs. One young couple held Franz's attention for more than a moment. They were both small and delicately made, both of them looking scrupulously clean. They were dressed in very well tailored brand-new hippie garb: he in leathern jacket and corduroy trews, she in a beautifully faded blue denim suit with large pale splotches. They looked like children, but his neatly trimmed beard and the demure outdenting of her tender bosom proclaimed them adult. They held hands rather like dolls, as if they were used to handling each other very carefully. One thought of prince and princess on a masquerade planned and supervised by graybeards.

A very aware and coldly calculating section of Franz's mind told him that he was not one bit safer here than out in the dark. Nevertheless his fears were being lulled as they had been when he'd first arrived at Beaver Street and later, a little, in the cab.

And then, just before entering the concert hall, he glimpsed at the far end of the foyer the backs of a rather small man, gray-haired, in evening dress and a tall slender woman in a beige turban and pale brown, flowing gown. They seemed to be talking animatedly together and as they swiftly turned toward him, he felt an icy chill, for the woman appeared to be wearing a black veil. Then he saw that she was black, while the man's face was somewhat porcine.

As he plunged ahead nervously into the concert hall, he heard his name called, started, then hurried down an aisle to where Gunnar and Saul were holding a seat between them in the third row.

"It's about time," Saul said darkly as Franz edged past.

As he sat down, Gun said from the seat just beyond, grinning somewhat thinly and momentarily laying his hand on Franz's forearm, "We were beginning to get afraid you weren't coming. You know how much Cal depends on you, don't you?" Then a puzzled question came into his face when the glass in Franz's pocket clashed as he pulled his jacket round.

"I broke my binoculars on Corona Heights," Franz said shortly. "I'll tell you about it later." Then a thought came to him. "Do you know much about optics, Gun? Practical optics—instruments and such, prisms and lenses?"

"A little," Gun replied, with an inquiring frown. "And I've a friend who's very much into it. But why—?"

Franz said slowly, "Would it be possible to gimmick a terrestrial telescope, or a pair of binoculars, so a person would see something in the distance that wasn't there?"

"Well . . ." Gunnar began, his expression wondering, his hands making a small gesture of uncertainty. Then he smiled. "Of course, if you tried to look through broken binoculars, I suppose you'd see something like a kaleidoscope."

"Taffy get rough?" Saul asked from the other side.

"Never mind now," Franz told Gunnar and with a quick, temporizing grimace at Saul (and a quick glance behind him and to either side—crowded concertgoers and their coats made such an effective stalking ground), he looked toward the stage, where the half dozen or so instrumentalists were already seated—in a shallow, concave curve just beyond the conductor's podium, one of the strings still tuning thoughtfully. The long and narrow shape of the harpsichord, its slim bench empty, made the left end of the curve, somewhat downstage to favor its small tones.

Franz looked at his program. The Brandenburg Fifth was the finale. There were two intermissions. The concert opened with:

> *Concerto in C Major*
> *for Harpsichord and*
> *Chamber Orchestra*
> *by Giovanni Paisiello*
>   *1. Allegro*
>   *2. Larghetto*
>   *3. Allegro (Rondo)*

Saul nudged him. He looked up. Cal had come on stage unobtrusively. She wore a white evening frock that left her shoulders bare and sparkled just a little at the edges. She said something to a woodwind, and in turning, looked the audience over without making a point of it. He thought she saw him, but he couldn't be sure. She seated herself. The house lights went down. To a spreading ripple of applause the conductor entered, took his place, looked around from under his eyebrows at his instrumentalists, tapped the lecturn with his wand, and raised it sharply.

Beside Franz, Saul murmured prayerfully, "Now in the name of Bach and Sigmund Freud, give 'em hell, Calpurnia."

"And of Pythagoras," Gun faintly chimed.

The sweet and rocking music of the strings and of the softly calling, lulling woodwinds enfolded Franz. For the first time since Corona Heights he felt wholly safe, among his friends and in the arms of ordered sound, as if the music were an intimate crystal heaven around and over them, a perfect barrier to paranatural forces.

But then the harpsichord came in challengingly, banishing cradled sleep, its sparkling and shivery ribbons of high sound propounding questions and gaily yet inflexibly commanding that they be answered. The harpsichord told Franz that the concert hall was every bit as much an escape as anything proposed on Beaver Street.

Before he knew what he was doing, though not until he knew well what he was feeling, Franz had got stoopingly to his feet and was edging out in front of Saul, intensely conscious yet regardless of the waves of shock, protest, and condemnation silently focused upon him from the audience—or so he fancied.

He only paused to bend his lips close to Saul's ear and say softly but very distinctly, "Tell Cal—but only after she's played the Brandenburg—that her music made me go to find the answer to the 607 Rhodes question," and then he was edging on quite rapidly, the back of his left hand very lightly brushing backs to steady his course, his right hand an apol-

ogetic shield between himself and the sitters he passed in
front of.

As he reached the end of the row, he looked back once
and saw Saul's frowning and intensely speculative face,
framed by his long brown hair, fixed upon him. Then he was
hurrying up the aisle between the hostile rows, lashed on—
as if by a whip strung with thousands of tiny diamonds—by
the music of the harpsichord, which never faltered. He kept
his gaze fixed steadily ahead.

He wondered why he'd said "the 607 Rhodes question"
instead of "the question of whether paramentals are real,"
but then he realized it was because it was a question Cal had
herself asked more than once and so might catch its drift. It
was important that she understand that he was working.

He was tempted to take a last look back, but didn't.

XXIV

In the street outside the Veterans Building, Franz resumed
his sidewise and backward peerings, now somewhat random-
ized, yet he was conscious not so much of fear as of wari-
ness, as if he were a savage on a mission in a concrete jungle,
traveling along the bottoms of perilously walled, rectilineal
gorges. Having taken a deliberate plunge into danger, he felt
almost cocky.

He headed over two blocks and then up Larkin, walking
rapidly yet not noisily. The passersby were few. The gibbous
moon was almost overhead. Up Turk a siren yelped some
blocks away. He kept up his swiveling watch for the paramental of his binoculars and/or for Thibaut's ghost—perhaps
a material ghost formed of Thibaut's floating ashy remains,
or a portion of them. Such things might not be real, there
still might be a natural explanation (or he might be crazy),
but until he was sure of one or the other, it was only good
sense to stay on guard.

Down Ellis the slot which held his favorite tree was black,

but streetside its fingered branch-ends were green in the white street lights.

A half-dozen blocks west on O'Farrell he glimpsed the modernistic bulk of St. Mary's Cathedral, pale gray in the moonlight, and wondered uneasily about another Lady.

He turned down Geary past dark shop fronts, two lighted bars, and the wide yawning mouth of the De Soto garage, home of the blue taxicabs, and came to the dingy white awning that marked 811.

Inside the lobby there were a couple of rough-looking male types sitting on the ledge of small hexagonal marble tiles below the two rows of brass mailboxes. Probably drunk. They followed him with their dull eyes as he took the elevator.

He got off at six and closed the two elevator doors quietly (the folding latticed and the solid one) and walked softly past the black window and the black broom closet door with its gaping round hole where the knob would have been, and stopped in front of his own door.

After listening a short while and hearing nothing, he unlocked it with two twists of his key and stepped inside, feeling a burst of excitement and fear. This time he did not switch on the bright ceiling light, but only stood listening and intent, waiting for his eyes to accommodate.

The room was full of darkness (dark gray, rather) with the moon and with the indirect glow of the city's lights. Everything was very quiet except for the faint, distant rumbles and growls of traffic and the rushing of his blood. Suddenly there came through the pipes a solid, low roaring as someone turned on water a floor or two away. It stopped as suddenly and the inside silence returned.

Adventurously, Franz shut the door and felt his way along the wall and around the tall clothes cabinet, carefully avoiding the work-laden coffee table, to the head of his bed, where he turned on the light. He ran his gaze along his Scholar's Mistress, lying slim, dark, and inscrutably silent against the wall, and on to the open casement window.

Two yards inside it, the large oblong of fluorescent red cardboard lay on the floor. He walked over and picked it up.

It was jaggedly bent down the middle and a little ragged at the corners. He shook his head, set it against the wall, and went back to the window. Two torn corners of cardboard were still tacked to the window sides. The drapes hung tidily. There were crumbles and tiny shreds of pale brownish paper on his narrow desk and the floor at his feet. He couldn't remember whether or not he'd cleaned up those from yesterday. He noted that the neat little stack of ungutted old pulps was gone. Had he put those away somewhere? He couldn't remember that either.

Conceivably a very strong gust of wind could have torn out the red cardboard, but wouldn't it also have disordered the drapes and blown the paper crumbs off his desk? He looked out to the red lights of the TV tower; thirteen of them small and steady, six brighter and flashing. Below them, a mile closer, the dark hump of Corona Heights was outlined by the city's yellowish window and street lights and a few bright whites and greens in snaky curves. Again he shook his head.

He rapidly searched his place, this time not feeling foolish. In the closet and clothes cabinet he swung the hanging garments aside and glanced behind them. He noticed a pale gray raincoat of Cal's from weeks back. He looked behind the shower curtain and under the bed.

On the table between the closet and bathroom doors lay his unopened mail. Topmost was a cancer drive letter from an organization he'd contributed to after Daisy had died. He frowned and momentarily narrowed his lips, his face compressed with pain. Beside the little pile was a small slate, some pieces of white chalk, and his prisms, with which he occasionally played with sunlight, splitting it into spectrums, and into spectrums of spectrums. He called to his Scholar's Mistress, "We'll have you in gay clothes again, just like a rainbow, my dear, after all this is over."

He got a city map and a ruler and went to his couch, where he fished his broken binoculars out of his pocket and set them carefully on an unpiled edge of the coffee table. It gave him a feeling of safety to think that now the snout-faced paramental couldn't get to him without crossing broken glass, like that which they used to cement atop walls to keep out intruders—until he realized just how illogical that was.

He took out Smith's journal too and settled himself beside his Scholar's Mistress, spreading out the map. Then he opened the journal to de Castries's curse, marveling again that it had so long eluded him, and reread the crucial portion:

> The fulcrum (0) and the Cipher (A) shall be here, at his *beloved* 607 Rhodes. I'll be at rest in my appointed spot (1) under the Bishop's Seat, the heaviest ashes that he ever felt. Then when the weights are on at Sutro Mount (4) and Monkey Clay (5) [(4) + (1) = (5)] *BE his Life Squeezed Away.*

Now to work out, he told himself, this problem in black geometry, or would it be black physics? What had Byers said Klaas had said de Castries had called it? Oh, yes, Neo-Pythagorean metageometry.

Monkey Clay was the most incongruous item in the curse, all right. Start here. Donaldus had maundered about simian and human clay, but that led nowhere. It ought to be a *place*, like Mount Sutro—or Corona Heights (under the Bishop's Seat). Clay was a street in San Francisco. But Monkey?

Franz's mind took a leap from Monkey Clay to Monkey Wards. Why? He'd known a man who'd worked at Sears Roebuck's great rival and who said he and some of his lowly coworkers called their company that.

Another leap, from Monkey Wards to the Monkey Block. Of course! The Monkey Block was the proudly derisive name of a huge old San Francisco apartment building, long torn down, where bohemians and artists had lived cheaply in the Roaring Twenties and the Depression years. Monkey—short for the street it was on—Montgomery! Another San Francisco street, and one crosswise to Clay! (There was something more than that, but his mind hung fire and he couldn't wait.)

He excitedly laid the ruler on the flattened map between Mount Sutro and the intersection of Clay and Montgomery Streets in the north end of the financial district. He saw that the straight line so indicated went through the middle of Corona Heights! (And also rather close by the intersection of Geary and Hyde, he noted with a little grimace.)

He took a pencil from the coffee table and marked a small "five" at the Montgomery-Clay intersection, a "four" by Mount Sutro, and a "one" in the middle of Corona Heights. He noted that the straight line became like a balance or scales then (two lever arms) with the balancing point or fulcrum somewhere between Corona Heights and Montgomery-Clay. It even balanced mathematically: four plus one equals five— just as was noted in the curse before the final injunction. That miserable fulcrum (0), wherever it was, would surely be pressed to death by those two great lever arms ("Give me a place to stand and I will stomp the world to death"—Archimedes) just as that poor little lower-case "his" was crushed between that dreadful *"BE"* and the three big capitalized words.

Yes, that unfortunate (0) would surely be suffocated, compressed to a literal nothing, especially when "the weights" were "on." Now what—?

Suddenly it occurred to Franz that whatever had been the case in the past, the weights were certainly on *now*, with the TV tower standing three-legged on Mount Sutro and with Montgomery-Clay the location of the Transamerica Pyramid, San Francisco's tallest building! (The "something else" was that the Monkey Block had been torn down to clear a site first for a parking lot, then for the Transamerica Pyramid. Closer and closer!)

That was why the curse hadn't got Smith. He'd died before either structure had been built. The trap hadn't become set until *later*.

The Transamerica Pyramid and the 1,000-foot TV tower— those were crushers, all right.

But it was ridiculous to think that de Castries could have predicted the building of those structures. And in any case coincidence—lucky hits—was an adequate explanation. Pick any intersection in downtown San Francisco and there was at least a 50 percent chance of there being a high rise there, or nearby.

But why was he holding his breath then; why was there a faint roaring in his ears; why were his fingers cold and tingling?

Why had de Castries told Klaas and Ricker that prescience, or foreknowledge, was possible at certain spots in megacities? Why had he named his book (it lay beside Franz now, a dirty gray) *Megapolisomancy*?

Whatever the truth behind, the weights certainly were on now, no question.

Which made it all the more important to find out the real location of that baffling 607 Rhodes where the old devil had lived (dragged out the tail end of his life) and Smith had asked his questions . . . and where, according to the curse, the ledger containing the Grand Cipher was hidden . . . and where the curse would be fulfilled. Really, it was quite like a detective story. By Dashiell Hammett? "X marks the spot" where the victim was (will be?) discovered, crushed to death? They'd put up a brass plaque at Bush and Stockton near where Brigid O'Shaunessy had shot Miles Archer in Hammett's *The Maltese Falcon*, but there were no memorials for Thibaut de Castries, a real person. Where was the elusive X, or mystic (0)? Where *was* 607 Rhodes? Really, he should have asked Byers when he'd the chance. Call him up now? No, he'd severed his connection there. Beaver Street was an area he didn't want to venture back to, even by phone. At least for now. But he left off poring over the map as futile.

His gaze fell on the 1927 San Francisco City Directory he'd ripped off that morning that formed the midsection of his Scholar's Mistress. Might as well finish that bit of research right now—find the name of this building, if it ever had one, if it had, indeed, become a listed hotel. He heaved the thick volume onto his lap and turned the dingily yellowed pages to the "Hotels" section. At another time he'd have been amused by the old advertisements for patent medicines and barber parlors.

He thought of all the searching around he'd done this

morning at the Civic Center. It all seemed very far off now and quite naive.

Let's see, the best way would be to search through the addresses, not for Geary Street—there'd be a lot of hotels on Geary—but for 811. There'd probably be only one of those if any. He began running a fingernail down the first column rather slowly, but steadily.

He was on the next to last column before he came to an 811. Yes, it was Geary too, all right. The name was . . . the Rhodes Hotel.

XXV

Franz found himself standing in the hall facing his closed door. His body was trembling very slightly all over—a general fine tremor.

Then he realized why he had come out here. It was to check the number on the door, the small dark oblong on which was incised in pale gray, "607." He wanted to see it actually and to see his room from the outside (and incidentally dissociate himself from the curse, get off the target).

He got the feeling that if he knocked just now (as Clark Smith must have knocked so many times on this same door) Thibaut de Castries would open it, his sunk-cheeked face a webwork of fine gray wrinkles as if it had been powdered with fine ashes.

If he went back in without knocking, it would be as he'd left it. But if he knocked, then the old spider would wake . . .

He felt vertigo, as if the building were beginning to lean over with him inside it, to rotate ever so slowly, at least at first. The feeling was like earthquake panic.

He had to orient himself at once, he told himself, to keep himself from falling over with 811. He went down the dark hall (the bulb inside the globe over the elevator door was still out) past the black broom closet, the black-painted window of the airshaft, the elevator itself, and softly up the stairs two flights, gripping the banister to keep his balance, and under the peaked skylight of the stairwell into the sinister black room that housed under a larger skylight the elevator's motor and relays, the Green Dwarf and the Spider, and so out onto the tarred and graveled roof.

The stars were in the sky where they should be, though naturally dimmed somewhat by the glare of the gibbous moon, which was in the top of the sky a little to the south. Orion and Aldebaran climbed the east. Polaris was at his unchanging spot. All round about stretched the angular horizon, crenelated with high rises and skyscrapers marked rather sparsely with red warning and yellow window lights, as if somewhat aware of the need to conserve energy. A moderate wind was from the west.

His dizziness gone at least, Franz moved toward the back of the roof, past the mouths of the air shafts that were like walled square wells, and watchful for the low vent pipes covered with heavy wire netting that were so easy to trip over, until he stood at the roof's west edge above his room and Cal's. One of his hands rested on the low wall. Off a short way behind him was the airshaft that dropped straight down by the black window he'd passed in the hall and the corresponding ones above and below it on the other floors. Opening on the same shaft, he recalled, were the bathroom windows of another set of apartments and also a vertical row of quite small windows that could only let into the disused broom closets, originally to give them some light, he supposed. He looked west at the flashing reds of the Tower and at the irregularly rounded darkness of the Heights. The wind freshened a little.

He thought at last, this is the Rhodes Hotel. I live at 607 Rhodes, the place I've hunted for everywhere else. There's really no mystery at all about it. Behind me is the Transamerica Pyramid (5). (He looked over his shoulder at it where its single red light flashed bright and its lighted windows were as narrow as the holes in a business-machine card.) In front of me (he turned back) are the TV tower (4) and the crowned and hunchbacked eminence (1) where the old spider king's ashes lie buried, as they say. And I am at the fulcrum (0) of the curse.

As he fatalistically told himself that, the stars seemed to grow dimmer still, a sickly pallor, and he felt a sickness and a heaviness within himself and all around, as if the freshening wind had blown something malignant out of the west to this dark roof, as if some universal disease or cosmic pollution were spiraling from Corona Heights to the whole cityscape and so up to the stars, infecting even Orion and the Shield—as if with the stars' help he'd been getting things in place and now something was refusing to stay in its appointed spot, refusing to stay buried and forgotten, like Daisy's cancer, and interfering with the rule of number and order in the universe.

He heard a sudden scuffing and scuttling sound behind him and he spun around. Nothing there, nothing that he could see, and yet . . .

He moved to the nearest airshaft and looked down. Moonlight penetrated it as far as his floor, where the little window to the broom closet was open. Below that, it was very dimly lit from two of the bathroom windows—indirect light seeping from the living rooms of those apartments. He heard a sound as of an animal snuffing, or was that his own heavy breathing reflected by the echoing sheet-iron? And he fancied he saw (but it was very dim) something with rather too many limbs moving about, rapidly down and up.

He jerked his head back and then up, as if looking to the stars for help, but they seemed as lonely and uncaring as the very distant windows a lone man sees who is about to be murdered on a moor or sink into the Great Grimpen Marsh at dead of night. Panic seized him and he rushed back the way he'd come. As he passed through the black room of the elevator, the big copper switches snapped loudly and the relay arms clashed grindingly, hurrying his flight as if there were a monster Spider snapping at his heels at a Green Dwarf's groaning commands.

He got some control of himself going down the stairs, but on his own floor as he passed the black-painted window (near the dark ceiling globe) he got the feeling there was something supremely agile crouched against the other side of it, clinging in the airshaft, something midway between a black panther and a spider monkey, but perhaps as many-limbed as a spider and perhaps with the creviced, ashen face of Thibaut de Castries, about to burst in through the wire-toughened glass. As he passed the black door of the broom closet, he remembered the small window opening from it into the shaft, that would not be too small for such a creature. And now the broom closet itself was right up against the wall that ran along the inside of his couch. How many of us in a big city, he asked himself, know anything about what lies in or just on the other side of the outer walls of our apartments—often the very wall against which we sleep?—as hidden and unreachable as our internal organs. We can't even trust the walls that guard us.

In the hall, the broom closet door seemed suddenly to bulge. For a frantic moment he thought he'd left his keys in his room, then he found them in his pocket and located the right one on the ring and got the door open and himself inside and the door double-locked behind him against whatever might have followed him from the roof.

But could he trust his room with its open window? No matter how unreachable the latter was in theory. He searched the place again, this time finding himself compelled to view each volume of space. Even pulling the file drawers out and peering behind the folders did not make him feel embarrassed. He searched his clothes cabinet last and so thoroughly that he discovered on its floor against the wall behind some boots an unopened bottle of kirschwasser he must have squirreled away there over a year ago when he was still drinking.

He glanced toward the window with its crumbles of ancient paper and found himself picturing de Castries when he'd lived here. The old spider had doubtless sat before the window for long hours, viewing his grave-to-be on Corona Heights with forested Mount Sutro beyond. And had he previsioned the tower that would rise there? The old spiritualists and occultists believed that the astral remains, the odic dust, of a person lingered on in rooms where he'd lived.

What else had the old spider dreamed about there? rocking his body in the chair a little. His days of glory in pre-

Earthquake Frisco? The men and women he had teased to suicide, or tucked under various fulcrums to be crushed? His father (Afric adventurer or hayseed printer), his black panther (if he'd ever had one, let alone several), his young Polish mistress (or slim girl-Anima), his Veiled Lady?

If only there were someone to talk to and free him from these morbid thoughts! If only Cal and the others would get back from the concert. But his wristwatch indicated that it was only a few minutes past nine. Hard to believe his room searches and roof visit had taken so little time, but the second hand of his wristwatch was sweeping around steadily in almost imperceptibly tiny jerks.

The thought of the lonely hours ahead made him feel desperate and the bottle in his hand with its white promise of oblivion tempted him, but the dread of what might happen when he had made himself unarousable was still greater.

He set the cherry brandy down beside yesterday's mail, also still unopened, and his prisms and slate. He'd thought the last was blank, but now he fancied he saw faint marks on it. He took it and the chalk and prisms lying on it over to the lamp at the head of his couch. He'd thought of switching on the 200-watt ceiling light, but somehow he didn't like the idea of having his window stand out that glaringly bright, perhaps for a watcher on Corona Heights.

There *were* spidery chalk marks on the slate—a half dozen faint triangles that narrowed toward the downward corner, as if someone or some force had been lightly outlining (the chalk perhaps moving like the planchette of a ouija board) the snouted face of his paramental. And now the chalk and one of the prisms *were* jumping about like planchettes, his hands holding the slate were shaking so.

His mind was almost paralyzed—almost blanked—by sudden fear, but a free corner of it was thinking how a white five-pointed star with one point directed *upward* (or outward) is supposed in witchcraft to protect a room from the entry of evil spirits as if the invading entity would be spiked on the star's upward (or outward) point, and so he was hardly surprised when he found that he'd put down the slate on the end of his piled coffee table and was chalking such stars on the sills of his windows, the open one and the locked one in the bathroom, and above his door. He felt distantly ridiculous, but didn't even consider not completing the stars. In fact, his imagination ran on to the possibility of even more secret passageways and hiding places in the building than the airshafts and broom closets (there would have been a dumbwaiter and a laundry chute in the Rhodes Hotel and who knows what auxiliary doors) and he became bothered that he couldn't inspect the back walls of the closet and clothes cabinet more clearly, and in the end he closed the doors of both and chalked a star above them—and a small star above the transom.

He was considering chalking one more star on the wall by his couch where it abutted the broom closet in the hall, when there sounded at his door a sharp *knock-knock*. He put on the chain before he opened it the two inches which that allowed.

XXVI

Half of a toothy mouth and large brown eye were grinning up at him across the chain and a voice saying, ''E-chess?''

Franz quickly unhooked the chain and opened the door eagerly. He was vastly relieved to have a familiar person with him, sharply disappointed that it was someone with whom he could hardly communicate at all—certainly not the stuff crowding his mind—yet consoled by the thought that at least they shared the language of chess. Chess would at least pass some time, he hoped.

Fernando came in beaming, though frowning questioningly a moment at the chain, and then again at Franz when he quickly reclosed and double locked the door.

In answer, Franz offered him a drink. Fernando's black eyebrows went up at sight of the square bottle, and he smiled wider and nodded, but when Franz had opened the bottle and poured him a small wineglass, he hesitated, asking with his mobile features and expressive hands why Franz wasn't drinking.

As the simplest solution, Franz poured himself a bit in another wineglass, hiding with his fingers how little, and tilted the glass until the aromatic liquid wet his closed lips. He offered Fernando a second drink, but the latter pointed towards the chessmen, then at his head, which he shook smilingly.

Franz set the chessboard somewhat precariously on top of the piled folders on the coffee table, and sat down on the bed. Fernando looked somewhat dubiously at the arrangement, then shrugged and smiled, drew up a chair and sat down opposite. He got the white pawn and when they'd set up the men he opened confidently.

Franz made his moves quickly, too. He found himself almost automatically resuming the "on guard" routine he'd employed at Beaver Street while listening to Byers. His watchful gaze would move from the end of the wall behind him to his clothes cabinet to the door, then past a small bookcase to the closet door, across the table crowded with the unopened mail and all, past the bathroom door to the larger bookcase and desk, pause at the window, then travel along his filing cabinets to the steam radiator and to the other end of the wall behind him, then start back again. He got the ghost of a bitter taste as he wet his lips—the kirschwasser.

Fernando won in twenty moves or so. He looked thoughtfully at Franz for a couple of moments, as if about to make some point about his indifferent play, but instead smiled and began to set up the men with colors reversed.

With deliberate recklessness Franz opened with the king's gambit. Fernando countered in the center with his queen's pawn. Despite the dangerous and chancy position, Franz found he couldn't concentrate on the game. He kept searching his mind for other precautions to take besides his visual guard. He strained his ears for sounds at the door and beyond the other partitions. He wished desperately that Fernando had more English, or weren't so deaf. The combination was simply too much.

And the time passed so slowly. The large hand of his wristwatch was frozen. It was like one of those moments at a drunken party—when you're on the verge of blackout—that seem to last forever. At this rate it would be ages before the concert was over.

And then it occurred to him that he had no guarantee that Cal and the others would return at once. People generally went to bars or restaurants after performances, to celebrate or talk.

He was faintly aware of Fernando studying him between the moves.

Of course he could go back to the concert himself when Fernando left. But that wouldn't settle anything. He'd left the concert determined to solve the problem of de Castries's curse and all the strangeness that went with it. And at least he'd made progress. He'd already answered the literal 607 Rhodes question, but of course he'd meant a lot more than that when he'd spoken to Saul.

But how could he find the answer to the whole thing anyway? Serious psychic or occult research was a matter of elaborate preparation and study, using delicate, carefully checked-out instruments, or at any rate sensitive, trained people salted by previous experience: mediums, sensitives, telepaths, clairvoyants and such—who'd proved themselves with Rhine cards and what not. What could he hope to do just by himself in one evening? What had he been thinking of when he'd walked out on Cal's concert and left her that message?

Yet somehow he had the feeling that all the physical research experts and their massed experience wouldn't really be a bit of help to him now. Any more than the science experts would be with their incredibly refined electronic and radionic detectors and photography and whatnot. That amid all the fields of occult and fringe-occult that were flourishing today—witchcraft, astrology, biofeedback, dowsing, psychokinesis, auras, acupuncture, exploratory LSD trips, loops in the time stream, astrology (much of them surely fake, some of them maybe real)—this that was happening to him was altogether different.

He pictured himself going back to the concert, and he didn't like the picture. Very faintly, he seemed to hear the swift, glittery music of a harpsichord, still luring and lashing him on imperiously.

Fernando cleared his throat. Franz realized he'd over-looked a mate in three moves and had lost the second game in as few moves as the first. He automatically started to set up the pieces for a third.

Fernando's hand, palm down in an emphatic no, prevented him. Franz looked up.

Fernando was looking intently at him. The Peruvian frowned and shook a finger at Franz, indicated he was concerned about him. Then he pointed at the chessboard, then at his own head, touching his temple. Then he shook his head decisively, frowning and pointing toward Franz again.

Franz got the message: "Your mind is not on the game." He nodded.

Fernando stood up, pushing his chair out of the way, and pantomimed a man afraid of something that was after him. Crouching a little, he kept looking around, much as Franz had been doing, but more obviously. He kept turning and looking suddenly behind him, now in one direction, now the other, his face big-eyed and fearful.

Franz nodded that he got it.

Fernando moved around the room, darting quick glances at the hall door and the window. While looking in another direction he rapped loudly on the radiator with his clenched fist, then instantly gave a great start and backed off from it.

A man very afraid of something, startled by sudden noises, that must mean. Franz nodded again.

Fernando did the same thing with the bathroom door and with the nearby wall. After rapping on the latter he stared at Franz and said, *"Hay hechicería. Hechicería ocultada en murallas."*

What had Cal said that meant? "Witchcraft, witchcraft hidden in walls." Franz recalled his own wonderings about secret doors and chutes and passageways. But did Fernando mean it literally or figuratively? Franz nodded, but pursed his lips and otherwise tried to put on a questioning look.

Fernando appeared to notice the chalked stars for the first time. White on pale woodwork, they weren't easy to see. His eyebrows went up and he smiled understandingly at Franz and nodded approvingly. He indicated the stars and then held his hands out, palms flat and away from him, at the window and doors, as if keeping something out, holding it at bay— meanwhile continuing to nod approvingly.

"Bueno," he said.

Franz nodded, at the same time marveling at the fear that had led him to snatch at such an irrational protective device, one that the superstition-sodden (?) Fernando understood instantly—stars against witches. (And there had been five-pointed stars among the graffiti on Corona Heights, intended to keep dead bones at rest and ashes quiet. Byers had sprayed them there.)

He stood up and went to the table and offered Fernando another drink, uncapping the bottle, but Fernando refused it with a short crosswise wave of his hand, palm down, and crossed to where Franz had been and rapped on the wall behind the couch and turning toward Franz repeated, *"Hechicería ocultada en muralla!"*

Franz looked at him questioningly. But the Peruvian only bowed his head and put three fingers to his forehead, symbolizing thought (and possibly the Peruvian was actually thinking, too).

Then Fernando looked up with an air of revelation, took the chalk from the slate beside the chessboard, and drew on the wall a five-pointed star, larger and more conspicuous and better than any of Franz's.

"Bueno," Fernando said again, nodding. Then he pointed down behind the bed toward the baseboard it hid, repeated, *"Hay hechicería en muralla,"* and went quickly to the hall door and pantomimed himself going away and coming back, and then looked at Franz solicitously, lifting his eyebrows, as if to ask, "You'll be all right in the meantime?"

Rather bemused by the pantomime and feeling suddenly quite weary, Franz nodded with a smile and (thinking of the star Fernando had drawn and the feeling of fellowship it had given him) said, *"Gracias."*

Fernando nodded with a smile, unbolted the door, and went out, shutting the door behind him. A little later Franz heard the

elevator stop at this floor, its doors open and close, and go
droning down, as if headed for the basement of the universe.

XXVII

Franz felt a little as though he imagined a punchdrunk boxer
would. His ears and eyes were still on guard, tracking the
faintest sounds and slightest sights, but tiredly, almost pro-
testingly, fighting the urge to slump. Despite all the day's
shocks and surprises, his evening mind (slave of his body's
chemistry) was taking over. Presumably Fernando had gone
somewhere—but why? to fetch what?—and eventually would
come back as he'd pantomimed—but how soon? and again
why? Truly, Franz didn't much care. He began rather automatically to tidy around him.

   Soon he sat down with a weary sigh on the side of his bed
and stared at the incredibly piled and crowded coffee table,
wondering where to start. At the bottom was his neatly layered current writing work, which he'd hardly looked at or
thought of since day before yesterday. *Weird Underground*—
it was ironic. Atop that were the phone on its long cord, his
broken binoculars, his big, tar-blackened, overflowing ashtray (but he hadn't smoked since he'd got in tonight and wasn't
moved to now), the chessboard with its men half set up,
beside it the flat slate with its chalk, his prisms, and some
captured chess pieces, and finally the tiny wineglasses and
the square bottle of kirschwasser, still uncapped, where he'd
set it down after offering it a last time to Fernando.

   Gradually the whole jumbled arrangement began to seem
drolly amusing to Franz, quite beyond dealing with. Although his eyes and ears were still tracking automatically
(and kept on doing so) he almost giggled weakly. His evening
mind invariably had its silly side, a tendency toward puns
and oddly mixed clichés, and faintly psychotic epigrams—
foolishness born of fatigue. He recalled how neatly the psychologist F.C. MacKnight had described the transition from

waking to sleeping: the mind's short logical daytime steps becoming longer by degrees, each mental jump a little more farfetched and wild, until (with never a break) they were utterly unpredictable giant strides and one was dreaming.

He picked up the city map from where he'd left it spread on his bed and without folding it he laid it as if it were a coverlet atop the clutter on the coffee table.

"Go to sleep, little junk pile," he said with humorous tenderness.

And he laid the ruler he'd been using on top of that, like a magician relinquishing his wand.

Then (his ears and eyes still doing their guard rounds) he half-turned to the wall where Fernando had chalked the star and began to put his books to bed too, as he had the mess on the coffee table, began to tuck in his Scholar's Mistress for the night, as it were—a homely operation on familiar things that was the perfect antidote even to wildest fears.

Upon the yellowed, brown-edged pages of *Megapolisomancy*—the section about "electro-mephitic city-stuff"—he gently laid Smith's journal, open at the curse.

"You're very pale, my dear," he observed (the rice paper), "and yet the left-hand side of your face has all those very odd black beauty marks, a whole page of them. Dream of a lovely Satanist party in full evening dress, all white and black like *Marienbad*, in an angelfood ballroom with creamy slim borzois stepping about like courteous giant spiders."

He touched a shoulder that was chiefly Lovecraft's *Outsider*, its large forty-year-old Winnebago Eggshell pages open at "The Thing on the Doorstep." He murmured to his mistress, "Don't deliquesce now, dear, like poor Asenath Waite. Remember, you've got no dental work (that I know of) by which you could be positively identified." He glanced at the other shoulder: coverless, crumble-edged *Wonder Stories* and *Weird Tales*, with Smith's "The Disinterment of Venus" spread at the top. "That's a far better way to go," he commented. "All rosy marble under the worms and mold."

The chest was Ms. Lettland's monumental book, rather appropriately open at that mysterious, provocative, and question-raising chapter, "The Mammary Mystique: Cold as . . ." He thought of the feminist author's strange disappearance in Seattle. Now no one ever could know her further answers.

His fingers trailed across the rather slender, black, gray-mottled waist made of James's ghost stories—the book had once been thoroughly rained on and then been laboriously dried out, page by forever wrinkled, discolored page—and he straightened a little the stolen city directory (representing hips), still open at the hotels section, saying quietly, "There, that'll be more comfortable for you. You know, dear friend, you're doubly 607 Rhodes now," and wondered rather dully what he meant by that.

He heard the elevator stop outside and its doors open, but didn't hear it going off again. He waited tautly, but there was no knock at his door, no footsteps in the hall that he could hear. There came from somewhere through the wall the faint jar of a stubborn door being quietly opened or closed, then nothing more of that.

He touched *The Spider Glyph in Time* where it was lying just below the directory. Earlier in the day his Scholar's Mistress had been lying on her face, but now on her back. He mused a moment (What had Lettland said?) as to why the exterior female genitalia were thought of as a spider. The tendriled blot of hair? The mouth that opened vertically like a spider's jaws instead of horizontally like the human face's lips or the labia of the Chinagirls of sailors' legendry? Old fever-racked Santos-Lobos suggested it involved the time to spin a web, the spider's clock. And what a charming cranny for a cobweb.

His feather-touching fingers moved on to *Knochenmädchen in Pelze (mit Peitsche)*—more of the dark hairiness, now changing to soft fur (furs rather) wrapping the skeleton girls—and *Ames et Fantômes de Douleur*, the other thigh; de Sade (or his posthumous counterfeiter), tiring of the flesh, had really wanted to make the mind scream and the angels sob; shouldn't *The Ghosts of Pain* be *The Agonies of Ghosts*?

That book, taken along with Masoch's *Skeleton Girls in Furs (With Whips)*, made him think of what a wealth of death was here under his questing hands. Lovecraft dying quite swiftly in 1937, writing determinedly until the end, taking notes on his last sensations. (Did he see paramentals then?) Smith going more slowly some quarter-century later, his brain nibbled by little strokes. Santos-Lobos burned by his fevers to a thinking cinder. And was vanished Lettland dead? Montague there (his *White Tape* made a knee, only its paper was getting yellow) drowning by emphysema while he still wrote footnotes upon our self-suffocating culture.

Death and the fear of death! Franz recalled how deeply Lovecraft's "The Color Out of Space" had depressed him when he'd read it in his teens—the New England farmer had his family rotting away alive, poisoned by radioactives from the ends of the universe. Yet at the same time it had been so fascinating. What was the whole literature of supernatural horror but an essay to make death itself exciting?—wonder and strangeness to life's very end. But even as he thought that, he realized how tired he was. Tired, depressed, and morbid—the unpleasant aspects of his evening mind, the dark side of its coin.

And speaking of darkness, where did Our Lady of Same fit in? (*Suspiria de Profundis* made the other knee and *De Profundis* a calf. "How do you feel about Lord Alfred Douglas, my dear? Does he turn you on? I think Oscar was much too good for him.") Was the TV tower out there in the night her statue?—it was tall enough and turreted. Was night her "treble veil of crape"? and the nineteen reds, winking or steady, "the fierce light of a blazing misery"? Well, he was miserable enough himself for two. Make her laugh at that. Come, sweet night, and pall me.

He finished tucking in his Scholar's Mistress—Prof. Nostig's *The Subliminal Occult* ("You disposed of Kirlian photography, doctor, but could you do as well with the paranatural?"), the copies of *Gnostica* (any relation to Prof. Nostig?), *The Mauritzius Case* (did Etzel Andergast see paramentals in Berlin? and Waramme smokier ones in Chicago?), *Hecate, or the Future of Witchcraft* by Yeats ("Why did you have that book destroyed, William Butler?"), and *Journey to the End of the Night* ("And to your toes, my dear.")—and wearily stretched himself out beside her, *still* stubbornly watchful for the tiniest suspicious sounds and sights. It occurred to him how he had come home to her at night as to a real wife or woman, to be relaxed and comforted after all the tensions, trials, and dangers (Remember they were still there!) of the day.

It occurred to him that he could probably still catch the Brandenburg Fifth if he sprang up and hurried, but he was too inert even to stir—to do anything except stay awake and on guard until Cal and Gun and Saul returned.

The shaded light at the head of his bed fluctuated a little, dimming, then brightening sharply, then dimming again as if the bulb were getting very old, but he was much too weary to get up and replace it or even just turn on another light. Besides, he didn't want his window too brightly lit for something on Corona Heights (Might still be there instead of here. Who knew?) to see.

He noted a faint, pale gray glitter around the edges of the casement window—the westering gibbous moon at last beginning to peer in from above, swing past the southern high rise into full view. He felt the impulse to get up and take a last look at the TV tower, say good night to his slender thousand-foot goddess attended by moon and stars, put her to bed, too, as it were, say his last prayers, but the same weariness prevented him. Also, he didn't want to show himself to Corona Heights or look upon the dark blotch of that place ever again.

The light at the head of his bed shone steadily, but it did seem a shade dimmer than it had been before the fluctuation, or was that just the pall cast by his evening mind?

Forget that now. Forget it all. The world was a rotten place. This city was a mess with its gimcrack high rises and trumpery skyscrapers—*Towers of Treason* indeed. It had all tumbled down and burned in 1906 (at least everything around this building had) and soon enough would again, and all of the papers be fed to the document-shredding machines, with or without the help of paramentals. (And was not humped, umber Corona Heights even now stirring?) And the entire world was just as bad; it was perishing of pollution, drowning and suffocating in chemical and atomic poisons, detergents and insecticides, industrial effluvia, smog, the stench of sulfuric acid, the quantities of steel, cement, aluminum ever bright, eternal plastics, omnipresent paper, gas and electron floods—electro-mephitic city-stuff indeed! though the world hardly needed the paranatural to do it to death. It was blackly cancerous, like Lovecraft's farm family slain by strange radioactives come by meteor from the end of nowhere.

But that was not the end. (He edged a little closer to his Scholar's Mistress.) The electro-mephitic sickness was spreading, had spread (had metastasized) from this world to everywhere. The universe was terminally diseased; it would die thermodynamically. Even the stars were infected. Who thought that those bright points of light meant anything? What were they but a swarm of phosphorescent fruit flies momentarily frozen in an utterly random pattern around a garbage planet?

He tried his best to "hear" the Brandenburg Fifth that Cal was playing, the vastly varied, infinitely ordered diamond streamers of quill-plucked sound that made it the parent of all piano concertos. Music has the power to release things, Cal had said, to make them fly. Perhaps it would break this mood. Papageno's bells were magic—and a protection against magic. But all was silence.

What was the use of life anyhow? He had laboriously recovered from his alcoholism only to face the Noseless One once more in a new triangular mask. Effort wasted, he told himself. In fact, he would have reached out and taken a bitter, stinging drink from the square bottle, except he was too tired to make the effort. He was an old fool to think Cal cared for him, as much a fool as Byers with his camp Chinese swinger and his teen-agers, his kinky paradise of sexy, slim-fingered, groping cherubs.

Franz's gaze wandered to Daisy's painted, dark-nested face upon the wall, narrowed by perspective to slit eyes and mouth that sneered above a tapering chin.

At that moment he began to hear a very faint scuffing in the wall, like that of a very large rat trying very hard to be quiet. From how far did it come? He couldn't tell. What were the first sounds of an earthquake like?—the ones only the horses and dogs can hear. There came a louder scuff, then nothing more.

He remembered the relief he'd felt when cancer had lobotomized Daisy's brain and she had reached the presumably unfeeling vegetable stage ("the flat effect," neurologists called it as if the soaring house of mind became a lightless and low-ceilinged apartment complex) and the need to keep himself anesthetized with alcohol had become a shade less pressing.

The light behind his head arced brightly greenish white, fluttered, and went out. He started to sit up, but barely lifted a finger. The darkness in the room took forms like the Black Pictures of witchcraft, crowd-stupefying marvels, and Olympian horrors which Goya had painted for himself alone in his old age, a very proper way to decorate a home. His lifted finger vaguely moved toward Fernando's blacked-out star, then dropped back. A small sob formed and faded in his throat. He snuggled close to his Scholar's Mistress, his fingers touching her Lovecraftian shoulder. He thought of how she was the only real person that he had. Darkness and sleep closed on him without a sound.

Time passed.

Franz dreamed of utter darkness and of a great, white, crackling, ripping noise, as of endless sheets of newsprint being crumpled and dozens of books being torn across at once and their stiff covers cracked and crushed—a paper pandemonium.

But perhaps there was no mighty noise (only the sound of Time clearing her throat), for he next thought he woke very tranquilly into two rooms: this with the this-in-dream superimposed. He tried to make them come together. Daisy was lying peacefully beside him. Both he and she were very, very happy. They had talked last night and all was very well. Her slim, silken dry fingers touched his cheek and neck.

With a cold plunge of feelings, the suspicion came to him that she was dead. The touching fingers moved reassuringly. There seemed to be almost too many of them. No, Daisy was not dead, but she was very sick. She was alive, but in the vegetable stage, mercifully tranquilized by her malignancy. Horrible, yet it was still a comfort to lie beside her. Like

Cal, she was so young, even in this half-death. Her fingers were so very slim and silken dry, so very strong and many, all starting to grip tightly—they were not fingers but wiry black vines rooted inside her skull, growing in profusion out of her cavernous orbits, gushing luxuriantly out of the triangular hole between the nasal and the vomer bones, twining in tendrils from under her upper teeth so white, pushing insidiously and insistently, like grass from sidewalk crack, out of her pale brown cranium, bursting apart the squamous, sagittal, and *coronal* sutures.

Franz sat up with a convulsive start, gagging on his feelings, his heart pounding, cold sweat breaking from his forehead.

XXVIII

Moonlight was pouring in the casement window, making a long coffin-size pool upon the carpeted floor beyond the coffee table, throwing the rest of the room into darker shadow by contrast.

He was fully clothed; his feet ached in his shoes.

He realized with enormous gratitude that he was truly awake at last, that Daisy and the vegetative horror that had destroyed her were both gone, vanished far swifter than smoke.

He found himself acutely aware of all the space around him: the cool air against his face and hands, the eight chief corners of his room, the slot outside the window shooting down six floors between this building and the next to basement level, the seventh floor and roof above, the hall on the other side of the wall beyond the head of his bed, the broom closet on the other side of the wall beside him that held Daisy's picture and Fernando's star, and the airshaft beyond the broom closet.

And all his other sensations and all his thoughts seemed equally vivid and pristine. He told himself he had his morning mind again, all rinsed by sleep, fresh as sea air. How wonderful! He'd slept the whole night through (Had Cal and the boys knocked softly at his door and gone smiling and shrugging away?) and now waking an hour or so before dawn, just as the long astronomical twilight began, simply because he'd gone to sleep so early. Had Byers slept as well?—he doubted that, even with his skinny-slim, decadent soporifics.

But then he realized that the moonlight still was streaming in, as it had started to do before he slept, proving that he'd only been asleep an hour or less.

His skin quivered a little, and the muscles of his legs grew tense, his whole body quickened as if in anticipation of . . . he didn't know what.

He felt a paralyzing touch on the back of his neck. Then the narrow, prickly dry vines (it felt—though they were fewer now) moved with a faint rustle through his lifted hairs past his ear to his right cheek and jaw. They were growing out of the wall . . . no . . . they were not vines, they were the fingers of the narrow right hand of his Scholar's Mistress, who had sat up naked beside him, a tall, pale shape unfeatured in the smudging gloom. She had an aristocratically small, narrow face and head (black hair?), a long neck, imperially wide shoulders, an elegant, Empire-high waist, slender hips, and long, long legs—very much the shape of the skeletal steel TV tower, a far slenderer Orion (with Rigel serving as a foot instead of knee).

The fingers of her right arm that was snaked around his neck now crept across his cheek and toward his lips, while she turned and leaned her face a little toward his. It was still featureless against the darkness, yet the question rose unbidden in his mind whether it was just such an intense look that the witch Asenath (Waite) Derby would have turned upon her husband Edward Derby when they were in bed, with old Ephraim Waite (Thibaut de Castries?) peering with her from her hypnotic eyes.

She leaned her face closer still, the fingers of her right hand crept softly yet intrusively upward toward his nostrils and eye, while out of the gloom at her left side her other hand came weaving on its serpent-slender arm toward his face. All her movements and postures were elegant and beautiful.

Shrinking away violently, he threw up his own left hand protectively and with a convulsive thrust of his right arm and of his legs against the mattress, he heaved his body across the coffee table, oversetting it and carrying all its heaped contents clattering and thudding and clashing (the glasses and bottle and binoculars) and cascading with him to the floor beyond, where (having turned over completely) he lay in the edge of the pool of moonlight, except for his head, which was in the shadow between it and the door. In turning over, his face had come close to the big ashtray as it was oversetting and to the gushing kirschwasser bottle and he had gotten whiffs of stinking tobacco tar and stinging, bitter alcohol. He felt the hard shapes of chessmen under him. He was staring back wildly at the bed he'd quitted and for the moment he saw only darkness.

Then out of the darkness there lifted up, but not very high, the long, pale shape of his Scholar's Mistress. She seemed to look about her like a mongoose or weasel, her small head dipping this way and that on its slender neck; then with a nerve-racking dry rustling sound she came writhing and scuttling swiftly after him across the low table and all its scattered and disordered stuff, her long-fingered hands reaching out far ahead of her on their wiry pale arms. Even as he started to try to get to his feet, they closed upon his shoulder and side with a fearfully strong grip and there flashed instantaneously across his mind a remembered line of poetry—"Ghosts are we, but with skeletons of steel."

With a surge of strength born of his terror, he tore himself free of the trapping hands. But they had prevented him from rising, with the result that he had only heaved over again through the moonlit pool and lay on his back, threshing and flailing, in its far edge, his head still in shadow.

Papers and chessmen and the ashtray's contents scattered further and flew. A wineglass crunched as his heel hit it. The dumped phone began to beep like a furious pedantic mouse, from some near street a siren started to yelp like dogs being tortured, there was a great ripping noise as in his dream— the scattered papers churned and rose in seeming shreds a little from the floor—and through it all there sounded deep-throated, rasping screams which were Franz's own.

His Scholar's Mistress came twisting and hitching into the

moonlight. Her face was still shadowed but he could see that *her thin, wide-shouldered body was apparently formed solely of shredded and tightly compacted paper*, mottled pale brown and yellowish with age, as if made up of the chewed pages of all the magazines and books that had formed her on the bed, while about and back from her shadowed face there streamed black hair. (The books' shredded black covers?) Her wiry limbs in particular seemed to be made up entirely of very tightly twisted and braided pale brown paper as she darted toward him with terrible swiftness and threw them around him, pinioning his own arms (and her long legs scissoring about his) despite all his flailings and convulsive kickings while, utterly winded by his screaming, he gasped and mewed.

Then she twisted her head around and up, so that the moonlight struck her face. It was narrow and tapering, shaped somewhat like a fox's or a weasel's, formed like the rest of her of fiercely compacted paper constrictedly humped and creviced, but layered over in this area with dead white (the rice paper?) speckled or pocked everywhere with a rash of irregular small black marks. (Thibaut's ink?) It had no eyes, although it seemed to stare into his brain and heart. It had no nose. (Was *this* the Noseless One?) It had no mouth—but then the long chin began to twitch and lift a little like a beast's snout and he saw that it was open at the end.

He realized that *this* was what had been under the loose robes and black veils of de Castries's Mystery Woman, who'd dogged his footsteps even to his grave, compact of intellectuality, all paper work (Scholar's Mistress indeed!), the Queen of the Night, the lurker at the summit, the thing that even Thibaut de Castries feared, Our Lady of Darkness.

The cables of the braided arms and legs twisted around him tighter and the face, going into shadow again, moved silently down toward his; and all that Franz could do was strain his own face back and away.

He thought in a flash of the disappearance of the gutted old pulp magazines and realized that they, crumbled and torn to bits, must have been the raw material for the pale brown figure in the casement window he'd seen twice from Corona Heights.

He saw on the black ceiling, above the dipping black-haired muzzle, a little patch of soft, harmonious ghostly colors—the pastel spectrum of moonlight, cast by one of his prisms lying in the pool on the floor.

The dry, rough, hard face pressed against his, blocking his mouth, squeezing his nostrils; the snout dug itself into his neck. He felt a crushing, incalculably great weight upon him. (The TV tower and the Transamerica! And the stars?) And filling his mouth and nose, the bone-dry, bitter dust of Thibaut de Castries.

At that instant the room was flooded with bright, white light and, as if it were an injected instant stimulant, he was able to twist his face away from the rugose horror and his shoulders halfway around.

The door to the hall was open wide, a key still in the lock, Cal was standing on the threshold, her back against the jamb, a finger of her right hand touching the light switch. She was panting, as if she'd been running hard. She was still wearing her white concert dress and over it her black velvet coat, hanging open. She was looking a little above and beyond him with an expression of incredulous horror. Then her finger dropped away from the light switch as her whole body slowly slid downward, bending only at the knees. Her back stayed very straight against the jamb, her shoulders were erect, her chin was high, her horror-filled eyes did not once blink. Then when she had gone down on her haunches, like a witch doctor, her eyes grew wider still with righteous anger, she tucked in her chin and put on her nastiest professional look, and in a harsh voice Franz had never heard her use before, she said:

"In the names of Bach, Mozart, and Beethoven, the names of Pythagoras, Newton, and Einstein, by Bertrand Russell, William James, and Eustace Hayden, begone! All inharmonious and disorderly shapes and forces, depart at once!"

As she was speaking, the papers all around Franz (he could see now that they *were* shredded) lifted up cracklingly, the grips upon his arms and legs loosened, so that he was able to inch toward Cal while violently threshing his half-freed limbs. Midway in her eccentric exorcism, the pale shreds began to churn violently and suddenly were multiplied tenfold in num-

bers (all restraints on him as suddenly gone) so that, at the end
he was crawling toward her through a thick paper snowstorm.

The innumerable-seeming shreds sank rustlingly all around
him to the floor. He laid his head in her lap where she now
sat erect in the doorway, half-in, half-out, and he lay there
gasping, one hand clutching her waist, the other thrown out
as far as he could reach into the hallway as if to mark on the
carpet the point of farthest advance. He felt Cal's reassuring
fingers on his cheek, while her other hand absently brushed
scraps of paper from his coat.

XXIX

Franz heard Gun say urgently, "Cal, are you all right?
Franz!" Then Saul; "What the hell's happened to his room?"
Then Gun again; "My God, it looks like his whole library's
been put to the Destroysit!" but all that Franz could see of
them were shoes and legs. How odd. There was a third pair—
brown denim pants, and scuffed brown shoes, rather small;
of course—Fernando.

Doors opened down the hall and heads thrust out. The
elevator doors opened and Dorotea and Bonita hurried out,
their faces anxious and eager. But what Franz found himself
looking at, because it really puzzled him, was a score or
more of dusty corrugated cartons neatly piled along the wall
of the hall opposite the broom closet, and with them three
old suitcases and a small trunk.

Saul had knelt down beside him and was professionally
touching his wrist and chest, drawing back his eyelids with a
light touch to check the pupils, not saying anything. Then he
nodded reassuringly to Cal.

Franz managed an inquiring look. Saul smiled at him easily and said, "You know, Franz, Cal left that concert like a
bat out of hell. She took her bows with the other soloists and
she waited for the conductor to take his, but then she grabbed
up her coat—she'd brought it onstage during the second in-

termission and laid it on the bench beside her (I'd given her your message)—and she took off straight through the audience. You thought *you'd* offended 'em by leaving at the start. Believe me, it was nothing to the way she treated 'em! By the time we caught sight of her again, she was stopping a taxi by running out into the street in front of it. If we'd have been a bit slower, she'd have ditched us. As it was, she grudged us the time it took us to get in.''

"And then she got ahead of us again when we each thought the other would pay the cab driver and he yelled at us and we both went back,'' Gun took up over his shoulder from where he stood inside the room at the edge of the great drift of shredded paper and stuff, as if hesitant to disturb it. "When we got inside she'd run up the stairs. By then the elevator had come down, so we took it, but she beat us anyway. Say, Franz,'' he asked, pointing. "Who chalked that big star on your wall over the bed?''

At that question, Franz saw the small brown scuffed shoes step out decisively, kicking through the paper snow. Once again Fernando loudly rapped the wall above the bed, as if for attention, and turned and said authoritatively, *"Hechicería ocultada en muralla!"*

"Witchcraft hidden in the wall,'' Franz translated, rather like a child trying to prove he's not sick. Cal touched his lips reprovingly, he should rest.

Fernando lifted a finger, as if to announce, "I will demonstrate,'' and came striding back, stepping carefully past Cal and Franz in the doorway. He went quickly down the hall past Dorotea and Bonita, and stopped in front of the broom closet door and turned around. Gun, who had followed inquisitively behind him, stopped, too.

The dark Peruvian gestured from the shut doorway to the neatly stacked boxes twice and then took a couple of steps on his toes with knees bent. ("I moved them out. I did it quietly.'') and took a big screwdriver out of his pants pocket and thrust it into the hole where the knob had been and gave it a twist and with it drew the black door open and then with a peremptory flourish of the screwdriver stepped inside.

Gun followed and looked in, reporting back to Franz and

Cal, "He's got the whole little room cleared out. My God, it's dusty. You know, it's even got a little window. Now he's kneeling by the wall that's the other side of the one he pounded on. There's a little shallow cupboard built into it low down. It's got a door. Fuses? Cleaning stuff? Outlets? I don't know. Now he's using the screwdriver to pry it open. Well, I'll be damned!"

He backed away to let Fernando emerge, smiling triumphantly and carrying before his chest a rather large, rather thin gray book. He knelt by Franz and held it out to him, dramatically opening it. There was a puff of dust.

The two pages randomly revealed were covered from top to bottom, Franz saw, with unbroken lines of neatly yet crabbedly inked black astronomical and astrological signs and other cryptic symbols.

Franz reached out shakily toward it, then jerked his hand sharply back, as though afraid of getting his fingers burned.

He recognized the hand that had penned the Curse.

It had to be the Fifty-Book, the Grand Cipher mentioned in *Megapolisomancy* and Smith's journal (B)—the ledger that Smith had once seen and that was an essential ingredient (A) of the Curse and that had been hidden almost forty years ago by old Thibaut de Castries to do its work at the fulcrum (0) at (Franz shuddered, glancing up at the number on his door) 607 Rhodes.

XXX

Next day Gun incinerated the Grand Cipher at Franz's urgent entreaty, Cal and Saul concurring, but only after microfilming it. Since then he'd fed it to his computers repeatedly and let several semanticists and linguists study it variously, without the least progress toward breaking the code, if there is one. Recently he told the others, "It almost looks like Thibaut de Castries may have created that mathematical will-o'-the-wisp— a set of completely random numbers." There did turn out to be exactly fifty symbols. Cal pointed out that fifty was the total number of faces of all the five Pythagorean or Platonic solids. But when asked what that led to, she could only shrug.

At first Gun and Saul couldn't help wondering whether Franz mightn't have torn up all his books and papers in some sort of short-term psychotic seizure. But they concluded it would have been an impossible task, at least to do in so short a time. "That stuff was shredded like oakum."

Gun kept some samples of the strange confetti—"irregular scraps, average width three millimeters"—nothing like the refuse of a document-shredding machine, however advanced. (Which seemed to dispose of the suspicion that Gun's Shredbasket, or some other supersubtle Italianate machinery, had somehow played a part in the affair.)

Gun also took apart Franz's binoculars (calling in his optical friend, who among other things had investigated and thoroughly debunked the famous Crystal Skull) but they found no trace of any gimmicking. The only noteworthy circumstance was the thoroughness with which the lenses and prisms had been smashed. "More oakum picking?"

Gun found one flaw in the detailed account Franz gave when he was up to it. "You simply can't see spectral colors in moonlight. The cones of the retina aren't that sensitive."

Franz replied somewhat sharply, "Most people can never see the green flash of the setting sun. Yet it's sometimes there."

Saul's comment was, "You've got to believe there's some sort of sense in everything that crazies say."

"Crazies?"

"All of us."

He and Gun still live at 811 Geary. They've encountered no further paramental phenomena—at least as yet.

The Luques are still there, too. Dorotea is keeping the existence of the broom closets a secret, especially from the owner of 811. "He'd make me e-try to rent them if he knew.

Fernando's story, as finally interpreted by her and Cal, was simply that he'd once noticed the little, low, very shallow cupboard in the broom closet while rearranging the boxes there to make space for additional ones and that it had stuck in his mind (*"Misterioso!"*) so that when *"Meestair Jues-*

tón'' had become haunted, he had remembered it and played a hunch. The cupboard, by the stains of its bottom, had once held polishes for furniture, brass, and shoes, but then for almost forty years only the Fifty-Book.

The three Luques and the others (nine in all with Gun's and Saul's ladies—just the right number for a classic Roman party, Franz observed) did eventually go for a picnic on Corona Heights. Gunnar's Ingrid was tall and blonde as he, and worked in the Environmental Protection Agency, and pretended to be greatly impressed by the Junior Museum. While Saul's Joey was a red-haired little dietitian deep into community theater. The Heights seemed quite different now that the winter's rains had turned it green. Yet there were surprising reminders of a grimmer period: they encountered the two little girls with the Saint Bernard. Franz went a shade pale at that, but rallied quickly. Bonita played with them a while, nicely pretending it was fun. All in all, they had an enjoyable time, but no one sat in the Bishop's Seat or hunted beneath it for signs of an old interment. Franz remarked afterward, ''I sometimes think the injunction not to move old bones is at the root of all the para . . . supernatural.''

He tried to get in touch with Jaime Byers again, but phone calls and even letters went unanswered. Later he learned that the affluent poet and essayist, accompanied by Fa Lo Suee (and Shirl Soames too, apparently), had gone for an extended trip around the world.

''Somebody always does that at the end of a supernatural horror story,'' he commented sourly, with slightly forced humor. ''*The Hound of the Baskervilles*, etcetera. I'd really like to know who his sources were besides Klaas and Ricker. But perhaps it's just as well I don't get into that.''

He and Cal now share an apartment a little farther up Nob Hill. Though they haven't married, Franz swears he'll never live alone again. He never slept another night in Room 607.

As to what Cal heard and saw (and did) at the end, she says, ''When I got to the third floor I heard Franz start to scream. I had his key out. There were all those bits of paper swirling around him like a whirlpool. But at its center they hugged him and made a sort of tough, skinny pillar with a nasty top. So I said (*pace* my father) the first things that came into my mind. The pillar flew apart like a Mexican *piñata* and became part of the paper storm, which settled down very quickly, like snowflakes on the moon. You know, it was inches deep. As soon as I had got Franz's message from Saul, I'd known I must get to him as quickly as I could, but only after we'd played the Brandenburg.''

Franz thinks the Brandenburg Fifth somehow saved him, along with Cal's subsequent quick action, but as to how, he has no theories. Cal says about that only, "I think it's fortunate that Bach had a mathematical mind and that Pythagoras was musical."

Once, in a picky mood, she speculated, "You know, the talents attributed to de Castries's 'father's young Polish mistress' (and his mystery lady?) would correspond quite exactly with those of a being made up entirely of shredded multilingual occult books: amazing command of languages, learned beyond measure in the weird, profound secretarial skills, a tendency to fly apart like an explosive doll, black polka-dotted veil of crape and all—all merciless night animal, yet with a wisdom that goes back to Egypt, an erotic virtuoso (really, I'm a bit jealous), great grasp of culture and art—"

"Far too strong a grasp!" Franz cut her short with a shudder.

But Cal pressed on, a shade maliciously, "And then the way you caressed her intimately from head to heels and made lovey talk to her before you fell asleep—no wonder she became aroused!"

"I always knew we'd be found out some day." He tried to pass it off with a joke, but his hand shook a little as he lit a cigarette.

For a while after that Franz was very particular about never letting a book or magazine stay on the bed. But just the other day Cal found a straggling line of three there, on the side nearest the wall. She didn't touch them, but she did tell him about it. "I don't know if I could swing it again," she said. "So take care."

Cal says, "Everything's very chancy."

THE DRAGON REBORN

Sequel to *The Great Hunt*

Book Three of *The Wheel of Time*

by

Robert Jordan

Praise for *Eye of the World*

"A powerful vision of good and evil...fascinating people moving through a rich and interesting world." —Orson Scott Card

"Richly detailed...fully realized, complex adventure."
—*Library Journal*

"A combination of Robin Hood and Stephen King that is hard to resist...Jordan makes the reader care about these characters as though they were old friends." —*Milwaukee Sentinel*

Praise for *The Great Hunt*

"Jordan can spin as rich a world and as event-filled a tale as [Tolkien]...will not be easy to put down." —*ALA Booklist*

"Worth re-reading a time or two." —*Locus*

"This is good stuff...Splendidly characterized and cleverly plotted...The Great Hunt is a good book which will always be a good book. I shall certainly [line up] for the third volume."
—*Interzone*

The Dragon Reborn
coming in hardcover in August, 1991